To Claim What is Ours

A Legacy of Light

Book One

Kyah Merritt

ISBN: 978-1-7355459-0-5

Cover art created using postermywall.com

Published by Northern Horizon Books

Table of Contents

Introduction

Far back in the mists of time (or at least 2011), at the age of sixteen, I wrote a short school paper about Pharaoh Tutankhamun and his unexpected death, which, at that point, was believed to have been the result of a chariot accident. In 2014, a new "virtual autopsy" of his remains strengthened the theory that he had lived with a clubfoot and several other physical challenges, which made a chariot wreck somewhat less likely, but presented the opportunity for other types of drama. Then, in 2015, Spike TV produced a highly-fictionalized biographical miniseries simply titled *Tut*.

My earlier interest in this historical figure, the compelling new information about him, and the entertaining Shakespearean soap opera converged in a story of my own. Through 2018-20, this story grew into a piece of historical fiction that has captivated me, kept me company through the coronavirus pandemic— this generation's historical event— and taught me more about Egyptian history, the Bible, and myself, than I ever could have dreamed.

During the writing process, I found more kinship with Tutankhamun and his family than I ever would have expected. And I am honored, grateful for, and moved by the experience of getting to know a person who was, in some ways, very much like me, and whose family was, in some ways, very much like mine. I hope my readers will be as intrigued as I have been as I seek to answer the questions of this famous Pharaoh's life and death.

1 Good Morning

It was morning. Pharaoh Tutankhamun opened his eyes, the new day greeting him with pain as his foot realized that it was exactly the same as it had been when he had gone to bed.

Even despite the pain, he smiled as he saw movement under the fine, white linen bedsheet; his cat Bastet was waking up. Slowly she appeared, her gray back bending deeply as she stretched, first rising as she lowered her head, then arching like a cobra about to strike as she yawned, baring her tiny pointed teeth and digging her tiny front feet into the bed.

"Good morning, kitty," he said, reaching out and petting her. It was nice to be able to begin the day with a smile. Now… now it was time to locate someone to help him get ready for the day.

Yawning, he sat up and looked blearily around the room for the bell he would summon a servant with. The bed he was curled up on was made of gold-plated wood, the four feet carved in the shape of a lion's paws, representing the strength and power of mighty Pharaoh. He lay on a mattress filled with wool, made even more comfortable with various other handmade pillows, some made by the palace staff, some gifts from the governments of neighboring countries. Beside the bed was a small wooden chest of drawers where he kept things like cosmetics, an oil lamp centered on top of it, next to his bronze mirror. Every inch of the little chest of drawers was decorated with written wishes for the King's good health. As if.

"Sleep all right?" he asked his cat conversationally. She just looked at him. Although it almost seemed like she could understand him, she never talked back.

"You know what today is, don't you?" Tut asked his furry little friend. Bastet looked up at him with large, thoughtful eyes, as if to say that of course she knew. The Pharaoh chuckled. Tribute Day was nothing that the Royal Cat had to worry about.

Tutankhamun's eyes roved around his room as he continued to hunt for his bell. Every wall was decorated with beautiful paintings, most depicting the Pharaoh and his Queen. On one wall hung a sword and shield that he would probably never use, and a fan of ostrich feathers, a reminder of a fun hunting trip a few years back. Carved columns painted like lotuses helped support the walls, and gauzy linen curtains rippled in the gentle breeze that was entering the room with the warm morning sun.

Tut finally found the bell, calling for his morning assistance.

"You rang, My Lord?" the valet asked, hurrying into the royal chambers and immediately throwing himself to his knees. His clothing, of course, was not nearly as elaborate as what he was going to help the King put on, but it looked nice— a white linen tunic with a rather plain sort of belt made of blue fabric, a short braided wig that hung to just past his chin, and classic eye makeup— kohl around his eyes, blue eye-shadow over his lids and up to his eyebrows.

Barely older than the King, Semerkhet was the son of a scribe and deeply honored to be one of the King's personal staff. Despite his youth, he was a skilled and conscientious employee; his name meant "attentive friend," and he had proven himself to be one. Except that… slaves were not really "worthy" to be considered a "friend" of the Pharaoh.

Beside him knelt Kahotep, a short, fat, old valet who was not nearly as friendly as Semerkhet, but he did a good job.

8

It was still strange to have male servants coming in to help Tut get ready for the day. Ever since he had been left the poor orphan boy symbolically in charge of Egypt, he had been looked after by Hetepheres, a sort of all-purpose nanny. But she had joined the gods just a month ago, after many decades serving the palace. And now her responsibilities fell to Kahotep and Semerkhet, Hetty's former assistant and one of the palace's more recent hires. Since her passing, the young man had received a promotion, to King's Valet, and many more responsibilities. At eighteen, after all, the Pharaoh was really too old to have a nurse. As a man, he was now old enough to command a manservant or two.

"Good morning, Semerkhet, Kahotep," Tut said, trying to muster all the cheerfulness he could. The servants popped to their feet and stood at attention. "I'm ready to get dressed," the King continued.

"As you wish, O Great Morning Star." Semerkhet crossed to the archway that led into the storage room where all the Pharaoh's various pieces of finery were kept. In there were a series of chests where most of his clothing was kept, reappearing throughout each week fresh and clean after he wore each item, leaving it in a heap on the floor when it was dirty. And, of course, a rack of shoes, a shelf of wigs, and a rack of walking-sticks. "What would His Majesty like to wear today?"

"Just a tunic for now," he said. After disappearing into the storage room, Kahotep returned to the King's bedside with his arms full of clothing and shoes.

Even getting dressed was a struggle… Tutankhamun swallowed his pride and, unable to change his clothes while standing, adjusted his sleeping-tunic so he was no longer sitting on it, and silently raised his arms. Semerkhet slipped the tunic over his head, leaving him sitting in his loincloth, then brought him a jar of sweet-smelling ointment that would protect his skin from the hot sun and the dry air. Then the King put on his frankincense-based deodorant, and cleaned his teeth with natron paste. He had to smell nice today, after all.

If he had had a beard, now would have been the time to let Semerkhet shave it for him. But at eighteen, he did not yet have very much facial hair to speak of. Oh, well. Maybe next year.

Now Semerkhet took this morning's tunic of finely-pleated white linen from Kahotep's waiting hands and held it at an accessible height. Tut weaved his arms through the sleeves and pulled it over his head, silently imagining what it would be like to be able to dress himself.

Then he sat and let Semerkhet put his sandals on his mismatched feet. Tutankhamun hated to look at his left foot. His ankle curved inward so that when he walked, he put most of his weight onto the outer edge of his foot. His heel also did not touch the ground, or the sole of his shoe, so when it came to his left foot, he walked with an off-balance tiptoe. And not only was his foot an unstable foundation on which to put the weight of his tall frame; it had been painful for the past year, causing him to wince with every slow, limping step he took. The gods had seen fit to give him this disability, and the doctors did their best to help him, but even then, he still had to struggle every day through aches and pains and the slow work of walking from one side of the palace to the other.

Thank the gods for walking-sticks.

His feet did not match, and neither did his sandals; the Shoe-maker to the Pharaoh had designed them specially to fit the

10

different shapes of his two feet. Each shoe was constructed with an edge that wrapped all the way around the back of each foot, and tight straps over the top of each foot kept him from walking right out of them as he shuffled around the palace with the help of his walking-stick.

Tut had over eighty pairs of shoes in a series of chests. His favorites were the two pairs that actually had cushioned soles; they were by far the most comfortable. Others made a political statement, their soles illustrated with pictures of enemies like the Hittites, enemies he got to stomp on all day as he walked. Then there were the literally gold-plated ones, which he only ever wore to special events. When he wore them, he was wearing art. Not that they had ever touched the ground— he wore them while parading around in his palanquin, or they were carried by a servant, basically announcing to the populace that the Pharaoh owned gold-plated and jewel-encrusted shoes. Because that sort of thing was important. The ones he had on today were elaborately beaded, but they were at least wearable. And he knew that he would not have to walk very far in them.

His work done, Kahotep gave a silent bow and disappeared. Tut hardly noticed him leave.

"Are you ready for your kohl?" Semerkhet asked, choosing a cosmetic palette and application tool. Tut nodded and closed his eyes, sitting very still as he felt the pointed tool gently trace his eyes, outlining them and creating the graceful, catlike line elongating the outer corners. After darkening the King's eyebrows with kohl, Semerkhet filled in the area between Tut's eyelashes and eyebrows with the blue-green paint he wore every day. Semerkhet's own makeup, which he had applied himself early that morning, was just as neat as the King's, but Tut knew that he would have to excuse himself to touch it up every few hours, because with his budget, he couldn't afford the royal-quality products he was carefully applying to the Pharaoh's face. Tut's makeup would stay exactly where it was until a servant washed it off that evening... whenever they finally got home.

"Are you happy with the look?" Semerkhet asked, handing Tut his bronze mirror. The King turned his face from side to side, examining the valet's work. He smiled at the mirror, then closed his lips over his large, prominent front teeth. He would have to try not to grin at anyone. Or lisp, as he was wont to do on long, tiring, stressful days like this was sure to be.

"Very nice, Semerkhet," he said, giving the mirror back. The valet turned away too slowly to hide his grin of delight at the compliment. Satisfied with his cosmetics, Tut completed his look by choosing a black, braided wig, and... choosing a cane.

They stood in rows, in a specially-built wooden rack painted with lotuses. Tut gave a tired sigh and scanned them with his eyes. He had canes in every color from ebony to ivory, some made of wood, others of precious metal. Some were elaborately carved, some painted, some inlaid with precious stones. They were beautiful. But oh, was it hard to appreciate them.

"That one," he said dully, flicking a finger in the direction of a well-worn one decorated with a tiny model of the head of an Asiatic warrior. He already symbolically stepped on his enemies as he hobbled around in his elaborately decorated sandals; now he could punish them as he pounded with his stick. Each morning, he decided who to honor that day by using their gift. Why did every ambassador he met at a diplomatic event, every loyal subject he encountered at a festival, insist on giving him another cane as a gift?

At his last count, he had had 131. And if he had had his way, he would have owned zero.

But he didn't have his way, and he did own 131 canes. Tut held out his hand for it, the one he had used so many times, and slowly rose to his feet, wincing as the left one took his weight. He was dressed. Time to greet the day.

And what a day it was. Today the Pharaoh was to receive tribute from near and far. That would involve sitting immobile in the hot sun for nearly six hours. So much to look forward to.

And so many people. Certainly dozens, probably several hundred, walking by to greet him one after the other, all the livelong day. So many people. And so much noise, so much busyness, so much chaos. Tut felt his heart begin to beat harder at the very thought, gulping as his hands began to sweat. He wasn't afraid of people... he just didn't enjoy dealing with large quantities of them all at once. If it had been up to him... he would have spent most of the day in his study, reading with Bastet. His sister, his valet, and his cat were company enough.

But he was the Pharaoh. Today, this was one of his responsibilities. And he would do his duty.

Ankhesenamun woke up, and immediately her heart thudded with worry. Today was Tribute Day, the most difficult day of the year for her poor husband, dear brother. And she couldn't help him, because it was his day, not hers.

With a sigh, she sat up and stretched. Meresankh had clearly continued tidying up after the Queen had gone to bed; all the shoes she had been trying on had been put away, as had the jewelry. She smiled. Her handmaiden was good at her job. The Queen's bedroom looked much like the Pharaoh's, with graceful columns, elaborately painted walls, and ornate furniture. Time to get up.

Ankhesenamun rang her bell, and Meresankh appeared, kneeling before the Queen, clasping her hands before her heart, and bowing until her face nearly touched the floor. She was in her mid-twenties, and a terrible gossip... in the best way. Beside her knelt Tia, a maidservant. They had only been assisting her for the past few months; since switching from a nanny to a team of handmaidens the day she had become Queen, Ankh had been served by many maidservants. But Meresankh was her favorite of all of them.

"Good morning, My Lady," Meresankh said as she raised her head. It took her a moment to get up; her dimples and rounded curves were endearing, but occasionally they slowed her down just a tiny bit.

"Good morning, Meresankh," Ankh yawned. She slid out of bed, wrapping her sleeping-tunic closer around herself. "Suppose I'm ready to get dressed."

"As you wish, My Lady." Meresankh and Tia got to their feet and disappeared through the archway that led to the secondary storage room. The two helped her into her favorite dress, with wide, starched sleeves. The belt that sat high on her waist was red and blue, long ribbons of fabric falling as far as the hemline of the dress, floating as she walked. Today was going to be hot, but her dresses were breezy. She would manage.

"And which wig would you like?" Ankh considered her large collection of wigs, which she chose to display in a corner of the room and which ranged from simple, chin-length arrangements to elaborate affairs that reached nearly to her waist.

14

"Oh, that one," she said, choosing one of the simpler ones and sitting down so her handmaiden could reach to put it on her. Carefully Meresankh placed it on her head, arranging the fine, delicate braids around her face with her dimpled little fingers.

"And for jewelry?" the handmaiden asked.

Ankhesenamun pointed. "That necklace… and I think I'll wear my diadem today too."

"As you wish, My Lady." After Tia fetched them, Meresankh arranged the heavy, beaded collar around the Queen's neck and placed the small gold diadem on her head, the cobra-headed *uraeus* peeking out at the world. The Queen had more jewelry than she could keep track of, but the only pieces that were truly meaningful to her were the ones that had belonged to her mother and sisters. Like this necklace. It had belonged to Meritaten. Ankh stroked the delicate beads, remembering.

Then she smiled with an idea. "And my blue lotus perfume." Something to make her husband happy.

Meresankh caught on, sharing the Queen's smile. A dimple showed in the handmaiden's round cheek. "Excellent choice, My Lady."

Finally Ankhesenamun let Meresankh do her eye makeup, then cleaned her teeth with natron. Ready for the day, the Queen admired herself in her polished bronze mirror. "Lovely," she said with an appreciative smile. Meresankh grinned at the compliment.

Ankh got up with a sigh. "Time for breakfast."

Tut limped out of his bedroom, past Ankh's room, which was across the hall from his, and into the grand dining room of the palace, a great open hall large enough to accommodate many guests during a feast, supported by brightly painted pillars and walls decorated with gods, kings, plants, and animals of all descriptions. Ankh was still at the table, enjoying a plate of fresh bread and dried figs, dates, and raisins. That did look good.

"Good morning," he said, shuffling to the table.

"Good morning, darling," she replied with a smile. Seeing that the King was about to sit down, a servant silently hurried to pull out his chair. Leaning his walking-stick on the edge of the table, Tut planted his hands on the table for balance and waited until the chair was in place before collapsing into it, weary already. Seconds later, there was a huge plate of bread and fruit in front of him, a plate from which Semerkhet pulled a fragment of bread and picked a bit of fruit to make sure they weren't poisoned, just like he always did with the Pharaoh's wine. They weren't.

He looked worried, Ankhesenamun thought as she watched her brother come in for breakfast. There was a tightness to his jaw, a stiffness to the way he moved.

She smiled as he sat down beside her at the table. Not everyone would call him handsome, with his long nose and his receding chin, but if anyone said his nose wasn't attractive, they were calling the Queen ugly too, because the royal brother and sister had exactly the same nose. But he was the handsomest man the Queen knew, with his bright eyes, warm, brown skin, and fine, narrow jaw. His dark eyebrows, which, when the moment required it, could grow as stern as thunder and lightning, reminded her of their Father, and the way he had used his powerful eyebrows to command the politicians around him. They were good for a Pharaoh to have. But as stern as his eyebrows could make him, they also made him handsome. And he was hers. Brother and husband all at once.

16

Tut picked at his breakfast, his stomach filled with an annoying combination of worry and frustration.

"Are you looking forward to today?" Ankh asked tentatively, gently placing her soft, cool little hand on his. As anxious as he was about today, he could not help but take a moment to admire her outfit. She was also wearing a very sexy perfume that smelled like the intoxicating blue lotuses that grew in the reflecting pools on the palace grounds. Although he wasn't in the mood. He looked up at her with an unhappy smile and shook his head.

"No," he sighed. "How will I do? How am I supposed to show the people the Pharaoh they think they have? If I stumble even once, or let myself lisp, I'll ruin everything. Then they won't know what to believe, and I'll be labeled a heretic just like Father." Whatever he believed personally, whatever he doubted, he couldn't do that to his beloved people. Let them keep their precious illusions of their powerful, perfect King who was in the same league as Ra and Horus. Deities who had never done anything perceptible for him. He gave a wry chuckle. "And I am not... looking forward to the crowds."

She squeezed his hand and looked into his eyes. "Well, what can you do to make sure things go as well as possible? I always feel better about an event when I know I have a plan to follow. You can bring your fanciest walking-stick, so it looks like you just want to look regal. And you can ride down to the courtyard in your palanquin. Same thing, they'll look at you and think how stately you look. The Pharaoh is so special..." Ankh paused as if she were considering her words. "The Pharaoh is so special that he doesn't even have to walk if he doesn't feel like it." She looked down as if she were afraid to meet his eye, worried that she had hurt his feelings.

But he just sighed. She was right. Gently he took her hand, and she looked up again. He smiled at her, and she smiled back, letting her shoulders drop with a tiny sigh and looking relieved. He gave a sarcastic smile and shook his head. "I am the Pharaoh, and I don't want to walk today."

The King returned to his chamber to let Semerkhet change him into his fanciest purple outer robe and put on his best *nemes* head-cloth and the heavy, red-and-white double crown of the united Egypt that always gave him a headache. He was all for celebrating the union of Upper and Lower Egypt, but it seemed a shame that the representation of their unity brought him only pain. And the towering series of crowns made him feel like he was about to topple over. Would Egypt as a united country cease to exist if he collapsed in an undignified heap on the floor? He just hoped he didn't sneeze.

Three other servants had joined them, three silent young men holding the jewelry Semerkhet was about to put on the Pharaoh. They looked all alike, from their neat wigs to their simple uniform-tunics. Their names might as well have been One, Two, and Three. Silently they stood there, letting Semerkhet take each item as he was ready.

The *uraeus* peeked out from the front of the blue-and-gold striped *nemes* head-cloth on the Pharaoh's head, symbolizing the protection of Wadjet, the snake goddess who had somehow failed to do anything useful for Tut that he was aware of. Beside it crouched the vulture goddess Nekhbet, the mother of all that was divine about Tut (if anything was at all). His rather ostentatious headgear in place, he fastened on the elaborate false beard of magnificence. The cord was itchy.

Then came the jewelry. Tut stood like one of the many statues in the palace, hands planted firmly on the walking-stick that was holding him up, as Semerkhet decorated him with an elaborate falcon-shaped necklace, inlaid with feathers of turquoise, carnelian, lapis lazuli, and colored glass. Tut stood as straight as he could, but he could still feel the heavy collar-necklace resting more heavily against his left shoulder; not only were his feet misshapen, but his back had a curve in it, a curve that kept his right shoulder higher than his left. The necklace in place, Semerkhet placed long, beaded earrings in Tut's ears, then festooned his thin arms with gold bracelets inlaid with blue glass and his fingers with ornate rings.

Now he was almost too heavy and off-balance to move. But he was fashion-coordinated. The blue and gold color scheme of his jewelry matched the blue and gold stripes of his *nemes* and walking-stick, and of the crook and flail he would hold crossed over his chest as he received all the visitors. The symbols he held would demonstrate to them that as Pharaoh, he would guide them like a shepherd, but he would also discipline those who needed it. Or, more likely, Grand Vizier Ay would. He took care of most things.

Hands empty, the three servants bowed from the waist and filed out with murmured wishes for the Pharaoh's long life, prosperity, and health. Tut hardly noticed them go.

"Well done, Semerkhet," Tut said, giving the servant a small smile. His smile got bigger as he saw Semerkhet lap it up; to actually be the King or Queen's valet or handmaiden was a dream many young men and women had but few saw come true. Even having the opportunity to carry the Pharaoh's sandals or stand beside him with an ostrich-feather fan was something to be envied. Contrarily, Tut envied the opportunities that servants, and even peasants, had to live the lives they wanted.

Tut looked in the mirror, taking in the full look. "I am the Morning and the Evening Star," he told himself. He tried to believe it.

There was a soft *mrrrow* from around his ankles. Tut smiled and looked down to see Bastet rubbing her soft, furry, gray body against his legs. She was wishing him good luck.

Ankh stood in the hallway, her thoughtful expression turning into an encouraging smile when she saw him come into view. Stepping toward him, she held out her hands, and he extended the one that wasn't busy with his cane for a squeeze.

"Good luck today," she said, stepping closer and putting her arms around him. Wrapping his free arm around her, he held her close, giving his sister a warm hug— even as he was careful not to hit her with his false beard.

"Fank you," he said, then bit his tongue. That lisp. Swallowing, he tried again. "Thhhank you."

"Tell me all about it when you get back," she said.

He nodded. "I will." Again, he gave a wry chuckle. "But it's on days like these… that I wonder what it would be like to be a peasant."

Walking out of the palace and into a little mud hut on his own two feet, he would not be turning his back on much that he loved. As long as he could take Ankh. Then maybe they could live as the siblings they were, rather than the royal couple they had to be in order to produce the Pharaoh who would succeed Tut. Then they

20

could each choose a spouse they were attracted to, rather than bound to by family ties and politics. They might not even live together. Being neighbors would be sufficient.

They had been married nine years ago upon their father's death, at the ages of nine and fourteen. They loved one another more than anything else in the world, and it brought them great joy to stand together as the symbolic leaders of their country, but sometimes, Tutankhamun still wondered what it would have been like to fall in love with a stranger.

Tut did have to walk to the front atrium of the palace, but that was all the further he had to go. Six servants, smartly dressed in their uniforms of starched white linen kilts, wide collar-necklaces of bright beads, and simple white head-cloths stood silently around his palanquin, a long litter of gold-plated wood swathed in gauzy linen curtains that would conceal him from his curious subjects. When he got out, he told himself, the people would merely remark at how grand he looked, and how majestic with his golden staff that was almost as fancy as the *was*-scepter he carried during the most important religious ceremonies. He was the King. He could get around how he pleased.

Standing outside the palace, he could hear a faraway bustle, a buzz of human sound. He squinted into the distance, over the far-away houses and marketplaces of Memphis, which lay in the valley beneath the palace, so close, and yet so far. He rarely even thought about the city outside the palace, beyond the wall; he had everything he needed, so why bother with whatever was out there? Outings like this were quite enough. Ay and the other Viziers had everything under control.

Tut handed his cane to one of the servants, who placed it in the litter for him. Now came the hard part; he was so much taller than most of the staff that it was tricky for them to help him move. First he took off his giant crown and handed it to another servant; it was so tall that he would not have fit into the litter with it on. With help, he climbed into the rectangular space and reclined as comfortably as he could, settling himself onto the cushions. He got his cane and crown back, and laid them beside him. Then he laid his head back with a sigh. He was exhausted. And they weren't even there yet.

The Queen looked out the window, watching them go. Slowly the palanquin moved away from the palace, toward the large courtyard where Tribute Day would take place. What a day her husband had ahead of him.

He hadn't even noticed the blue lotus perfume, she observed. He was stressed. In her heart, she prayed that he would have the best day possible. But somehow… even praying to the gods she loved did not make her feel any better.

2   Tribute Day

O nce they arrived at the wide, sandy courtyard where Tribute Day was going to take place, the bearers set the litter down, and Semerkhet opened the curtains and helped Tut to his feet, cane in hand. Then he helped him get his crown on. The blinding morning sunlight immediately made the Pharaoh squint. This was going to be difficult. "Fank you," he said to Semerkhet, and immediatcly bit his tongue. The beginning of the day, and he was already lisping. This was not encouraging. Tut swallowed and prepared himself. They started to walk, the King trying hard not to let his giant crown make him lose his tenuous balance as he clung to his cane. Time to show the people the god they thought he was.

Tut collapsed into the gilded throne that had been dragged out here for him and placed on a dais that elevated him above all the common folk who were going to be visiting him today. Even climbing up the equivalent of one stair-step had been a hassle. Carefully, he tucked the hem of his robe around his feet. Nice as his shoes were, he did not want to advertise the fact that the god-king of Egypt had something wrong with him to political neighbors hungry to find a weakness to exploit. He would keep his feet to himself.

Squinting, he looked wearily at the line of people that stretched out of sight across the dusty courtyard that felt as wide and hot as the desert. The figures in the distance actually appeared to be wavering in the oppressive heat. From downtown Memphis all the way to Kush, they had come to show their adoration and bring things they hoped would bring joy to him and his court. The party was for him, but the King didn't want to be there. He took the crook and flail from a servant with a sigh, crossing them majestically over his chest.

His heart began to thump, but he told it to be calm. Here came the people. He did what he could to prepare himself… and re-minded himself that in a few hours, it would be over. In a few hours, he could go back to the safety of the palace, the quiet of his own chambers, the peace of interacting with only one or two people at a time. He just had to get through the next few hours, and that would be his reward. The thought made him smile. He could do this.

His entourage stood around him, Semerkhet and another valet, four scribes who stood ready to record the gifts he would receive today, and ten or twelve other servants who would be responsible for actually taking the gifts and helping each one find its place in the pile. An empty corral stood waiting, just in case anyone had decided to bring the Pharaoh a live animal. In the distance, Tut wondered if he could hear a cow mooing.

"And from Cyprus, eight measures of the finest copper," a representative was announcing. Tut forced his face into a closed smile and gave a rather pathetic little wave with the flail, which jin-gled. The man bowed and moved on, to be replaced by an envoy from Retjenu in the east, which had brought with them a live bear for the King, with light brown fur, white claws, and a bad attitude. What would he do with that? He could feel a headache coming on.

"Thank you," Tut said politely to some official from Retjenu, who had brought a whole basket full of shimmering blue lapis lazuli stones. He kicked himself mentally as he felt his mouth forming the lisped version that began with "F;" he managed to

24

force the "Th" out just in time. If only there was another phrase of gratitude that did not begin with such a tricky sound. Then it came to him— the Royal We. If ever there was a time to drag that out, it was now. Dressed in elaborate red and blue robes, the bearded men of Retjenu presented their gifts of furniture, horses, precious stones, golden jewelry, animal skins, vases… a lion cub…

Person after person filed past the King, men, women, and children offering gifts of every description for their beloved Pharaoh and his court. Donkeys and camels plodded by, laden with oil, wine, honey, spices, perfumes, handicrafts, musical instruments, walking-sticks (yay!), exotic furs, textiles, live animals… The air filled with smells and sounds as their gifts clogged the courtyard. Fruits, vegetables, cheeses… Tut saw coconuts, mulberries, melons…

"…with wishes for all life, prosperity, and health," another official was saying, brushing sand off his robe as he rose from his groveling bow. Tut tried to smile. Life, prosperity, and health. Sounded good.

Today he had received eight beautiful brand-new walking-sticks, bringing his running total to 139. He struggled not to roll his eyes at the thought, imagining what Ankh would say if she was sitting next to him— *does the Pharaoh roll his royal eyes?* He managed to restrain himself.

Tut's head pounded as the sun beat down; the thin linen canopy he sat under (which had been installed on extra-long poles to account for the absurd height of his crown) did little good in terms of shielding him from its rays. His father Akhenaten had worshiped the Sun, called it the Aten, why did its life-giving rays now feel like death?

25

Tut's hidden foot ached and his legs began to cramp up, he could not attend to what people were saying. All there was was the heat, and the sweat, and the pain. His skin burned from the raging sun. His head pounded in a terrible headache. He felt sweat dripping from his body, running down his forehead and stinging his eyes, making the gold-plated handles of the crook and flail slippery in his hands, making his burning-hot metal jewelry slick against his skin, making the hairline of his heavy wig damp and itchy. Hopefully it would not make his makeup run.

His shoulders ached under the weight of the heavy pectoral collar. And his neck ached under the weight of everything he was wearing on his head. The wig was heavy and hot enough, but today he had to wear it with not only a *nemes* but the full double crown of Egypt. Whoever had invented this fiendish custom deserved to have his name desecrated far more than his father did.

Why was it so hot today, he implored the gods. Why? This was supposed to be the cool half of the year, and here he sat sweating like it was the broiling month of Thoth. What was he being punished for?

The throne he sat on was not comfortable. Tut kept shifting restlessly, placing more pressure on one hip, then the other as he struggled to keep his legs from cramping. The throne was breathtakingly beautiful; fifteen craftsmen had worked for months to carve its wooden frame from the headrest to the lion heads on the arms and the four lion-paw-shaped feet, carefully gild it, and apply hundreds of little pieces of bright-colored precious stones and colored glass, but it was as hard as a rock. It was hard to be grateful sitting on an unforgiving piece of metal.

So… many… people. Again the Pharaoh squinted at the endless line of visitors, stretching out into the invisible distance. Today, he thought, represented about a year's worth of interactions.

He could hardly see. The air moved gently nearby; a servant girl was fanning him with a large ostrich-feather fan with a gold handle. It was actually a rather embarrassing fan; the golden center to which the feathers were affixed was engraved with an illustration of he himself, hunting the very animals the feathers had come from. He loved hunting, he really did, but it was so much work simply to get into the chariot that it was a rare treat.

The servant girl's skin was as brown as the sand; just like the billions of grains of sand in the desert around them, she was one of many, all alike, with a single purpose: to serve the Pharaoh. If only she could stand a little closer and shade him with the fan instead of just blowing hot air toward him, hot air that smelled like sweat and smoke and horse manure and a thousand cloying perfumes and exotic spices that stuck in his thirsty throat. A few yards away, another servant was burning incense to try to combat the assortment of stenches, but all it was doing was adding another note to the general smell of the day. Even he stank. He was the Pharaoh, the King of the world, a deity in human form, and his sweat stank.

The people of Alashiya had sent him ten of their finest cows and a large shipment of gleaming copper. Babylonia, Assyria, the Mitanni, the vassals of the city of Kadesh and the other towns in Amurru… all had come to pay tribute to Egypt and her King. Off to the side stood four scribes, busily recording every gift the King received on endless scrolls of papyrus as ten or twelve servants worked to arrange them into some sort of temporary order, occasionally herding live animals into the growing zoo inside the corral.

Ankh was not here. The people had come to see the Pharaoh, and on such a blazing hot day as this, his sister-Queen had chosen to stay in the cool dimness of the palace. If only he could send his *ka*, his life force, home, keeping only his *ba*, or personality, here to deal with the people. If he had to sit here much longer, his life force was in danger of taking flight. He was about to go out of here and fly west with the setting sun.

When did I sign up for this? When? Tell me and I'll take it back, were the only thoughts that pounded through his aching head as he sat in the punishing sun, trying to smile (without flashing his teeth) as one dignitary after another passed by in robes and headdresses of bright colors, offering their best wishes and an example of local goods from handmade shoes that wouldn't fit to exotic birds whose shrill squawks did a fantastic job at making his headache even worse. *What could I possibly have done to deserve this?*

The Morning and the Evening Star rested his aching head on his hand, closing his sore, gritty eyes. Sand and dust were blowing everywhere from the movement of the crowds, and that fan wasn't helping any.

Slowly the day passed. The endless river of humanity, seemingly longer than the mighty Nile itself, made its slow way past the throne, piling their gifts around him with deep, groveling bows that more often than not involved touching their faces to the sandy ground, short speeches, and polite disregard of his non-matching feet.

Then from Kush, under the administration of Viceroy Amenhotep and Governor Hekanefer, arrived baskets and baskets of bright ivory, dark ebony, lush ostrich feathers like the ones in that embarrassing fan, and sweet palm fruits. Piles and piles of fine gold rings, bags of gold dust, trays of precious stones. Animal skins, elegant furniture, bows, arrows, and shields that he would probably never use… a number of long-horned cattle… a small live giraffe that towered a head above the man leading it… even a brand-new gold-plated chariot with six-spoked wheels. Even the Princess of Kush had come to honor him, riding in a chariot pulled by oxen, identical to the chariot she had brought him. He smiled and waved. "We are grateful for your gift," he intoned graciously, glad that even though it was obnoxiously pretentious, it didn't have any of the more difficult sounds.

The Hittites, however, did not appear. Egypt's northeastern neighbors brought them nothing at all. No surprise, though. From what Tut knew, if the Kingdom of Hattusa had brought them a gift, it would have been a beautiful knife… used to stab him in the back.

But his feet remained hidden from them all. Tucked behind his purple robe, they stayed just out of sight, their presence offering no distraction to the allies and potential allies, trading partners and future trading partners, who were filing by the Pharaoh as he sat on his majestic throne. He was a politician, and that was all. And his royal scepter was just for show.

He sat up straight. And he smiled and waved and thanked people grandly. And somehow, he fooled the entire world into thinking he was not in pain.

The blazing sun reached its painful zenith, then slowly sank, transitioning from scorching his back to pounding the top of his head to baking his face and intensifying his throbbing headache. Sitting rigidly in his hard metal throne for so many hours had turned all the muscles of his back and shoulders into a painful, stiff board. In the distance, he could hear the cows mooing and the birds and monkeys, of which he had received six, shrieking.

It got worse. After a time it was almost painful, the thumping of his heart, the compulsive swallowing, the sweating of his hands, the way his tense body almost seemed to shake. It was almost as if his body were preparing to run, to run away from all these sensations that were assaulting him from every angle. He did feel himself curling inward, shrinking back from the world, his body trying to protect him by getting him as far away from all of it as possible, shield him from this crazy world in some small way.

It was too much. Just too much. The sounds pressed on his ears, the blazing sunlight and bright colors hurt his eyes, all the smells around him were making him queasy, his sweaty clothing itched and scratched, his crown and jewelry were so heavy, his chair was hard as a rock. It was all he could do not to drop his crook and flail and press his hands over his ears, tucking his head in toward his chest, closing his eyes, and shutting out the world. Or curl into a ball, hiding his face in his knees as he wrapped his arms around his shins, making himself as small as possible. He wanted to go home, wanted to leave this chair and retreat to the safety of the palace, his own room, his own bed, wanted to hide from the world in the dark and the quiet.

I won't come out for a week, he promised himself. *I'll eat something, have a shower, go to bed, and stay in my room for a week.*

Maybe he would never lead the armies of Egypt on the battlefield, but he was going to have to fight to get through this day. And when it was all over, he was going to have to recover.

The Queen sat in her room, staring out the window. How was he doing, she wondered. Was he drinking enough water, was he managing to stay grand and formal despite the pain, would he be able to make it to the end of the day? She just hoped that he came back safe, and satisfied with the way the day had gone. This was his day, and his satisfaction or dissatisfaction with the result was all that mattered. But she hoped he would be happy.

Apart from a sip or two of wine every hour or so and a short lunch break, Tutankhamun and his entourage did not bother to eat. Tribute Day only happened once a year. They could not insult any of the hundreds of people who had traveled miles to offer their gifts to the Pharaoh by turning their attention to food. After all, the Pharaoh was a god in human form, wasn't he? He presumably neither hungered nor thirsted nor suffered from migraines, and was not painfully affected by the sun, the heat, the sandy wind, or any one of the thousands of sounds and smells that assaulted him from every angle. He was divine.

"We're finished, Your Majesty," Semerkhet said gently. Tut's head jerked and his eyes snapped open; he had fallen from a daze into a drowse. The last hour had gone by in a meaningless, unmemorable blur, person after person smiling at him, bowing, kissing his hand, offering their gift… Looking back, he hoped that no one had been insulted by his inattentiveness. But at least his relative silence had prevented him from showing off his lisp to anyone.

Tut took a deep breath and sat up a little straighter. Now that the sun was going down, it was no longer blasting directly into his face. What a relief. And the pervasive noise was over, leaving echoing near-silence. Every part of him still felt jangled, like a bell that had just been rung, and he had never felt so exhausted, but he no longer felt like crying or throwing up. The moment he had been waiting for had come. The day was over.

"Good. Let'th go home." The lisp escaped too late for him to correct it, but it didn't matter; he was just among his own staff now, and they all knew he lisped. In the distance he could still hear the cows and monkeys; he looked over to see a group of servants beginning to herd them towards home while others worked on organizing his gifts on sledges for transport back to the palace. It looked as though the baby lion had tried to bite one of them, and the giraffe appeared very confused. The servants would have a very busy day sorting things tomorrow.

Slowly Tut handed the crook and flail to a servant, feeling the joints of his fingers creak stiffly as they opened after clutching the handles all day. Semerkhet and another servant prepared to help him to his weary feet, carefully untangling them from the bit of robe that had concealed them. Gentlemen One, Two, and Three had helped him get ready this morning, now Gentlemen Four, Five, and Six were helping him get home. This was not quite according to etiquette; technically servants always had to ask permission before touching the King, and avoided eye contact out of respect (and out of fear of being incinerated by his royal gaze). But they all knew that at the end of such a long day, Tut would not be offended by a silent offer of help. They lived to serve him, they were his possessions, gained their identity and meaning from being the instruments of his will.

Without a word, he clung to their hands and hauled himself to his feet with a grunt of pain, groping for his stick once he was on

32

his feet. He groaned as he bent to begin standing; his back was so stiff that he could barely move. The Pharaoh paused, wiggling his feet inside their sandals to try to get his blood flowing again as his knees and hips whined at him after so long at right angles. Time to go.

Trying not to let his precarious crown knock him off balance and symbolically throw all of Egypt into disunited chaos, he stumbled off the dais, then took the few steps toward the litter, making all sorts of faces as he went. Thankfully all the guests were gone, so no one would see how much pain the god-king was in. Together, the servants guided the boy to his waiting palanquin, taking his heavy double crown, helping him lower himself onto the cushions and settle in, then closing the curtains around him and directing the bearers to begin the march back to the palace.

Tut lay back in the cool, dark little chamber, letting the cool, soft cushions embrace his tired body, and closed his eyes, sun-burned, thirsty, achy, and utterly worn. A little smile came to his face. In here it was quiet, it was dark, it was no longer hot, and it was enclosed. With a deep sigh of relief, he let his weary body re-lax, so very, very grateful that the day was over. Soon he would be home, and then he could go to bed.

He did not remember the ride home.

The next thing he knew, the palanquin was resting on the ground again, and Semerkhet was pulling back the curtains as two or three other servants handed Tut his cane and hauled the ex-tremely tall young King to his feet in the most dignified manner possible. With a firm grip on his arms, they helped him make his way through the deepening night to stumble up the two treacherous steps into the torch-lit palace, bent over his walking-stick like an old man. The day was over.

3   Relief

He was home. The King staggered into the grand front hall of the palace, his bleary eyes barely taking in the stately columns, the fabulous paintings on every wall. Tut sighed as he sank down in his favorite chair, which had randomly appeared in the front hall, padded with soft pillows from his bedroom. Slowly he placed one of his tired, sore feet, then the other, on a convenient footstool, feeling them almost sigh in relief as he propped them up. Finally he set aside his cane.

He felt himself give a groan of relief as his aching body collapsed into the chair, his exhausted legs finally disengaging after the short but painful walk that had capped off this perfectly ridiculous day. This divine day. In the cool shade of the dim palace, he could feel how sunburned he was. Thankfully, since he had not yet taken every bit of the Pharaoh's responsibility, he could occasionally be excused from going to the Temple of Amun-Ra for the ceremony that marked the end of the day. On a similar note, the best thing about spending this long day in the hot, blinding, crowded courtyard had been missing the daily bull-slaughter that also took place in the Temple of Amun-Ra.

Around him servants who had been busy at the palace all day buzzed back and forth like so many locusts, taking the *nemes* head-cloth from his tired, aching head, silently offering him wine, bread, a bit of meat. Semerkhet wove around and between them, pointing, directing. Gentlemen One, Two, and Three might have been among them, but Tut wasn't sure— it was somewhat hard to tell the servants apart. They ran around busily taking care of him, but none of them actually spoke to him, or even looked directly at him.

Semerkhet brought him a terracotta cup of red wine, tasting it before he presented it with the usual ritual phrasing, the promise that if it was poisoned, he would take the harm upon himself. Once it had been declared not poisoned, Tut took it and sipped it, feeling great relief as it flowed down his parched throat, finally easing the thirst that had been nagging him all day. After the wine was gone, he had a servant refill it three times with plain water, then with cool, sweet licorice *mai-sus*. They didn't usually drink it in the month of Meshir; it was usually enjoyed in the hot parts of the seasons of Harvest and Inundation, but he was the Pharaoh, and if he wanted it, he could have it. Oh, what relief to be out of the sun. Inside it was cool, it was dim, it was quiet, and he could rest.

Then the servants disappeared, and there was blessed silence. Tutankhamun was alone for the first time since early this morning, at peace. His ears were tired after the constant dull roar of humans, animals, and vehicles, and the sudden silence was as comfortable as a pillow.

Slowly his headache began to ebb, and his stiff back and neck began to relax. Finally free of the heavy double crown, his head felt like it was about to touch the ceiling. The flower arrangements in the corners of the room went in and out of focus and even changed number as his tired eyes tried to fall shut on him. The flowers smelled much better than he did. Tut laid his weary head on the back of the chair, his body sinking into its solid embrace. Now that he was safe, was home, his heart quit pounding, slowing into the calm rhythm of feeling secure, surrounded by what was familiar. And he felt his eyes closing.

Ankhesenamun heard the servants bustling around in the front hall of the palace, heard the familiar uneven footsteps and groan of weary pain. Her brother was home. Heart filling with both joy and worry, she hurried out to greet him.

He was lying sprawled in his chair, feet propped up on a foot-stool, head resting on the back of the chair, eyes wearily closed. Breathing slowly, softly, he looked as though he might actually have drifted off out of sheer exhaustion. Ankh bit her lip, shaking her head with a sad little smile. Poor tired, brave darling.

"How was your day, darling?" Tut heard Ankh whisper. He felt the sensation of waking up, and realized that in a matter of seconds, he had nearly drifted off. Slowly Tutankhamun opened his weary eyes to see her walking toward him, holding out her little hands in a gentle, sympathetic welcome, an almost sad little smile on her pretty brown face. She looked clean, cool, and comfortable, her crisp white robe hanging gracefully from her body, and she smelled good. No hot, sweaty, miserable day in the sun for her. Only her love for him could have kept her from wrinkling her cute little nose at his aroma of sweat, smoke, and manure.

He rolled his weary head toward her and gave her a wry smile under half-closed eyes. "Divine," he said sarcastically. "I got eight walking-sticks. And a bear. How wath your day?" Tut swallowed carefully. Another lisp had escaped his tired mouth.

She shook her head with another little smile of sympathetic concern. "Quiet. I missed you. Thought about you all day."

He reached out and squeezed her hand, returning her smile a little more warmly than before. "And I missed you. Well, I'm home now, finally. Everyone from Babylonia to Kush had a look at me and brought me beautiful things we'll have to figure out where to put. I fink there may be a lion cub in there thomewhere, too.

And we'll have to figure out where to keep the monkeyth… I'll have a bit to eat… and then I'll go rest. Have a wash at some point."

Gently Ankh took the heaviest of his collar-necklaces from his weary shoulders, then kissed the sweaty hairline between the heavy wig and his shaved scalp. "I'm really glad you're home," she whispered, lovingly squeezing his stiff shoulders. Involuntarily, he gave a little sigh as he felt his exhausted body relax at her touch.

"Tho am I," he whispered. He barely noticed his own lisp this time. At this point, it no longer mattered.

She kissed his cheek, then gave a soft chuckle. "Monkeys?" she asked.

Tut felt his face break into a tired smile as he slowly nodded. "Thikth."

Ankhesenamun kissed her weary husband goodnight and watched him hobble down the hall to bed with a catch in her throat. Now his valet would get him his shower and put him to bed, and he would sleep, recovering from this long, weary day. She just hoped he would be able to rest well.

Slowly Tut limped into his bedroom and made his way to the bed. Carefully, he sat down, then set aside his cane and slowly lay down on his back, his exhausted body sinking into the bed, a cloud of comfortable nothingness. He closed his eyes, the comfortable dark embracing him, shutting out even the peaceful, reassuring familiarity of his bedroom ceiling. He didn't need to look at anything right now.

He sighed as he felt his legs and back disengage, his aching muscles relaxing, feeling like he might float away. Just to rest. Just to rest felt so good. And to be alone, alone in the dark and the silence, felt just as good. His mind and body were still buzzing with all the noise, all the activity, and he would have to rest for awhile before the overstimulation finally faded.

But the stress was gone, the anxiety. He was finally receiving the reward he had been looking forward to all day, lying here alone in his room, resting in the dark and the quiet. And he promised himself that he would rest until he felt alive again, until he was ready to return to the rest of the world.

There was the whisper of something furry moving through the air, and Bastet gracefully leaped up onto the bed. She padded over to her master and sniffed him, then sneezed. Tut chuckled. He must really stink. Bastet apparently forgave him for coming home smelly, curling up beside the King with a purr. "Good kitty," he whispered, slowly reaching out a tired hand to pet her. "Good kitty."

For nearly an hour, all he could do was lie on the bed, sinking into the mattress and soft pillows, resting his painful feet and his weary legs, trying to regain enough momentum even to move. He didn't even have the energy to take off his wig, sandals, and heavy jewelry, which was now weighing him down, pressing him into the bed. He was sinking so deeply into the bed that it felt like he would never leave. Heat radiated from his sunburned skin. His face itched from the dried sweat and the makeup he had been wearing since this morning. Every muscle ached.

It was totally dark in the room; he had not asked anyone to light his lamps, but he didn't care. His eyes were closed anyway. And the dimness was a relief after the scorching sunlight he had been squinting in all day. But despite the darkness of the room and the softness of the bed, he knew he wasn't going to just fall asleep lying here— he was too uncomfortable. He wanted a shower before he went to bed.

"Semerkhet?" he called. Ten seconds later, the boy hurried into the room, ready and waiting for anything his lord and master might possibly need. Day or night, Tut knew he would rush in the moment he heard the King call him. If he did happen to need his valet in the middle of the night, Tut rang his bell for one of the guards who patrolled in front of his room, and they ran down to the servants' quarters, where the Pharaoh had never been, and brought Semerkhet back.

Semerkhet looked down politely at the weary King, the younger boy, lying on his back in the bed, without batting an eye (or wrinkling his nose at the smells of sweat, manure, and smoke). During the King's little lie-down, Semerkhet appeared to have had a shower of his own (or maybe he'd gone for an invigorating moonlit swim in the Nile) and enough of a break that he appeared refreshed.

"Yes, Master?"

Tut slowly sat up with an effort, sending Bastet hopping lightly back to the floor, and took his walking-stick in his hand, stiff, aching fingers closing unwillingly around it after so many hours clutching the crook and flail. This one was an old favorite (if any of his canes could be called a favorite), a much simpler staff decorated with a familiar lotus motif. "I would like to take a shower."

Semerkhet inclined his head. "Of course, Master."

Tut sat in exhausted silence, barely aware of what was going on, as Semerkhet slipped one arm, then the other, out of his outer robe,

40

then carefully removed his wig and jewelry, taking some of the weight off of the Pharaoh's tired body. The valet lifted away all the jeweled collars, relieving the pressure on Tut's aching shoulders, and pulled off ring after ring along with his ornate bracelets and false beard of magnificence. Finally off came the heavy earrings that, along with the heavy double crown, had been pulling Tut's chin toward his chest all day.

With each item gone, Tut felt lighter, freer. But wearing them all day in the hot and the bright and the noise had done its damage. He was still stiff and exhausted. As Semerkhet took each piece of jewelry off the King, slowly stripping him of everything that made him the Pharaoh, one of another three servants who had appeared out of nowhere took it to clean it of the accumulated sand and sweat and put it away for next time. Tut hoped that that would be many days in the future. Wearing all of it at once was too much work. Sitting here while Semerkhet patiently undressed him made him wonder what it would be like to do it himself.

As he slipped the King's shoes off, Semerkhet's face did not change; all the staff knew the King's feet didn't match, but it was their job to act like they didn't notice. His legs didn't match either; the left one was much thinner than the right because he could hardly put any weight on his left foot. But right now that didn't matter. Both of his legs were equally tired. He sat for a moment on the bed in just his under-tunic, girding himself up for the journey ahead.

Tut's legs groaned in protest as he stood up again, but Semerkhet helped him rise and hobble across the room, leaving his cane behind. Together they went into the royal shower room, a small room with limestone walls and a wooden bench. Again the King felt his legs breathe a sigh of relief as he sat down.

Old Kahotep came in with several basins of water. After helping the King finish undressing, setting aside a pile of ill-smelling laundry that was stiff with sweat, embedded with smoke, and full of sand, he carefully poured the cool water over him. Then Semerkhet washed him from head to toe with soap made from natron mixed with oil. Tut sighed as the servant washed away the dust and sweat of the day, as well as his makeup, the cool, refreshing water soothing his sunburned skin and the gentle scrubbing relaxing his tired body, calming the remaining jangling of his nerves. At last he was clean. Sitting here naked, he had been washed clean of everything that made him the Pharaoh.

They couldn't be more different, these two servants on either side of him, Tut thought with a chuckle. Semerkhet was only two years older than the King and almost as tall, and he had a bright spirit and a willing smile, while dour Kahotep, who was almost old enough to be Tut's grandfather, was short, almost as fat as the Chief Physician, and as cranky as a hungry crocodile. But they both did their jobs well, serving him faithfully as they met every need.

Although it was still strange, sad, not to have Hetepheres, dear old Hetty, looking after him.

Kahotep poured one last basin over the Pharaoh, then wrapped him in a soft, white linen towel. Semerkhet and Kahotep, one on each side of the tall young King and with a firm hold on his arms, helped him back into his bedroom, where a clean loincloth and sleeping-tunic were waiting. The dirty laundry had disappeared, as had the other servants, leaving the room neat but silent. Blissfully quiet.

Before leaving, one of the servants had lit the oil lamps that were scattered around Tutankhamun's room; their warm light gave a cozy evening look to the room that made Tut even sleepier. One of the servants had also lit some incense for him. He caught a glimpse of himself in his copper mirror, hobbling along in a towel, without any wig or makeup, supported by the two valets, and could do nothing but chuckle vaguely to himself. He looked like his sister; he had the same long, prominent nose, the same slightly elongated head shape that their sisters had shared. Although Ankh had more chin than he did. He didn't think he was ugly, by any means, but with his long nose and receding chin, he thought he looked better from the front than in profile.

Then he paused. He saw his face and Semerkhet's reflected side by side, the same dark eyes, the same warm brown skin, and if he crossed his eyes, they melded into one. As if they were the same person. Not as if one was a god and the other was his lowly slave. They looked like they could be brothers.

In five months of being served by Semerkhet, he had never seen him as another human being.

The evening air was cool on Tut's shaved scalp; it was a lovely feeling after wearing his hot, heavy wig all day and his even hotter, even heavier *nemes* and double crown half the day. Finally free of his heavy jewelry, his body felt much lighter. And much to his delight, freshly showered, he was now free of the smells of sweat, smoke, manure, and stale perfumes that had been clinging to him all through this weary day. The incense that the servants had lit while he'd been in the shower smelled much better.

Having been inside the cool dimness of the palace for a good two hours and drunk his fill of wine, water, and *mai-sus*,

Tutankhamun's headache was also finally disappearing, an enormous relief. The overwhelmed buzzing had finally faded, his mind and body letting go of all the things he had experienced since that morning. He had made it to the end of the day. And he was back on his way to feeling not so bad. Time for bed.

They arrived at the King's bedside (the bedding and pillows having been replaced with a fresh set) and the servants helped Tut sit down, then released the firm, supportive hold they'd had on the King's upper arms as they had helped him limp from the bathroom to the bedroom without his cane, putting most of his weight on his strong leg.

Kahotep gave an elaborate, rather groveling bow, huffing and puffing as he bent his fat body, lowering his head toward the floor. The fat old man expressed a fervent wish that Tut would live forever, and retired after the King dismissed him with a vague word of thanks, silently hoping that he would live to the end of the week. Finally seated, off his exhausted legs, Tut sat in weary silence as Semerkhet helped him into his loincloth, the most intimate of tasks. He also brought him the natron paste he used to clean his teeth.

Oh, Tutankhamun thought, what he wouldn't give just to be able to look after his own needs in privacy. Given the choice, he would have preferred to be a common peasant with a healthy body rather than a Pharaoh who could barely walk. Some might see being waited on literally hand and foot as an honor, but for Tutankhamun, it was a daily frustration. Imagine that, if he was a simple peasant with two strong legs, he could have just jumped in the Nile for a refreshing swim. Of course, as Pharaoh, he wasn't allowed to; being waited on hand and foot came with the territory regardless of his health. Furthermore, he knew that it was an honor for Semerkhet to have the opportunity to care for him, but was that really an honor Tut wanted to bestow on anyone?

The only reason this boy had so much work to do as his valet was because of how frail Tut was. He did have more help than he needed when it came to showering; he needed someone to pour water over him, but he could easily have scrubbed himself. Although of course, when he was stupid tired like this, it was nice to be able to just sit there and let it happen. Except for when he remembered why he needed help.

Tut roused himself from his frustrated reverie with a blink. Across the room, Semerkhet was selecting a sleeping-tunic for him, but was going to wait to offer it until the King asked for it.

He ached all over. Tut's weary body wanted to go to bed, but right now, he was in too much pain. He would never get to sleep like this. There was one thing he needed first.

"Semerkhet," he said, and the young man turned to him, eager to attend to his next task. "Would you give me a massage?" He didn't know why he said it as a question; the Pharaoh could have anything he wanted (other than a brand-new pair of legs, of course) and didn't technically have to "ask" for anything. Maybe it was some subconscious effort to affirm that he and this other boy were equal in a way, equally human. Because… reflected side-by-side in the mirror, as alike as brothers, it was clear that they were.

He was not a god. He was a King, but he was a boy just like Semerkhet.

Semerkhet nodded with a polite, willing smile. Of course he did, what other choice did he have? "Of course, Master. Make yourself comfortable." Silently Tut chuckled, trying not to let his mouth twist into a wry smirk. Having a massage was the only thing that was going to make him comfortable.

Wearily, Tut lay down on his stomach in his loincloth, leaving his back and limbs accessible. His aching body already sinking into the bed, he closed his exhausted eyes with a sigh. He heard Semerkhet pick up the little ceramic jar of scented ointment and scoop a little into his hand with a little alabaster spoon, letting the solid coconut oil melt in his palm. The room filled with the fragrances of spikenard and frankincense. The King smiled. That one was his favorite.

Semerkhet perched on the edge of the bed and paused. Softly, the Pharaoh heard him ask, "May I?"

He just nodded into the pillow. Gently Semerkhet rested his hands on the King's tired back. Tut smiled sleepily as the valet began kneading his tense shoulders, digging his thumbs into the stiff muscles and slowly loosening them up.

As his body relaxed, sinking into the bed, Tut felt himself give a sigh of relief. The day was finally over... and it was ending in the nicest way imaginable.

"Fank you," Tut breathed as Semerkhet worked the muscles in the middle of his back that were always so stiff because of the way his spine curved. He didn't know why he said it; the Pharaoh never had to thank anyone for anything, but he wanted Semerkhet to know how grateful he was for bringing him this comfort, and allowing him, he was sure, to get to sleep.

"You're welcome, Your Majesty," Semerkhet replied, a hint of a chuckle in his voice. He did not expect to be thanked, and he was delighted.

"How was your day?" Semerkhet asked softly, gently rousing Tut from the drowse he was descending into as the valet's hands made their way down his back.

"All right," he murmured into the pillow. "Lotth of people. Got a giraffe."

He heard Semerkhet give the ghost of a chuckle. "Really."

"We're proud of you," Semerkhet said carefully as he gently rubbed the King's head, relieving whatever remnants of his headache had managed to hang on this long. "All of us. We know… we know it wasn't easy, a day like this."

Tutankhamun shook his head against the soft pillow. "No. It'th my job… but it's not eathy." He paused, trying not to drift off in the middle of this conversation with his concerned valet. "I'm glad you were there."

He could hear Semerkhet's smile in his intake of breath, feel the pride radiating from him. "Thank you, My Lord."

"What are we doing tomorrow?" Tut asked as Semerkhet gently worked his stiff arms and hands, his poor, tired legs, and his sore feet, replacing the day's misery with heavenly relief.

"Nothing you don't want to do," the servant replied.

Tut smiled. "Then I'm sleeping til noon."

Now that Tutankhamun's body was filled with such heavenly relief, he realized again just how tired he was. Too tired to keep his eyes open; he had closed them long ago. Too tired to stay awake. And he smiled as Semerkhet's hands returned to his back, his fingertips following one another down Tut's spine in an endless, sleepy rhythm.

And the King was asleep.

4   New Ideas

Tutankhamun awoke at noon, refreshed and in little pain. Time to greet the day… today he actually felt like it. Wasn't that nice. Semerkhet got the Pharaoh dressed in a soft white tunic and simple blue outer robe, one of his favorite wigs, his most comfortable shoes, and no crown or jewelry, then helped him dab on some of his favorite perfume. Ready for the day, Tutankhamun made his slow way out to the royal feasting hall, Bastet purring at his heels. He was delighted that today didn't look to be nearly as hot as yesterday. He actually wanted to wear a tunic and robe today, rather than just a kilt. This was much more seasonable for the end of the month of Meshir.

Ankh looked up from her lunch of roast duck, cheese, stewed onions, and red wine as she heard the familiar tapping of a cane, the familiar shuffling footsteps. He was up. Good. She smiled, feeling slightly concerned as she wondered how he would be. *I hope he's feeling better.*

He came into view, the cat following him. Ankh smiled as she saw him, seeing that he looked very refreshed. The wanness in his face was gone, the dark shadows under his eyes had faded. He looked so much better than when he'd gone to bed last night. He had gotten the rest he had needed.

"Good morning, love," she said, getting up and opening her arms. He stepped into her embrace, putting his free arm around her as he bent to kiss the top of her head. "You look better."

"I *feel* better," he said with one of his adorable toothy smiles, one of the ones he never wanted to show anyone but her. "Sometimes there's nothing for it but to sleep til noon."

His sister chuckled. "Well, I suppose the Pharaoh can sleep as late as he likes." She gave him another squeeze, then stepped back. "Want some breakfast?" she said, nodding toward the table. She chuckled again. "Or lunch?" He smiled again and sat down, actually feeling like he had an appetite today. Getting thoroughly tired and then having a good, solid night's sleep had made him hungry.

Breakfast was good, fruit and bread and a cup of tea, all tested for poison by Semerkhet. None today, of course. As the Pharaoh ate, his wife finished her breakfast, then came over to kiss his head and tell him that she was going for a short walk, leaving him to finish eating. A fly buzzed by his face and Tut swatted at it, snagging a long fingernail on one of the tiny braids of his wig and tearing it. Wincing, he held it up to examine it. It wasn't bleeding; he had just ripped the tip of the nail. Better see the royal manicurist. He looked down at his feet. Maybe he could get a pedicure while he was at it.

Tut rang his bell and Semerkhet hurried back to his side, standing at attention. In the brighter light of the airy royal feasting hall, the Pharaoh could see that his valet was also looking better after yesterday's exhausting adventure. He, too, must have gotten a good, solid night's sleep.

"Yes, Master?"

"Bring me Kemsit, please. My nails need doing."

"Yes, Master." Semerkhet bowed and left the room, returning a few minutes later with the small, delicate young woman whose tiny, nimble hands made her the perfect manicurist. Her dress was of white linen just like the Queen always wore, but of course, it was much simpler, as was the neat wig that framed her face. No starched bird-wing sleeves for her. A necklace graced her long neck, but it was a simple pendant, not an elaborate collar made of hundreds of tiny gemstones. And her makeup, as nicely as it was done, would surely require multiple touch-ups throughout the day, just like Semerkhet's. But it was impressive how well-put-together someone could look even on a more modest budget.

"Presenting Kemsit, Manicurist of the Great House." She knelt, clasped her hands, and bowed to the floor, then slowly rose, standing before him with her tools in her hands, waiting for her instructions. Her head was lowered respectfully, her eyes on her own feet.

"My nails need cutting," he explained, showing her the ragged one.

She bowed again from the waist. "Of course, Your Majesty. I brought my kit."

At the table was as good a place as any to do it, Tut offered his hand, and she rested it on a small board to keep it steady. She took out a small flint knife and carefully pared down his nails, beginning with the damaged one.

He watched her as she worked. Tut was suddenly ashamed to realize that he had never really *looked* at her; he had always simply thought of her in terms of what she could *do* for him. She was an individual, unique among all the servants, among all the women in Egypt, among all women everywhere. He watched her, taking in every detail, her tiny, pointed chin, her pointed little nose, the roundness of her ears, the attitude with which she bent professionally over her work, the focus, and yet the ease, with which she was taking care of his nails. She was a girl, a woman, just like the Queen.

Then this beautiful, unique young woman whose heart and mind brimmed with beautiful, unique hopes and dreams of her very own

50

knelt on the floor and moved to his feet, politely ignoring the fact that they didn't match, just like every member of the palace staff did. And he refused to be embarrassed.

Though still a little embarrassed that she thought he was a god. But what was he going to do, issue an edict declaring that the Pharaoh was just a boy like thousands of others?

She began by washing his feet, carefully removing his sandals, then pouring water over his feet from a pitcher, which was caught in a basin. Both containers had been brought by another servant, a silent young man, and they disappeared just as quickly as the man slipped back into the shadows without a barely audible wish for Tut's long life, prosperity, and health. Then Kemsit dried the Pharaoh's feet with a linen towel. One by one, she rested his feet on her knee, using the same little knife to carefully cut his toenails.

The last step was the henna nail color. Tut let Kemsit take first his left hand, and then his right, and dip his fingertips into a small alabaster container of red henna dye. Just like everything else about his appearance, this would show everyone that he was not a commoner.

Her own nails were incredibly neat, he noticed, both her fingers and her toes, although, of course, she wasn't wearing any henna. That was not for commoners. Although if everyone was a unique individual... how could anyone be described as "common?" He wondered if she had done her nails herself... then wondered if that was even possible.

"There you are, Your Majesty." His nails were done. Kemsit gathered her materials and offered another deep bow.

"Thank you," Tut said, and she blushed furiously.

"Y-you're welcome, Your Majesty," she stammered, looking at her feet. "All l-life, p-prosperity, and health." Then she was gone. He smiled. A simple thank-you could make anyone's day.

Tut sat in his favorite chair in his bedroom and pondered as he slowly petted Bastet. He was human. So was Semerkhet. It was only a trick of fate, the whim of the gods, that he had been born a Prince and Semerkhet a commoner. They could have been switched; Semerkhet could be Pharaoh and Tutankhamun could be hobbling through the dust, slave to a master of his own. Tut thought of the long-ago Hebrew Prince. How had he felt when he, too had discovered that those who served the palace were people too?

He had murdered an abusive taskmaster and run away to the desert. That showed how he had felt. Maybe Tut would not take it to quite that extreme.

Tut was not a god. And Semerkhet was not a piece of dirt, and not an automaton who existed only to serve him. One was a King, the other, his servant. But they were just alike. Just like the King, Semerkhet had interests, wishes, goals, cares of his own.

And it was time to find out what they were.

But even these new thoughts were temporarily interrupted by one of Tut's most important obligations: the daily prayers and sacrifices in the Temple of Amun-Ra that protected all of Egypt from falling into chaos and destruction. Taking up his walking-stick, he headed off to the temple on the grounds. It felt like it was a mile away from the palace, past all the gardens, almost as far as the stables. No one was with him, which worried him slightly; if he collapsed somewhere on this endless pathway while most of the servants were at lunch, would anyone hear him yelling for help, and if not, how long would it take them to find him?

But even as he struggled to make the long walk to the temple, the Pharaoh felt his spirits rise as he passed the royal gardens. Tut smiled as he saw two or three little brown birds fluttering among the beds of bright flowers, pecking for seeds and twittering loudly. The garden proliferated with a rainbow of blossoms— white daisies, pink roses whose sweet fragrance wafted toward him in the gentle breeze, red poppies, tiny, white jasmine blossoms, anemones of all colors. But the garden offered more than color and beauty, it offered sweet fruit to eat— stately rows of graceful peach and pomegranate trees, jujube shrubs, date palms, and grapevines. This early in the year, most of the trees were only flowering, few had yet borne fruit.

The peaches would ripen in a few months, but the grapes wouldn't be harvested until the hot month of Paophi, the pomegranates even later, in Athyr, when the year had begun to get cool again, and the jujube in the chilly month of Sholiak. He smiled as he thought of the pomegranate, his favorite fruit; its puckery taste, its tiny, berry-like sections gleaming like red jewels. A breeze rippled the surface of the lotus-pool he had just passed, ruffling the leaves of the trees.

Someone had gone to a lot of thought to design this garden, Tut thought; it was arranged geometrically, with the largest lotus-pool in the very center, surrounded by a rectangle of flowerbeds, flanked by a larger rectangle of fruit trees. Elsewhere in the enormous garden the pattern was repeated, with smaller lotus-pools surrounded by borders of trees or flowerbeds.

All through the pattern walking paths were laid out, and a jaunt around the entire palace was something the King had not attempted since he was about twelve, although the families of other government officials certainly enjoyed the walking opportunities.

Around the garden, around the entire palace grounds, there was a wall, providing privacy, shielding the royal peace of the palace from the dirt and noise of the city outside it. And he had not ventured outside that wall for a very long time.

In the distance he could hear servants chattering as they went about their daily work; even further away he could dimly hear the bustle of the town of Memphis, where he had never been, even though it was right outside the palace gates. The Grand Vizier had discouraged it. Even further away, a group of half-built statues of his grandfather Amenhotep the Third recalled the Hebrew slaves of his day, the slaves who had all disappeared one day, never to be seen again. They had left their building projects, left their bricks, left their hovels, and gone… somewhere else.

Nearer to hand, six guards marched by on their regular patrol of the palace grounds, their spears in their hands, daggers at their belts. Just in case something should happen. Although nothing ever did.

Tut limped down the long, long path of packed earth that stretched as straight as an arrow between two courtyards, watching the alabaster temple slowly, slowly grow larger, squinting at it as the sunlight reflected dazzlingly from the white walls and columns. Almost there. After much too long of a walk, by which time his left foot was throbbing with every step, he completed his journey, finally pausing at the doorway of the white, gleaming building to center himself, preparing for an encounter with the divine.

Slowly he entered the temple, where High Priest Parannefer was waiting, a spotted leopard skin draped over one shoulder over his white robes of fine, pleated linen. He was as bald as Ay— the priests bathed and shaved constantly to maintain their purity. Tutankhamun sighed with relief as the shadows of the temple closed over him. Away from the blinding brightness of the midday Sun, he could open his eyes beyond a squint.

And yet, shielded from the warmth and light of the Sun, the temple was dark. Cold. To his surprise, Tut felt himself shiver.

"The god delights in the presence of Pharaoh Tutankhamun," the High Priest greeted him, giving a little bow. He stepped aside, and the Pharaoh walked into the depths of the dimly-lit temple, past high walls painted with strange animal-headed gods, dimly illuminated by the cold, shivering light of flickering oil-lamps. The air was heavy with the fragrance of incense.

He stopped before the image of Amun-Ra and respectfully lowered his head. This was the only time that he bowed to anyone. He raised his hands in worship, pausing a moment in prayer, a prayer for the well-being of everyone around him. Servants included. After all, they were people too, weren't they?

Make me strong, he prayed finally. *Make me the strong Pharaoh I'm supposed to be.*

Then it was time to ask his questions. The King looked up at the statue of Amun-Ra, standing silently above him, gazing out solemnly into the middle distance.

"O great god Amun-Ra, will the harvest be good this year?" he asked.

The High Priest looked up at the statue, brow furrowed in concentration. Could he hear something the King couldn't?

"The great god announces that the harvest will indeed be good this year, My Lord," the High Priest said with a smile.

Tut nodded. Good. "O great god," he continued, "will I become a strong Pharaoh?"

Again the High Priest looked up. "Amun-Ra agrees that Pharaoh Tutankhamun will be remembered as a great Pharaoh."

He smiled. Time for... time for one more question. "O Amun-Ra," he asked softly, "will I have an heir?"

The High Priest's face went solemn. He knew why the Pharaoh was asking. For the final time he looked up at the statue for what to say. "The great god Amun-Ra urges Pharaoh Tutankhamun not to give up hope," he said simply.

Tut sighed. That was not an answer.

He inclined his head before the statue of the god. Now it was time for the part of prayer-time that he had been glad to miss on Tribute Day. He and the High Priest left the temple, blinking in the bright sunlight and sudden warmth, to find another priest leading a large, black-and-white bull. The bull stood in a paddock scattered with sand. Sand that could easily be replaced.

"O Great Morning Star, we sacrifice this bull in the name of Amun-Ra, an offering to all the gods that they may pour out their protection upon Egypt and bless us with *ma'at*, truth, harmony, and justice," the Royal Butcher said. His copper blade gleamed in the bright midday sun as the bull stood there peacefully, looking like he wished there was some grain nearby for him to eat.

Tut nodded, stomach twisting. "Let it be done."

And he looked away as the bull was sacrificed, blood splashing onto the sand.

With farewells to the priests, his daily intercessions were done. Time to get back to his day.

Nothing seemed to have happened, he thought as he slowly made the long journey back to the palace, not entirely sure if he was hungry anymore. His words to Amun-Ra had simply echoed back to him. And he knew that the answers to his daily questions really came from the High Priest. Had he even been heard?

The Sun was bright and hot, and he found himself squinting as he walked. But there was something real about it, something true, as the warm rays stretched down from the heavens to touch him... as if to tell him that he was loved. The world the Sun shone on felt very different from the cold, dark world inside the temple.

"She's got more jewelry than she knows what to do with... but she can't even put it on without me!" Meresankh was giggling to Persenet as they stood chatting in the hallway during their break. "The Queen wears the crown, but she doesn't know how to put it on."

"They're the gods," Persenet agreed, "but what do they really do all day?"

"I'm happy helping," Meresankh said with a shrug, "but I don't really know... if we'll ever be friends. Or if it even matters. It's a good job... but it doesn't feel like being with people like me... or even being with people at all. I wonder how different it is from the priests' jobs, putting clothes and makeup on the images of the gods and giving them their meals!"

And they laughed together.

Ankhesenamun kept walking. She didn't know Meresankh very well... but she had just learned a lot about what her handmaiden thought about her.

Then the Queen paused. The sound of Meresankh and Persenet's laughter echoed inside her heart, awakening a memory. A memory of similar laughter, shared by six sisters so long ago. Laughter that had sounded exactly like that of these two servants.

Quietly, Ankh turned back around, watching Meresankh and Persenet as they continued to walk.

And it hit her. They were people too.

They were not living dolls with no purpose other than to serve her. And she was not a goddess.

She was a human. And so were they. With thoughts and cares just like hers.

The Queen shook her head as the ladies' laughter faded. What an idea.

The Queen also went to the temple for prayer. Head bowed before the image of Tawaret, the goddess of fertility, she asked, as she had too many times for her aching heart to count, to be blessed. And to bless her husband with an heir.

Someday, that was. When they were both ready.

Because they were not. It was still too soon.

But as she turned to go back to her day, returning to the warmth of the Sun after the shadowy chill of the temple, she was not sure she had been heard.

Tawaret had never responded. Would she now?

After lunch, lamb with a salad of lettuce and peas, Tut and Ankh walked out to the garden, arm-in-arm. The sun was bright but not harsh, the sky was a clear blue scattered with fluffy clouds, and a cool, gentle breeze blew, ruffling the surface of the lotus-pools and embracing them with the sweet fragrance of the bright flowers. And it blew the braids of Ankh's wig away from her face, jingling her red beads, and made the Pharaoh wrap his blue outer robe closer around himself, huddling comfortably into it. The year was still cool, and the breeze could be chilly, especially when the sun went behind the clouds. Today the Queen wore a long-sleeved dress, keeping off the chill.

In the distance, the gentle sunlight sparkled on the surface of the lotus-pools. Meshir was a beautiful month, the second month of the Season of Emergence. The days were slowly getting longer, giving them more time to enjoy this lovely weather. Even after Tut's long walk, it was such a beautiful day that he wanted to stay outside.

One of the servants brought out their *seega* gameboard and silently set it on a nearby table. Tut smiled. He and Ankh sat down to play.

"I'm trying to remember what Father always said about the servants," Tut said as he placed two of his game pieces on the square board, which was organized into twenty-five spaces, five one way and five the other. He was placing them rather randomly, he had to admit. He still hadn't figured out that part of the strategy.

Ankhesenamun answered his move, advancing toward a victory, adding her twelve pieces to his using an arcane but effective tactic, then capturing his pieces one by one by flanking them with hers, removing one of his pieces after another from the board. Tutankhamun shook his head. His wife always won. More knowledge, more wisdom, more experience made her the better player.

"He said that they were just like us," she said. "And that we were all the servants of the Lord of Light." She paused. "And that if the Hebrew slaves, who called Him I-AM, could grow to become a great nation of free people, there really was no difference between us."

Tut looked at the board, considering his next move. "Well, I don't know about the Lord of Light," he said, "but I think he was right about the servants. I've been thinking... when Semerkhet gave me my shower last night—"

Ankh giggled, her cheeks coloring with a blush. One did not talk about bathing while sitting outdoors in the middle of the day.

"Oh, come on," he said, rolling his eyes with a chuckle. "Anyway, we were passing by my mirror, and I saw the two of us reflected side-by-side. We looked just the same. And so I think Father was right... we're all people, royalty and servants."

"I've been thinking too," Ankh said. "About my maidservants. About the way they walk, the way they talk. And they're just like me."

"I do wonder, though," he said thoughtfully, "why I'm so tall. I'm the tallest person I've ever seen."

"Well, you were the first boy," his wife said. "And even... even though things were hard for you, you were the heir the minute you were born. Mother and Father were not very traditional," she said, "but when it came to that... Mother may have become Pharaoh after Father died, after she was co-regent, but it was not as though they could have made Meritaten the heir, even though she was the oldest. She was..." Ankh smiled. "She was Mother's Queen instead. But you were the first boy, the only boy, and they did everything they could to take good care of you so you could grow up big and..." She paused, swallowing. "So you could grow up to be Pharaoh."

60

Tut smiled. "They saw us as all equal. We were all children. They had six daughters and a lame son, but that didn't change how much they loved us."

She shook her head, tears sparkling in her eyes. "No. It didn't." Ankh sighed as she looked back into the memories. "They brought wet-nurses for you, and making sure you were well-fed was their only job, because you were hard to feed. You had different ones over the years, but Maia was always my favorite. I remember she carried you around all day so she could feed you whenever you were hungry, and you weren't weaned until you were nearly five."

He smiled. "I remember her. I always loved the songs she sang. Just like... Hetepheres." He gulped, trying to blink back his unmanly tears. Because his heart still ached when he thought of his old nurse.

Ankh nodded. "And we gave you cow's milk, and goat's milk... We had a sweet little goat brought to the palace, just for you. And as much fruit as you wanted... Even if something was out of season, we did our best to have it brought for you. We all worked hard to make sure you ate well. You were the youngest, and you had six big sisters to love you and play mother with you. And because you ate so well, and Grandfather was tall, you were tall too." She stroked his cheek with a little smile. "So really, you're tall because we all love you so much."

Tut smiled wistfully, heart warming with gratitude. They had all worked so hard to take care of the tiny baby with the mismatched feet and the mouth that struggled to swallow. And they had succeeded.

"You were always there for me, all six of you," he said a little later, looking up from their half-played game. His sister just smiled. "I remember when Auntie Hennutaneb's children would tease me, and you would quote the *Instruction of Amenemope*.

> *Do not jeer at a blind man nor tease a dwarf,*
> *Neither interfere with the condition of a cripple;*
> *Do not taunt a man who is in the hand of God,*
> *Nor scowl at him if he errs."*

"Amenemope was called wise for a reason," Ankh said, making another move. "He knew that no one can know another person's destiny, and no one has the right to judge another person based on their differences. We are all..." She swallowed, eyes falling for a moment. "We are all made the way we are for a reason. And we are all meant to do something unique. We are all provided with a future that only we can accomplish."

She looked up at her brother with a little smile, and then he was the one looking down, blinking away the feelings in his heart. She was right. But when would he discover the purpose for which he had been sent to Earth in this body?

Then he looked up again. And in her eyes, he saw determination. And he saw hope. And he knew that one day, they would find it. The thing that only he could do.

After Ankh beat Tut at *seega* and decided to go have a little walk among the reflecting pools, Semerkhet came outside and sat down across from the King, turning to gaze out at a flock of birds flying by. Tut looked at him, his profile, so like his own (except that Semerkhet had more chin), the darkness of his kohl-outlined eyes, the warm brown of his skin. They were exactly the same.

"Semerkhet," he said softly, wondering how to say what was on his mind.

"Yes, Master?" his valet replied, turning to look at him, or at least his chin, if he was not yet ready to make full eye contact.

"I have to tell you something." He swallowed. "I... I'm not a god. I'm a boy, just like you."

Semerkhet shook his head with a little smile. "I know, My Lord. All the servants know. It's a secret we all keep. It's a beautiful thought, but... whatever the gods are like, they are not walking among us. You... you are the Pharaoh, and we love you and we honor you. And we honor the traditions that say the Pharaoh is a god. But we know." Semerkhet bent forward and whispered dramatically into the King's ear. It felt like something a friend would do, telling a secret. Then it hit him— he and Semerkhet were friends. "It's a big conspiracy." Together the two friends dared to almost chuckle over the strange secret.

And that was when Tut noticed Ay striding away with a very odd expression on his lined, venerable face.

5   Gratitude

Going back inside, Tut sat and looked at all the things, all the *stuff*, that he had accumulated in his bedroom. Ten wigs (the one he had on today wasn't his favorite, but that was at the delouser, being cleaned), endless laundry that was always clean and neatly folded… How was it always clean, anyway? Someone… someone was responsible, taking the dirty laundry at the end of each day, washing it, folding it, bringing it back fresh and clean and starched and sparkling white. Someone cleaned his shoes. Someone polished his jewelry.

He didn't even feed his own cat.

How many people, Tut wondered, did it take just to take care of the things he owned?

"Who washes the clothes, Ankh?" Tut asked at lunch, a filet of fish in garlic sauce with a side of fresh asparagus. Prayer-time with Amun-Ra had been just as silent as always, and the sacrifice of the bull had been worse than usual. He had had to change his sandals. But he knew that nothing would go wrong with today's lunch— Semerkhet had tasted it for him and declared it free of poison.

Ankh took a sip of wine and shrugged. "The servants." She glanced around at the five or so who stood around them at this very moment, silently waiting to refill a cup or plate at a nod from Semerkhet, who directed them.

"But… who? Like, which person? Probably takes more than one person. And how do they do it?"

His wife chuckled. "I think they haul it out to the Nile and wash it there, but I've never seen it done."

Tut chuckled too, at the image of clothing essentially being bathed. He was going to have to do some poking around.

"Kahotep?" he asked. Immediately the portly servant was at his elbow, ready for whatever the King wanted him to do (as long as it didn't involve any running). As the old man caught his breath, winded from even that brief trot, Tut caught a whiff of the anise, myrrh, and marjoram medicine that Kahotep used on his decaying teeth.

"Yes, Glorious Lord?"

"Who does the laundry?"

Kahotep paused. "The Chief Washers of the Palace and Handlers of Royal Linen, O Great Morning Star, and the Chief Bleacher."

Tutankhamun nodded. "I would like to speak with them."

The servant frowned, his face blanching. "Is there a problem with your clothing, O King for Whom the Sun Rises?"

Tut shook his head. "No. I just want to thank them for doing my laundry."

And Kahotep blinked and went to find someone.

"Presenting Khenut, Superintendent of the Clothes of the King," he said a moment later. A nervous young woman stepped forward, eyes on the floor, and knelt before him, clasping her hands before her heart and bowing to the floor. She was unique, just like Kemsit; she was a little shorter than the manicurist, a little heavier, and just like the King, she had imperfect teeth. She was visibly shaking— she looked like she thought she was about to be executed.

Tut smiled at her and extended his hand, which she kissed.

"I just want to thank you for doing my laundry," he said.

Still on her knees, she burst into tears. "My f-family has b-b-been washing the Pharaoh's c-clothing for f-five generations," she sobbed, makeup running down her face. "F-family b-business. It's our honor and p-p-privilege."

After she left on the supporting arm of a maidservant, still sobbing heartily, Tut sat and thought. Maybe he should find a different way of thanking people.

And now, when he died, he would not be able to promise the goddess Ma'at, who demanded the correct answers to forty-two questions about how a person had conducted themselves in life, that he had not made anyone cry. Would this moment speak against him, weighing down his heart and making him unworthy of spending eternity in the Field of Reeds?

As she went, her sobs still audible long after she was out of sight, it occurred to him that Khenut would make a very good wailing woman at a funeral.

"Are you happy working here, Meresankh?" Ankh asked as her handmaiden helped her get ready for bed. She was sitting on the bed in her sleeping-tunic, enjoying the feel of the cool night air on her bald head after so many hours under her hot, heavy wig.

The servant paused in folding up the Queen's linen dress.

"Of course, Your Majesty," she said slowly. She sounded slightly uncomfortable, as though she was worried she was about to be called out.

"I hope you are," Ankh continued. "Because I caught a few words between you and Persenet, and it sounded to me like you resented me for…" She paused. "Not being able to put on my own jewelry."

Meresankh bowed her head, cheeks reddening in a blush of shame. "I'm sorry, My Lady," she whispered. "I was out of place."

Ankhesenamun raised an eyebrow. "Just a little." Then she smiled. "I want you to be happy here," she said softly. "And… I don't want to annoy you. Because…" She paused, thinking how to go on. "Because even though I'm Queen… I'm just like you. Only human. And you're just like me. And I want you to be happy."

Meresankh looked up, cautiously yet boldly meeting the Queen's eyes with her own. Eyes that were so like the Queen's and those of the sisters she remembered, eyes that proved that Ankh and Meresankh truly were both human. And Meresankh smiled. "Thank you, Your Majesty."

Ankhesenamun gave a little sigh. "Maybe…" She chuckled. "Maybe you could teach me to style my own wigs. Make me a little more… independent."

Meresankh gave her Mistress another hint of a smile. "If you like, My Lady."

Ankh sighed. "But please… don't spread a negative attitude. Attitudes are catching, and if everyone starts whispering about how the Pharaoh and the Queen are incompetent fools, soon everyone will be grumbling. If you ever have a concern, please, please tell me, but please don't… spread it around."

Meresankh nodded. Her face cleared; the Queen could see she knew she was forgiven.

"Yes, My Lady," she said with a bow. And with a little smile, she turned away to put away the day's jewelry.

Ankhesenamun smiled. A problem solved… with good communication and no hard feelings. If only politics could be so simple.

But even as his life seemed to brighten before him with the prospect of so many new things to learn, Tut still had to attend to the mundane. And he had to submit to his weekly checkup from the Chief Physician. It was just as bad as always; embarrassingly detailed, painful in places, and utterly pointless. Now he sat on his bed, trying to keep his helpless frustration from leaking out of his eyes.

"What's wrong, darling?"

It was Ankhesenamun, standing quietly in the doorway of Tut's chambers, her long, white linen dress rippling around her, the delicate black braids of her wig cascading over her tiny brown shoulders, a golden diadem identical to his setting off her look. Tutankhamun turned his face to her.

"Another awful doctor's appointment," he said with an angry sigh. "I don't know what the point is of him coming every week. Nothing he ever does makes any difference, it just hurts, and the medicines are disgusting. I'm juth tho tired of all this, Ankh! My foot hurts, it never lets up, and it's all 'doom and gloom' when he cometh, like I'm going to die next week, and he knows it, only he's not letting on because he wants me to *suffer*!" With a cry he put his face down and wrapped himself in his arms, trying not to show her his tears.

Gently she sat down next to him and put her cool little arms around him. She was almost a foot shorter than he was, but she was strong. Sniffling, he took her hand, and she pulled him half-way into her lap and stroked the tiny black braids of his wig.

"I know. I know. Tomorrow's going to be better. You'll see."

He gulped and felt her smooth face on the back of his neck. "Thank you. I know things'll get better; it's just so hard to *wait*."

68

"I know." That was all she said, but that was all he needed. "I know."

Or almost all he needed. He gave another heavy sigh, wiping away his angry tears.

"What's the point of all of this?" he whispered. There was so much pain in the question. And he was really asking.

She squeezed his hand, fighting back her own tears. "Life is about what is. Figuring out what you can change, and what you can't. And living with it all, whatever it takes."

He closed his eyes, relaxing into her arms. He let go of the anger, letting it fade into sadness… and a strange, dissatisfied acceptance.

The Queen smiled as she took care of her husband, her brother. He was so brave, so patient. It was so unfair that he was burdened with daily pain, hobbling like an old man with his walking-stick. But who could divine the will of the gods, or their purpose in sending the Pharaoh to Earth in this body.

But there was a purpose, she knew. If only they could find it. And for now, it was her joy to bring him comfort.

That night the Pharaoh sat on his bed as usual, letting Semerkhet help him get into his loincloth and sleeping-tunic. The task complete, Semerkhet stepped away, his eyes respectfully lowered.

"Thank you," Tutankhamun said gently.

Semerkhet blushed, visibly restraining himself from making eye contact with the King. "You… you're welcome, Master," he whispered.

Tut smiled. But there was still so far to go. Semerkhet had accepted his gratitude, but he still seemed uncomfortable with it. And he wasn't yet making eye contact. However, as Tut reminded himself with a chuckle, at least he had not made Semerkhet cry by thanking him.

Now that Tutankhamun was starting to grasp the fact that everyone who worked at the palace was just as human as he was, he wanted to understand the different responsibilities they had. It transpired (after a long mission that sent Semerkhet from one end of the palace to the other with a sheet of papyrus and a pen), that the creation and maintenance of Tut's wigs was a governmental department unto itself, including such roles as the Wig-Maker of Pharaoh and the Upper and Under Wig-Makers of the King, led by the Superintendent of the Wig-Makers. The Chief Metal-Worker and Chief Artist for the Care of the Royal Jewels designed, crafted, and looked after his jewelry, the Custodian of Sandals kept track of the King's eighty pairs of shoes, and the Keeper of the Diadem, Who Adorns the King, a member of the wig department, kept his crowns and circlets clean and shiny.

Even the care of the Pharaoh and the Queen's nails required an entire department, with the Manicurist of the Great House, the Caretaker of Nails, the Attendant to the Nails, and the Supervisor of the Manicurists in the Royal Palace. And now he knew the titles of Gentlemen One, Two, and Three who helped Semerkhet dress him: the Handlers of Royal Linen and the Handlers Of Crowns And Headdresses. The King blushed to learn that there was even a Director of Royal Loincloths.

Not to mention Semerkhet's official title, which made the King chuckle— The Washer of Pharaoh. Of course, his other titles included Director of the King's Dress, Master of Cosmetics, Who Adorns the King, Chief of the Scented Oils and Pastes for Rubbing His Majesty's Body, Attendant of the Lord of the Two Lands, Masseur of Pharaoh, Who Adorns Him, and Groom of the Bedchamber. The job titles were so comically specific; at least that meant that people knew what they were getting into when they applied for a palace job.

And every single one of those people who looked after him, his clothes, or the palace in which he lived had a name. A name of their very own. Every single one of those people was a unique individual with their own thoughts, wishes, hopes, and dreams.

"It seems we owe gratitude to rather a lot of people," Tutankhamun commented to Ankh, looking down at the list on the table as they sat in their pavilion one cool morning, watching the birds between games of *seega*. Out of five games, he had only won one. A gentle breeze blew, making the green beads on Ankh's wig jingle under her golden diadem, sending a flutter through her long linen sleeve, and making Tut pull his warm, yellow robe closer around himself. Their guards, too, were warmly dressed. A murmur of conversation told them that the Treasurer's little girl and her nanny were out for a walk, stopping every few feet to smell the flowers.

"We do," Ankhesenamun agreed, scanning the list of which people worked in which departments. "No one ever told me that there was a whole department just for wigs!"

Tut chuckled. "That's what I was thinking. But how can we show people we're grateful?"

"You mean, without making them cry?" she said, raising an eyebrow.

He nodded. "Exactly."

She tapped her chin. "Hmm. Mother and Father always made a point of telling the servants how grateful they were for their work. Reminding them that we were all the servants of the Lord of Light. So, really, just telling them."

Tut sighed, giving himself a wry little smile. "Maybe that's the power I have," he said. "The power to make people smile when I tell them thank you. Let them know how grateful I am... how what they do for me every day really matters." He shook his head. "Even cutting my nails. Kemsit cut my nails earlier, and it seems like such a small thing, but that matters too. I can't do it myself."

Ankhesenamun nodded. "That sounds like a good move, Your Majesty."

Tutankhamun sighed, looking down into the depths of one of the reflecting pools. Three little fish swam up to the surface, looking up at him curiously as if hoping to be fed, and he smiled. Fish could be just like cats, they begged just like Bastet. "I have more political power than anyone else in Egypt," he said slowly, "or I will soon. But I feel like I have less power over my actual life than the average fisherman." He sighed.

"This is your power," she said, putting her little hand over his.

He looked up and smiled at her. "I wake up feeling like I'm in a deep, dark hole because of the things I can't control," he said. "Maybe this can keep me out of it."

"It will," she said with a nod. "Focus on the things you do have power over. Even little things like saying *thank you*. Making people smile."

"When will Ay step back?" Tut asked his sister with a frustrated sigh. "He's been Vizier since before I was born, before you were born, and regent since I was crowned. I'm eighteen now... When will he stop being regent? Give me the crown?"

"Sounds like you need to talk to him about that," Ankh said, running her thumb over his knuckles. "Lord of the Two Lands."

"So *there* you are!" came a sudden angry voice. The King and Queen jumped, then looked up to see the Treasurer's wife striding out into the garden, the long sleeves of her fine linen dress trailing behind her and a tiny dog yapping under her arm. "Hemetre! Why did you think this was a good time for a walk? Mayamenti is late for her dress-fitting. Get inside, both of you." And she removed Mayamenti's hand from her nanny's and took it in hers, beginning to almost drag the little girl inside. She followed her mother, but looked regretfully behind her at the beautiful day and the abandoned walk.

"Yes, My Lady," the servant said, inclining her head. And with a sigh, she followed them.

"They might be rich," Ankh said as they disappeared into the palace, "but I don't think they're happy."

Tut sighed. She was right. And gratitude was one of the things the Treasurer's family was missing. "Saying *thank you* is so small, so easy," he said with a little chuckle. "How can two words give anything back to everyone who works so hard for me, does so much for me?"

"Well, you will be surprising people," she said, nodding at the list. "Nobody expects the Pharaoh to say *thank you* when they serve him lunch."

"I'll just have to hope I don't make anyone cry again," he said dryly.

"Indeed." Ankh leaned over and put her hand on his shoulder. "So, you see, you do have power."

He smiled. "And I'm going to own it. I will be the King who may never have ridden into battle but who made his staff smile and feel needed. Because where would I be without them?"

Ankh sighed. "Where indeed?" She paused. "And at the same time... where would they be without us? Our lives are all so deeply interconnected... they serve us, we employ them. It's to the point where I don't think we could exist without one another."

He nodded. "That's true. We need them, and they need us. So we have to take good care of them while they take good care of us." He smiled, looking down at the list in front of him. "And I'm going to learn everyone's names, and make sure they know we're grateful."

The sound of laughter blew in on a sudden breeze, the braying of a donkey, the lowing of a cow, even a snatch of music. Tut looked up, peering over the garden wall, down at the city of Memphis below. A city that was full of people who were just as real as all the servants at the palace, each with their own names, personalities, hopes, and dreams. The world beyond the wall.

"There's a whole city down there, Ankh," he said. "A whole city full of real people living real lives. And somehow, we're responsible." He sighed. "Would be fun to visit someday... but I'm sure Ay wouldn't want us to."

She smiled and squeezed his hand again. "Who says we have to ask?"

Tut and Ankh sat at lunch after the King's visit to the temple, snitching dates and almonds (from Tribute Day) from one another's plates as they chatted. Across the room, Semerkhet facilitated the meal while a harpist entertained them. As always, Tut's loyal valet had checked the food before the Pharaoh had begun to eat. No poison today.

Ankh's handmaiden Meresankh picked up the Queen's empty cup, slowly carrying it over to Semerkhet. He took a wine jug and refilled it just as slowly. The King and Queen couldn't help but notice the way they were looking at one another.

They tried to hide their giggles.

The King slowly walked past Ay's chambers and paused as he heard voices. He stopped just out of sight, peering through the half-open door. Ay was in there, sitting at his desk across from Treasurer Maya. Hunched with age, he was bent over a document like a vulture picking its meal down to bare bones. Picking over the details of his plans for the future of Egypt, plans he had not discussed with the actual Pharaoh.

"...and so I believe we should raise the prices of the grain we sell to our neighbors," Maya was finishing.

The Grand Vizier nodded his old, bald head. "Let it be done, in the name of the Pharaoh." And bending over the document, they both appeared to sign it, marking it with their signet-rings.

Tut grumbled to himself as he kept walking. In the name of the Pharaoh? But without having discussed it with him first? Who was Pharaoh, him or Ay?

Here he was, gazing out at the long expanse of adulthood that lay before him. Things were going to change.

6   Pushback

Tutankhamun looked down, admiring the delicate white pleats of his tunic. He and the Vizier were sitting in the Pharaoh's study that morning at the beginning of the cool month of Phamenoth, as Ay had been going through a long, long list of Tut's ancestor Thutmose the First's accomplishments with him, a list of who and what a Pharaoh should be. Tall, strong, warlike, a conqueror of distant lands, expander of the great Egyptian empire. Even as Tut gritted his teeth at the impossible standard set by his great ancestor, he hoped that the facts he was learning would help him lead his country one day.

"Khenut and her staff do a good job," he said appreciatively.

Ay's bag-rimmed eyes snapped open, his lined face blanching for an instant as he accidentally began to crumple the papyrus he'd been reading from in his dull monotone. He swallowed, visibly calming his expression and letting go of the wrinkled document, slowly, deliberately beginning to smooth it out again. And paused. A moment later, looking down at the page as he pressed it with his old, gnarled fingers, he finally said,

"How do you know Khenut, O Great Morning Star?"

"Well, I've been talking to the Queen, and my valet…"

"Sennefer?"

"Semerkhet," the King corrected him. "His name is Semerkhet. And we got to talking about how the laundry gets done, and I got to meet Khenut."

Ay nodded, thoughts hidden. Finally he looked up, making eye contact. "Interesting way of spending your days, My Lord."

Tut shrugged. "Well, it's my kingdom, and if I'm going to be ruling it, I want to understand how it works."

76

Ay nodded again. "Indeed."

Tut walked back to his room at the end of the day. He was exhausted, and was looking forward to spending a few minutes chatting cheerfully with his valet.

"Semerkhet?" he said, coming into the room. He smiled. There he was, standing at the end of the bed—

Tutankhamun paused. Who was that? Shorter, wider, older than Semerkhet. A totally different person. Although he was dressed in the same uniform as the King's usual valet.

"Who are you?" he asked, politeness forgotten in shock.

"Nuya, O Mighty King," the man said nervously, gulping as he folded his hands in front of him, avoiding Tut's eyes just like all the staff did. He knelt down before the Pharaoh as if he was more comfortable down there.

"May I ask where Semerkhet is?" the King asked.

"I believe the Grand Vizier had him transferred to work as a scribe, O King for Whom the Sun Rises."

"Hmm." Tut shook his head. Something to deal with tomorrow. "Well, thank you for being here. I suppose I'm ready for bed now."

Nuya gave a deep bow from where he knelt, face to the floor. "As you wish, Glorious Lord."

And the Pharaoh let Nuya help him get ready for bed as his mind filled with plans.

The next morning Nuya was still there. Tut was polite to him, let him do everything he was getting used to having Semerkhet do, helping him with his moisturizer and perfume, slipping him into the day's outfit. The Pharaoh sat on the bed looking at the replacement valet as Nuya went to get his shoes; the man was dressed in the same uniform as Semerkhet always wore, but he had something tucked into his belt. Silently the Pharaoh squinted at it.

It was a piece of papyrus, covered in lines and lines of graceful hieroglyphics and scribal hieratic script in neat calligraphic style. It wasn't words, it was rows upon rows of repeated characters, each more beautiful than the last, arranged as if Nuya was practicing his technique. Had Nuya written all that himself? The King didn't say anything, but kept turning it over in his mind as Nuya came back with his shoes, then helped him select a walking-stick for the day, one of the more formal ones, of the type he might carry while holding court. Then came a chin-length wig of delicate black braids and the Pharaoh's small gold circlet. Tut's only slight complaint about Nuya's work was how his hands were steady when he was writing but not when he was putting kohl on someone else; as a result, the King's eye makeup wasn't as neat as Semerkhet always made it look. Finally he was ready for the day, ready to get breakfast.

Ready to talk to his Vizier.

Nuya followed him into the royal feasting hall, where he pulled out his chair for him and stood at his elbow, ready to bring him more bread or fruit or refill his tea. And of course, he began the meal by testing Tut's food for poison. The King had to admit he really was good at his job. But he wasn't Semerkhet. He wasn't the one who had helped him begin to discover the world around him. Wasn't the one he was delighted to be able to call his friend.

"Good morning, Vizier," Tutankhamun said as the old man came in, bent over his finely-carved walking-stick, the sleeves of his robe swaying like the heavy wings of a vulture.

"Good morning, Your Majesty," Ay responded with a bow.

"Interesting thing," Tut said casually, taking a bite of an apple. "Apparently Semerkhet has been turned into a scribe. And apparently you know something about it."

Ay swallowed, glancing down at the Pharaoh's plate as if he was thinking about what he wanted for breakfast. "I believed his skills would be better used somewhere… else in the palace, Glorious Lord," he said. His gravelly old voice was not quite as clipped and courtly as it usually was.

Tut raised a black eyebrow, letting it just begin to get dark and dangerous. He knew he had powerful, sometimes frightening, eyebrows, and sometimes they made an effective tool… or weapon. "Really. May I ask why?"

"He is so… talkative, Son of Ra. I feared his gossip would… distract you from your kingly duties." The Vizier sounded uneasy, almost wheedling.

"Really. But is it not my duty to be informed about the running of my country?"

Ay gave a little smile, still wheedling as the wrinkles around his mouth deepened. "The running of your country is your sphere of concern, Great Morning Star. Not laundry."

"Perhaps I feel I can be a better Pharaoh if I at least understand how laundry works," Tut countered.

"As you wish," he said, inclining his bald head. His smile had faded. He had no comeback to that.

"And as Pharaoh, I believe I am ultimately responsible for all hiring and firing, and for making sure that each member of the palace staff is assigned to the best department based on their skill set," the Pharaoh continued. "And it is our royal wish that Semerkhet be returned to his position as our valet. Immediately."

He glanced at the replacement valet. "Nuya," he said. The servant jumped to attention, ready for whatever the Pharaoh might be asking for. "Would you like to be a scribe?"

Nuya gave a delighted gasp, eyes lighting up as they almost strayed to the King's face. "I've always *dreamed* of being a scribe, Your Majesty!"

Tut gave a satisfied smile. His deduction had been correct. Mission accomplished. He nodded. "There. Nuya can have the scribe job Semerkhet was transferred to, and Semerkhet can be my valet again. It's settled."

"I... I'm not sure..." Ay stuttered.

"It is," Tut said with a nod, letting the thunder behind his eyes just begin to rumble, threatening lightning. "It's settled." He turned to Nuya, who straightened up. "Nuya, go to the scribes and tell them you're there to take Semerkhet's job, and send him back to me. Thank you."

"Thank you, O Great Morning Star," Nuya said with a deep bow, and hurried off at once, sandals flapping loudly on the stone floor in his joyous haste. Smiling to see his excitement, Tut immediately forgave him for forgetting to deliver the farewell wishes of life, prosperity, and health.

Tut continued eating his breakfast, refusing to look at the Vizier. Suddenly it all tasted very good. It tasted like victory.

Five minutes later, Tutankhamun heard a familiar footstep on the polished floor. He looked up with a smile to see Semerkhet hurrying in, adjusting the tunic he'd just thrown on over the scribe's kilt. There was rather a lot of ink on his fingers.

"You called, My Lord?" he asked with an expression of relief.

"Hello, valet," Tut said, grinning as his servant, now his friend, made eye contact with him, even if it was only for an instant. "It's good to see you again."

And Semerkhet smiled as he took his familiar place at the King's elbow.

Only Ay frowned.

The morning went on, and Tut went for a little walk through the palace, stretching his legs. He passed one of the smaller audience chambers, not the grand throne room where he very occasionally held court when something extremely important needed to be approved, but a smaller meeting room.

He heard voices from inside. And he paused just out of sight, planting his walking-stick on the floor and peeking in through the half-open door.

Grand Vizier Ay was sitting on the throne-like chair at the head of the room, speaking to what looked like a delegation of some sort. Tutankhamun thought he recognized the Viceroy of Kush.

"...and so the yearly tribute from Kush will be increased to one thousand cattle, seven hundred measures of ivory, and five hundred measures of gold," Ay was saying.

"As you wish, Your Grace," the viceroy said with a bow. Together the two applied their signet-rings to a document, and Tut heard Ay say,

"Let it be done, in the name of the Pharaoh."

Suddenly Tutankhamun understood. Ay was conducting his morning audience-time, the audiences that an older Pharaoh would be expected to run himself.

Tut walked away. Someday. Someday very soon.

"What happened at breakfast?" Ankhesenamun asked her brother as they sat down for their lunch, side-by-side at the enormous table in the grand feasting hall. Tut smiled as Semerkhet took a bite of his molokhiya soup, declaring it free of poison, then a sip of his wine. Also good.

"Thank you, Semerkhet," he said pointedly.

His valet chuckled, smiling back at him. "You're welcome, Master." And looking extremely pleased about something, he walked across the feasting hall to find something else to get done.

The Queen watched him go. Then she turned back to her brother, still waiting for the answer to her question. Clearly this new chemistry between the Pharaoh and his valet had something to do with the odd events she had received a vague report on earlier.

Tutankhamun looked at his sister. And he smiled again. "Politics happened," he said with satisfaction.

Ankh raised an eyebrow as she spooned up a bite of green soup. He was telling her that "politics" had happened?

"Please elaborate," she said with almost a little chuckle of incredulous surprise, slurping down a mouthful of smooth, leafy molokhiya soup, seasoned with chicken broth and garlic.

"Well, yesterday I was telling Ay about everything I've been learning, and how Semerkhet was helping me gather the information I needed. And then last night, when I went to my room to get ready for bed, he wasn't there."

His sister gave a heavy sigh as she looked at him, as if to say that as a politician, she had suspected as much.

"It was a man named Nuya," Tut went on. "And he's nice, he really is, and he did a fine job helping me get ready for bed, and get ready this morning. But he's not Semerkhet. Not... my friend."

He took another bite of soup, then wiped a stray bit of greens from the corner of his mouth as his sister silently smiled to hear him describing his valet as a friend. "So this morning at breakfast," he finished, "I told the Vizier that who worked where was my decision to make, and I got Semerkhet back from the scribe department where Ay had put him, and made Nuya a scribe instead, because that's what he wants to do anyway, instead of being a valet. So everyone's happy... except for Ay."

Ankh looked at her brother, the silver beads of her wig tinkling as she shook her head with a smile.

"You, my love, are a politician," she said, bumping him playfully. "I'm proud of you." Then she paused. "Just remember... getting someone's job switched is the least that someone as powerful as the Vizier can do. We won this time... but politics is a dangerous game." She squeezed his hand. "And the game's not over yet. It's just beginning."

The Pharaoh smiled. "Am I ready to play?"

She grinned. "I think you are."

"Vizier," Tut said as they played *seega* in the garden that afternoon, "I'm eighteen now."

Ay made his move, the little ivory game piece clicking on the wooden board as he captured one of the Pharaoh's pieces between two of his own. "You are, Glorious Lord."

Tut answered the Vizier's move with his own, retreating with one of his two remaining pieces toward the corner of the board. "So I'm wondering... how much longer are you going to be my regent? When do..." He swallowed. "When do I start getting to make the decisions myself?"

Ay smiled warmly at him, his wrinkled face making the Pharaoh think of a mummy. Silently he slid one of his pieces into the one space Tut had not considered, claiming the Pharaoh's piece before it had reached safety. "Your mother, before she died, told me that in the event that she journeyed to the next world while you were yet a child, to place you in full power when I thought you were ready."

Tut made another move, trying to avoid capture by the old man's pieces, but noticing too late that his final piece was trapped. "So, am I?"

The Vizier smiled again, finishing the game in victory. "Almost, My Lord. Almost."

"'Almost,' he says," Tut said, flopping down in frustration on the couch in his sitting room, putting his arm around Bastet as she hopped up beside him, sensing his distress. "But of course he didn't give me a date. He makes it sound like it's completely up to him, whenever he decides I'm 'ready.' For all I know, that could be never." He gave a deep sigh, running his hand over Bastet's back, hearing her purr. "Now what am I supposed to do?"

"Show him you are 'ready,'" Ankh said immediately, getting up from where she'd been sitting at the desk, reading a volume of history. "That you're mature, that you're wise, that you can make decisions on your own." She smiled. "You already have, getting Semerkhet back from the scribe department."

She stepped closer and took his hand. "Keep looking for those opportunities," she said. "And impress him. And he will see."

Tut squeezed her hand, giving her half a slightly unsatisfied smile. Then he nodded. "Sounds like a plan."

"I'm so sorry," Tut said that night as Semerkhet helped him get ready for bed. It was still a bit strange, even a bit lonely, to have a valet, rather than old Hetty, putting him to bed. Semerkhet, after all, did not offer to tell him a story or sing to him, which he either would have declined with a playful eye-roll, or, if he was under the weather, gratefully accepted.

His valet looked up from the sleeping-tunic he was unfolding for the Pharaoh.

"About what, Master?"

He gave a sad little laugh. "About how the Vizier turned you into a scribe. I'm sorry I couldn't stop him."

Semerkhet shook his head with a forgiving shrug. "It's not your fault, Master. I'm just glad... I'm just glad I got back in one piece!" He sighed, looking into his own thoughts. "Bit awkward, though. I saw my father. And neither of us knew what to say." His voice dropped to a murmur; a reflective whisper Tut was not convinced was meant for his ears. "Although I'm glad he switched from alcohol to work." Then Semerkhet smiled again. "But it's nothing compared to what might have happened."

"Indeed," Tut agreed. "And I'm so glad to have you back. I won't let him do that again, I promise."

Semerkhet just chuckled again, and for the briefest, briefest instant, his eyes flickered up toward the Pharaoh's face. They didn't quite meet Tut's, but they were no longer trained carefully on the floor. "Thank you, Master."

And Tut smiled.

Hetepheres' funeral was that week. The Pharaoh joined the palace staff in remembering her long, loyal life, trying not to let himself cry in front of all the strangers. Together they honored her, recounting in gratitude all the things she had done for them. And life went on.

Later that week Tutankhamun had another history lesson in Ay's study. The Vizier's reading voice was not always very engaging, but Tut did his best to stay focused and listen dutifully.

"...he cultivated friendships with the Mitanni, the Assyrians, the Babylonians, and the Hittites," the Vizier droned. He was reading about Amenhotep the Third, Tut's own grandfather. "His reign will be remembered for its peace and prosperity."

"Did you miss a section?" Tutankhamun asked, looking up. Ay looked at him as though he had not been sure the Pharaoh was still awake. Sometime when he couldn't sleep, he should make Ay read history to him, Tut thought. That would probably knock him out immediately.

"Miss a section, Great Morning Star?" Ay asked, blinking at him, eyes bright over their wrinkled bags. There was something almost uncomfortable in his expression.

Tut nodded, sitting up from his slouch. "About the Hebrews. And how they disappeared. And how my father changed everything because he thought..." Tutankhamun's heart warmed as he remembered the stories his father, and his father's mother Grandmother Tiye, had whispered to him, Meritaten, and Ankh, cautious of being heard by any of their courtiers. "Because he thought, with everything that had happened, with the Nile and the insects and the hail and Uncle Thutmose dying and the army disappearing, that the Hebrew Prince had been right all along." Tut shook his head. "Why is that not written down in our records?"

Ay swallowed, setting the papyrus carefully aside, gnarled old fingers moving delicately, as though it were sticky.

"My dear boy," he said carefully, "...some things are better left in the past. The Hebrews are gone, and we have nothing to do but move forward without them."

"So was my father only telling me stories, or did it really happen?" Tut asked his Vizier. But Ay had already excused himself and walked out of the room.

Who could he ask, Tut wondered, if Ay didn't want to discuss it with him?

7   Decisions

One morning as Tutankhamun sat in his study looking at the list of servants and their roles and ticking off who he'd met and thanked so far, Ay's secretary brought him some documents to authorize with his signet-ring. All Tut's life Ay had been making the decisions, just having the Pharaoh approve them and make them official. And every day he held meetings with people from far and near who had questions and concerns, meetings that would one day soon be Tut's responsibility. Whenever the Vizier decided to hand over, that was.

Tut had never really thought about it, the decisions the Vizier made in his name. He just signed what he was given, trusting in Ay's infinite wisdom. He shook his head. As Pharaoh… as Pharaoh, he really ought to be taking the time to understand the things he was signing. He really ought to be making sure that he wanted to sign them.

He picked up one of the papyrus documents and looked more closely at it. This one was a budget; they were ordering a thousand Arabian horses for the army, three tons of cedar-wood lumber, and… five hundred slaves from Nubia.

Tutankhamun set down the papyrus without stamping the wax seal. He was going to have to talk to Ay about this.

"Ankh, I'm worrying about something," Tut said as they played *seega* in the pavilion outside. It was cooler today, overcast and breezy, a relief after the horrible heat and oppressive sun of Tribute Day.

She moved a game piece, flanking one of his and removing it from the board. This early in the game, and he could already see

88

that he was doomed. Well, he had just slapped his pieces into rather random starting positions, still not sure of how to strategize in that first stage of the game. She looked up at him with a concerned frown.

"What is it, darling?"

"Ay… and some of the decisions he makes. I got some paperwork to authorize earlier, and I saw that we're importing five hundred slaves from Nubia. I didn't sign it yet… but I don't want slaves from anywhere. We have enough servants at the palace, and they're all paid. Why should we have slaves?"

She shook her head, the delicate braids of her wig swinging with the movement. "I don't think we should. And… how can we be moving toward slavery again so quickly when all the Hebrews ran away from our own grandfather? I'm not sure that's wise."

He nodded, making his next move in the game, which didn't help much— only maneuvered his piece into a spot where it was safe, but could no longer move without being captured. "I don't think so either. But… how do I stop him?"

"Just don't sign it."

"But how do I just not sign it?"

Ankhesenamun gave a sarcastic little chuckle. "Tutankhamun, you are the Pharaoh, if I remember correctly. You don't have to sign anything you don't feel comfortable with. You're of age, and these decisions are yours now. It's time for you to take your power. Start with this, and then next week, do something else. Look at the taxes and see if they need to be changed. Maybe… maybe your legs aren't strong, but your mind is. So think for yourself. And don't let Ay make the decisions for you any longer."

Tut nodded and smiled at his wise wife. "Thank you."
Calling for the document and a pen, he proudly wrote "denied"
over the listing of slaves. Then he stamped the wax with his signet-
ring. Horses and cedar-wood they could use.

The Queen smiled as Tut walked away after quite surprisingly
winning the game. Her baby brother was growing up.

Later that day, Ay came to visit the Pharaoh as he sat in his
study, Bastet curled up in his lap and a cup of tea in his hand. Tall
even as he bent over his cane, Vizier Ay cut an impressive figure, a
gaunt, bald old man whose outward frailty housed an infinite well
of wisdom. Since the death of Tut's parents, Ay had guided the
young King, carefully steering him in sensible directions. Tut was
grateful for every minute of it, and trusted the man completely. Or
at least, he always had…

"O Great Morning Star," Ay said with a deep bow, "there is a
matter I wish to discuss with you."

Tut looked up. "What matter, Vizier?"

"My secretary brought me the budget you approved," he said,
holding it up for Tut to see. Tut nodded. "And I see that you made
some… adjustments. It appears that we are not importing slaves
from Nubia."

"That is correct," Tut said sweetly with a little nod.

Ay swallowed. "May I ask why?"

"Because the Pharaoh is not convinced that Egypt requires slave
labor. The paid palace staff meet all our needs, and even the
conscripted laborers and soldiers receive a wage. We do not need
unpaid slaves. And we are not going to have any. Or have you
forgotten the disaster with my grandfather's Hebrew slaves? I have

90

Egypt's best interests at heart here. I don't want to bring ten more plagues down on our heads."

"The slaves are not people, My Lord," Ay said unctuously. "They are... slaves. Besides, it would cost too much to pay everyone working in Egypt. We are accustomed to a... certain lifestyle, after all." He ran a be-ringed hand over his finely-pleated white linen tunic. "And that is precisely why we need more slaves," he continued, his mouth quirking in a slight grimace. "To replace those who left so... precipitately. Only by importing slaves from Nubia and other neighbors of ours have we been able to rebuild, go on with life without, for example, the Treasurer having to wash the palace floors. We need a solid workforce, O Great Morning Star. Slaves are slaves, wherever they come from, and importing them has allowed us to go on without feeling a... pinch."

Tut raised an eyebrow, dark and stern. He let it get just the slightest bit intimidating. "So you're saying that when the Princess adopted the Hebrew baby who grew up to go mad in the desert and help the slaves escape, he wasn't a real person, and neither were they? What was he, then? Slaves are people. And people deserve a wage. I want you to work on that. From now on, everyone working in Egypt will receive a wage. There will be no more unpaid slavery." He paused, thunder rumbling in the darkness of his kohl-lined eyes. "And there will be no more signing things for me 'in the name of the Pharaoh'."

Ay swallowed again, Adam's apple jumping in his skinny neck that was just like a vulture's, hung with droopy, wrinkled skin. "Indeed, My Lord." He stood there, shifting his weight from foot to foot as if he didn't feel the conversation was over, but wasn't sure what to say next.

"Do you have any questions?" Tut finally asked.

"No, My Lord," Ay said uncomfortably.

"Then you are dismissed. The budget has been finalized as it currently stands."

He looked at Ay, holding his gaze with slightly unnerving intensity in his dark eyes and stern eyebrows until the Vizier finally looked away.

"Yes, O Great Morning Star," he said slowly. And with a deep bow, he left the room with a wish for Tut's long life, prosperity, and health.

Tut lay back in his chair, petting the cat. That had felt good.

He had never dismissed his Vizier before.

"I still feel like I don't really understand the government." Tut was sitting with Ankh in her private sitting room, petting the cat as they chatted.

"Tell me what you know," she said with a shrug. "And I'll fill you in."

He thought. "Hmm. Well, there's the Treasurer, named... Maya. He's in charge of the money. General Horemheb is in charge of wars, and the Viziers, especially Ay, are in charge of... everything else. And I'm..." He gave half a smile, half a sarcastic little chuckle. "I'm the symbol of Egypt."

Ankh leaned over and took his hand. "But you can be more. You're eighteen. And when you see Ay or Horemheb or any of the others do something you know isn't right... say something. Show them that you're not going to leave all the decisions to them anymore. You're the Pharaoh. And they're not."

Tutankhamun looked at his sister. "This is the year," he said with a smile. "The year that I step forward. Take my power."

His sister squeezed his hand. "I can't wait to see it."

That afternoon, the King and Queen took a walk in one of the courtyards outside the palace, strolling slowly through the gardens, between the lotus-pools. Cane firmly in one hand, he had the other arm linked with hers, and, small as she was, she was bearing some of his weight. Sometimes it was good to get out in the fresh air and get a little exercise. Slow as he walked, it felt good to get tired enough to get a good night's sleep, rather than tossing and turning after a long, quiet day of inactivity. And it always felt good to get out and look at the flowers on a cool, refreshing day in Pharmouthi.

In the distance he could see two tall women walking arm-in-arm, with matching wigs, matching dresses, matching jewelry. They looked familiar; he was pretty sure they were the wives of General Horemheb, although he didn't remember their names. It was nice, really, that at least the other members of the government and their families got to enjoy the enormous gardens. He squinted at two other figures standing near the largest pond on the grounds and recognized the Treasurer's little girl standing next to what appeared to be her nanny. The child clearly wanted to take a boat ride across the pond, but that wasn't on the agenda.

Between the palace grounds and the city, there was a high wall. A wall that kept the city out... and the members of the royal family and its court in.

"Have you ever been outside the grounds, Ankh?" Tut asked as they made their slow way down the garden path.

She shook her head. "Not for a long time. By the time we moved here, we didn't have a lot of childhood left," she said, adjusting her hold on him. He had to look where he was going, but he admired the garden as they went, the tall date palms and peach trees, the peaches, nectarines, and plums just beginning to flower, the winding grapevines waiting to be harvested by the winemakers in the month of Paophi, the riotous colors of the flowers. Their guards stood at a distance, giving them privacy to walk and chat while keeping an eye on them. "Meritaten, Meketaten, and I were born in Thebes, and Tasherit, Rure, Setepenre, and you were born in Akhetaten, the city he had built far away in the desert. Although I don't remember it very much."

He shook his head, the images he did remember passing through his mind like the pictures of the deceased in a tomb. "Neither do I. Mother moved us here right after Father died." He paused. "Does anyone still live there?"

She shook her head with a sad smile. A shadow passed over her face as they walked under a sycamore tree. "I don't think so. We had to move as soon as Father died. It must look so sad... I remember the courtyards where the Sun would shine in, and Mother and Father would stand together and sing hymns... and it still shines there, but I'm sure all the walls are crumbling. I heard they've been using the stone for other buildings." She swallowed, tears sparkling in her eyes without falling. "I always wanted to go back... but now I don't think I'd want to see what it looks like now."

They had stopped walking. Tut squeezed his sister's hand. All his memories of Akhetaten were from before his sixth birthday, but they were the same as hers: bright, sunny courtyards, joyful hymns sung by Mother and Father, sweet incense. But no images to bow to. There had never been any idols of the Aten. Only pictures of the King and Queen at worship, the Aten Himself represented as the life-giving rays of the Sun.

"They loved the Sun," Ankh said, as if she had heard her brother's thoughts. "They called it the *Aten*, and they said…" She lowered her voice, as if not wanting the guards who were shepherding them at a distance to hear her. "They said that He was the only true God, the God of the Hebrew slaves who had left us to become a great nation of their own.

"That was what they named you," Ankh continued. "Tutankhaten. *The Living Image of Aten*. And they named me Ankhesenpaaten, *Her Life is Of the Aten*. But we changed them to *Amun* when we…" She chuckled. "Got married. Because the priests took us back to the old traditions."

"Was Father right?" Tut asked his sister. "About the Aten, the Lord of Light, being the same as I-AM of the Hebrews? Were his stories true, about the insects, the Nile turning to blood, the darkness, the reason…" He swallowed. "The reason Uncle Thutmose died?"

Ankhesenamun bowed her head as a breeze rippled the diaphanous linen of her long-sleeved dress. "I don't know," she whispered. "I think… he believed he was right. And so did Mother. And something, something, must have happened, to make them change everything so suddenly. But I don't know what."

Tut sighed. "I wonder if we'll ever know."

His sister gave half a smile. "So do I." They looked quietly around the gardens, feeling the breeze blowing their wigs, then smiling as the Sun touched their faces.

"So, yes, I have been outside the grounds," she said with a sigh, bringing the conversation back to his question as they slowly resumed their stroll, walking past a glorious rosebush whose sweet scent carried halfway across Memphis, "but not for a long time."

He smiled at her. "Would you like to?"

"Where would we go?" she whispered in a conspiratorial voice. "Greece? Arabia?"

He shook his head. "No, I mean to just go out into town, into Memphis. Have a look around. See how Ay is taking care of things and what we need to change, now that we're in charge."

"*You're* in charge," she said. "You're the Pharaoh, and I'm the Great Royal Wife." Then she winked. "Technically. Even if I do tell you what to do."

Tut chuckled and squeezed her hand again. "Yes. You've always guided me— you're smarter than I am."

"Well, I am your big sister," Ankh chuckled. She brushed away a fat, black fly as it buzzed by, then reached up to tuck a stray braid of his wig behind his ear. Big sister indeed.

Tut smiled at her. "And I need your help. I need my Queen at my side, serving her country with her intelligence. Even… even if the dynasty ends with us, Egypt herself can be our child. And she's going to need two parents to take care of her."

Ankh looked pensive for a moment, her gaze dropping to her empty arms, then sighed and looked up at him with a grin. "Assignment accepted, Your Majesty. So, when should we plan our little trip?"

"I was thinking tomorrow morning," Tut said. They were almost back; the palace gate loomed closer with every step they took, and the servants milling around the door looked at them silently, leaving the Queen to carry on helping the King until they heard otherwise. The guards took the same approach. "Ay is going to On for a series of meetings, and if we get back before dinner, he won't ever know we went."

Ankh smiled. "Let's do it. I'm excited. It's fun being the King and Queen, figuring out how to take good care of our people."

Tut smiled back, leaning his tired body on her shoulder as they reached the gate, walking more slowly than ever. It was time to go in. "I think so too."

"What is Memphis like, Ay?" Tutankhamun asked over dinner. He wanted to hear the Vizier's perspective, feel him out. Compare what the Vizier told him to what he actually saw.

"What do you mean, Your Majesty?" Ay asked, plucking two or three figs from one of the bowls on the table. All around them servants stood silently, ready to refill a plate or cup at a word from Semerkhet, who stood overseeing every aspect of the meal— including testing it for poison. All clear tonight. A harpist played gently in the corner.

"I mean, just out in the town. What are the houses like?"

"The houses vary, Great Morning Star," Ay said carefully, "based on the economic status of their owners. But the city is strong and prosperous. Your country is the greatest in the world." The Vizier paused, a question on his lined face. "Why do you ask, Glorious Lord?"

"Oh, it's just I've never been out there," Tut said casually, giving a little shrug as he reached over to grab a handful of pistachios out of a bowl. "Just curious."

"Please let my words satisfy your curiosity," Ay said, putting a wrinkled, caring hand on Tut's shoulder. "You know you're not strong enough to leave the palace grounds. I would not wish for you to get hurt. Do not trouble yourself with the affairs I am managing in your stead."

"Thank you, Ay," Tut said, giving the Vizier a sweet smile. "I know that you manage things very effectively. And that you will until I'm... ready."

"I have always done my best, O King for Whom the Sun Rises," Ay said, dipping his bald head, "and I always shall."

"When I was little, you always told me not to worry about what was out there," the King said. "Not to bother about it."

"And you still don't have to, Glorious Lord," Ay said warmly. "You are eighteen, barely of age. One day, you will stand alone, taking full responsibility for your country. But not yet. Cherish these days," the Vizier said, "before you bear that burden alone."

Tutankhamun smiled. "Thank you, Ay."

8 The Outside World

The next morning, Tut had Semerkhet get him up early, and Ankh had Meresankh do the same. They got dressed and had their breakfast, then headed outside, where ten uniformed servants waited by the extra-large palanquin, the one they could both ride in. They each had a little purse jingling on their belt— going out into the marketplace, they just might want to buy something. Ever the big sister, Ankhesenamun had suggested they not go empty-handed.

Semerkhet helped the Pharaoh climb in, then helped the Queen get in beside him.

Tut had never been to town. For a moment, he wondered how he would do, how loud and bright it would be, how big the crowds would be, how it would compare to Tribute Day. But he would be inside the palanquin, he reminded himself. Observing from a slight distance, shielded from some of the intensity by the curtains around him, while still able to observe, gathering data that would help him become a better Pharaoh. It would be tiring. But it was too important to not do it because he didn't want to get a headache. He had a duty to his citizens. And this was part of fulfilling it.

"Just a quick look around town, please," Tut ordered, and slowly, the palanquin was hoisted into the air by the litter-bearers. A moment later they were off, down one of the paths between two courtyards, toward the high wall that separated the palace from the world. It was a smooth ride, much smoother than either riding in his chariot or going horseback riding. In front of the palanquin and its ten bearers marched six spear-bearing guards, ready to protect the Pharaoh and the Queen on their little jaunt through town.

"Can you see, darling?" he asked, reaching over to adjust the fine linen curtains that shrouded them from the view of the populace, opening them just enough to get a good glimpse of the outside world.

"Yes, that's fine," Ankh said. She grinned and squeezed his arm, leaning closer to him. "Oh, I'm excited. I haven't been out in such a long time."

"Open the gates!" a servant cried, and the large gates in the wall that separated the palace grounds from the city of Memphis began to creak. Slowly they swung open, and the King and Queen were out.

Out in the world.

They headed away from the palace, past the fine villas of various high-ranking government officials. White or creamy-tan stone, crisp, clean lines, gardens of fruit trees and bright flowers, reflecting pools... They were smaller than the palace, but houses like this were still run by staffs of their own.

"I wouldn't mind living in one of those," Tut mused as they went by one barely a third the size of the palace. "Oh, what a nice garden they have."

"Mmm, you can smell the flowers from here," Ankh sighed, taking a deep breath. "When we get back, we'll have to tell them we want a garden like that."

Before too much longer, the graceful villas began to give way to smaller, plainer houses, those of business owners, doctors, teachers. Even those were nice. They were... quaint.

In the distance a crowd appeared. Tut sat up straighter, peering ahead. What was happening?

"I think this must be the marketplace," Ankh said.

Tut smiled, feeling his heart begin to beat a little faster as the sound of the crowd grew louder with every step the litter-bearers took. "I bet you're right. This should be... should be fun."

They entered the marketplace, the litter jostling through the bustling crowd, a crowd that was so busy with its shopping that it barely looked up at the fine people who must be riding in this litter. The Pharaoh took a deep breath, willing his heart and mind to settle as all the sounds, all the smells, all the people, threatened to overwhelm him.

Then he felt a soft, warm little hand touch his. And he smiled, feeling the overstimulation dissipate. His sister was beside him. And this would... *would* be fun. And very informative.

He began to look around. And he saw stalls and stalls of cucumbers, lettuce, onions, radishes, artichokes, apples, and, of course, dried figs and dates. This early in the season, most fresh fruit was a delicious hope to look forward to. But the vegetables were booming. All around him was the fruit of the labors of the citizens who milled around them, the everyday people who worked hard and earned what they ate. And it wasn't just fruits and vegetables— he saw fish caught from the Nile that very morning, spices from faraway lands, fresh bread and roasted meat, and handmade goods one couldn't eat— woven baskets, pottery painted in bright colors, and handmade textiles. The beauty of what people could make— real, everyday people who were not professionally trained artists employed by the palace— took his breath away.

Tut's stomach grumbled as he smelled the delicious street food. They never had anything quite like that at the palace. Children ran by, chasing one another gleefully, pointing out things they wanted their parents to buy for them. The occasional donkey plodded by, loaded down with groceries, led by a shopper with a basket of bread or a clay jug of water carefully balanced on his or her own head.

"Should we get something?" Ankh asked. "I do like that shawl."

"And I like the way that lamb kebab smells," Tut said, his stomach growling as the hot, smoky fragrance of the roasting meat blew their way on the cool Pharmouthi breeze.

She chuckled, beaded braids jingling just like her laughter. Today's beads were solid gold, just like her diadem. "Let's do it."

They stopped in front of the clothing stall, and the Queen placed her order via one of the guards. Then the Pharaoh did the same for the lamb kebab. Ankh sat happily smoothing the heavy, blue-and-purple striped shawl in her hands, and Tut carefully held the skewer of spiced meat so it wouldn't drip. He was getting hungry, but he wasn't quite ready to eat yet.

Ankhesenamun saw the woman before he did. Doing her shopping, working hard to provide for her family. With six happy little children trailing along behind her, and another one on the way, her curved belly full of life.

Tutankhamun took his wife's hand as she looked down, eyes closed but gazing blindly at her own flat stomach, her empty arms. And they remembered. Remembered the hope. And remembered the pain.

That woman looked just like their own mother, so long ago, in the good old days when a happy family had lived life one long, laughing day at a time, a mother and father and their seven children, safe from the knowledge of what would one day tear them apart.

When they had stood like that, six sisters laughing and teasing, little Tutankhaten, as he had first been named, safe in his mother's belly, they still had five happy years ahead of them. And when Ankh herself had stood that way, cradling her belly and the little life within, once, and then twice, they had not known that it would be only weeks before their joy would be stolen from them.

So they took a moment, there in their little refuge in the middle of the crowded marketplace, and remembered together.

The moment came to an end with a deep breath, a hand-clasp. And again they looked out from between the curtains of the palanquin at the outside world, the citizens of the country they had never seen. They passed through the market without buying anything else, but taking with them the memories of the rich sounds, sights, and smells. This was a day to remember.

The houses got even smaller as they continued past the marketplace. But they saw people, peasants, in the yards, families working in their gardens, which were more the sort that produced vegetables to eat rather than proliferating with flowers that were nothing more than decoration, playing with pets, playing ball games, laughing together. They were simply dressed, but they looked happy. Happier than Tut and Ankh often were in their palace.

Then Tut saw his wife cover her nose with a grimace. It hit him half a second later, the smell of garbage.

The palanquin paused. Tut understood, the guards and the litter-bearers could see where they were headed and wanted to see if the royal couple wanted to turn around before it got too nasty.

But they didn't want to turn around. They wanted to see it for themselves.

"Continue," he ordered. They resumed, and the King and Queen looked around in growing concern at tiny, tiny houses, no, cottages, no, huts, no, hovels, that appeared to be made of mud bricks. They were crowded together, all built right in a row. Some were barely bigger than the King's bedroom. Tut swallowed as they passed. *I once wished I could live in a "little mud hut." But that was before I ever saw one. Now I take it back.*

The streets were narrow here, bumpy and rough, scattered here and there with garbage. A communal dump was visible a few streets away; that was the source of the smell. It was an irrigation canal, but it was full of rotting garbage and waste of all descriptions, and rats were picking through it. Tut tried not to gag at the sight.

A stray cat ran by, its fur patchy and matted, its ribs visible. Tut gulped as he thought of Bastet. It had no one to take care of it.

Cats… they weren't just cherished pets. They were holy animals, sacred to the goddess Bastet, after whom Tut's own beloved kitty had been named. Families whose pet cat had died shaved their eyebrows in grief, and carefully mummified their treasured companion so they would be reunited in the afterlife. And killing a cat carried the death penalty. So how was it possible that right here in Memphis, this cat was hungry and alone, dirty and flea-bitten, with no family to love and honor it? Why had no one taken it home?

Doors here opened right onto the street. But right now they were all closed. Closed like the King and Queen's eyes had been until today, closed like the eyes of the Vizier and the courtiers who listened to him, who had elected to do nothing about the problems they had so carefully hidden from the Pharaoh and his Queen. Problems that were right at their doorstep.

Then they saw a person. A very small person. A little girl, around ten years old, wrapped in a very dirty white linen tunic, carrying a very old doll. She was barefoot. Hunger showed in her face, her prominent cheekbones and wristbones, a lonely, courageous independence wrought of necessity showed in her haunting, hollow eyes. And she was all alone.

"Stop," Tut said in a commanding voice. The litter came to a halt, and Tut opened the curtain, revealing himself and the Queen to the child. She stared at the bejeweled couple as if she had no idea who they were. Or what they were. They might as well have been a god and goddess.

Tut held out the delicious-smelling kebab. "Come here," he whispered, holding it out. "This is for you. You must be hungry."

"Take this too," Ankh said, offering her brand-new shawl.

The child just stared, catlike eyes wide with shock, suddenly wrapped in a soft shawl, a good meal in her hand. And all they could do was leave her staring.

Then they turned around. Tut sat staring into space, pondering everything they had seen. His jewelry suddenly felt very heavy. His empty stomach growled, complaining at not having received the spiced lamb it had been waiting for, but the discomfort was a grain of sand compared to the hunger that little girl dealt with every day. And along with the discomfort of his empty stomach came pain that such suffering even existed.

He could still see her eyes. He would never, never forget those haunting eyes.

He was tired. And he did have a headache. But he barely no-ticed. Dealing with what they had seen was much too important for him to attend to how overstimulated all the sounds, all the colors, all the smells, all the crowds, had made him.

Beside him, Ankh softly began to cry. With a sigh, Tut put his arm around her shoulders, drawing her close to him. There was nothing to say. What they had seen today was worth crying about.

These were real people. Not just numbers, statistics, recorded on a piece of papyrus. They were real, and their needs and their suffering were real. And Ay and his policies were not taking very good care of them.

9 To Claim What is Ours

"**. . . A**nd you can imagine how shocked we were to discover our people living in tiny mud huts, suffering in abject poverty at the edge of the royal city!" Tut finished. His words echoed off the stone walls of the throne room as he hauled himself to his feet for emphasis, looming over the Vizier who stood before him.

Ay swallowed, avoiding the Pharaoh's eye. "I tried to protect you from this, Glorious Lord."

"You mean you tried to hide it from me!"

Smoothly, Ay continued. "It was never my intention that you or the Queen should be disturbed by the sight of the... less fortunate."

The King flung his arm wide, red robe billowing through the air. "Disturbed?! Disturbed is right— how you knew about this all these years and never did anything. Your policies, your neglect of our people's suffering, are only making all these problemth worse."

"But My Lord, I thought—"

"Be still! Pharaoh speaks!" Tut roared.

Ay blanched, visibly recalculating. And even as he teetered on the edge of rage, the Pharaoh could see that the Vizier was asking himself how he would regain control of the young King who until now, had been his naïve, innocent little puppet.

Tut sighed heavily, anger pounding a warlike drumbeat in his temples as a red haze began to throb before his eyes, a strange rushing filling his head. He turned away, wishing he was able to pace angrily up and down. "I can't believe you hid all this from us… you've been keeping me in a cage for eighteen years!"

"Keeping you safe, O King for Whom the Nile Floods."

The Pharaoh scoffed. "Keeping me *ignorant!*" Tut swung back around, gesturing with his free hand as the words tumbled out, tripping over one another as he began to lisp. "Well, I don't *want* to be safe, I want to be *Pharaoh!* All those thingth you kept from me… I know them now. And I'm going to use them ath *I* lead *my* people as Pharaoh. You can't put me back in that cage, Vizier. Because now I know that'th what it is."

"May I ask whatever it was that possessed you to go out into town in the first place?" the Vizier asked. "All these years, I have assured you that things are well in hand." He swallowed. "And they are. Why do you no longer trust me to do my job?"

Tut's rage had begun to calm, but his voice rang out as he proclaimed to the Vizier exactly how things were going to go. "Because your job is to carry out the wishes of the Pharaoh. And you are not doing so. And we went," he said, eyebrows darkening again, "because you've always insisted that we not worry about the world outside the palace walls. We wanted to see for ourselves, be able to judge for ourselves, whether you were doing a satisfactory job caring for the people in our stead.

"And now," Tut's nostrils flared in anger as the horror of what they had seen that day rose in his pounding heart, "we have our answer. The welfare of the people is our responsibility, Vizier. And we will ensure that those who are carrying out our wishes provide our people with an Egypt in which they need not fear starvation. We are going to lead our country into a future where tiny children will not wander the streets in rags and go to bed hungry."

108

"If you insist upon being treated as an adult, you'd best prepare yourself for what that will mean," Ay spat, dropping his attempt at placation. "The world of politics is a dangerous place. I will not play this game gently because you are the Pharaoh, or because you are young. If you wish to be treated as an adult, you will take the good with the bad. And I will not sacrifice my own aims out of respect for your office, until you demonstrate to me that you deserve my respect. I don't offer respect to my fellow adults automatically. You must earn it, Glorious Lord."

Pharaoh and Vizier locked eyes, neither backing down. They stared. They waited.

The words the Vizier had just spoken came back to him. *You must earn it.* That was what Ankh had said. *Show him you are "ready…" that you're mature, that you're wise, that you can make decisions on your own.* And… He smiled. *Show them that you're not going to leave all the decisions to them anymore. You're the Pharaoh. And they're not.* Tut felt himself taking a deep breath, and the pounding of his heart began to slow, the belligerent pounding in his head to fade. He was back in control of his mind, his body. Now it was time to recover control of this situation.

The Pharaoh dropped his gaze. Even as he remained firm in his claim to the authority that was his, could he salvage this mess, make himself appear deserving of the Vizier's respect and support, by being the one to end the fight?

"Glorious Lord," Ay said again, more softly, "the kingdom's resources are limited. If we could have done anything for the less fortunate, we would have already."

"Less fortunate— that's right," Tut scoffed, clenching his walking-stick in a death-grip. "The little girl we saw out there, all she had, all she had on was a linen sack, just like one of my bedsheets. That was it. And she was hungry, and dirty, and all alone. People are starving out there. Struggling to survive. Little children, alone in the streets with nothing but a doll for company. We have to do something." He swallowed. Ay had chosen to ignore this crisis for years, so Tut didn't feel he was the best person to consult, but he was the most experienced, the most knowledgeable. "What can be done?"

Ay seemed to choose his words carefully. "There are many things that the Pharaoh could do," he said slowly. "Lower taxes, distribute baskets of food to the indigent, loan the unemployed money to get by until they find something, hire more palace staff or undertake a building project solely for the purpose of creating jobs…"

"Yes. See to it. Do it all," Tutankhamun said, nodding emphatically. "And not just in Memphis. In Upper and Lower Egypt, from Tamiat to Napata."

"Your new policies may bankrupt the country you are endeavoring to feed, Glorious Lord," Ay said softly.

The Pharaoh shook his head. "It would be better to go bankrupt taking care of the people I've been made responsible for than to grow our economy at their expense. I can't sit here surrounded by gold while they starve."

"It will take time," Ay finally said.

Tut nodded. "As long as it starts immediately. And time is the thing I have the most of. These new policies will be in force when I celebrate my Sed Festival."

The Pharaoh sat back down grandly, exuding power.

"All life, prosperity, and health." Ay bowed and excused himself.

110

Ankh trailed back to her bedroom, eyes still full of tears, heart aching. Poor little girl… all alone, hungry, dirty, with no way to get any of the things she needed. The shawl Ankh had given her could not elevate her lot in life. The Queen looked around at all the beautiful things she owned— golden jewelry, dresses of fine, delicate white linen, jars and jars of makeup and perfume, countless elegant wigs— and thought of how many of them she would be delighted to give away to help that little girl and all the other little girls just like her.

"What's wrong, Your Majesty?" came a soft voice. Ankh turned her head to see Meresankh glimmering beyond the tears in her eyes.

The Queen wiped her eyes and swallowed. "The Pharaoh and I went out into Memphis today," she said in a choked voice. "And the things we saw… I never imagined how hard it is for people, the peasants; they're hungry, and dirty, and their houses aren't even as big as this room. I gave the shawl I'd just bought to a little girl, and the Pharaoh gave her the lamb kebab he'd just gotten. But how much of a difference can that have made?" Ankhesenamun sniffed, looking into Meresankh's eyes. "What can we do?"

"Talk to the Pharaoh," her handmaiden suggested, lowering her eyes slightly, not quite comfortable with the eye contact. "He trusts you. Discuss it together, and have him present your plan to his court." She smiled, raising her eyebrows. "He may be the official decision-maker, but he relies on you. You're not just his Queen; you're his big sister."

Ankh gave a watery chuckle. "Thank you, Meresankh."

She took the idea to heart, just as if it had been a piece of advice from a good friend. Maybe it had been.

The King found himself still fuming as he sat down in his room with Ankhesenamun, their two chairs set facing one another. It was so much quieter here in the palace than it had been out in town, but he wasn't lying down with something to read, resting his overwhelmed mind and body and relishing the silence. What they had seen needed to be discussed immediately.

"He doesn't understand because he doesn't want to," he sighed, resting his head on the back of the jewel-inlaid chair whose lion-paw feet matched those of his bed. "He doesn't go out either, because he knows how bad it is, and he doesn't want to see it." Tut beat at the air in an angry gesture, voice taking on Ay's mincing tone. "And he says he's 'not going to respect me until I show him I deserve it'… What's that supposed to mean? Until I give up on everything and just do what he says like I have been my entire life? Go back inside my cage?"

"No," Ankh said gently, shaking her head. Her braids clinked. "Not at all. You hold onto your plans and don't let anyone change them. But…" She paused, a hint of a smile creeping into her voice. "I do think you need a different approach."

He raised his head to look at her. "Like what?"

She gave a tiny chuckle and raised her eyebrows. "Like not shouting. I heard you." He bit his lip, but she continued without actually telling him off. "Like showing him you're mature enough to be taken seriously— mature enough and with enough self-control to get your point across without yelling. And once he starts taking you seriously, he'll see that your ideas are good. Be that adult you want him to see you as. And things will change."

112

Tut gave his sister half a smile. "Worth a try. You're pretty smart."

She grinned. "I am your big sister, after all." Then the Queen chuckled. "The secret to effective politics is being civil and sneaky. Not scaring anyone off or making them angry with aggressiveness that might make them feel threatened. But making your point and pushing it through all the same, while making friends with your enemies. Or making them knuckle under without even realizing it. Making things happen before they even know it. Being sweet and deadly, courageous and cunning, civil and sneaky. What it comes down to is... you need to learn to fight like a girl."

The Pharaoh laughed. "I do." He smiled. "I thought of you, actually." She blushed, chuckling as he went on. "When we were... arguing. That that's what I need to do. Earn it, like he said. Like you said, show him that I'm ready, that I can make my own decisions... and let him know that I'm going to start making them."

Then he gave a sigh. He shook his head sadly, not sure of how they could even proceed— how could he even obtain the chance to demonstrate to Ay what a mature adult he could be? "It's like not only do they not expect me, us, to be involved in politics; they expect us *not* to. And I don't know how to break in." Tut gave a heavy sigh and swallowed. "I wish Meritaten was here. I'd make her Vizier in a minute, fire Ay."

Ankh took his hand as they remembered together. "She'd be a good one."

The King gave half a smile. "Better politician than either of us. Had so much practice, being Queen when Mother was Pharaoh. I think the three of us could have made all this work, no problems."

Ankh nodded. "I know she could." She swallowed. "You're not the only one who had a wise big sister."

"She had a foot like mine," the King said, remembering. "But even more, and on both sides. She could barely walk at all, could she?"

"Not for very far," the Queen said, shaking her head. Sometimes the chiming of the golden beads in her wig sounded like merry laughter, but now they sounded like funeral bells. "But she had her canes, and her litter, and she got around. Didn't let it stop her. She was a politician. Everything she fought with was in her mind and her heart, and her feet didn't really matter."

They sat in silence for a moment hand in hand, lost in their own thoughts. The cat appeared from under the bed, having laid claim to a bracelet Semerkhet hadn't been able to find yesterday.

"Do you suppose that little girl likes the shawl?" Ankh asked Tut.

He leaned over and picked up the gilded bracelet Bastet was playing with, then smiled.

"I'm sure she does. It'll keep her warm."

She shook her head, and again the bells sounded, the sound of sadness for the plight of the people of their country. "At least you gave her one good meal."

He nodded, looking down at the shining bracelet in his hand. It represented how rich they were, but it didn't bring him a lot of joy, didn't mean all that much to him. It didn't mean as much to him as a solid meal would mean to a hungry person, as much as a new robe would mean to someone who was cold.

But they had given both to that little girl. Her stomach would be full tonight. And the shawl would keep her warm on the cold days and nights ahead.

114

Tutankhamun sighed. "We could have given her our jewelry, but it wouldn't have been any use to her. Throwing gold at people is not going to fix these foundational problems. You can't eat jewelry. And someone would probably assume she stole it. What a gift that would be." Getting up, he hobbled over to one of his highly-decorated storage chests (the one that offered countless wishes for his long, healthy life) put the bracelet away, and got out a little ball of shredded linen that Bastet could play with. "People need food. And jobs. And education. How can people get good jobs outside of unskilled labor if they don't have any education?"

"We need more schools," she agreed. She smiled. "Ones that accept both male and female students. Being a woman is about more than homemaking, after all. If women can own property or get a divorce just like men, they should have the same access to education and employment."

"You, my dear, are a genius," the King said, walking over and kissing her in the middle of the forehead. "Keep the ideas coming. I can't do this without you."

Ankh took a deep breath as she, too, rose to her feet. Her golden beads tinkled again— now the bells were full of hope. "We can replace the foreign slave labor with a workforce of Egyptians who went to a trade school. Architects, doctors, teachers… we can rebuild our economy through education, not on the backs of slaves. Some sort of minimum wage needs to be established, too, so people can be sure of earning enough to support themselves. And like I said earlier, maybe the taxes need to be adjusted."

"What about giving baskets of food to people who can't afford it, to help tide them over, or giving loans to the unemployed?" Tut asked, adjusting his grip on the cane he was leaning on. "That's what the Vizier said when I asked him what could be done. And he talked about lowering taxes, adding staff, and starting new building projects, too, just like you said."

Ankh frowned. "What? No! Those are terrible ideas! Not mine," she said hurriedly when he frowned at her in confusion. "But the loans and the bread lines... Sounds good on the surface, but not sustainable at all. Those are bad ideas, and he knows it."

The Queen shook her head with a sigh as if she'd expected as much. "The Vizier has presented you with a mix of good ideas and unsustainable ones. He's trying to set you up for failure, so when those things don't prove helpful in the long run, he can blame you and your youth and make the case that you're not wise enough to rule. But we don't have to let him," she said before her brother could get upset. "We can take the ideas that will work and leave the rest."

She stood up straighter, and Tut did too, readying his mind for the wise piece of instruction he knew was coming, the explanation of why the good ideas were good and the bad ones were bad.

"People being able to support themselves is the key part— just receiving food or a loan does nothing for their self-worth and isn't sustainable. But with a minimum wage, people will be able to feed themselves.

"And we can expand our staff to create jobs. We need more gardeners, and I'm sure that bringing in some new cooks would also bring in some fresh ideas. You know, building these schools will create jobs in itself, because we'll need to hire architects to design it and laborers to build it. And we need to expand trade... and encourage immigration. There is a lot of empty space in Goshen that we could pay people to farm." She swallowed. "I've never been there, but I know it's completely empty. The Hebrews left one day… and they never came back." She gave half a chuckle. "Left their half-finished statues, buildings, all their bricks made of straw. And went… somewhere else. Are they still walking through the wilderness?" She shook her head. "And the army never came back either. Not a single soldier."

Tut shuddered. Such a mystery… a mystery that might never be solved. Then he smiled, looking up from the papyrus he was busily scribbling on. "Let me get all that down, and I'll give it to Ay. I believe you'll save Egypt yet."

She took his free hand and squeezed it. "It's time to claim what is ours."

10   The Conference

Tut limped down the hall to the throne room, where Ay and a number of other courtiers were waiting. Ay had asked him to take part in a meeting; apparently there were some "issues" that needed discussing. So he had had Semerkhet put his false beard of magnificence on him, and in the hand that wasn't busy with his walking-stick, he had his crook and flail. On his head he wore his kingly striped *nemes*, on his body a graceful white tunic and blue robe, and over his chest dangled one of his larger, more elaborate pectoral necklaces. He was looking extremely royal.

Grand Vizier Ay, Treasurer Maya, General Horemheb, General Nakhtmin, and secondary Viziers Usermontu and Pentu were waiting in or by the chairs they'd had brought in, all facing the King's throne.

Whispering. Tut paused at the entrance, just out of sight.

"What kind of approach should we take?" Maya was asking Ay. "You know him best. Will he execute us if we dissent?"

Ay shook his head with a little smile. "No. Our Pharaoh is so tenderhearted he would never have anyone executed, not even for high treason. His weeping for the poor is the reason we are all here today."

Tut stepped through the doorway, into their field of view. As one, Ay and Maya stepped apart, returning to their seats.

"Good afternoon, gentlemen," he greeted them, careful to keep his face quiet. He must give no sign that he had heard anything.

They all rose as the King entered, bowing from the waist until he got himself seated on the throne, which stood on a dais between graceful stone columns carved and painted like lotuses, which

118

supported walls covered in fantastical paintings of gods, kings, plants, and animals. This was the same throne as he had spent the day sitting in on Tribute Day, every inch of the surface he sat on tiled in hard, unforgiving pieces of colorful inlaid glass or metal.

But today, he had to demonstrate his majesty. So he sat on the throne.

Tut struggled up the two steps that led to the dais, foot protesting as his weight bore down on it, and, supporting himself with his walking-stick, turned around to finally sink down onto the throne. There. First step of the meeting accomplished.

Six members of his council stood before him, quietly returning to their seats now that he had settled himself on the throne. Somehow that felt like a lot, especially so soon after the thronging crowds of Memphis. He was still tired, still longing for some solitude in which to recover. But this was much too important for him to put himself first. The Pharaoh swallowed. And he thought about the purpose of the meeting. And the thought of what this conference could accomplish made him smile. Second step complete.

"I was interested to hear you request a meeting," Tutankhamun said by way of opening. He held the crook and flail crossed over his chest, just like on Tribute Day. And as much as his foot was throbbing from going up even two stairs, he proudly concealed his pain, just as he had on Tribute Day. He was the Pharaoh. The Pharaoh did not have aches and pains. He was divine.

Ay nodded, the wrinkles hanging from his throat wobbling. "Yes, O Great Morning Star. The Treasurer and I have had some observations we wish to share with you. Although first we are pleased to report that the baskets are being prepared to feed the indigent, and Treasurer Maya has made arrangements for loans to be distributed to those in need."

"Actually," the Pharaoh said, sitting up a little straighter, the crook and flail grasped tightly in his hands, "I'm canceling the loans and the baskets. I've been speaking with someone whose judgment I trust completely, and have concluded that such measures would be unsustainable and would not fix any of the underlying problems that have resulted in such levels of poverty." The men blinked, as though they were about to offer a rejoinder, but he beat them to it. "Now, what observations did you wish to share with me?"

Treasurer Maya stood up. A strong, well-fed man, he had broad, muscular shoulders but a touch of softness to his stomach under his finely-pleated robes of delicate white linen. The heavy ring that identified him as Treasurer gleamed on his hand, which was smooth, free of calluses, and had finely-manicured nails, and like all the other courtiers gathered here today, he wore a finely crafted pair of sandals.

"If I may, Glorious Lord," he began in his deep, rumbling voice. Tut nodded, giving him permission to proceed. "The Grand Vizier and I have some concerns... some reservations... about some of the new policies you've proposed. We appreciate the fact that you are concerned for the poor of Egypt, but we, in turn, are concerned about the approach you are taking to remedy these issues. The way you suggest we redistribute wealth is... interesting. Opening schools, adding palace jobs, establishing a minimum wage, and lowering taxes are all very laudable, but if we proceed in this way, we may find our own budgets... tightening somewhat. The taxes you levied a year ago to support the newly-reopened temples have

120

not yet borne fruit. Would it not be more prudent to simply begin importing slaves again and restore normality?"

Tut looked down at him steadily, focusing every word, every gesture, on being the adult he was going to have to be to gain genuine leadership of his country. "Tell me, Treasurer, which will do more to ease human suffering, lowering taxes and creating jobs, or capturing slaves?"

Maya swallowed, eyes flickering. "Whose suffering are you referring to, O Ruler of Truth? Do not forget how those of us who have been... blessed with prestige... would suffer if the status quo were to change in the ways you are proposing."

Tut nodded politely, then offered his counterargument. "I believe that it will be easier for us to adjust slightly than for those who are currently poor to continue struggling to survive in their current circumstances, and even easier than for slaves we might capture to adjust to living without freedom. I've been speaking with the Queen—"

"Your wife?" Maya interrupted, bushy eyebrows rising incredulously as he rose to his feet. Tut fixed him with a look of thunder and lightning, and he stopped.

"Yes," the Pharaoh continued. Maya looked away, then sat back down, his mouth a hard line. "My incredibly brilliant wife, and she had some excellent ideas I think we should implement. She is the one whose wisdom helped me see that however altruistic they may be, handing out food and loans would not ultimately be helpful. So we've devised a different approach. First, we need to open trade schools throughout Egypt, trade schools open to both men and women. Then we will be able to replace the foreign slave labor of my grandfather's day with a paid workforce of Egyptians who went to a trade school. Architects, goldsmiths, teachers... We can rebuild our economy through education, not on the backs of slaves. It would also bring me great joy to open a medical school."

His audience was starting to look uncomfortable, shifting in their seats at the end of every sentence he uttered as if they were desperately hoping he would stop. But he did not. He went on.

He repeated his sister's plan to them verbatim, from expanding the palace staff and opening co-ed schools to repopulating Goshen with the skilled laborers whose hard work was going to lead Egypt into the future, a future made even more secure by the promise of decent wages and moderate taxes.

Tutankhamun paused. The older adults looked at him, considering their response.

"I believe the Pharaoh... and the Queen... show wisdom beyond their years," Pentu said, standing up. He was older than the King, but young for a Vizier. No taller than most women, and with a pointed nose, pointed chin, pointed elbows, and pointed knees, he didn't cut an impressive figure. But Tut was sure that the compassion he had seen Pentu show to everyone from local children to little old ladies would bring this Vizier to his side of the argument. The only thing that annoyed Tut slightly was how Pentu used his Vizier's staff to get up— for him it was only a symbol, and it hurt to see another young man hauling himself to his feet with the help of a cane when he didn't need it. Another symbol all three of the Viziers wore was a large pectoral necklace, a large green scarab set in gold.

"All of these recommendations would serve to expand the economy and help lead us back to prosperity..." Pentu swallowed. "Without slaves. And without prolonging these underlying problems with unhelpful quick fixes like bread lines." He swallowed again, looking down, and Tut wondered if Pentu had been the only one present who had dissented when it came to the preparation of the food baskets and loans. "Do not," he said to those gathered, "discount the ideas of the young. Age does not always equal wisdom."

Tut felt his heart warming as the young Vizier dared to give him a little smile. He, Ankh, and Pentu were young. They had much experience to gain. But their ideas were capable of changing the world. And together, who knew what these young politicians could accomplish.

Now Usermontu stood up. With a little difficulty. He actually needed his staff of office to get up. A grandfatherly sort, he was round and plump, the jolly sort of man who would have loved to bounce a child on his knee if his large belly had left any space. But his was a joyful, comfortable sort of corpulence, full of satisfaction and gratitude for the prosperity that had allowed him to get fat, not the sweaty, plodding sort of obesity that Kahotep dragged around with him.

The old man spoke, offering his views on the Pharaoh's plans.

"I agree that all these proposals are worthwhile, Lord of Perfect Laws. And I agree that they are more likely to work in the long term than simply handing out food and money. Perhaps we could begin by implementing the… less extreme… changes, and then, as time goes on, continue revisiting the others." He cleared his throat, and Tut caught a whiff of the cumin, frankincense, and carob paste that he used on his bad teeth. "May I recommend we begin by, over the next five years, opening two trade schools in Thebes and two in Memphis, possibly to be followed by a medical school in Thebes, and by examining the areas in which we might expand the palace workforce? I also propose we defer the purchase of any more slaves until next year. We can reassess the other proposals—reevaluating taxes, establishing a minimum wage, resettling Goshen— in a year or so."

"As long as the trade schools will not keep good fighting men out of Egypt's army," Horemheb assented. The King had rarely heard him speak; the tall, broad warrior was not given to verbosity. Ever the soldier, Tut noticed that the General had worn his military uniform to the meeting. The heavy leather cuirass covering his upper body would presumably protect him against any stinging words that might be exchanged today. Unlike Maya's, his broad hands were rough and callused, with little attention having been paid to his nails, and looked strong enough to throttle an attacking lion. Shaking his head, Horemheb continued. "Rebuilding our armed forces since your grandfather's day has not been easy, and I would not wish to deter a single strong fighting man from serving his country."

Beside Horemheb, General Nakhtmin stood up. Like Pentu, he was young for a high-ranking government official. He was the son of Vizier Ay, and looked just like him, except much shorter. If anything, his short stature made him more menacing; when he looked at you with those hooded eyes under their arrogant arched eyebrows, it was like looking at a cobra about to strike. A rather lazy cobra at times, but a dangerous one nonetheless.

"Your Majesty," he said in his characteristic drawl, "How can we replace slave labor with paid work? I mean, look around you." He glanced around the throne room. "Our wealth, our infrastructure, is based on a steady supply of slaves. Eliminate them, and…" He scoffed. "All this goes away. And, I might add, I believe that the locals are doing quite well enough with their current wages."

His lip curled into a haughty sneer. "It's not as if the peasants really need all that much, is it? I mean, what do they eat? Lentils... bread... beer... more beer... It's not very expensive, is it? Poor people are, well... poor, and that's what they're used to. So why should we worry about changing it?" He sneered again. "The only problem with poverty is when beggars stop you in the street, er... begging. Do as you choose, but if I was on that throne, I would be importing slaves every year, and... testing our border with the south of Nubia, which has so much lovely gold..."

And he sat down, reclining back in his chair with one foot resting on the other knee, regarding the room under half-closed lids. Ostentatiously he brushed a speck of dust from his robe with a hand that was as manicured as Maya's. The sunlight streaming through the window gleamed on his extravagant jewelry— two rings, a bracelet, and a heavy collar-necklace inlaid with hundreds of tiny pieces of glass and precious stones. Everything but a crown. He almost outshone the King, although, unlike with the Viziers, none of his shiny things denoted his position. He was just rich. And he wore a lot of perfume.

Maya had blinked when Tut had said that the schools would be open to both men and women, but he said nothing now, only nodded grimly.

"I believe we are at an accord, O King for Whom the Nile Floods," Ay said smoothly. "We shall begin by building the schools you have requested, and, over time, examine how we might add palace jobs, establish a minimum wage, and lower taxes. The purchase of any additional slaves will also be deferred until next year. No baskets of food are to be prepared, and no loans are to be offered."

125

The Pharaoh nodded. He had expected some opposition, but he sensed victory. The Queen's changes were on their way.

Together, they drafted a document outlining the details of the new schools and the agreement that no slaves should be purchased until the following year. And one by one, they applied their signet-rings, signing it into law.

"Thank you all for taking the time for this discussion," he said, slowly rising. Sensing dismissal, his courtiers also rose, bowing from the waist as they intoned,

"Hail to thee, Ruler of Truth; all life, prosperity, and health!"

Slowly they rose, filing out of the throne room. As they went, Tut thought he could see Maya scowling, Usermontu looking indulgently proud of the dear young royal couple, Nakhtmin looking contemptuous, Horemheb looking slightly blank, but satisfied— as long as he had the military budget he needed, the other decisions didn't matter much to him— and Pentu looking excited. He could not read Ay's face.

The King slowly and carefully descended from the dais and hobbled from the throne room, satisfied with the day's work. Things really were going in sensible directions, directions that would help improve the economy and the general welfare of all the human beings in Egypt.

Speaking of human beings… In the shadowy edge of the corridor he was walking down, a servant woman was kneeling on the floor, scrubbing it with a wet rag she kept dipping into a bucket. He paused, watching her work, work with the same focus and professionalism that Kemsit had demonstrated as she had cut his nails for him. She was cleaning the floors, but she looked proud of her contribution to the beauty of the palace, proud of the fact that if the

Pharaoh ever walked down this hallway, it would be clean, thanks to her.

"Thank you for your work," he said. She stiffened, dropping her rag into the bucket as she turned her kneeling position into a face-to-the-floor bow. He smiled down at her even though she wasn't looking at his face, trying not to feel awkward. "It looks beautiful."

And accepting the fact that she wasn't going to look up at him, he kept walking, carrying his own head a little higher, walking a little easier. That was one good deed done today.

The King and Queen stood on one of the balconies overlooking Memphis as the golden light of late afternoon melted into the soft pinks and reds of evening.

"How was the conference?" Ankh asked, leaning her head affectionately against his arm. The braids of her wig tickled his skin. She could see that he looked tired, as tired as if he had taken a walk around all four sides of the palace grounds. It had been a challenge for him. His cane set aside for the moment, he was leaning heavily against the stone railing of the balcony.

Tut smiled. "All right," he said with a satisfied nod. "I don't think they could see how scared I was when I first went in."

"Oh, darling." Ankh got up onto her tiptoes to peck him on the cheek. "I'm proud of you." Stepping away for a moment, she crossed over to the table in the corner, returning with a bright bouquet of lotuses and poppies. "My love."

With a smile, he accepted them with his free hand, bending his head to breathe in the sweet fragrance of the lotuses. And he felt the stressful day melt away as he focused his senses on their beauty, smelling their sweetness of the lotuses, marveling at the bright colors of the poppies. Already he felt better.

"Thank you, darling," he said. "Juth what I need." He was lisping, but he didn't care. It didn't matter when he was talking to his sister at the end of a long day.

She chuckled and patted his arm. "So, tell me about the conference. What policies did you finalize?"

He smiled a little sheepishly. "We're going ahead with the schools, and we're not going to buy any more slaves this year. And taxes are going to be lowered, eventually, at least, and we'll make the minimum wage official. That will be two trade schools here and two in Thebes, and a medical college in Thebes in a few more yearth." He yawned. "Just fink what that will mean." He bent to kiss the top of her head. "And it's all thanks to you. All I'm doing is presenting your ideas. I will sign anything you give me!"

His sister looked up at him with a little chuckle. "Well, thank you, darling, and I appreciate that you trust me... but I want you to approve my ideas because you understand them and agree with them, not just because I give them to you and I am always right. And I want you to develop your own ideas to present and pass."

She smiled at her brother. "I'll always answer your questions... but I want you to be able to answer your own questions, too. Someday, you will have the confidence in your wisdom, knowledge, experience, and judgment to not need to ask me what to do. And someday... we will come upon something that I feel we should handle one way, and you feel we should handle another. And the call will be yours to make. Because you are the Pharaoh."

Tut sighed, then smiled. "Well, I'll always need you, even if I live to be a hundred. Your experience and my signet-ring."

"That's why we make a good team," she said with a wink.

128

"Just like Mother and Father." Tut yawned again. "I can't wait to thee what we do next."

His sister just smiled up at her baby brother.

The King and Queen looked down at their capital city, where shadows were growing longer. They could see families heading to market to get something for dinner, leading donkeys, people pausing to chat with a neighbor, adults coming home from work, children playing. No words carried that far, but even from the balcony, they could hear the happy bustle of the city. The city that they loved, the city that they knew, the city that they had personally visited.

Men were lined up across the square near the palace, signing on to join a construction project— the building of the two new trade schools. Over the next five years, it would be joined by two more trade schools in Thebes, and a medical college. And all of them would be open to both male and female students.

Ankh put her arm around Tut's shoulder and pointed down at a little girl, who was leading a donkey. Beside her, her brother was pushing a wheelbarrow of what looked like vegetables.

"Look," she said with a smile. "Those little ones, right there, will have the opportunity to go to school. And someday, their children will too."

He just nodded. What a gift it was to be able to give the gift of a hopeful future to the next generation.

The King and Queen smiled and stepped into one another's arms. Together, they watched their world move toward the future.

He told Semerkhet that evening, about the conference, about the decisions he had had passed. And his valet... his friend... smiled as he helped the Pharaoh into his sleeping-tunic after his shower. Tut still missed Hetepheres, but he was used to it now, the routine of having Sem get him up in the morning and put him to bed at night. And it was all right.

"I knew you could," Semerkhet said proudly, handing Tut his walking-stick again so that he could turn down the covers for him. On the Pharaoh's dressing-table, the bright bouquet of poppies and lotuses seemed to glow even in the dark. "Maybe it wasn't easy… but you did it. And I'm proud of you."

Tutankhamun smiled as he got into bed and let Semerkhet tuck him in. Just what he'd said after Tribute Day. And it was still good to hear.

"General Nakhtmin doesn't think anything needs to change," Tut said with a yawn. "Thinks the 'peasants' are just fine as they are. And the Vizier… he doesn't want to stop using slaves. And Treasurer Maya wants more slaves too… and he doesn't approve of female students attending the schools."

Semerkhet rolled his eyes. "Clearly the Treasurer does not have a sister."

The Pharaoh nodded. "Indeed. But the others agreed with the Queen and me, generally, anyway. Especially Pentu. And we're moving away from slavery… lowering taxes… and 'stablishing a minimum wage…" He yawned again, closing his eyes with a satisfied smile. "And I think it's going to be a really good thing."

He felt Semerkhet adjust his blankets. And he could hear the smile in his friend's voice.

"I'm sure it will. And someday… someday you'll be in those history papyri the Vizier teaches you out of."

Tut just smiled again. And he was asleep.

11 The Bond

"**S**emerkhet got me a necklace," Meresankh said cheerfully one morning as she helped the Queen get dressed, the curvy little handmaiden bustling quickly around the room, gathering up garments. Her assistant Tia had already laid out the day's dress, wig, and jewelry and excused herself with a bow.

The Queen smiled. The handmaiden and the valet were so cute together.

"Did he?" she said.

Meresankh grinned, the dimple in her round cheek deepening. She took off the necklace, holding it up for the Queen to see. It was a small silver pendant with a tiny image of the goddess Isis, a pair of delicate feathered wings extending from her arms like sleeves. It was small, and simple, and cheap, and would probably tarnish before long. But it would mean more to Meresankh than most of the Queen's much more expensive pieces did to her.

"It's beautiful," Ankh said with a smile. And it was. Meresankh put it back on and began unfolding the dress she had brought for the Queen.

"Shows me how much he loves me," Meresankh said, but as she spoke, Ankh thought she caught the tiniest bit of discomfort, as though there was some fact about the necklace that bothered her.

"Semerkhet's sister's little boy is rolling over now," the handmaiden said conversationally.

The Queen froze before her mirror, a thousand memories coursing through her mind, through her body. A thousand hopes and dreams, a thousand wishes, a thousand, thousand tears. A thousand, thousand tears for each of them, each of the two precious ones who now lay in the tiny, tiny coffins that had been so carefully prepared by the royal craftsmen.

"Is he," she whispered, closing her eyes to hold back the tears. Even after so many months, the tears were just under the surface.

Then Meresankh bowed her head. "I'm sorry, My Lady," she whispered, sounding utterly mortified with herself. "So sorry. I wasn't thinking." She paused. "I… I'll go find you a dress."

The Queen didn't answer. Meresankh walked away to find a dress to offer her. Even though her arms were already full of clothing.

Tutankhamun saw it in her face at lunch. Something was wrong, a cloud of grief throwing her face into shadow. She wasn't really eating, just picking at the dates and sycamore figs on her plate that looked like teardrops.

And he knew. Knew what some careless comment had done. He put his arm around her, holding her close. "I know," he whispered. "I know."

But as they moved toward the future, the past was still with them. And it still hurt. Why, she asked herself, as she had a hundred, a thousand, ten thousand times before. What had happened to take their two daughters away, away from the parents who loved them so much? Was it her husband's health? Her health? Something she was doing, or not doing? Would they ever know?

All week the Queen mulled it over in her heart. The pain they had gone through. The questions they still had. And what unknown thing needed to change in order for them to bring a healthy heir into the world.

She went to the temple and prayed to Tawaret, goddess of fertility, as she had a hundred, a thousand, ten thousand times before. *Will I ever give him a son*, she asked, standing before the silent stone image of the grandly pregnant hippopotamus goddess of fertility, an image that might almost have been comical if her own flat stomach had not brought her such pain. Nearly every month her blood came, but although it meant that she was healthy, it meant that no tiny baby was taking shape in her womb. *Will I ever give my husband an heir? When will I fulfill my role, do what a Queen is supposed to do... give birth to the next Pharaoh?*

But there was no answer.

All week long, the Pharaoh had the same thoughts. A Pharaoh's greatest legacy was his heir, the Pharaoh to whom he would one day give his crown. How could he fulfill his duty, live up to who he was supposed to be as Pharaoh, if he never gave his Queen an heir? How could he fulfill his duty as husband if he never gave his wife a child to raise?

What had happened, he wondered as he had so many times before. Why had they said hello to their daughters only to say goodbye? And what could they do to protect themselves, and their future children, from the same tragedy happening again?

There were no answers. Only the silence. And the memories. And the pain.

They tried again that week. But even in their unity, they went to sleep in one another's arms without real satisfaction. Because they knew it had not happened.

"Why doesn't she respond?" Ankh sighed in frustration as she sat at her dressing-table one evening, Meresankh slowly lifting away her heavy necklace, earrings, bracelets, and wig to be put away for the next day.

"Who, My Lady?" Meresankh asked, placing the day's wig carefully on its stand, arranging the delicate black braids so they didn't tangle.

The Queen glanced toward the heavens. "Tawaret. I went to the temple today, prayed for… what I always pray for. Someday." She swallowed, looking down. "Will she ever answer?"

Her handmaiden sighed, stepping slowly toward her Mistress. "A… are you sure she's listening?" she asked softly.

Ankhesenamun frowned at her. "What do you mean? Of course she's listening. She's the goddess."

Meresankh swallowed, turning away to put away another item. She didn't say anything else. But as her face caught the glow of the oil-lamps that brought light to the evening, the Queen caught a glimpse of Light she thought she recognized.

A Pharaoh needed an heir in order to continue his dynasty. And she had not borne him one. Standing before her mirror, hands folded on her flat stomach, Ankhesenamun decided she loved her husband, and her dynasty, enough to let it be continued… by whatever means necessary.

The next day at dinner, the King was smiling, excited about everything they were about to do. Maybe smiling a little bit too much. He kept smiling at Persenet, the maidservant who kept refilling his wine, his new favorite from Tribute Day, and at Menhet, the flutist who was entertaining them with her acrobatic melodies.

Ankh noticed.

After they ate, she pulled him aside, into the far corner of the grand dining room. "Darling," she said, shifting her weight from foot to foot, "I couldn't help but notice you looking at Persenet and Menhet."

He nodded. "They take good care of us, don't they?"

She nodded with an unhappy little smile, not meeting his eyes. "Yes." Then she swallowed, twisting her hands together. But she didn't say anything else.

Tutankhamun frowned at his wife. "What's bothering you?" he asked softly. Getting a firm grip on his walking-stick, he slowly got to his feet. "Do you want to go talk?"

The Queen just nodded, tears sparkling in her eyes.

He followed her down the hall that led to the royal bedrooms, into hers. They stood together in her private sitting-room, safely secreted from any listening ears.

Ankh sighed. And Tut looked at her in concern. "Tell me what's going on," he invited.

She swallowed. And looking down at her folded hands, she began.

"You're of age now, and I just want to say… If you ever meet someone else… I will try very hard not to be jealous. Maybe she could give you an heir."

The King blinked, feeling lightheaded for an instant. "What?" Immediately he wrapped her in a one-armed hug, holding her to his heart. "No, no, no, Ankhesenamun. I would never look for another wife. I would never betray you like that. You're my wife, my sister, my friend, my advisor, my sun, my moon, the person I can always trust. You are all I need. Don't ever worry about that.

135

Ever." He kissed her, kissed her cheeks, her forehead, her lips. "We've been through too much together," he whispered.

"Just listen," she whispered back. "Darling, it's fine. You would not be betraying me. It's not possible for the Pharaoh to commit adultery. You could..." She chuckled. "You could have a wife for every day of the year. Thutmose the Third had six or seven wives, and Grandfather had about six as well. And that doesn't count concubines. So you wouldn't... wouldn't be doing anything wrong." Again, Ankh tried for a wry chuckle. "Love, you've been using the harem quarters of Grandfather Thutmose's palace in Thebes to store furniture, not house beautiful women. You could... you could have a whole classroom of little boys by now. You could." She swallowed back tears as her voice broke. "So why don't you?"

He swallowed. "Mother and Father," Tut said with a smile, "they only had each other. And that was all they needed. Why would I choose another wife after growing up with their example? They were enough. And you and I... we are enough."

Ankh just tried to smile.

"Why would I marry someone else?" he asked again softly, brushing her braids back from her face as he kissed her on the forehead. "You're all I need. All I've ever needed. And you're the only one in the world who I can trust no matter what."

She sighed, blinking back tears. And she came back in for another hug.

"We'll wait," he whispered. "Someday, we'll try again. In another season of life."

Ankhesenamun nodded. "Someday."

He wouldn't change it, he thought as he held her, one arm clasping her, other hand gripping his walking-stick but his arm still

136

wrapped around her. Even if he had had the opportunity to go out into the wide world and meet a stranger with whom he might become friends and slowly fall in love. From childhood, he and Ankhesenamun had known that they would marry one another. And they had. It was like she had always told him... Life was a combination of the things you could change and the things you couldn't.

But as wonderful as it might have been to "marry for love..." they had. Because they did love one another. And as brother and sister as well as husband and wife, they were closer than anyone else in the world. Because when it came down to it, they only had each other.

He didn't even really know anyone else. But his sister protected him. Always had, always would. With her at his side, he knew that everything would be all right. She would make everything all right.

How lucky he was, to have his big sister at his side as his Queen.

Ankh stood in Tut's arms, husband, brother. Marrying purely for the sake of romantic love could have been wonderful. But it wouldn't have been the same. She and another husband wouldn't have had the same bond, the bond she and her brother had shared since the day he was born. Standing beside her husband, beside her brother, she had everything she needed.

He was enough for her... and she was enough for him. He had loved her through all their pain... she had not failed him. Even if the dynasty ended with them. Ankh tried to smile. And accept the love he freely gave her as she freely loved him. She was his sister, and he was her brother. Now and for always. That was enough.

They traveled that week. The entire royal court packed up— or watched while their servants did— and loaded up into a grand caravan of horse-carts and camels, ready to make the long trek south to Thebes. The Pharaoh and his Queen divided their time between Egypt's two capitals, and when the month of Pharmouthi was nearly over, it was time to make their way to the palace that Grandfather Thutmose had had built in Thebes. It was time for the Pharaoh to see how the southern half of his country was faring.

The palace was beautiful. It was even larger than the one in Memphis, and it had a giant man-made lake the size of a harbor. Tut always enjoyed spending the Season of the Harvest in Thebes.

The month of Pashons arrived, the days lengthening until day and night stood in balance. They celebrated the Harvest Festival and the Festival of Isis, the members of the palace staff mingling with the rest of Thebes as all of Egypt thanked the gods for the beginning of a bountiful harvest.

Everyone except… Meresankh and her Granny, Ankhesenamun noticed. She could count every other one of the servants she knew, but her handmaiden and the old midwife she seemed to spend all her free time with were not there.

The Queen tried to have a good time anyway, listening to the music, watching the dancers. But she was curious.

The Harvest Festival and the Festival of Isis were just as loud and energetic as they always were. The Pharaoh attended with the Queen because as the Pharaoh, it was his job. But he was glad when it was time to go home. He was exhausted from the crowds, the sounds and smells, the hubbub, happy as it was. Glad that the people of Egypt were having such a wonderful celebration. But glad to go home, all the same. And ready to have his shower and go to bed. Because he was worn out.

"Oh, this watermelon is good," the Queen groaned appreciatively as they ate dinner in the royal feasting hall one night, taking a juicy bite and trying to keep the pink juice from dripping down her chin. "I've been waiting all year for this moment..."

And Tut smiled as he watched his sister devouring her favorite fruit. He, for his part, was about to start in on a peach. They were finally in season after months of dried dates and raisins, and he relished each sweet, juicy bite. And after that, he would enjoy a few sycamore figs. Fruit season had finally arrived. And they were going to enjoy every moment of it.

The days were getting longer. And as she did every year as one season gave way to the next, Ankhesenamun remembered. Remembered where she had been, two years ago, four years ago. When the days had stood in balance during the month of Pashons, she had been six months along with Mereneferet, then, two years later, four months along with Senebhenas. As she put on the first short-sleeved gowns of the season, she remembered putting them on in the distant past, the days before. Two years ago, four years ago, when day and night had stood equal during the month of Pashons, everything had been all right. Everything had been perfect.

Tut walked slowly out of his study, stretching after sitting too long. He shook his head and blinked; it was as if he could still hear Ay's voice in his mind, droning on as he went through every Pharaoh in history and their accomplishments. Mentuhotep the Second who had regained control of all Egypt after over a hundred years of leadership by local leaders, Senusret the Third who had made a former slave from Canaan his Vizier in a time of famine, Sobekneferu and Hatshepsut, rare female Pharaohs who had held their country together during good times and bad.

Tut had graduated from working with Sennedjem and other tutors years ago, but Ay still spent a few hours a week conducting lessons just for him, helping prepare him to be the best Pharaoh he could be. Tut loved history, he really did, and economics was fascinating, but he was sure that there must be a more engaging way of teaching them. Ay's dreary monotone all but put him to sleep as the skinny old man read from endless sheets of papyrus, knobbly old fingers pointing out graphs and charts for the King. With the Vizier's bald head and gravelly, croaking voice, Tut could not help but think of a vulture. He even had the same loose wrinkles on his throat, wrinkles that shivered and shook as he droned on and on. Perhaps this vulture's strategy was to bore its prey to death before eating it.

The month of Payni had arrived. But at least it was not too warm in the study, as hot as it would be in the middle of the Season of the Harvest, the early part of the Season of Inundation. Tut was disappointed, as he was every year, to lay aside his warm outer robes, then trade his long-sleeved linen tunics for short-sleeved ones and the tunics for kilts that extended only from his waist to his knees. It was also a bit sad, as it was every year, to set aside his

140

second blanket, then any blanket at all. But, all in all, he was grateful that it was not yet too hot to study.

But now he was done for the day, having lived through another lesson, and he could do as he liked for a few hours. He smiled. Time for a snack. Maybe an apricot. And then to find Bastet.

"How was your lesson?" Ankh asked as Tut appeared in the hallway, stretching broadly.

He shrugged, smiling at her kind gesture of asking.

"All right, I guess," he said, stretching again, one arm, then the other, switching his walking-stick from one hand to the other. The cuffs of his tunic, a long-sleeved one so far, fell back over his fore-arms, and he shook one arm, then the other, to get the fabric back into place. "We're going through the lists of Pharaohs. Let me see who I can remember…" Tut counted on his fingers. "Menes-Narmer who first united Upper and Lower Egypt, Djoser, who had the very first pyramid built, Djedefre, who commissioned the Great Sphinx, Pepi the Second, who they say reigned for ninety-four years… and they're only from the first six dynasties. And our own dynasty was founded about two hundred years ago when Ahmose the First reunited Egypt after over a hundred years of foreign rule by the Hyksos and different mini-dynasties ruling different parts of the country at the same time."

His sister nodded. "Did you learn about Merneith, the great-granddaughter of Menes-Narmer? She ruled for her son Den until he was old enough to take the throne. And there were the wives of the warrior-kings of Dynasty Seventeen, who took charge of the politics of Egypt while their husbands went off to fight— Queen Tetisheri, her daughter Ahhotep the First, and *her* daughter

Ahmose-Nefertari, the first Queen of our dynasty. And those are just four of them. There are about ten more."

Tut shook his head. "He told me about Hatshepsut, and he mentioned Sobekneferu. But I didn't hear about Merneith or Ahhotep."

Ankh rolled her eyes. Men. "Well, they were the mothers and wives who kept their dynasties in safe hands between men. Mother taught me all about them."

The Pharaoh shrugged, then gave his sister a smile. "It sounds as though I should be studying the Queen Lists as well as the King Lists. You'll have to fill me in."

She popped up onto her tiptoes and gave him a peck on the cheek. "Don't worry. I will. And that's the problem. There aren't any Queen Lists. You have to find out about them in relation to their fathers, brothers, husbands, and sons."

Tut gave his sister a smile. "Maybe you can fix that."

She just chuckled. "There is one, actually," she said. "Just one full list anywhere. Mother and Grandmother made it for us girls. I'll show you later."

Tut smiled at his sister. Then he sighed, reaching up a hand to rub at his stiff neck, and a question came to him that he hadn't thought about for a very long time. "Do you have lessons?"

The Queen smiled. "I had a lot of hands-on education watching Mother and Father and Meritaten. And we had teachers, too, all six of us girls, and lessons every day. Even... even little Setepenre and Rure were learning to read. They had their little writing palettes to hold their pens and ink, and they were learning to write their names."

Ankh closed her eyes, and Tut reached out to take her hand. Setepenre had only lived to be six years old and Neferneferure,

142

nicknamed *Rure*, had been seven. Having been only a year younger than Setepenre, Tut barely remembered them. He didn't remember Tasherit, as they called her, very much either— she had been eight when the epidemic had come. Or Meketaten, who had been ten. Most of his memories were of their oldest sister, Meritaten, who had died in the first year of his reign, not long after turning seventeen. What had been her nickname, what Father always called her when he mentioned her in a letter? *Mayati*. That was it.

Ankhesenamun gave a sigh, and when she opened her eyes, they were clear. "So, between what I learned at their feet, what I learned from my tutors, and what I've learned since our part of this journey started, I would say that I've had quite a… well-rounded education."

Tut nodded. "I should say."

"But specialized, too," she continued. "Focused on political science. I can conduct diplomatic correspondence, I know the proper etiquette for meeting with a delegation from Phoenicia or what not to say to a Babylonian, and I can tell a lie a mile off, in speech or in writing, but I never learned to cook, and I don't do my own makeup. The traditional activities of homemaking… have never been my sphere. Politics has been my world, and it always will be." She sighed. "Just like it was for Meritaten. Not that I regret it, it's just… very, very different from the lives of the women of Thebes and Memphis."

Then she smiled. "Mother taught me so much. The history of the women who came before us, holding our country together in the dark times between dynasties. How to be a woman in the world of politics, how to use my power through standing beside the throne rather than sitting on it myself. I could, I know I could, and

I know she did, but I'll accomplish a lot more by… advising the Pharaoh than I would by being the Pharaoh."

Tut smiled and squeezed her hand. "And this Pharaoh will accomplish so much more with you advising him than he would without your help. I don't know what I'd do without you. Ay is my advisor on paper, but really… it's you I rely on. You and everything you know."

She chuckled. "Politics… cooking… I think I have the best chance at changing the world where I'm at. Even if I can't boil lentils."

"Well, I can't cook either," Tut said almost teasingly. "Or dress myself. But I can hunt, and play *seega*… sort of, anyway," he said to his sister's smile that playfully reminded him that she always beat him, "and I can… represent our country to our neighbors. And I can…" He gave a dramatic sigh, imagining all the long days ahead of endless pages of history, every tiny bit of which was potentially useful, "I can be a good student and learn the King Lists backwards and forwards." He smiled. "And the Queens List, too."

His sister smiled back. "And you know the next step," she said, reaching up to run her fingers through the delicate braids of his wig, "is to apply what you've learned. Don't leave it in the classroom. Knowledge is power. What you learn here will help you become that great Pharaoh I know is waiting." Gently she poked her finger into his chest, toward his heart.

He gave her half a smile. "You really think so?"

"I know so," she said confidently, taking his hand. "Just you wait and see. With what you'll accomplish, you'll be in the King Lists you're reading. And you'll never be forgotten."

144

The next week was a difficult one. Together they marked the fourth anniversary of Mereneferet's birth, the day they had said hello only to be forced to say goodbye. Together they remembered, remembered the months of joyful hope that had been cut short with the onset of the labor pains Ankhesenamun had not anticipated for another four months. Together they remembered the silence that had fallen, the silence that still lay in the absence of the laughter of a four-year-old echoing through the palace. The emptiness that now filled their lives, the sacred space they had held in their lives and hearts for their daughter, that even now should be overflowing with the life of their child. The pitter-patter of little feet running through the palace was missing; so was the fulfillment her parents would feel in taking care of her, the relationship that would grow between parent and child as Mereneferet grew from a baby into a little girl.

Always, there was the pain. And the questions. All those sweet, beautiful months of hope, of anticipation, of joyful waiting… followed not by a child in their arms, but a funeral. There was a part of their hearts… that didn't understand. How could she have flown from their lives so suddenly, leaving only the imprint of the love they felt for her like the echo of a kiss?

Why had it happened to them? They knew that other couples had suffered the same losses. Was it wrong to hurt so much when other families were in even more pain? And was it wrong… what had they done wrong? Their hearts ached with the feeling that they should have done or not done something different… a terrible "if-only" that they knew was not really true. They had not done anything wrong.

Amid all the pain were the hopes and dreams and expectations they had had to put away, the aching longing that was always there, and a shame they could not silence. There was an empty space that belonged to their daughters that nothing could fill. And yet... they knew that they did not want it to be filled, because that emptiness was all they had. So even as the emptiness broke their hearts yet again, they chose to remember. And together, they remembered... the hope that one day, they would be reunited.

Her parents talked. And they comforted one another. And as the day passed, her mother found herself retiring to her room, putting her arms gratefully around Bastet, who had followed her, wide eyes full of concern. She held the cat. And she thought.

Even as she remembered Mereneferet, Ankh also remembered Senebhenas. She had been just five months on this date; her mother had smiled to feel her first kicks, kicks she had barely had the chance to feel with Mereneferet. At five months, there had been just under four months remaining. Four months of hope.

12 An Adventure

The King sat listlessly in his favorite chair one day in the middle of the hot harvest month of Epiphi, weighed down by his hot, heavy wig, sticky with sweat, and bored out of his skull. So many beautiful, perfect days had been spent trapped indoors on account of his "fragile health." This was one of them. And it wasn't even as if he was busy with important "Pharaoh stuff." What a waste.

Then an idea popped into his mind. A mischievous, life-threatening idea.

"Sem," he said quietly. A sort of nickname, it slipped out quite naturally, a name he had just given to his new friend. The servant looked up from adjusting one of the Pharaoh's massive necklaces on its stand.

"Yes, Master?"

"Let's go hunting."

Semerkhet raised his eyebrows. "Is that a good idea?"

"Of course not!" Tut gave his friend a toothy grin. "C'mon, let's go before they catch us!"

Semerkhet summoned three lower-ranking servants seemingly out of thin air, directing them to gather up the Pharaoh's bow and arrows. They disappeared just as quickly, with wishes for Tutankhamun's long life, health, and prosperity. Then Tut was off as fast as he could hobble, Semerkhet and the others hurrying along beside him. The hotter half of the year had begun, and the Pharaoh felt himself begin to sweat the moment they left the relative cool of the stone palace.

They snuck out to the royal stables as quietly as they could, keeping an eye out for any guards or members of the palace staff. All was quiet.

"This is going to be great!" Tut whispered as he stood in the stable, watching Semerkhet directing a groom to harness two chestnut horses to the hunting chariot. Semerkhet just shook his head and chuckled.

"Well, I suppose all this is yours, anyway."

"And I'm the Pharaoh! I can do anything I want!"

The groom guided the horses out of the stable, then Semerkhet helped the King clamber into place, glowing with excitement. This was going to be awesome.

A breath later, they were off with a heart-stopping lurch, the horses' hooves pounding on the packed earth. Tut threw his head back, feeling the wind in his wig and laughing with sheer delight. Hunting wasn't important. This was. The racing speeds, the wind in his face, the feeling of freedom he could never catch on his own two feet.

That was when they heard Ay's voice. Laughing, Tut turned his head to see the ancient Vizier puffing along, actually chasing them. Ay gave up three seconds later, panting, and Tut heard him shout,

"My Lord! Think of your health!"

"I am!" he hollered. "My mental health! I was about to go crazy! Faster, Sem, faster!"

Now the guards were after them. They were following them on horseback, grown-up faces full of disappointment at the way the Pharaoh was taking his life into his hands.

"Into the grasslands!" he shouted. "Faster, faster!"

"Hyaah!"

Semerkhet slapped the reins on the horses' backs and they galloped even faster, hooves thundering on the ground as the chariot rattled under the feet of the two boys. Together they screamed, howled, whooped for sheer joy, on a joyride with the palace guard after them.

"I think we lost them," Semerkhet panted a mile later. "Oh, look where we are."

Catching his own breath, Tut looked around as they slowed down to a smart trot. They had reached the grasslands, home of the ostriches. "Here," he panted. "Might as well hunt a little while as long as we're here."

In the distance, the ostriches were eating quietly, pecking for insects and stray seeds. They would have to approach carefully; once the birds knew that a fearsome hunter was on the prowl, they would begin to run, and even the horses would be hard-pressed to catch them. Semerkhet pulled the horses back to a walk, then brought them to a halt, letting them catch their breath. The King needed to catch his breath too.

Then it was time. Semerkhet flicked the reins against the horses' backs and they took off, plunging toward the ostrich flock.

Laughing, Tut put an arrow to the string and let it fly, hitting a bird squarely in the neck. It stiffened and fell, its fellows running away from the chariot in a panic, flightless wings flapping. They galloped on, the wind in the young King's face as he scanned the landscape for any more prey. He sighed. This was the only time he felt truly free, racing along at high speeds with the wind blowing his wig, his mind focused on his task, his body free from the effort of getting around.

There was one, running at full speed on its gangly legs, a picture of panic. It didn't run long, for Tutankhamun let another arrow fly, burrowing into the gigantic bird's body and sending it tumbling to the ground. They raced on, toward a marsh full of ducks sitting peacefully on the surface of the water. But not for long. As Semerkhet pulled the horses to a halt just where the ground began to get soft, giving way to the wetland, Tut turned and grabbed a throwing stick, aiming it at the nearest fowl. It arced through the air and hit its mark, sending the duck into the water with a splash. Hopping out of the chariot and splashing through the muddy water, Semerkhet retrieved it, dropping it on the floor of the chariot.

They hunted all that afternoon, and the King caught enough birds for a small feast. They rode along together, faces glowing, and he could see that truly... he and Semerkhet were both boys.

By the end of the afternoon Tut was tired; he hadn't been walking, but the sun, which was sliding toward the western horizon, shone heavily on their heads, and his eyes were starting to hurt. He was very hot.

"I think we've caught enough," he said to the servant as he wiped the sweat off his face. "Thank you."

"You're welcome," Semerkhet said, slowing the horses down. "I'll let someone know where the ostriches are, and they'll come back to pick them up later. Should we go back now? Face the wrath of Ay?"

"I suppose so," Tut said with a little chuckle. "Oh, that was fun. Have to do that again soon."

"If he doesn't barricade you in your chambers for the next ten years," Semerkhet said with a chuckle of his own.

"That is a possibility. Let's separate when we go in," the Pharaoh said as they entered the stable, handing the horses and chariot back to the groom.

"Why?"

"Because I don't want to get you in trouble. Technically I was risking my life, and you were letting me, and if Ay knows it was you, you'll get it worse than I will."

"Thank you. Well… good luck, I suppose, and I'll see you tonight."

"See you tonight!" Semerkhet helped the Pharaoh get out of the chariot, and Tut hobbled back toward the palace, ready to get into trouble. The sun was beginning to set, and mosquitoes began coming out, buzzing around his ears. Tut slapped at one on his arm and scratched an itchy bite.

"May I enquire what was going through your royal mind as you decided to risk your life on a joyride?" Ay asked, not looking up as the Pharaoh entered the study, leaning heavily on his walking-stick, reeking of sweat. Having so much fun was exhausting.

"I just needed some fresh air," he said lightly.

Now Ay turned around, gesturing with both wrinkled hands. "Which you might have obtained on a short walk around the palace! You do realize it's my job to keep you alive so you can have an heir?"

Ay sighed, anger fading. "You know you're not strong. You could have fallen and the whole chariot could have landed on you." He paused, expression changing in a way Tut couldn't interpret. Then he sighed, looking almost tenderly at his young charge, half a smile adjusting the wrinkles around his mouth. "Your parents…

your parents trusted me to keep you safe. Don't prevent me from keeping my promise."

He opened his arms, and Tut stepped into them, letting the Vizier wrap him in an extremely formal version of a hug. The large scarab-shaped pectoral necklace Ay wore, identifying him as a Vizier, was hard and cold against Tut's chest. And as he embraced the boy, his cold arms folded around Tut's shoulders like the crossed arms of a Pharaoh's mummy. "I suppose you may be excused the Sunset Ceremony tonight… although that does make twice this week."

Once he was free of the clasping arms, Tut gave the Vizier the least-adolescent smile he could.

"All right. I won't do it again… at least not for a long time."

This time Ay cracked a smile. Now Tut grinned, big teeth or no. He had won.

That evening Semerkhet gave Tut his shower, pouring water over him and helping him scrub away the sweat and dirt of their little adventure. He wasn't too tired to think, so he really could wash himself as Semerkhet slowly poured the cool water over him. The only part he couldn't reach was his back. For his part, Semerkhet appeared to have washed up during Tut's conversation with the Vizier and changed out of his wet, muddy tunic into a clean one.

"That was so much fun!" Tut whispered as Semerkhet wrapped him in his towel.

"I know," he agreed, carefully leading him to the bed. He was smiling; far from being demeaning, being able to bathe the King was a strange honor, and now, more than ever, a moment of care from a friend to a friend. And even as Tut felt some annoyance at never having any privacy, he had found it in his heart to say, *this is not what I'd prefer, but this is you taking care of me, and this is me being grateful.*

"Even if we never do it again… at least we'll have the memories, right?"

Semerkhet nodded. "Yes, we will."

Tut sat still while Semerkhet dabbed his moisturizer onto him, then got him into his loincloth and sleeping-tunic. The day finally over, washed, garbed in nightclothes, and pleasantly exhausted, he lay down in bed with a smile.

"Goodnight, Sem."

"Goodnight, Master."

Tut lay in the dark, chuckling over the day. What fun. What an adventure. The cat curled up beside him, her warmth making him sleepy. As he drifted off, mind and heart full of happy memories of the wind in his face, he half-noticed himself shivering in an unpleasant chill.

"Ankh?" Tutankhamun groaned. The bedsheets around him were wet with sweat, sticking to his skin. He shivered and tried to push them off, but he could hardly move his arms, he was so weak. He'd felt like this before; he probably had the ague from a mosquito bite, just like he usually caught every year or two. "Ankh, I'm sick."

The light of a small lamp bobbed through the dark as she ran into the room and hurried to his side, taking his clammy hand and peering down at him with an anxious frown. As sick as he felt, he tried not to chuckle at the sight of her without her wig. She was as bald as he was, smooth, brown head gleaming in the lamplight.

"What is it, darling?"

"Fink it'th the ague. Got a fever… Will you get the doctor?"

"Of course. Just a minute. Better stay put." She hurried out of the room.

He stayed in bed, feeling his head burning up when the rest of him was frozen. He wanted the blanket back, but it was nasty with sweat, and he was too hot, he didn't want any blanket, and anyway, he couldn't sit up to grab it. He could only wait, ill, and try to scratch that mosquito bite. Bastet curled up beside him, her soft furriness keeping him warm.

Ankh was back in a few minutes with the doctor, who also carried an oil lamp. Tut noticed that she now had a wig on, although it was a little crooked. Her brother seeing her with a naked head was one thing, the doctor was another.

"I'm so sorry to hear that Your Majesty is ill," the Chief Physician said, bowing low to the ground. Tut nodded, trying to be patient. Finally the doctor got up off the floor and set about examining him.

"What exactly have you been feeling?" he asked as he took Tutankhamun's wrist to check his pulse by the dim lamplight.

"I'm cold, but I know I have a fever, and I'm tho tired. Hardly even sit up. Fink it's the ague."

The doctor considered, thinking face barely visible in the shifting shadows. "Have you been bitten by a mosquito recently?"

Tut nodded.

"Then Your Majesty is right; it is the ague. But we can contend with it. I'll prepare a mixture for you."

Tutankhamun lay back quietly. The doctor knew what to do. Whatever medicine he was making would help him. He'd be over this case of ague soon. And until he was, Ankh would help take care of him.

154

"Have you taken your medicine yet?" It was Ankhesenamun, hovering over him, her little hands around one of his.

Tutankhamun slowly woke up from the afternoon nap he was taking on the third day of being sick.

"Yeth, this morning. Fank you for reminding me." He yawned, sitting up a little. Ankh sat down on the side of the bed, taking his other hand.

"I love you. You'll get better soon, I know it." Bending forward, she kissed him on the forehead. He smiled, and he wanted to kiss her back, but sometimes the sickness of one person spread throughout the house, and he didn't want her to get sick.

He closed his eyes against the thought, against the memories of what could happen when an illness swept through a palace. The echoes of sweet laughter rang through his mind, sweet laughter suddenly silenced as four sweet sisters ran merrily around a corner from which they would never reappear. Not for a thousand, thousand lifetimes did he want to live through that again. So he squeezed her hand.

The Queen sat with him all she could, helping him drink his tea, tucking him in with blankets when he got cold and taking them off when he was too hot. Ague, like he'd gotten every year or two since childhood. Just another thing for his body to handle, she thought sadly. Just another thing for him to fight through. But he always had fought through everything he had faced. He would get through this too.

She prayed for him as she looked after him, to Amun-Ra, Isis, Osiris. But just like when she prayed to Tawaret, all she heard in response was silence. And all she felt was her own hope.

Semerkhet took care of him too, bringing him his meals, bringing a basin of cool water and helping him almost have a bath even in bed, washing away the feverish sweat and helping him stay fresh and clean. And every day, Ankh brought him fresh flowers from the garden to brighten up his room. Between his sister and his valet, he had all the care he needed. Although he missed his mother, his five other sisters. And he missed Hetepheres.

Tut stayed in bed until he felt strong enough to sit up, then slowly slide out of bed and walk around the bedroom. Two weeks after becoming sick, he finally observed with a little smile that he was nearly back to normal.

Finally, he was able to leave his bedroom, able to at least putter around the palace. Walking-stick in hand, he hobbled down a hallway just for the sake of exercise… and paused with a sigh.

Here was a painting, a massive painting of his ancestor Thutmose the First smiting someone rather definitively. He had been an empire-builder, stretching Egypt's borders further than any Pharaoh before him. Tut looked up at his noble form and swallowed. *Look at the writings and artwork of all the other Pharaohs,* he thought. *They're so broad and strong! And I'm just a scrawny child who can barely walk from my chambers to the garden. The Boy-King. Youngest and most pathetic Pharaoh ever to rule.*

Tut sighed, turning away from the vision of perfection, the established standard of what a Pharaoh should be. Broad. Strong. Warrior. He gripped his walking-stick and kept going.

156

13 Ripples

Tut sat at his bedroom window, watching the bright-colored birds fluttering around the garden, roosting in peach and olive trees, pecking for seeds among the roses, poppies, and jasmine flowers, occasionally fighting one another for possession of a particular branch. It looked hot outside. Very hot. It was the month of Epiphi, after all. But the breeze that blew in through the window was cool. And the view was beautiful.

He'd been resting in bed on and off today, still not quite up to his full strength again. Some days he still took a nap. But in general, he was pleased to see that he was getting stronger again. Even if it was a slow process.

"Ankh?" he said. She got up from her ebony and ivory-inlaid chair, setting Bastet carefully on the floor, and walked over, putting her hand lovingly on his shoulder. It was such a hot day that not only was he only wearing a kilt and a necklace, the Queen was wearing a dress with no sleeves at all. And that meant that it was too hot to cuddle. Tut would have loved to have been curled up on the couch with his sister's arms around him, but they were both too hot and sweaty to feel like it.

"Yes, dear?"

"What happened to all those ostriches?"

"Ostriches?"

"The ones I hunted, right before I got sick. Semerkhet said he was going to have someone else go back and get them… but I never heard what ended up happening to them. I don't even know what we do with ostriches, other than hunt them. Did they get cooked? And next time, could we have the meat given to the poor?" He swallowed, looking up at her. "If the servants are people just like us… what about the animals? Do birds have feelings? Do they have families? Is hunting really a good thing for me to be doing?"

Ankhesenamun smiled at her little brother. "Look at your fan, dear," she said, pointing across the room to where it hung on the wall near his sword and shield. "What kind of feathers are those?"

Tut looked, and nodded. "Ostrich."

She nodded, the blue beads on her wig chiming. "That's right. Those feathers right there came from an ostrich you hunted. I remember when they made it, year before last. And right before it was made, I remember my handmaiden telling me how delicious the roasted ostrich had been in the servants' hall. How grateful they all were to you for hunting it for them." She squeezed his shoulder. "Nothing goes to waste. And everything is interconnected. We live in the middle of a web… with the whole world around us. Staff, peasants, the animals we hunt… all interconnected."

Tut turned his head, pressing his cheek against his sister's hand. "All interconnected."

"It's like the ripples of a flower dropping into one of the reflecting pools," she said. He looked out the window again; he could see one of the pools from where he sat, the surface covered in flower petals. "Everything works together. Society, nature, the whole world. You hunted that ostrich, and the craftsmen made the feathers into a fan for you, and the servants ate the meat. The servants perform work for us, and we give them the opportunity to work. And all the work, and all the… bureaucracy… that takes place in Thebes and Memphis allows the whole country to function. And Egypt has her place among all the nations of the world.

And the world we live in stands under the sky, and above the underworld, within the waters of Nun that surround everything we know. And the gods created it all and guide it as they see fit."

The Pharaoh blinked, mind feeling about to explode from the sudden dose of cosmic transcendence.

"Everything works together," he repeated. "So we have to take good care of the people we've been made responsible for."

"That's right."

Tut nodded. "Father didn't care what anyone else thought. He led according what he thought was right." He smiled. "And I can do the same."

Now that he could get up, Tut could go down to the royal feasting hall for meals. The month of Epiphi brought a new variety of fruits and vegetables into season; alongside his usual entrees of beef, chicken, mutton, antelope, or the occasional ostrich, he got to enjoy plums, leeks, and a variety of melons. And of course, his sister consumed at least three watermelons with each week that went by. That was always fun to watch.

"Semerkhet," Tut said as his valet touched up his makeup after lunch, as the sweat that was dripping down his face was making it run, "there's something I wanted to ask you."

"Yes, Master?" he asked.

"You know, back a couple of weeks ago now, when we went on that... on that hunting trip..." In the bronze mirror, Tut could see Semerkhet's mouth quirk unhappily at the memory of the little adventure that had gotten his Master so sick. "Well, I... I was wondering how you felt about what I called you. *Sem*. Is that... is that all right? Do you want a nickname? I just thought… since we're… friends… that you might…" Tut found his words trailing off as he looked earnestly at his valet, anxious to hear his response.

Semerkhet put away the kohl and got out the eye-shadow. And Tut saw the tiniest shadow of a smile on his face. A smile that grew as he nodded in agreement. And a real smile, not just a polite one put on for the Morning and the Evening Star.

"I like it," he said with a grin, tentatively making eye contact for a brief moment. "And I'm… I'm honored that you wanted to give me a nickname."

Tut laughed, feeling his worry and embarrassment melt away. He almost… almost wanted to reach out and squeeze Semerkhet's hand. But maybe they weren't quite to that level of casual friendship yet. Not quite.

"Sem," he said with a smile. And his valet's… his friend's… eyes lit up. "Thank you, Sem."

His friend just chuckled. And they went on with the King's makeup.

Lessons went on, now that Tut was well again. From the Vizier, and from his sister. She taught him their names over the next weeks, of those mothers, wives, sisters, daughters, who had ruled Egypt just as capably as any man. Regents and Pharaohs, Sobekneferu and Hatshepsut reigning in equal stature to any man, Nimaathap, Khentkaus the First, Iput, standing in the gap at the end of the Second, Fourth, and Fifth Dynasties. And together, they waited to see how Ay would tell their stories.

"He's finally well," Ankhesenamun said to Meresankh as her handmaiden helped her get ready for bed, putting away her jewelry, helping her shower, and getting her into her sleeping-tunic.

"Oh, that is good to hear," Meresankh said, putting away the Queen's wig. Ankh sat on the bed, the evening air cool on her shaved scalp. They were all bald under their wigs. "The ague can take a long time to get over."

Ankh nodded, then swallowed. "I just wonder… next time… will he be able to get through it? He's never been strong; you can see how much it took out of him. He's thinner, he walks slower. He's better, but how long before he's really, truly back to normal?"

Meresankh sighed, forehead wrinkling sadly. "Sometimes… sometimes things don't go back to normal, My Lady. Sometimes they have to settle into a new normal."

Ankh closed her eyes. "But how many times can that happen?"

"As many times as the Divine decides," Meresankh said simply.

Ankhesenamun nodded, eyes still closed. She knew Meresankh was right… although her word choice, "the Divine," had been rather unusual.

And she knew that an unknown purpose still awaited discovery. It was there. If only they could find it. One day, everything would be clear.

"Your legs are stronger than I had expected, Your Majesty," the therapist said in her creaky old voice. Tutankhamun was lying on his back in bed as she gently guided his legs through their range of motion, examining how they had been affected by his time stuck in bed. "Your strength hasn't deteriorated very badly at all."

"Good," he said. "I can feel myself getting stronger." He lay there silently as she helped him stretch, feeling the warm support of her strong, wrinkled, old hands. He looked up at her, her kind, lined face, her neat wig of black braids, and thought what a wonderful, sweet grandmother she must be to some lucky children. Then a sudden thought popped into his mind. A thought that seemed perfectly ridiculous, as he realized it had never occurred to him before. Even though she worked on him every single week. Shame, shame. "What's your name?" he asked her.

She paused in stretching his leg, eyes flickering to his face for half an instant as she restrained herself from fully making eye contact. "Rahonem, Your Majesty."

"Rahonem," he repeated. "I just want to thank you for everything you do. You're the one who helps my legs stay strong enough to keep walking."

Rahonem blushed, looking down. "It's my honor, Your Majesty."

The King walked down the hall after lunch, feeling refreshed by simply being able to get up and walk again, slow work though it was. He was still recuperating, still convalescing, but each day he truly did feel a little stronger. Tomorrow he might actually be able to go to the Temple of Amun-Ra for prayers, stand by while the bull was slaughtered. Not that he was looking forward to it. The part he was looking forward to was being able to walk outside.

Out of nowhere, Bastet streaked past in a gray blur, dashing after a mouse. Suddenly Tut's walking-stick was out of his hand, and he was flying forward, about to break his teeth on the nearest stone pillar.

162

A pair of strong arms caught him. An instant later Tut felt himself being righted, supported by someone tall and strong.

"Wh—" Tut blinked at whoever this was, then realized that he recognized him as a member of the palace staff, although not someone he knew by name. "Thank you," he said finally.

"Y-you're welcome, Your M-majesty," the young man stuttered. Trying to establish a respectful distance, he allowed the Pharaoh to hold his shoulder as another servant picked up Tut's walking-stick and carefully returned it to him.

Tut got his balance, then smiled at both of the young men who stood before him, with matching uniforms, matching sandals, matching wigs, matching looks of terror. And then were suddenly kneeling before him, faces to the floor.

"Rise, please," he said, beckoning grandly with his free hand. Bastet had disappeared; apparently not having any idea that her antics had nearly killed her master, she had continued her mouse-hunt. Slowly the young men stood, quaking in their sandals, and stood in silence, hands folded, eyes on their own feet. Not on his feet, and certainly not on his face. "What are your names, so I know who to thank?" he asked.

"Amenmose, Your Majesty."

"Raherka, My Lord."

"Amenmose, Raherka, thank you for keeping me from breaking my nose," he said with a warm smile. They just stared at their feet, looking utterly terrified. He sighed, a little disappointed. So much for thanking the people who looked after him. And how could they see his smile if they were afraid to look at him? "Well, enjoy your day," he said after an awkward silence, and walked away. Halfway down the hall, he paused and subtly looked over his shoulder; both the servants had disappeared. As if they had run away in fright.

Ankhesenamun blinked as the words she had spoken to her brother about the interconnectedness of all things circled back to her with new meaning. She thought of Meresankh, the sweet, kind, cheerful handmaiden who had served her for the past year. And about how little she actually knew about her.

Meresankh was across the room, arranging freshly-cleaned wigs on their stands. The Queen looked over at her, wondering how to begin the conversation. All she could think of was,

"Meresankh… where do you live?"

The handmaiden settled a wig onto its stand and looked up. "In the staff quarters, My Lady. The west wing of the palace. I have a lovely little suite."

Ankh smiled. "How about your family?"

Meresankh paused, carefully untangling one of the delicate braids from the others. "My parents are gone, My Lady. I was raised by Merneith the midwife, and she got me a position here."

The Queen blinked back pain at the word "midwife" even as she remembered that the Chief Physician had been the one attending her four years ago, two years ago. And as her heart ached for her orphaned handmaiden, Ankh lowered her head with a sigh. She wanted… she wanted to give Meresankh a hug. But she restrained herself to extending her hand, giving a little smile when Meresankh took it and squeezed it, as embarrassed as she looked to be touching the Queen's hand. Although she was making eye contact, for almost the first time that Ankh could remember. "I'm sorry," the Queen whispered.

164

"She's very good to me," Meresankh said, her voice lightening as if she was worried she had disturbed the Queen with her sad story. As if she wanted to reassure her that she really was happy. She smiled. "And I'm so glad to be working here."

Ankhesenamun nodded. "I'm glad you're here too. And I want you to know... just how grateful I am for everything you do." She chuckled. "I'm not sure if I could even dress myself without your help!"

Meresankh smiled again, and this time it was a real smile, the dimple deepening in her round cheek. Together they remembered the time Meresankh had said the same thing, back before their eyes had begun to open. "It's my pleasure, My Lady."

Ankh smiled as Meresankh went on with her work. *Merneith.* So that was the name of the sweet old lady the handmaiden was always with. And who, as the Queen now understood, had raised her. What a powerful name, Ankh thought. The same name as the second dowager Queen Regent to rule Egypt, the great-grand-daughter of Menes-Narmer who had served as regent for her young son Den. To have such a name, so many centuries later, this midwife must be a truly formidable person.

Ankhesenamun wanted to meet her.

14 Learning

Tut sat gratefully at his desk, his head resting on his folded arms as his valet rubbed his neck. The weather was changing, and he had such a headache. But he could rely on his faithful servant… his faithful friend… to ease it for him. The cool, refreshing peppermint oil Semerkhet was using would probably help too.

Suddenly there was a knock at the door. Semerkhet turned his head as much to their surprise, it actually began to open, even though Sem had not formally answered it. Apparently the guard who patrolled the hall had not perceived a threat.

"Excuse me," the valet said in a slightly confused tone, leaving his Master to see what servant apparently had a death-wish.

Tut slowly sat up, curious as to the events that were about to unfold. It was Kahotep. The fat, cranky old servant stood there without a hint of shame, and immediately asked Semerkhet where the dust-rags were.

"What do you think you're doing? Get out of here!" Semerkhet whispered through clenched teeth. "You know where they are," he hissed angrily, shepherding him back out into the hallway with horror on his face. "Ask Amenmose if you can't find them. Now get out."

He shut the door very firmly in Kahotep's confused face before the old man could even offer his wishes for life, prosperity, and health, turning back to his Master with his own face full of embarrassment and shame. So much embarrassment that he couldn't meet his eye.

"A thousand apologies, Your Majesty," he mumbled, bowing more deeply than he had since before Tribute Day. "Kahotep has

166

been… more forgetful lately. But that's *no* excuse for disturbing the royal peace."

Tutankhamun just chuckled. "Well, he's royally forgiven. I suppose…" He shook his head with a little laugh. "I suppose we could make a sign for the door, for, uh, royal downtime. Something like, 'don't even knock until such-and-such time or you'll be fed to the crocodiles!'" He tapped his chin. "Or maybe we could just lock the door."

Semerkhet echoed the smile, locking the door with a satisfying click. Then he returned to his place behind the Pharaoh's chair, hands floating above his shoulders.

"May I?" he asked.

Tut smiled. "Oh… yes. Thank you, Sem." Again he rested his head on his folded arms.

And they returned to royal downtime. Tut smiled, sighing as his stiff neck loosened up, Sem's hands and the peppermint oil both doing their job. His headache was almost gone.

Tut was still getting his energy back, although he gained strength every day. So here, during the hottest part of the year, he found himself lying on his back on his bed in the middle of the day, feeling as though steam was radiating from every inch of his body. Indoors, and he felt almost as bad as he had during Tribute Day. Although there were far too many mosquitoes outside for him to want to sit outside. Thank the gods that there was a breeze blowing in through the window.

He closed his eyes and thought of Sholiak, Tybi, Meshir, Phamenoth, Pharmouthi, the months that didn't make him feel like bread being baked, the months that were cool enough for him and his sister to sit together and cuddle like they always had when they were little. The months when he could wrap up warm in his cozy outer robes and enjoy shivering in the chilly breeze, listen to the rain, which was always a bit of a novelty, wrap his hands around hot cups of tea, sleep under two or three blankets. Good days, cozy nights. Not like these hot, sticky, blazing days when everyone smelled worse than usual, no one wanted to touch anyone else, and most people slept on their roofs to get even a breath of cool air, a wisp of a breeze. He thought of the cool days, the cold nights. And he was homesick for them.

They would be here soon enough. But first he and the rest of Egypt had to get through the end of the Season of the Harvest and the first half of the Season of Inundation like they did every year. His birthday gift every year, in the month of Paophi, was that the hot season was soon to end. And he was always delighted to receive it.

He sat up. No use lying here hot and miserable. Maybe Semerkhet could go down to the kitchens and get him something cold to drink. Tut picked up his walking-stick and went to go find him.

"Why do all the servants act like they're afraid of me?" Tut asked as Semerkhet did his makeup the next morning. It was another bright, sunny, hot day, and Bastet was trying to catch the motes of dust that danced in the beams of sunlight streaming in through the window. Kahotep had held out the day's kilt and jewelry for Sem to put on the King and brought the requested pair of shoes... on his third attempt. First Kahotep had brought the wrong pair, then a mismatched pair of one correct and one incorrect sandal, before finally coming back with the "mate" of the comfortable, bead-encrusted pair with padded soles and helpful

168

straps. Finally, Kahotep had excused himself with a bow. But Tut wondered whether, when he had gone back down the hall, the old man had gone the right way.

Semerkhet carefully lined the King's eyes with kohl, thinking. "Because you are the Pharaoh. And because they know the power that the Pharaoh has. If anyone so much as looks cross-eyed at you, you could have them executed. So they're terrified of doing something wrong."

Tut sighed. Didn't the people understand that he would never execute anyone for anything but the most grievous offense? "It's like I've lived in a bubble for so many years. I never knew anyone's name but yours, never even knew how laundry worked. Never even thought about it. And now I'm finally starting to wake up. I'm astounded by all the jobs I never even knew existed because I never thought about them. They just... happened."

"Well, it is our job to be invisible," Semerkhet said, removing the Pharaoh's chosen wig from its stand and gently placing it on his head, carefully arranging the tiny braids that framed his face. Then he set Tut's small golden circlet over the wig, its little *uraeus* peeking out just above the bangs of the wig. "Our sphere and yours are totally separate. We take care of these things so you don't even have to think about them, don't even have to know about them. So you can focus entirely on your sphere, leading the government and taking care of all of us."

"Am I really doing that?" Tut asked almost sarcastically. "Or am I just the figurehead?"

Semerkhet shook his head with a chuckle. "You lowered Egypt's taxes, limited slavery, established a generous minimum wage, and you're building five schools," he reminded him. "I think you're more than just a figurehead."

Sem smiled, looking remarkably satisfied with his lot. "Keeping the meaning of our jobs in mind helps on a hard day," he said. "Remembering that every little bit helps, that we're all doing our part. If a low-ranking servant cleans the floor and that makes a low-ranking official smile, and his good mood makes his superiors feel more cheerful, and they're all more productive than they would have been otherwise, and that cheerful attitude makes it all the way up to the Pharaoh… paperwork just might get signed that day that could prevent a war. It's like the magical fountain in the old fable, that flows up instead of down. It's *ma'at*, the balance and order of the whole universe. So Egypt belongs to all of us, and it's everyone's responsibility. And every success belongs to all of us, because in some small way, we were all part of it. By extension. Like… like ripples." Semerkhet smiled. "And that makes us proud."

Tut smiled. There were those ripples again. "It's sad, though, that it seems like some of the staff can't accept my gratitude," he said with a sigh.

Semerkhet nodded. "Well, they'll get used to it," he said with a smile. "When they realize that you really do mean it and that you're not going to have them executed for looking at you cross-eyed."

"I'm glad I know about these things now," Tut said, taking the day's walking-stick from Semerkhet and slowly standing up. "I need to think about them, and learn about them, so I can understand how it all works, and I can properly appreciate everything everyone does for me. I feel like I've been a baby for eighteen years. I really don't know much of anything."

170

Semerkhet smiled, stepping toward the bedroom door to open it for him. "Well, you have a long time to keep learning."

As he walked down the hall, the Pharaoh noticed a woman merrily humming as she mopped the floor. She was doing her bit, just like Semerkhet had said. And that made her happy. Because who knew how far the ripples of that floor being clean might go. That clean floor might save the world.

Sitting on the bed, Tut looked over at the fabulous Nubian shield hanging on the wall of his bedroom, the graceful sword beside it. Would he ever fight?

He looked down at Ankh, who was sitting on the floor throwing dried flower-heads for Bastet to chase. He sighed. Just to be able to sit on the floor if he wanted to, without being afraid he could never get up again…

"Horemheb told me he thinks we'll be at war with the Hittites within the year," he said.

Ankh looked up with a frown. "Isn't there anything they can do?"

Tut shrugged and shook his head, sighing sadly. "He says they've tried. But at the rate we're losing land to them in the northeast, soon we'll be taken over. They've already taken Kadesh, and other parts of Amurru, where you were saying they used to pay tribute to our grandfather. If it's not us, it'll be the Mitanni— they're in worse shape than we are, and right now, their army isn't as big as ours, isn't as powerful. Although we should be grateful our army is as big as it is, with how it got wiped out when the

Hebrews disappeared." He swallowed. "I just wish I could fight. How can I be a strong Pharaoh if I can't fight?"

Ankhesenamun gave a little smile, tossing another flower-head. It rolled under a chair, and Bastet dived underneath, fishing for it with her paw. "You *are* strong. Maybe you'll never ride into battle, but your mind is strong, and you have the strongest heart I've ever seen. If you can't be a King of war... then be a King of peace. If you foster peace with the countries around us, maybe war can be avoided."

The King shrugged again. Maybe she was right. Or... maybe war was just a male thing.

"It's not just fighting, though," he said with a sigh. "It's every-thing to do with getting around. How am I ever going to make the ritual run around the courtyard for my Sed Festival when I reach my thirtieth year on the throne? I don't even know if I can hobble all the way around it." He gave a wry chuckle. "Might take me thirty years just to get around it. I hope I live to *be* thirty."

Ankhesenamun got up from the floor and sat beside him, putting her arm around him so his head rested on her strong little shoulder. The cat approached the bed and put her paws on Tut's knees, also wanting to be petted. "If I know you, you'll do more in three years than most Pharaohs can do in thirty." She smiled. "There's a purpose, baby brother. And someday, we'll know what it is."

172

15   Cranky Crocodiles

Tut and Ankh sat watching Kahotep bustle around the King's bedroom one hot afternoon toward the end of Epiphi, puffing as he dusted with a linen rag. Sweating under his wig, he gave the room a grimly satisfied nod, waddling away to attack the next dusty room. Why he was in here right now, Tut didn't know. It was a bit awkward. No one ever cleaned the Pharaoh's room while he was sitting in it. Most of the servants were terrified to risk disturbing the royal peace.

Tut chuckled as they watched him go. When he was safely out of earshot, the King turned to his wife.

"You know, some people, the meaning of their name really matches their personality," he whispered. "But doesn't his name mean 'peaceful essence'?"

Ankh giggled. "Yes. It does. Doesn't really line up."

"More like Kasobek," he laughed. "Essence of Cranky Crocodile God."

"Essence of Cranky…" Ankh couldn't help it; she rocked back and forth on the bed, guffawing with that whinnying laugh that Meketaten had always teased her about, made her call Ankh *Shadow* after Mother's horse. Alarmed, Bastet jumped to the floor and retreated to a corner, where she started inspecting the fine linen curtains for mice or insects.

"Or Tawaret!" Tut yelped, biting his lip to keep from laughing too loudly. Ankh squealed with delight at the terrible joke.

"I think I left my rag in here…" Kahotep was back, waddling heavily back into the room, his heavy trod audible throughout the palace.

"Shh…" The King and Queen shushed one another, biting back their laughter. The servant found his rag and excused himself again, and they cracked up again, glad that with all the strange things they were facing, one thing they could share was laughter.

Then there was a knock at the door.

"Come in," the Pharaoh said. Semerkhet came in, offering a bow to the King and Queen. Tut noticed that he was avoiding eye contact even more than usual. What was wrong?

"I beg your pardon for the interruption… Was Kahotep in here?" he asked, a hint of anxiety in his voice. Or was it embarrassment?

"Yes, just now," Tut replied.

Semerkhet grimaced, looking ashamed. "A thousand, thousand apologies, Your Majesties," he said, bowing again, even more deeply. He looked like he was about to get on the floor like he always used to before he and Tut had become friends, seeing one another as fellow human beings. "The Pharaoh should never see his room being cleaned. Kahotep is… I fear he is getting senile. I have been in the process of making a decision about him, but I fear I have left it too late… I will have him removed."

Tutankhamun looked at his servant with sudden anxiety. "Well, don't kill him! He wasn't bothering us. It was just a little… unexpected."

"No, no," Semerkhet said, shaking his head so hard that the tiny braids of his wig swung across his face, hitting him in the nose. "I merely meant immediate retirement. It is our job to be invisible… and Kahotep clearly cannot do his job anymore. He will not disturb you again."

The Pharaoh nodded, relieved. "Thank you. When you dismiss him… please thank him for all his years of service."

174

This time a hint of a smile touched Semerkhet's face. This was the valet, the friend, that Tut knew. "I will, Master." And with another bow, a little less dramatic this time, and a wish for life, prosperity, and health, Sem was gone. Tut chuckled. Having to talk to the Queen always brought out maximum formality in his valet. And having to apologize for the behavior of another servant probably had something to do with it, too.

Tutankhamun turned to his wife with a shrug. "I never *have* seen anyone cleaning my room before. It always just... happens."

Ankhesenamun shook her head. "Neither have I. Poor Ka-hotep..."

"Well, I hope he enjoys his retirement," Tut said. "He's served us for a long time."

Tut walked down the hall on his way to lunch after going to the temple, admiring the paintings on the walls, the graceful columns and pillars that supported the walls and ceilings. Semerkhet walked beside him, making doubly sure that the King got to lunch safely after two weeks stuck in bed. He was strong again, he really was, but Sem wanted to be careful, especially after the incident with the Royal Cat. And Tut was grateful for his friend's concern.

The month of Mesori, the last of the Season of the Harvest, had begun, as hot as Epiphi had been, and as hot as Thoth would be. As they walked down one of a hundred endless hallways, Tut gave a chuckle as a funny thought popped into his mind.

"Sem," he asked, glancing at him as they walked, then returning his eyes to the floor in front of him, cautious of any marauding cats, "how big is the palace?"

"How big is the palace?" Semerkhet repeated. "Oh, you wouldn't believe me if I told you. You and the Queen each have your own suite of rooms, of course, and you know the entrance hall, the royal feasting hall, the throne room, your study… but then you have the kitchens, and the staff quarters, and the studies that belong to the Viziers, the scribes' offices, the physicians' quarters, where they keep all their crocodile-eyeball concoctions…"

"And where they make things?" Tut asked.

Semerkhet nodded and continued, counting off departments on his fingers. "Then you've got the wig department, laundry department, jewelry department, shoe department, and the storerooms where the cleaning crews keep all their things so they can keep the rooms dusted and the floors shiny… and outside, all the storage for the gardeners' equipment so they can keep the grounds looking beautiful, and the gardens themselves, and the stables, and the lake…"

The King paused, smiling and closing his eyes as he imagined all these rooms, all buzzing with busy servants. And all for him and the Queen.

"I'd like to see more of it," he said with almost a sad little chuckle. "But it would probably take me three days to walk through all of it." He sighed, remembering. "We moved here when I was six… and I ran around as well as I could during those three years when Mother was Pharaoh. But then… since I've been crowned, it's been nothing but lessons, and I haven't had the time or the energy to explore very much."

His valet smiled. "Well, maybe this is your chance to explore a bit."

Tut smiled back. "Maybe it is."

176

"More beef," Ay said at lunch, snapping his gnarled fingers.

"Yes, sir," a servant said, bowing and taking the Vizier's plate to refill it.

"And you," he said, gesturing at another young man. The Pharaoh recognized him; he was one of the ones who had helped him when he had tripped over the cat.

"Me, sir?"

"Yes, you, whatever-your-name-is. Shut the curtains. The sun is making my headache worse. And bring me some of that white wine. I don't like this." The servant silently took the nearly-full cup of red wine back to the kitchen with a look that showed that this was exactly how he expected the Vizier to treat him. He was used to it.

Tutankhamun silently looked askance at his fractious Vizier. That was not the way to treat the human beings who happened to be employed to serve them.

"Thank you, Amenmose," he said for Ay as the young man came back with the Vizier's white wine. Ay glanced at the King in confusion as Amenmose contracted in embarrassment at being acknowledged.

"Yes, thank you, young man," the Vizier said stiffly. "This is much better." And he frowned at the King again before accepting his refilled plate of beef and returning to his meal.

Tut took a bite of beef with a little smile, then a cool sip of sweet licorice *mai-sus*. That was one good deed done today.

The interconnectedness of every element of his world ran through the Pharaoh's mind as he sat on the bed, watching Se-merkhet arrange several freshly-cleaned wigs on their stands.

Suddenly a question popped into his mind, a question that surprised him. Now that his mind was waking up, he could hardly believe that he'd never thought of it before. Semerkhet was a person, just like him, with a life of his own. He had to live somewhere. But where?

"Sem," he said slowly, "where do you live?"

Semerkhet straightened the wig and looked over at the Pharaoh. "In the staff quarters, in a nice little suite of rooms."

Tutankhamun nodded. "Good. I'm glad it's nice."

Semerkhet chuckled. "Only thing that sometimes gets annoying is being across the hall from General Nakhtmin."

Tut gave a little shudder. "I don't think he sounds like a very nice neighbor." He paused. "I could get you moved to another part of the palace, if you want. Or I could have him moved."

The valet chuckled again. "It's all right, Morning Star. I can handle it."

"Does he have a valet?" Tut asked.

Semerkhet shook his head sadly. "Poor Neferkare. He needs a lot of encouragement."

Tut smiled. "I'm sure you keep him smiling."

"I do encourage him... a lot. The General is not an easy person to look after. Neferkare can hardly keep up with the messes he makes in his quarters." He paused. "Kahotep used to live just across the hall. He made a... more cheerful neighbor than General Nakhtmin, but he was a bit of a..."

"Cranky crocodile?" Tut asked with a chuckle.

Sem looked up and laughed. "Exactly. A cranky crocodile."

"Ankh and I thought of that," Tut said, "back when he retired. And we came up with a nickname for him..." He chuckled again. "Kasobek."

Semerkhet's eyebrows rose as he laughed in spite of himself. "Essence of Cranky Crocodile God," he chuckled with a little nod. "Yes. That fits."

The Pharaoh sighed, then looked at Semerkhet again. "I'd like to see *your* quarters sometime."

Semerkhet grinned. "Someday, if you really want to."

Tut tapped his chin, other questions about his valet's life arising in his mind. "And what do you like to do when you're not working?"

The valet arranged a wig on its stand, then turned back with a smile. "I like to play field hockey," he said. "I play on a local team. The royal team, actually. They always make an announcement before a game thanking you for supplying all the equipment."

Tut looked up. "I'm sponsoring a sports team? Why am I the last to know?"

Sem looked like he wasn't sure whether to chuckle or not. "It's traditional, isn't it? I suppose they would have wanted to keep it going, keep some continuity."

"I'll have to get involved now," Tut said thoughtfully. "Now that I know I own a hockey team."

Semerkhet put another wig away. "We beat a team from Gebtu just last week, five goals to three. And sometimes... sometimes I race chariots. You know that, though," he said with a chuckle.

Tut smiled as he thought back to the little adventure they had shared hunting ostriches. And he smiled to think of his valet... his friend... playing field hockey.

"I'll have to come to a hockey game sometime," the Pharaoh said. "And a horse race."

Sem just looked down with a chuckle. "If you wish, Morning Star."

Tut tapped his chin again. Now that he was on a roll, and he and Semerkhet had come to be so comfortable simply chatting, what other questions could he ask him? "And how many siblings do you have? I know you have a sister."

Semerkhet nodded. "Just Nofret and me anymore." He swallowed. "Mother's been gone... five years now. Ague. And I had a baby brother... Nedjes. Died just back in Paophi, on his first hippopotamus hunt. Was only thirteen. And Father..." He sighed. "I've hardly seen him since then. And my sister... she advises her husband just like someone else I can think of."

Very carefully, Tut returned his smile.

Semerkhet paused, returning to his neatening-up. "Bit of family news, actually," he said a minute later. "Nofret had her baby. Healthy little boy. They're calling him Ahmose."

Tutankhamun closed his eyes, breath catching in his throat as if he had been violently pushed, like he'd been kicked in the chest, kicked in the heart. Suddenly he was back in time, back to those terrible days, four years ago, then two years ago. The days when all their hopes and dreams had been snatched from him and his dear, brave wife, their world shattering into a thousand, thousand fragments of grief. And the day, all those months of hope and fear later, when it had happened again. And all the days they had wondered if they should ever try again. Because how could they live through it a third time?

Semerkhet saw the Pharaoh react, and looked at the floor, looking ashamed. "I... I'm sorry, Your Majesty," he whispered. "I... wasn't thinking. I... I just remembered a question I needed to ask Khenut about the laundry..." And he was out of the room with a whispered blessing, leaving the Pharaoh alone with his thoughts, and his grief.

It was her grief. Tut had felt his hopes and dreams growing as their two precious children had grown more and more visible each day, but it wasn't his belly they were growing in. Wasn't him that they were keeping awake with their kicks. Wasn't him that could almost tell what their personalities would be as the bond grew stronger and stronger with every passing hour.

It was his wife. And when everything they had been hoping for by day and dreaming of by night was stolen from them not once but twice, it was her grief. Tut grieved for what might have been, and he grieved for his wife's pain. But it was *her* pain. Her grief.

And so now, as his heart seared again, the still-aching wounds stinging as the tears stung his eyes, he didn't go to his wife and put his arms around her so *she* could comfort *him* in *his* grief.

Instead he held out his arms to Bastet, and his faithful little cat padded across the bed to curl up in his lap and rest her warm, furry back against his aching heart. And she purred as he held her like a baby, dropping tears onto her gray fur.

He held her. And she comforted him.

Then he thought again about what his wife, his sister, had said. That as Pharaoh, he had to have an heir. And that as Pharaoh, he could have as many wives and concubines as he chose.

He thought of it; a whole wing of the palace filled with the prettiest young women in the whole kingdom, half of them doing their hair and makeup in the hopes of catching his eye that evening and the other half cradling curved bellies or dandling babies or toddlers that were the evidence of his superior manliness, all of them busy spinning flax and weaving linen when they weren't busy with the children in their arms or the children they still hoped for. And he shook his head. He could have that, yes, if he wanted it. He could have a harem full of women whose dearest wish was to get pregnant by him… pregnant with the son who could carry on his dynasty.

Then he thought of Ankh again. Sister, wife… He chuckled. Mother, some days. And he sighed. They had been through so much together. And she was the only woman he had ever really known, ever loved. It would be so strange to have another person in his life, to share the joys and sorrows of life with a woman who hadn't been part of his life for as long as he could remember, the only woman in his life for the past ten years, other than dear old Hetty. They had only had each other for so many years. And they only needed each other.

As Pharaoh, the task he had to perform in order to establish his legacy was to sire a son. And he would. When the time was right.

His valet had a sister, and a fractured relationship with his father. His mother was gone, and so was his baby brother. Tut suddenly knew more about Semerkhet and his family than he ever would have imagined learning.

And now his heart ached as he thought of his own family, the parents and sisters he had not seen for so long. Sem, too, had lost family. As he remembered his beloved sisters, suddenly it occurred to the Pharaoh that he wondered what having a brother would be like. Another boy to relate to, not being passed around like a doll because his sisters wanted to play "mother," not being scolded, very gently, for getting into their things because he wanted to put on their makeup. Someone he could hunt with, share secrets with, talk to about the things that only another boy would understand in precisely the same way. Someone who would offer concern and compassion on a bad day without necessarily mothering him into oblivion. Someone with whom he didn't even always have to share a conversation to know he was understood. Someone who got it.

Someone like Semerkhet.

16   Wisdom

The Pharaoh slowly walked down the hall one day after lunch, and paused when he heard voices. Angry voices. His heart began to pound as he recognized Nakhtmin's voice spewing out an angry torrent of words at the servant who cowered before him, backed against the wall.

"Just because you're the Pharaoh's valet doesn't mean you can get away with getting mud on my—"

And that was when Tut realized that the person being shouted at was Semerkhet.

Angry heart beginning to pound in his temples, Tut swung his walking-stick out ahead of him and strode over to the pair as fast as he could limp.

"What is going on here?" he bellowed right into the middle of Nakhtmin's tirade. The little snake jumped, looking over his shoulder like a guilty child. Semerkhet, who had been hunched into himself under the onslaught of angry words, practically pressed against the wall of the hallway, straightened back up and wiped away the flecks of spittle that had landed on his face.

"I was just correcting your valet's atrocious clumsiness and sloppiness," Nakhtmin said in an unctuous voice that barely concealed his sneer. Slowly he unclenched the fist he had been brandishing in Semerkhet's face. "I'm afraid his impression of a camel has gotten mud all over my new robe. You might want to think about replacing him. Sending him to work in the stables, perhaps. The horses won't mind his carelessness."

The Pharaoh got between Semerkhet and Nakhtmin, attempting to shield his friend from the wrath of the Vizier's son. And as the thunder began to rumble behind his eyes, dark, dangerous

184

eyebrows lowering like stormclouds, a wiser man than Nakhtmin would have excused himself and run.

"It doesn't matter what he's done. He's my valet, and I decide if he's going to be punished or not. And if you think you can—"

"Glorious Lord?" a new voice asked from a few feet behind the Pharaoh. Tut turned around to see General Horemheb arriving with rather a concerned expression on his face. "Is everything all right?"

"Everything is most certainly *not* all right," Tut spat, turning back around to Nakhtmin, who was sneering at the silent Semerkhet, whose eyes were trained on the floor. His head was still pounding, a strange rushing filling his skull, and his vision was throbbing red as lightning flashed from his eyes. "Nakhtmin's been threatening Semerkhet over getting mud on his stupid robe, *and* he called him a camel, and if anyone deserves to be beaten, it'th him—" Well beyond clear thinking, Tut grabbed for the wall so he could raise his walking-stick into the air and swipe at the offender. Nakhtmin stepped back.

"Sounds like quite the situation," Horemheb said calmly. He turned to Nakhtmin. "General, may I ask what you have to say for yourself?"

"Nothing," Nakhtmin spat, lip curled contemptuously. "Except that in my opinion, the Pharaoh's valet is nothing but a—"

"No one athked for your opinion!" Tut shrieked, again attempting to lambaste Nakhtmin with his walking-stick. Across the hall, Semerkhet stood as still and silent as a statue, hands clasped at waist height as he continued to stare at the floor. Three other servants considered walking by with their various baskets of goods, thought better of it, and selected a different route to their respective destinations.

Gently, Horemheb cleared his throat. "It sounds to me as though a decision needs to be made. Your Majesty?"

Seething, Tut had stepped back, planting his walking-stick back onto the stone floor of the hallway. He did not look at Nakhtmin. Very deliberately, he swallowed.

"Nakhtmin," he said stiffly through gritted teeth, "your robe will be replaced. You will stop persecuting Semerkhet, and neither of you will be punished. Now get out of my sight."

For a moment the little General appeared to be considering a comeback, then thought better of it as he saw what a firm grip the King still had on his stick, as well as Horemheb's posture, tall, strong, and ready to break up a fistfight. Nakhtmin gave a snort like an angry cat, grumbled a wish for the Pharaoh's well-being, turned on his heel, and was gone.

Tut put his head down, supporting himself on his walking-stick and taking long, deep breaths as his heart stopped hammering and his head stopped pounding, his vision clearing as the rage passed. Now he was shivering, despite the warmth of the day, and his teeth were chattering. He could feel the cold sweat standing on his face, making his hand slide on his cane. And his knees felt strangely weak. Nothing ever made him that angry. And why had Nakhtmin's behavior caused him to lose control like that? He had witnessed the Vizier's son shouting at many servants over the years. And although it had always struck him as unreasonable, he had never lost his temper over it before.

Then he knew why. This hadn't been just any servant. This had been Semerkhet. Tut's friend. He could not bear the sight of Nakhtmin being such a bully to his friend.

"Are you all right, Great Morning Star?" came a gentle voice from beside him. Tut stood up straight to see Horemheb standing there, looking as calm as ever.

The Pharaoh took another deep breath. "I am now," he said with a little nod. "He just makes me so—"

"I know," Horemheb said softly. "That is the great challenge of the Pharaoh. Using righteous anger to create positive change, rather than declaring war. Not using one's authority to have little jackals like that executed." Bending toward the Pharaoh, he lowered his voice even more to a conspiratorial whisper. "You know, sometimes I want to kill him, too!"

Tut almost laughed. Little jackal? Kill him too? Horemheb must feel the same way about Nakhtmin as he did.

Then he sighed again. It was hard. And with all that screaming and carrying on and trying to hit Nakhtmin with his walking-stick like he'd hit Kahotep that horrible day when he was ten, he had failed. Failed to be a King of peace. "How do you do it?" he asked softly.

Horemheb smiled with the ghost of a chuckle. "Practice, My King." And with bow and a wish for life, prosperity, and health, he was gone.

Tut sighed again. And he looked over at Semerkhet, who was still standing there, looking less shaken than before, but still uncomfortable.

"I'm sorry," the Pharaoh whispered.

Sem looked up with a dismissive little smile, a little shake of his head. "It's all right, Morning Star. He didn't hurt me."

Tutankhamun nodded. "Well, he's lucky, then. Because if he *had* hurt you..." Tut's hand tightened on the handle of his walking-stick and he felt his teeth begin to clench as his heart began to beat faster again. With another sigh, he let go of the image. No one had been hurt. And no one would be hurt.

He tried to smile at his friend. "I am sorry, though. Sorry he shouted at you... and sorry I lost *my* temper."

Sem shook his head with an awkward little smile of his own. "I'm... I'm not. Well, I'm sorry the whole thing happened; I'm sorry I got mud on his robe in the first place. But I'm... I'm honored. Because... my friend would step in like that. Because my friend... doesn't want anyone to bully me." His eyes flickered toward the Pharaoh's face, not enough to make eye contact, but almost.

Tut gave a shaky little chuckle. "No," he said. "He doesn't. And he won't let anyone bully you ever again."

"I'm honored," Semerkhet almost whispered again, "to see how much you care."

The Pharaoh smiled, almost wanting to reach out and squeeze Semerkhet's hand. "Of course I care," he said softly. "You're my friend."

Suddenly Semerkhet seemed to remember who they were to one another and gave a deep bow.

"Thank you for protecting me, Your Majesty." And with a wish for life, prosperity, and health, he too was gone.

Tut watched his friend go. And he thought about how much he had learned in the past five minutes. About how to handle obnoxious people maturely, about himself, about Sem. About his friend. And about General Horemheb. He was... he was truly grateful that the General had stepped in when he had. And he looked forward to availing himself of Horemheb's wisdom and experience in the future.

188

He told his sister. About what a bad boy he had been. And how ashamed he was. But she... she wasn't ashamed of him. She said she was proud. Of how much he was learning. How much he was growing. And of the brave, wise young Pharaoh he was becoming.

But when would he be wise? At eighteen, the closest he could seem to get to real wisdom was the acknowledgment of how wise he was not. Not yet. Wisdom took awhile to develop. As the *Teaching of Ptahotep* reminded them, the young needed to go to the old for guidance, for no one could be born wise.

Tutankhamun sighed to himself. If no one could be born wise, what was he to do? Keep learning, that was what. And he would seek the guidance of those he knew to be wise already. He would keep studying with Ay, keep learning from his sister how to apply all those facts, ask the experienced old General for advice. And one day... one day, he would be wise. He had taken the first step today.

Finally Tut was well enough to go outside just because he wanted to. It was sprinkling with rain, but it was a relief to smell the fresh air, see the flowers, feel the largeness of the outdoors after so many days of walls and ceilings. The walls and ceilings offered comfort and protection, yes, but confinement as well. Walking outdoors, he could feel a few minutes of freedom.

These were the longest days of the year, here during Mesori. And some of the hottest. So it was a relief to feel this rain, this gift of cool respite in the middle of the hottest season of the year. The gentle rain whispered on the leaves of the willow and tamarisk trees, fell in glistening, quivering drops on the petals of the daisies and anemones, made ripples on the surfaces of the reflecting pools just like the ripples that moved in their own lives, dripped from the eaves of the palace. Sometimes a rainy day could be lovely. The rain fell on everyone, the King thought. And watered everyone's gardens, palace, rich, poor. And no one had to pay for it. The rain was generous. It saw everyone as alike.

The guards he had to take with him whenever he left the palace did not know why he had wanted to go walking in the rain, especially so soon after being sick, but he was the Pharaoh, and he got what he wanted. So they stood there, blinking away the raindrops as they waited for him to be ready to go back in.

Refreshed and ready for a rest, he turned to go back inside. Suddenly, an angry voice made him pause. Ay? Who could the Vizier be shouting at?

"Just look at all the mud in the front hall!" Ay was barking at a young man who stood silent and cowering before the wrath of the Vizier, hands folded, eyes on the ground. "It's an absolute disgrace. Get inside. That's ten lashes for being a lazy slob, and be grateful it's not more." Ay pushed the boy, who caught his balance with a little gasp, too afraid to speak a word. And he and Ay disappeared inside.

The King decided that rain or no rain, he needed to take another turn around the garden. Grasping his walking-stick, he kept walking, past date palms, fig trees and acacia trees, daisies, and grapevines, garden walls and graceful columns. They were all so beautifully maintained by the hardworking staff. The hardworking staff that, come to think of it, he sometimes heard the Vizier shouting at for failing to keep the plants properly pruned and shaped. He may have said it was all in the interest of maintaining the magnificence of the palace, but Tut had to admit that some-

190

times Ay… just wasn't very nice. And neither, he reminded himself, was Nakhtmin.

Shouting at servants for poor gardening… having them beaten on account of a muddy floor on a rainy day… The Pharaoh was going to have to make sure that Ay knew that now that Tutankhamun was Pharaoh, things were going to be different, and staff members were going to be treated as the humans they were. Nakhtmin already knew, but he, too, was not going to be allowed to forget.

Satisfied, Tut walked back toward the palace, followed by the grateful guards. He would just have to make sure his shoes were clean before he went inside. He didn't want to get anyone else in trouble.

Ankhesenamun walked down the hall to lunch one warm day, quite simply wondering what was for lunch. Suddenly, a voice stopped her.

"My Lady?"

Ankh paused to see the Vizier. Tall and thin, he must have been quite a specimen back when the pyramids were being built. Now creases lined his fine-featured face, and loose wrinkles wobbled at his throat as his gnarled old hand gripped his walking-stick.

"Yes, Vizier?" she asked politely.

"My Lady," he said softly, and the Queen suddenly felt the inside of her heart frowning. There was something in his tone that she did not like. "Recently the Pharaoh met with myself, Viziers Usermontu and Pentu, General Horemheb, and Treasurer Maya. And we discussed… the Pharaoh's generous new proposals."

Ankh smiled. That wasn't too bad of a beginning to the conversation, actually. "Yes," she said proudly. "I believe that the increased minimum wage, limitations on slavery, decreased taxes, additional hiring at the palace, and new schools will make a big difference."

The Vizier swallowed, Adam's apple jumping in his skinny old throat. "Indeed, My Lady." He paused. "My Lady… the Pharaoh told myself and the other members of our government that many of his proposals were, in fact, your ideas."

The Queen smiled again. Her sweet brother… telling them that she'd helped. "Yes, they were," she said.

Ay swallowed again. "I see," he said. Again he paused, shifting his weight from foot to foot as the heavy sleeves of his linen robe rippled like the wings of a vulture. "My Lady," he said, "I can see that you are having a large impact on our young Pharaoh. And I want to urge you, My Lady… to be Queen. Not King." He looked at her with just a hint of ice in his gaze.

Ankhesenamun returned his gaze with the flashing eyes of Isis. And she turned herself to stone. Only by remaining perfectly calm would she retain her credibility, only by being courageous and cunning, civil and sneaky, sweet and deadly could she show herself to be the mature politician who truly merited her place at her husband's side. And carefully, she crafted her response. "Thank you for your suggestion, Vizier," she said coldly. "But I can only imagine how disappointed my mother would be if I made no effort to follow in her footsteps. Good day." And she continued down the hall, long linen skirt rippling behind her.

She was twice as hungry as before.

"It's just not fair," she said that evening as Meresankh helped her take off her jewelry.

192

The handmaiden paused as she unclasped the Queen's heavy necklace.

"What's not fair, Your Majesty?" she asked, her concerned frown reflecting in the bronze mirror on the dressing-table.

"The Vizier, and his ideas about what a Queen should be," she said with an angry sigh. Meresankh set the necklace aside and stepped around to face her Mistress.

"What did he say?"

Ankh shook her head. "That my ideas were having a big impact on what my brother does, and that I should be Queen... not King." She thought back to how her stomach had plummeted at those words. "And I said that my mother would be very disappointed if I didn't follow in her footsteps, and kept walking."

Meresankh smiled. "Sounds like you handled it very well. Some people... some people don't fail to understand because it's hard for them. They choose not to understand. And that... that's never your fault." In the mirror, Ankh saw her handmaiden's hand hovering an inch above her shoulder, as if Meresankh were about to gently touch it... like a friend would. But an instant later, it was withdrawn. Ankh did not turn her head, gave no sign that she had noticed.

But she was glad. Glad that Meresankh wanted to reach out to her. As a friend.

"Thank you, Meresankh," she said. "You're right. And maybe he will understand... when he sees everything that my little brother accomplishes because of me." In the mirror, she smiled at her friend.

Meresankh smiled back.

The longest day of the year arrived, the solstice. And out in Thebes, the people celebrated the Wadjet Ceremony. Carried in a palanquin, the Pharaoh and the Queen attended just long enough, helping officiate the yearly ceremony, get the festival started. They even spent a little time in town, admiring the market, which was quite similar to the one they'd visited in Memphis. Men and women of all social classes haggled at stalls for fruit, vegetables, fish from the Nile, imported spices, fresh bread and roasted meats, and handicrafts like baskets, pottery, and woven fabric in bright colors and patterns. Plum season was just beginning, and they noticed a few grapes, stacked like purple jewels among large, round watermelons, figs of different varieties, the last apricots of the season, and cucumbers.

Ankh chuckled as she saw the watermelons.

"We've got plenty of watermelons at home," Tut said teasingly before she could suggest buying one.

"Don't know if the guards would appreciate having to carry it home!" she said with a laugh. And they passed the watermelons by.

They did not visit the outskirts of Thebes, where they knew that stray cats and hungry orphans roamed. But they knew they were there. And they hoped that their new policies would help them.

And worn out with even a short outing, Tut needed to go home.

Again they found Meresankh and her Granny, working quietly together in the palace, away from the festivities. And again they wondered why.

194

17 A Royal Tour

"**A**re you ready, Master?" Semerkhet asked as he adjusted the Pharaoh's wig and circlet. Ptahmose, the new secondary valet, stood silently handing each item to Semerkhet. "Ready to see the palace?"

Tut smiled, slowly standing and making sure that his white kilt was properly arranged. Another blazingly hot day. Mesori was usually the most miserably hot month of the whole year, and it wasn't over yet. "Lead on."

They set off— rather slowly— down the familiar hallway that led past Ankh's room, past the grand painting of Thutmose the First, who looked rather disappointed as Tut passed beneath his gaze, past the study and its scrolls of papyrus, down to the royal feasting hall.

"Each section of the palace is run by its own overseer, in addition to each department having a leader," Semerkhet explained as they went. "It's like a city that has a mayor, a treasurer, and overseers."

Tut just nodded and smiled, focusing on keeping up, his stick tapping on the polished floor. Semerkhet wasn't going too fast, but still, the King was about to get some very good exercise.

"Want to see the kitchen?" Semerkhet asked almost mischievously. Tut grinned, choosing not to hide his teeth.

"Of course."

Sem led on, across to the far end of the royal feasting hall, past the elegant tables, standing quietly ready for the next meal. They came to a small, unassuming door near the corner of the room, one the King had never noticed before. Semerkhet opened it for the King. "Welcome," he said, sweeping his arm out grandly.

Tutankhamun's stomach began to rumble as a thousand delicious smells hit his nose, the mutton they were going to have for lunch, seasoned with garlic, onion, and thyme, the honey and dates that were going to go into the cake for dessert. Half-plucked ducks, well-fattened by force-feeding, hung on hooks, ready for the next round of roasting, huge jars of olive oil and linen sacks of emmer-wheat flour sat on shelves, along with baskets of eggs and rounds of cheese wrapped in linen. The fragrant smoke from the roasting mutton rose up a chimney, but still, with all this cooking and all these cooks, it was hot.

In the far end of the kitchen, large amounts of bread dough were being shaped into loaves, and massive quantities of lentils, beans, and chickpeas were being cooked in large metal pots over a fire, probably for the servants themselves.

He... remembered the kitchen, he thought. From one bored, curious afternoon as a seven-year-old. How strange, now, to think that it had taken him nearly twelve years to come back to it.

All around them servants in simple, white-and-blue uniforms and aprons buzzed, chopping vegetables, piling slices of plums and cubes of watermelon into bowls, stirring pots over cooking fires, tasting, pouring, directing one another and receiving directions. No one seemed to know that he and Semerkhet were there.

The King chuckled. A little too loudly. The man who was bent over the fireplace, turning the spit on which the mutton was roasting, looked up. Saw who was chuckling at him. Blanched. And fell to his face on the floor. "Hail to thee, Lord of All, O Great Morning Star! All life, prosperity, and health!" With horrified gasps and looks of terror, all the cooks dropped what they were doing and flung themselves to their knees, prostrating themselves before Pharaoh, shaking with fear.

"Rise," he said grandly, beckoning. Slowly they got to their feet, carefully avoiding his eye. Now they stood in neat ranks, stiffly at attention, sure that some horrible mistake they had made was about to be revealed and get them all executed. But he just smiled down at them benevolently, trying to keep his hungry stomach from growling too loudly. And hoping that through interrupting them, he wouldn't cause something to burn.

"I just wanted to see what was for lunch," he said awkwardly. No one laughed. Slowly he turned back toward the door, not wanting to disturb them further. "It looks delicious. Carry on." And he and Semerkhet left the kitchen behind, leaving terror and confusion in their wake. With all that, lunch might be served late today.

"So that's the kitchen," Tut said reflectively as they walked back through the grand dining room, ready to attack the next corridor. He was starting to get tired. "Maybe… maybe we can find a room where no one's actually working. That way we won't scare anyone."

Semerkhet chuckled. "Good idea."

Tut felt himself slowing down as he leaned more heavily on his cane, each step more difficult than the last. "Thanks for showing me," he said, a hint out of breath. "Maybe we can see the next bit after lunch."

"As you wish, Master," Semerkhet said, slowing his own steps to match the Pharaoh's pace. "Maybe the jewelry department. Or even my room, if you wanted to see it."

The King smiled. "Sounds good."

They sat down for awhile, then Tut made his slow way to the Temple of Amun-Ra. After prayers and sacrifices were complete, it was finally time for lunch (the roast mutton with garlic and thyme and the honey-date cake really were very good, and the meal was served right on time, with the usual accompaniment of flute music). As expected, Semerkhet's faithful food-testing indicated that no one had tried to murder the Pharaoh today. Tut's legs got a bit of a rest while he ate, and an hour later, he felt ready to attack the next part of the palace. Maybe he would never lead troops on missions of conquest, but this was an expedition, an exploration of the world in which he lived.

"Where is your room?" he asked Semerkhet as his valet led him down an unfamiliar hall in the western region of the palace where a series of doors seemed to lead to living quarters. Even here servants were working, dusting furniture, cleaning floors. Back in the areas of the palace more familiar to the Pharaoh, someone had even been touching up one of the glorious paintings that gleamed on every wall. As they walked, it suddenly occurred to the King how useful a map of the palace would be. Everyone who saw them stopped what they were doing and bowed.

As they entered the staff quarters, Tut saw a change. Everything was still perfectly neat, but the hallways they were walking down seemed to have grown narrower. They were also undecorated, not graced by images of gods and kings like those in the Pharaoh's sphere. And the windows in this part of the palace seemed to be fewer, smaller, and further apart. Everything was very serviceable, but it seemed... very plain down here.

Semerkhet was counting doors, looking for his own. On the floor in front of one door, Tut noticed a plum pit, just lying there.

They stopped at the next one. "Right here," Semerkhet said. They paused in front of it, and Semerkhet looked down with a little chuckle, poking the toe of his sandal against the carefully polished floor. "Your Majesty, my humble abode." Slowly he opened the door, letting the King into his suite.

Tutankhamun looked around with a smile. How cozy. Here was a suite of rooms much like his own, with a comfortable metal bed with a wool-filled mattress, crisp white linen sheets, and a soft pillow, a wooden chair and desk, a little dining area with a tiny table and a wooden stool, a corner for dressing, and a series of storage chests painted with patterns of brown birds and blue and red flowers. In one corner of the room, the Pharaoh saw Semerkhet's sports uniform, carefully folded, and his hockey stick. Fine white linen curtains rippled in the breeze at either side of a large window looking out onto the gardens, where the birds were twittering among the rosebushes.

There didn't appear to be a private shower room, but Tut supposed that when you weren't the Pharaoh, you had to take your turn in a communal one. Or just avail yourself of the swimming opportunities in the Nile, an opportunity he would personally never have.

At the edge of the desk was a small rack of reed pens, a container of ink, and a stack of fresh papyrus sheets. Tut also noticed a piece of papyrus Semerkhet had been writing on, which didn't really look like a letter, since the phrases on it were formed into short lines, almost like a poem. At the top, he caught the words "To my Sweet Meresankh," and quickly looked away, hoping Sem wouldn't notice his blush. Some things were better not looked at.

"It's nice," Tut said with an appreciative nod, turning his gaze to the other side of the room. "Looks very comfortable." Semerkhet kept looking down, looking embarrassed that the Pharaoh was actually in his room, looking at his things, walking on his floor.

"It works for me," his valet said. "I do like it. Uhh… grapes?" He gestured toward a chair and picked up a terracotta bowl of purple grapes from the table.

Tut sat down gratefully, resting his foot. "Thank you." He popped a grape into his mouth, feeling the cool sweetness filling his mouth as he bit into it. He looked around with another smile. "What a lovely room." Then he looked at Semerkhet, trying to make eye contact. He did for half an instant, now looking embarrassed that the Pharaoh was sitting in his chair. "Thank you for showing me." Tutankhamun sighed. "Thank you for showing me everything. Thank you for showing me the world, opening my eyes."

Semerkhet just smiled. "Your wish is my command."

Over the next week, they toured the rest of the palace, a section or two each day. Whenever they popped into a new department, the servants panicked, half of them lowering their heads and working twice as fast, the rest running around in a dither, all but shoving him into a chair, pressing a glass of wine or *mai-sus* into his hand, falling on their faces before him as they apologized for not being perfect.

Even the servants they passed in the hallways, walking to or from a task, carrying stacks of papyrus documents, royal wigs, or laundry baskets, which, like other baskets, were often carried on the head, stopped and bowed when they saw the Pharaoh coming

200

(or, quite possibly, heard his stick tapping), looking mortified to have been found idle. Occasionally bowing with a basket balanced on one's head resulted in the basket falling to the floor and the contents spilling everywhere. He wished they wouldn't act like that, really, but it couldn't be helped. Besides which, none of them were idle.

He smiled as they finally finished the tour with a visit to the stable, a happy reunion with the horses he had not seen since his hunting trip with Semerkhet, Stormy and Flash. He had seen almost every room of his grandfather's colossal palace, from the wig-making department to the workshop supervised by the Overseer of the Sandal-makers to the Royal Library, packed floor to ceiling with papyrus scrolls. The Pharaoh had even discovered the secret courtyard where laundry was hung up to dry, and blushed to see his own loincloths, freshly bleached, flapping in the breeze as they dried.

He'd walked through five perfectly nice meeting rooms the size of the throne room that he hadn't even heard of, and from the physicians' quarters to the sheds of the gardeners and the Beekeepers of Pharaoh who produced the honey that went into their cake. He had learned dozens of job titles, and thought with a chuckle that there were so many comically specific job descriptions that somewhere in this elaborate structure there was probably a Senior Undersecretary to the Vice-Treasurer. And his memory had been jogged, here and there, by places he had visited before, back when he was little. It was all run so efficiently, almost like a small city of its own.

And somehow, in some strange way, he owned all of it.

"Sem took me on a tour of the palace this week," Tut told his sister as they sat quietly in his private sitting room. The weather was changing, a rainy day coming, and he had another headache. So his sister was sitting on one of the couches, and he was lying nestled with his head in her lap, the cat curled up by his feet.

She chuckled. "Sem?"

"Nickname," Tut replied. "Since we're... we're friends now, it kind of just slipped out one day, and it stuck. Think he likes it."

Ankh nodded, red-beaded braids swaying. "Sem," she said again, tasting the single syllable. Then she looked down at her brother again.

"So how was the tour?" she asked.

"Long," he said dramatically. "I never would have imagined our home was that big. So many hallways, so many workshops, so many *people*... I had an idea of how many people it took to take care of us, from that list Sem made, but to actually see it..." He chuckled, shaking his head against his sister's knee. "It's beautiful," he said. "And it's all run so well. I just wish..." Tut sighed. "Wish people didn't always get scared when they saw me. The minute they saw me, everyone always acted like they thought they were doing something wrong, even if they were perfect. I wish I could... show them that we're all people."

Ankhesenamun chuckled. "Someday they'll see. And someday... you'll be a greater Pharaoh than Thutmose the First."

The year was ending. First there was a feast to celebrate New Year's Eve. Then they observed the Five Days Upon the Year, the five days that belonged to no month, but were dedicated to celebrating the birthdays of Osiris, Horus, Seth, Isis, and Nephthys. The Pharaoh had to go to the temple, protecting all of Egypt from

202

the wrath of the goddess Sekhmet with special prayers and ceremonies. But even as he left the silence of the temple without any fear of the goddess' wrath, he also left it without a sense of having been heard. Just like always.

But when the month of Thoth began, and the Season of Inundation with it, they celebrated the beginning of the new year with the Opening of the Year Festival, remembering the death of Osiris with ritual mourning and his rebirth with singing and dancing. As the flooding of the Nile began, the earth, too, would be reborn.

18   The Mighty Hunter

The Pharaoh still had his history lessons with Ay a few times a week, even as the study became more and more unbearably hot with every lecture. But it seemed that the lessons were getting shorter, each covering less material than the last. They were in the Eleventh Dynasty now, a key turning-point when Mentuhotep the Second had reunited all of Egypt after over a hundred years of civil war between two competing courts, one in Henen-Nisut and the other in Thebes, each with their own Pharaohs. But somehow, as the hot weather stretched out endlessly before them and Tut began to think about his upcoming birthday, they were slowing down, slogging through the events of their past as if they would never catch up with the present.

And as he tried not to yawn with the heat and the monotony of the Vizier's voice, Tut wondered why.

Tut sighed in annoyance one hot afternoon as Ankh won the third game of *seega* in a row.

"What am I doing wrong?" he asked, looking down at the pieces, still in position after her win. Three of his pieces had never had the opportunity to move out of their starting positions, remaining trapped by his sister's expert tactics.

"Hmm." She looked at them too, examining their arrangement. "I was thinking about your strategy," she said, "and I think part of it… is that you expect to lose."

He raised an eyebrow. "Expect to lose?"

She pointed at a few key pieces. "See, right here, you could have captured these pieces and stopped me, but you didn't. You're

204

not thinking about stopping me, and playing offense at the same time." Then she sighed. "And it's more than just in the game."

Tut looked up at her. "What?"

"You need to up your game," she said. "Not just here," she said, nodding at the gameboard, "but out there, with the rest of the politicians. Don't just slouch in the background, expecting to lose."

"I don't slouch," he said. His sister raised an eyebrow. And he sat up straighter.

She clenched her fist, raising it inspirationally. "Be active, take charge. Don't just let life happen around you. You're eighteen, and it's time to take your power."

He smiled. "Let's play again. And this time you tell me what to do. I need to learn to win!"

Ankhesenamun chuckled. "Yes, you do. And you will. You see," she said, "what you're doing is just reacting to my moves, and treating the moves as very disconnected from one another. It's very reactionary. The key is learning to think ahead several moves; hypothetical thinking, not just reactionary. Same thing in life. Staying a step ahead of everyone else, basing what you do on what you suspect they'll do next, not only on what they just did. That's why they call politics a game."

Tut nodded. That was an excellent point. Then he chuckled. Ever since they had been little, Ankh had played *seega* mercilessly, never just giving him a game.

He smiled. "That's what makes you different from everyone around us, different from the servants, different from how Ay always used to be. You challenge me, don't just let me win because I'm Pharaoh, or because you're sorry for me." He chuckled. "You must think I'm up to the challenge."

She squeezed his hand. "I know you are."

He tapped his chin as the Queen began putting her pieces into place for a new game. "I wonder… if you played against Ay, who would win?"

Ankhesenamun shook her head. "I don't know. Hmm. Now I wonder, too."

"You'll have to play sometime and see."

"Only after I make you a winner," she said. "Let's play."

The days were sunny and long, so as much as Tut enjoyed history, it felt like even more of a waste than ever to sit inside studying. At least there was a cross-breeze in the room. Otherwise, with the way temperatures were rising, he and his teacher would be stewing like poached ducks. Even so, Tut felt a drop of sweat slowly sliding down the back of his neck as he sat there in a sweltering haze in nothing but his kilt, struggling to listen to today's lesson.

"And Senusret the Third built the Great Canal, which brought great prosperity to the region of Fayum, just southwest of the Nile Delta, by allowing the region to fulfill its potential as farmland," the Vizier droned. "For seven years, the land yielded more plentiful crops than had ever been gathered in the same period of time."

Tut blinked. Seven years of plentiful harvests… Where had he heard that before?

"…under the direction of a Vizier who had risen from a position of slavery, Egypt stored its excess crops in silos for a period of famine that the gods had warned the Pharaoh of in a series of dreams. The seven years of plenty were followed by seven years of famine, but because of the quantity of grain they had stored, Egypt

206

was able to feed the known world during the famine. Also during this period of famine, an influx of Canaanite immigrants settled in Goshen, in the eastern Nile Delta, only to be eliminated by Ahmose the First when their numbers became too great…"

And there was that Canaanite Vizier again. And the foreigners who had taken over Goshen, only to be brought down… and then what? Cast out? Or enslaved?

The Pharaoh did not interrupt the Vizier with his questions. He kept them to himself.

Later that afternoon, after the day's lessons were finally over, Tut lay on his bed looking up at the ostrich-feather fan and bow and arrow that hung on the wall.

"Ankh," he said, sitting up. She looked up from throwing pistachio shells for Bastet to chase.

"Hmm?"

He looked at her with a smile, a toothy grin that made her chuckle.

"Let's go duck hunting."

She laughed. "Both of us?"

Playfully he reached out and shook her shoulder— not nearly as hard as he would Semerkhet, if they were ever friends like that, but just enough to make her laugh again. "Come on," he said in a teasing moan. "It'll be fun!"

The Queen got up, brushing pistachio shells out of her lap and onto the floor. And she kissed his forehead.

"I think it will be."

Half an hour later, they were squeezed into a tiny boat made of bundled papyrus reeds waterproofed with pitch, like the basket the Hebrew Prince had been found in, if that story was even true. A servant stood at the bow to navigate, Tut was settled on a comfortable stool, and Ankh sat merrily on the floor on a little cushion, her lap full of arrows. Tut held his bow in his own lap, his throwing-stick within easy reach. And off they sailed toward the marshes.

They sped along the Nile in the tiny boat, moving too quickly for the mosquitoes to settle. The day was hot, but the cool breeze off the water ruffled their wigs and made them laugh. As fast as they were going, Ankh managed to reach out and pick a few of the lotuses they were passing, breathing in their intoxicating sweetness.

The water here was swift but calm, not the wild, dangerous rapids full of man-eating beasts that made washing laundry in the great river a life-threatening endeavor. Fish darted through the sparkling water; along other parts of the Nile, the King and Queen knew that hippopotamuses were hiding among the bulrushes and crocodiles were sunning themselves on the banks. But they weren't hunting crocodiles today. Or hippos. They were hunting ducks.

And up ahead, there were ducks in abundance. Tut raised his hand to a prompt "Yes, My Lord," and the boat came to a halt, lying just far enough from the ducks that they noticed nothing, just went on muttering to one another and doing their own hunting for insects.

Ten seconds later, there was no peace. Tut laid hold of his bow, and began firing arrows in quick succession from where he sat on his stool. One after another, the birds fell, the rest taking flight in a startled flutter of wings. Ankh handed her brother arrow after

208

arrow, laughing along with him as the mighty hunter felled his prey.

"Throwing stick!" he said a moment later, and she put it in his hand. Tut sent it spinning through the air, striking two ducks on the wing and stunning them. Conveniently, they landed right at the Queen's feet.

Grabbing his walking-stick, Tut got to his feet, then bent to pick up his quarry with his free hand. Meanwhile, the servant was using the barge-pole to gather up the rest of the felled birds.

Laughing with pride, the Pharaoh held out the biggest duck for his wife to see. Raising her hands in mock surprise, she joined in his laughter.

"All hail the mighty hunter!" she sighed adoringly from where she sat at his knee. Tut just laughed even harder. He knew she was being sarcastic… but, at the same time, that she had real appreciation for his success. Then Ankh's nose wrinkled, her grimace just as playful as her smile. "But you are not bringing those dead birds in the palace!"

"Yes, dear," he chuckled, sinking back onto his stool. Carefully standing as the boat rocked, she stepped toward him, and he put his free arm around her— as soon as he'd dropped the dead duck in the pile of eight or ten. And as the sun began to set and turn the Nile into a river of topaz and carnelian, their lips met in a kiss.

He'd done well. So well. He was her hunter, her warrior, bringing home his quarry. He had worked hard, and he had been victorious.

But Ankh could see... how tired he was. How much it had taken out of him. How even since he had regained his strength after his bout with the ague, he was still not quite the same.

As they floated home in the deepening twilight, the Queen sat and thought. About the distant future, and the milestones that lay there. Because when a Pharaoh reached thirty years in power, it was time for them to renew their strength in the Sed Festival, the festival that proved the Pharaoh's continued capacity to rule with a ritual run. Ankh winced as she thought of it. Because she could picture it, her baby brother in all his finery, standing before all the assembled dignitaries, bravely setting off at the modest trot that was all he could manage, tapping along the track of packed earth with the help of his cane. The race would be an embarrassment— it would take him all day to limp around the track, and everyone gathered would feel awful sitting and watching him.

The Queen shook her head. And horribly enough, the struggle he would face in running the race on foot would have made the opposite point than the Sed Festival was intended to make. Watching him limp bravely around that track would, if anything, give Ay and the others reason to depose him as a pathetic weakling.

He was so strong. But not like that. So when he reached his thirtieth year on the throne, maybe he would find a different way of showing the people of Egypt that he still had it.

Then she had it. His chariot. She smiled, her heart warming. Of course. Her charioteer would run his Sed Festival race in his chariot. And his people would see how strong he was.

"I got something for Meresankh," Semerkhet said out of nowhere as he paused between chores that afternoon. Tut looked up from petting Bastet and smiled.

"What did you get her?" he asked.

"A necklace," the servant said, blushing. "With a picture of Isis. Because she's just as pretty as the Queen of all the goddesses." He paused. "C... cost me a week's wages. Hope she likes it."

The King just smiled. And Semerkhet hurried off to sort something.

It made the Pharaoh smile to think of his valet and the Queen's handmaiden sending one another gifts, shy little tokens of growing affection. But even as he smiled, a solemn festival was ready to be observed. In the middle of the month of Thoth, they commemorated the death of Osiris again, and the deaths of all those they wanted to remember.

That was how Tutankhamun found himself standing on the east bank of the Nile, arm-in-arm with the Queen, each of them holding a little paper boat as they fought back tears. One little paper boat for each of them, the tiny precious ones who had been gone for so long. And seven more already floating down the river, for their parents, their sisters.

He handed her the little boat he held, and they looked silently at one another, seeing the tears shining in one another's eyes. Then his wife carefully set the little boats afloat in the Nile where they joined hundreds of others, sailing toward the West bank and the setting sun, where they hoped their loved ones had found peace.

She stepped back up onto the shore and put her arm around him. And together they watched the boats float away, until they were lost in the distance and the tears that blurred their vision.

19   Competition

The Pharaoh couldn't help it. In the middle of a history lesson on a stiflingly hot day, he gave an open-mouthed yawn just as the Vizier was glancing up.

"Am I boring you, My Lord?" Ay asked, delicately setting the papyrus aside. He had been reading about the birth of the Middle Kingdom, the reunification of Egypt after over a hundred years of division and violence.

Tut shook his head enthusiastically, feeling the tiny braids of his black wig swinging across his face.

"No, no," he said, stretching as he spoke. "Very interesting. Very important. Just… it's getting so hot these past couple of weeks. And…" He chuckled, wondering what Ay would say to his suggestion. "I was wondering, why haven't I learned about Djoser's mother Nimaathap, and Khentkaus the First who might even have been Pharaoh, and Iput and Ankhesenpepi the Second, the regents? And of course, the legendary Nitocris? We were just studying the Sixth Dynasty not too long ago, and you seem to have missed them."

The Grand Vizier was starting to look very uncomfortable. He rolled up the papyrus scrolls from which he had been reading, carefully lining them up on his desk as if he was going to be judged for his neatness. "The education of a King should focus on… Kings, My Lord, not their… mothers."

"Even when their mothers are Pharaohs in their own right, or hold the country together with as much skill as anyone who ever held the crook and flail?" Tut asked, raising one eyebrow. "Like my mother?"

Ay swallowed, avoiding eye contact. He continued his careful adjustment of the scrolls, then finally looked up, appearing to have decided what to say.

"If the Pharaoh wishes, future lessons shall include regencies as well as the reigns of crowned Pharaohs," he said a bit stiffly.

"We're in the Twelfth Dynasty now, so Pharaoh Sobekneferu will be coming up," Tut replied with a smile.

The Vizier gave a little nod, nostrils flaring. "Indeed."

And the day's lesson was over.

"Well, I got Sobekneferu coming up," Tut said to his sister as they shared an afternoon snack of sliced plums, safe from the heat of the day and the clouds of mosquitoes in the cool of her private sitting room.

Ankh bit into a piece of fruit, giggling as the sweet juice ran down her chin. She wiped it away with a bit of linen and nodded.

"Good. You told him you wanted to hear a more balanced history?"

"I told him that those mothers were just like our mother. And that got him." Tut smiled and took a slice of plum for himself. "You got me excited about the Seventeenth Dynasty. I can't wait to learn about Ahhotep."

"She's fascinating," Ankh said, reaching out to pat his hand. "You'll love her. Even though she wasn't Pharaoh... she got a lot more done than most of them, while her husband was away fighting the Hyksos. A Queen doesn't have to become a King in order to lead her country... but if she does, she becomes part of one of the most elite legacies the world has ever known."

Tutankhamun chuckled, looking at his brave, wise big sister. "I can't wait to see what you'll do, following in their footsteps."

214

Ankhesenamun shrugged, giving her brother a smile. "I don't know. Only history will tell. But I do know that I'll always be here for you. And together... we'll do something history will never forget."

"Big day?" Sem asked that evening as he helped Tut remove his jewelry, slip out of his short-sleeved tunic for a quick wash, and put on his nightclothes.

The Pharaoh nodded with a smile. And with a little nod, the valet went to get the little pot of natron paste so Tut could clean his teeth. The snippet of conversation was over, fading back into the comfortable silence that often settled between them.

But it was enough. And somehow... Tut thought with a smile, it had felt like talking with a brother.

Tut sat in the stands of the arena, squinting out at the racecourse in the blinding sun. Beside him stood Raherka, who was steadily wafting the hot air with a fan of fresh ostrich feathers. Semerkhet was not at his side, attending him. Sem was out on the racecourse down below.

Again the Pharaoh squinted, leaning forward and shading his eyes as he tried to make out his friend among the ten charioteers in the distance. The metal accents of Semerkhet's fine chariot shone in the sun; the red and blue blankets on the horses' chestnut backs made them stand out. Stormy and Flash were the same team that had taken them on their ostrich-hunting trip.

An announcer was shouting out the names of the racers as they brought their chariots into position. And they were off.

Even in his seat, Tut could feel the rumbling of the chariot wheels, the pounding of the horses' hooves against the packed earth. The charioteers urged their horses on, two of them beating their steeds with whips that might have been more appropriate for cattle. Sem did not carry a whip. But he bent low over his horses' backs, maneuvering them skillfully between the chariots of two other racers whose animals were already flagging.

Around the bend they tore, Semerkhet's chariot tipping onto one wheel as he kept his eyes focused on what was ahead, kept the reins taut and his feet steady. Tut's heart jumped into his throat as his hand tightened around the handle of his walking-stick. Seconds later the chariot had settled onto two wheels again with an audible thump, and the Pharaoh couldn't help but let out a whoop of triumph. Two other racers were not so lucky; the crowd gave an audible groan as one charioteer flew out of his chariot, tumbling to the ground, and another found his horses running into one another, stumbling to a halt in a confused tangle of reins. Only eight racers were left.

The finish line was ahead, and Tut could see the concentration on his friend's face. Stormy and Flash were growing tired, but it was as if they, too, could sense victory ahead. With one more burst of speed they launched forward, straining at their harnesses as they fought past one, two, three of their competitors, leaving them choking in a cloud of dust.

Only two chariots stood between Semerkhet and the finish line. The other racers knew what they were doing; one kept zigzagging between the center of the track and the right edge, the other kept swerving from the left side to the middle, never giving Semerkhet a moment to burst through. Tut held his breath as he watched his friend take in the scene; the angles, the obstacles in his path. He

216

steered his horses to the right side of the track. And as he let out a "Yaah!" and slapped the reins against his steeds' backs, the horses knew what to do. With matching neighs of victory, Stormy and Flash took a sharp left, diving between the two chariots ahead of them not an instant too late.

The crowd went wild as Semerkhet's chariot thundered over the finish line. Tut grabbed his walking-stick and hauled himself to his feet, waving his free hand as he cheered for his friend. Semerkhet's face was glowing with sweat and pride as he beamed up at the crowd, accepting the winner's collar-necklace of blue beads as the second- and third-place racers received necklaces of red and white. The crowd continued to cheer appreciatively, honoring the valiant efforts of the losers even as they exalted the winner.

The celebrations seemed to last half the day. Finally the Pharaoh was able to get up, tottering down to the field with the help of Raherka. Those he passed fell silent, the crowd parting with deep bows and murmurs of "All life, prosperity, and health!"

There were no words. He just smiled at Semerkhet, who was drowning in fans. He reached out and grabbed his friend's hand, sweaty and dirty as it was, then clapped him on the shoulder. And as the raucous shouting of the spectators went on and on, his heart was full of his friend's victory.

A few yards away, Tut thought he saw a small, curvy woman with a silver necklace. And laughing, he stepped back so Meresankh could congratulate the man she loved.

The victory echoed through the next days, shining in Semerkhet's face as he smiled, coloring his conversations as he praised Stormy and Flash for winning the race. All he had done was guide them, he said.

But it wasn't long before the Pharaoh got the chance to see his friend's other pastime of hockey. And again, Tut sat in the stands, peering down at the arena below. No horses trotted onto the packed earth this time, rather, men with sticks stood in two lines of ten. Semerkhet's team were resplendent in blue tunics, faced off against a team from the town of Nekhen in red uniforms. At each end of the pitch there was a large net; each time one team got the ball into the other team's net earned them a point. The referee brought out the ball; a half-circle made of dyed leather stuffed with papyrus. The players watched him silently, waiting, choking up on their hockey sticks.

But before the game could begin, an announcer strode onto the pitch.

"Thank you all for joining us on this beautiful day for this competition between the Hawks of Nekhen—" Half the stands erupted in cheers— "and the Royal Stallions!" The other half roared their approval. Tut tried to whistle like the spectator behind him, but only managed an odd sort of sputter. So he hollered instead. "We want to thank our glorious Pharaoh for providing the uniforms and equipment that have made this game possible. All hail Pharaoh Tutankhamun! All life, prosperity, and health!"

And every voice in the crowd echoed the wish for Tut's well-being. He tried to smile graciously.

The cheering died down, and silence descended. Finally, the game was about to begin.

The referee pumped his fist into the air. "Play!" he bellowed.

And they were off. The red team took possession of the ball within seconds, and Tut deduced Semerkhet's role— goalie.

218

Rather than dashing out among the other players, fighting for control of the ball, he crouched before the net on the blue team's end, waiting.

With a clatter of sticks, Semerkhet's team took the ball, beginning to scoop and toss it toward the red team's goal. The crowd gasped as the ball soared through the air toward the net, but the red goalie dived, smacking it out of its trajectory and back out into the field.

The red team had the ball again. Slowly but surely they fought their way past Semerkhet's teammates, toward the goal where Tut's friend stood, bouncing on the balls of his feet, face calm, eyes focused.

A tall, broad man on the red team, a bulky brute who looked like he could take Horemheb in a fistfight, hooked his stick into the ball. And with a powerful swing, he sent it flying into the air, so high that it seemed it must overshoot the net and disappear into the stands.

Semerkhet's eyes were tracking the ball, his grip on his stick was tightening, his knees were bending, ready to spring. And as a gust of wind changed the trajectory of the falling ball, aiming it straight for the back of the net, he leapt, blocking the ball with his stick, crashing into it, and sending it flying almost all the way to the red team's goal.

The crowd leapt to its feet, screaming its enthusiasm. Tut waved his free hand as he cheered, heart soaring.

But that was only a moment. Seconds later, Semerkhet was back in position, eyes following the ball's every move as it passed from player to player, making its rounds around the entire field as players in red and blue darted and swooped in endless moves and countermoves. Back and forth it went, the supporters of the blue team cheering again as one of Sem's teammates smashed the ball into the red team's goal.

They won by two goals. And the Pharaoh cheered with the rest of the fans as his friend and his team high-fived one another, pumped their fists, and shouted themselves hoarse. They shook hands with the red team, and the crowd continued to applaud for them, honoring their valiant effort. Glowing with pride and dripping with sweat, Semerkhet's team went home with blue collars that matched their uniforms.

Over the weeks, Tut went to as many of his friend's horse races and hockey games as he could. It felt good to support him, and it was fun to see a side of him he had never known existed. And now they had another thing to talk about: how badly Semerkhet's team was going to beat their opponents in the next game.

That week brought a hard anniversary. Together, Ankhesenamun and Tutankhamun remembered the day that Senebhenas had come into the world, four weeks early. They remembered the strange wound on her back, the tiny feet that could not kick. And they remembered the five days and nights that they had had with her. Five days and nights into which they had poured all the love that filled their hearts, five days and nights that ached with every memory they lovingly examined. And they remembered the silence that had fallen, silence broken only by the tears they had shed together. Silence that remained unbroken by the merry commotion of the two-year-old who should be running around the palace after her sister. Silence that would remain until the day all of them were reunited.

220

There was still the silence. And silently, Ankhesenamun sat in her room, holding the cat in her arms, feeling her warmth, her soft fur, her purring. She held Bastet close. And she remembered.

It wasn't much longer before Mereneferet's fourth birthday, the day within the window of time when they had expected to welcome her into the world that they had selected to call hers. Lovingly, Ankhesenamun and Tutankhamun got down the basket of things they had collected for her; the soft swaddling, the rattle, the beads that would have adorned their daughter's first tunic. And her parents held one another's hands and smiled through their tears as they remembered the long years that may have separated them in time and space, but could not sunder them from the daughter they held in their hearts.

20 Practice

"Hey, Sem," Tut said as they sat in his study, swapping riddles over two cups of *mai-sus*. Scrolls and scrolls of papyrus outlining trade agreements, treaties, tax data, and history sat filed on shelves around them, but they weren't paying any attention to them right now.

"Yes, Master?" Semerkhet looked up. Tut was delighted to see him boldly but respectfully making eye contact in a way that looked almost comfortable. And he seemed pleased to hear the King use his nickname. Although he looked very hot. It was another blazing day toward the end of the month of Thoth, but although the Pharaoh could sit here wearing nothing but a simple linen kilt and a few pieces of jewelry, as a member of the palace staff, Sem had to sweat in his linen tunic that identified him as the royal valet.

"Funny question," Tut said. "Sort of an experiment, actually."

Semerkhet raised his eyebrows. "What is it?"

"I was talking to Ankh about, you know, me becoming a politician for real… and she said that shouting wasn't a good strategy," he said. Semerkhet silently nodded, ceding the Queen's point. "So I was wondering what would work better. And I thought of whispering. So I was thinking, you can pretend to be Ay, or some other politician who's not listening to me, and I can try it two ways, one kind of big and one real soft. Now, I'm not mad at you for anything, so please don't take it personally. Just tell me which one's scarier."

Semerkhet chuckled nervously, biting his lip. "All right." Both stood up, facing one another across the study. Tut winced as he put

222

weight on his weak foot, then found a good stance, resting enough of his weight on his cane to at least minimize the discomfort.

Tutankhamun made his face serious, getting into character. "All right," he said. "Be Ay. Say something I don't want to hear. Like, um, something I was telling you about from the conference."

Semerkhet paused. "Ah… we cannot lower taxes this year, O Great Morning Star; your generous building projects are threatening the military budget." The valet's impression of the Vizier was so accurate that Tut had to fight not to laugh. He stayed in character.

"Is that a problem?" he thundered, going full-on with the eyebrows of doom. "I am the Morning and the Evening Star, running my country as I see fit. You are the Vizier, carrying out my plans. Not the other way around. Now find a way to move forward with the schools without raising taxes, even if you have to cut your own pay. You're dismissed." In spite of himself, Semerkhet bowed deeply from the waist, just as Ay would have after that dismissal, but he looked like he wanted to get down on his face.

Now Semerkhet was standing very stiffly, eyes rather large. Tut grinned at him. "Scary?"

He shrugged. "A bit." Then he gave a nervous chuckle, releasing the visible tension in his shoulders as he bounced uneasily on the balls of his feet. They paused, taking a moment to breathe. Then the King said,

"And now soft." He nodded. "Go again. Be… be Maya this time." Semerkhet's face went still, then took on the attitude of the haughty Treasurer.

"Glorious Lord," he said snobbishly, "I wish to question the wisdom of accepting both male and female students into the schools you are having built."

In spite of himself, the King actually felt a bit of anger rising. Semerkhet had chosen both an issue that Maya was likely to argue against and something that was close to Tut's heart. He took a deep breath. Time for the sweet, deadly whisper.

"My dear Treasurer," he said softly, plastering a smile on his unwilling face, "I understand that this must sound... strange, and that you have concerns. But please understand that I have thought about this very carefully, and discussed it at length with my wife. As our Treasurer, it is your job to safeguard our budget and make sure it is used wisely."

He let just a hint of the thunder and lightning creep into his eyes, which he kept fixed unblinkingly on the not-Treasurer, turning up the intimidation just slightly. Slowly he approached not-Maya, gently passing beside him, walking-stick tapping softly as he went.

"And you do such a wonderful job. Practically every project you've ever led has come in at or under budget. But I want to let you know that as unique as it is to open a school that welcomes both male and female students, I don't believe it will be a waste of money. In fact, I believe it will be good for our economy. Releasing highly-educated adults of both genders into Egypt's workforce will allow for more people to possess higher-paying jobs, therefore being able to buy more goods, causing more money to circulate within the economy and helping us find our way back to prosperity."

Now he was behind Semerkhet, murmuring into his ear from over his shoulder. "So you see, Maya," Tut said finally, still in that soft, gentle near-whisper, "welcoming women into the new schools will be good for the economy. Thank you for coming to me with your concerns."

Coming back around to the front, he broke character and looked at Semerkhet, who was bent in a stiff bow, halfway through the automatic formation of the phrase, "Hail to thee, Ruler of Truth; all life, prosperity, and health!"

"What do you think?" he asked as Semerkhet rose, brushing his braids out of his eyes and looking up at him.

Semerkhet shivered, eyes darting away for an instant as if the Pharaoh was too frightening to look at. Then he nodded with a nervous little smile and another chuckle, letting his tense shoulders drop. "Kind of scary too. But different. Really made me want to do whatever you said, even more than the first one. It's… intimidating. But not like you're about to slap me, like the first one. It's… I don't know. But it works."

"Is that true, by the way, that most of Maya's projects have come in under budget?" Tut asked with a grin, showing his friend his teeth.

"I don't know," Semerkhet said, shrugging, "but it sounded good."

"Those points I was making actually sounded really good," Tut said thoughtfully. "I should write that down."

"You should," Semerkhet said, nodding. "Especially the bit about you talking about it with the Queen. That'll really bug him."

Tut smiled. Then he looked steadily at Semerkhet, extending his hand. Looking embarrassed, Semerkhet tentatively offered his own, letting the Pharaoh give it a friendly squeeze. "Thank you for doing that, Semerkhet," Tut said earnestly. To his delight,

Semerkhet maintained eye contact. "Having that practice will really help me. I'm glad to have someone… I can trust enough to do something like this with." He chuckled. "And I am sorry if I scared you."

Semerkhet laughed out loud. "That's all right, Your Majesty. The Pharaoh scaring you is part of the job."

Tut sighed. "Sem… why is the Queen so smart? Most of the ideas I'm trying to move forward were hers to begin with, and I just agree with her that they're good. Is she so smart because she's older, or because she's a woman?"

Semerkhet tried not to smile. "I'm not sure how to answer that question, Morning Star. But I will say that Father always said it was Mother's wisdom that kept us all warm and fed, not just the money he made. And my sister is the wisest person I know. She's older than me, too. And I know she's smarter than I am, because every time I do something stupid, even way back when I was little, she always said, 'I knew you were going to do that! Told you so!' And she's always right. She tells me not to do the stupid thing, like trying to pick up a scorpion, and in the last couple of years, I've finally started listening to her." He nursed one hand, as if remembering a painful sting. "Wish I would have started a long time ago." He smiled. "So being older… and being a girl… are probably both significant."

Tutankhamun rested his chin on his hand. "Then why is the Pharaoh almost always a man?"

Semerkhet just shook his head.

As they walked aimlessly down the hall, recapping the exercise they'd just gone through, Sem paused. A knot of young men about

226

his age were trooping along in the other direction, blue hockey uniforms scuffed with dirt and stained with sweat.

"You should have been there, Sem!" one exclaimed, stopping to give him a friendly pound on the shoulder. Semerkhet smiled, slapping him on the back. "We're going to annihilate Djerty next week!"

"I'll be at the next practice," he promised with a nod. And whooping and pumping their fists, the rest of the team continued on their way.

Semerkhet smiled at Tut, giving a little shrug, a little shake of his head. And they, too, continued, their feet finding their way to the kitchens. It was time for a snack, after all.

"Oh, Meresankh's such a gossip," Ankhesenamun chuckled as she and Tut played *seega* in his private sitting room, just off from his bedroom. In here it was like a cross between his bedroom and his study; a few chairs and a table, strewn with scrolls, but softer, more restful than the study, more of a place to relax and chat.

He moved a piece. Maybe… just maybe… there was a chance that he would win this time. The game looked like it was setting up in his favor. Already he had captured two of his sister's pieces.

"Really?"

She nodded. "She told me about a love poem a man in the shoe department wrote to another one of my maidservants. Tia didn't reply, of course, but I can tell she's pleased."

Tut smiled, as he thought of Semerkhet's love poem to Mere-sankh and wondered if he'd sent it to her, and as an idea occurred to him. A plan was forming in his mind. A plan that required a terrible gossip. "Ankh…" he said slowly, "can I actually talk to Meresankh? I need her help with something."

Ankh looked up at him in surprise, braids jingling. "What do you need her for?"

He chuckled. "I need her to spread some news."

Much to his delight, the King actually won the game. A minute later, Meresankh was kneeling before him, hands folded as she bowed to the floor.

"Your wish is my command, O King."

"Rise, please," he said, beckoning. Slowly she got up, avoiding his eyes as she waited for her instructions. She was so little, he thought. Almost a head shorter than the Queen, which meant that she barely came halfway up his chest. She was very curvy indeed, and there was a dimple in her round cheek. He also noticed with a smile that she was wearing the necklace Semerkhet had gotten her, a tiny silver pendant with an image of Isis.

The Pharaoh smiled gently as he tried to catch her eye. "Please… please look at me. It's all right." Slowly, unwillingly, she let her eyes flicker up to his face, as if she was not sure she would not be stricken blind or hit by lightning for the audacity. "The Queen has told me what a wonderful handmaiden you are," he said, "and what a good communicator."

She just blushed.

"I need you to deliver a message," he said. "To the whole staff, or everyone you work with, at least, and tell them to pass it on. I need you to tell them that by order of the Pharaoh, they are no longer forbidden to look at me. Actually, I'm encouraging them to. When I greet them, they can answer. When I smile at them, they can smile back. I don't want anyone to be afraid of me. I know you

228

can spread a message quickly, and this one is very important to me." He smiled, and boldly, she smiled back, then turned to smile at the Queen. "I appreciate your help."

She bowed again, but it was a bow of true respect rather than fear. "I am your humble servant."

"And I am your grateful Pharaoh."

The Queen smiled as Meresankh bowed and made her way back out of the room, off to begin delivering her message to the entire staff. This was one of the first times she had ever made actual eye contact with Meresankh, she realized. And as her eyes had touched her handmaiden's, she had been surprised. Because she could see there a light, a Light she recognized from the eyes of her parents, her sisters, in the days of the Aten.

What was it doing there? And what did it mean?

Still the Pharaoh's history lessons went on. They were in the Thirteenth Dynasty now, the beginning of a period of disunity between the strength of the lineages of Amenemhat and Senusret and the stability that they were enjoying here in their own time, which had begun with the reign of Ahmose the First, defeater of the Hyksos. And with every new fact he learned, Tut hoped he was growing not only more knowledgeable, but wiser.

"Is everything all right?" the Pharaoh asked his valet.

Semerkhet looked up from arranging a fresh bouquet of flowers on the dressing-table, arranging his solemn features into a smile as he brushed the back of his hand against his nose, swallowing loudly.

He nodded, even as he blinked back a certain brightness in his eyes.

"Just thinking," he said, and his voice was slightly choked. "This was the day... the day last year... that my father and I took my little brother Nedjes on that hunting trip."

Tutankhamun bowed his head. And slowly, cautiously, he reached out and put his hand on his friend's shoulder.

But there was no telling when the Vizier was going to hand the reins of Egypt to the Pharaoh (and his wife). So Tut had a lot of free time in which to read. And he and Ankh decided to spend it in the Royal Library.

"Anything?" he asked as they scanned scroll after scroll of history, searching for information on the Hebrews, or Hyksos, or whatever they were called, and their mysterious disappearance.

"'*Dfan'ty Pann'iah,* Overseer of the Storehouse of Abundance, He of the Excellent, Gracious Spirit,'" Ankh read. "Twelfth Dynasty. I... I would hazard to guess that this is the Canaanite Vizier. It does mention the seven years of plentiful harvests Ay was telling you about, which were followed by seven years of famine. But..." she said, turning to the next section, "although it talks about land in Goshen being given to the Canaanite Vizier's descendants, there's nothing else about the Hebrews. Only the 'Hyksos' appearing and starting to take power for themselves. And then..." She kept reading, then sighed. "Their sound 'defeat' by Ahmose the First. But there's nothing," she said, "about the enslavement of any Canaanites or their abuse, the murder of Canaanite children, the plagues, or the disappearance of thousands of slaves. Just... vague references to the way that 'Pharaoh'... it doesn't even say who... expelled the 'plague' of the Hyksos, and chased them into Sinai, where they were never seen again… Isn't that where the Hebrews are said to have gone?"

"I think so," Tut said, feeling a shiver running down his spine despite the heat of the day. Something was calling to him, something that felt like a true story he barely remembered, felt like the warmth of the Sun on his face.

Something that the Egyptian historians had not wanted the world to know.

"I never used to like hockey," Tut mused as he took a break from the research he hoped would make him a wise Pharaoh, sitting wearily at his dressing-table.

Sem looked up from dusting a box full of opulent rings and bracelets.

"Hmm?"

The Pharaoh shook his head. "No, I didn't," he said. "Or boxing, or the high-jump, or weightlifting…" He bit his lip, flexing his left foot. "Because I couldn't play."

Semerkhet went on cleaning the jewelry in silence, waiting for Tut to continue. There was nothing for him to add.

"The only one I can participate in is chariot-racing," Tutankhamun went on. "And I suppose it's still my favorite to watch. You were amazing the other day; you really were."

Semerkhet just went on, now rearranging the clean jewelry. But even as the valet kept his head bowed, Tut could see the smile on his face.

"But I like watching hockey now," he said with a smile of his own. "Because I like seeing you have fun."

Now Semerkhet looked up. But all he did was smile.

Tut paused as he walked down a long hallway one afternoon. General Horemheb was standing there. And he looked like he wanted to talk.

"Great Morning Star," the General said, dipping his head.

Tut smiled. "General."

Horemheb returned the smile. "Your Majesty... do you have a moment? There is something I was wondering... if we... could discuss."

Tutankhamun looked at Horemheb in curiosity. "Of course." They sat down together on a bench, and the Pharaoh looked at the General. "What is it?"

Horemheb looked down at his lap, twisting his hands together. And Tut began to worry. What could be wrong?

"Glorious Lord..." Horemheb said, as if he were searching for the right words, "I need your... wisdom."

Tut felt his eyebrows rise into his wig. "You... need *my* wisdom?" he asked a little incredulously.

"Yes," Horemheb whispered. Tut scooted closer, leaning in as the General bent toward him as if to whisper in his ear. "It's about... it's about my dear wives."

The Pharaoh sat up a little straighter. "What?" he whispered.

"Your Majesty... Your Majesty and the Queen are very young... but I envy you," Horemheb said.

Tut frowned. "Envy me?"

The General sighed as if in frustration. "I envy your relationship with the Queen," he said finally. "My wives... my wives are so..." He leaned even closer, mouth almost brushing the Pharaoh's ear, "...boring." Tut chuckled in confusion, but the General went on. "They never say anything interesting. They just want to know how

232

I am— they never tell me how *they* are. They're… they're my pretty little dolls, and I love providing for them and giving them things, but I feel like I don't really know them as people. I'm only home two weekends a month, and we have plenty of fun. But that's all we do together. There's no exchange of ideas. But you have that. How do you do it? What's your secret? How do you get to know them? How do you become friends with your wife?"

Tutankhamun scooted slightly away from the General with a sigh, formulating a response. "I suppose…" he said slowly, trying to put it into words, "that it's partly because we have grown up together. We're so close because we have spent so much time together. I think that's a big part of it. Spending time together. That's… that's the only way to get to know someone. Time. So I can't… can't really say anything else, but… the more time you spend with them, or anyone you want to get to know, the better."

General Horemheb gave a deep sigh. Now a small smile touched his face. "Thank you, My Lord," he said, inclining his head. "Your wisdom is profound." And with a wish for life, prosperity, and health, he got up, disappearing down the hall.

The Pharaoh sat there on the bench, shaking his head to himself. General Horemheb had turned to him for wisdom. Life truly was turning upside-down.

21   The Game Begins

Semerkhet appeared outside the pavilion one bright, breezy day, carrying Tut's favorite blue lotus cup on a tray. The month of Paophi was still hot, but not quite as bad as Epiphi, Mesori, Thoth. It at least offered the hope of cooler days ahead. This breeze, for example, gave a refreshing hint of the approaching Season of Emergence. And Tut's birthday was coming up… The chirping birds, pecking among the rosebushes and jasmine, sounded sweet and cheerful, their happy little voices promising a good day. Tutankhamun smiled at his valet, pleasantly surprised at the thoughtful gesture.

"Your Majesty," Semerkhet said. The valet took the cup, lifting it to his own lips as he did whenever he poured wine for the Pharaoh. "I taste your drink, Son of Ra… and if there be harm in it, let the harm fall upon me."

He took a sip, then smiled. "It's good." He bowed again, offering the cup. "Master."

Tut took the cup, the beads of his pectoral necklace clinking as he moved. Still too warm to really want to wear a tunic. Just a kilt. "Thank you, Sem."

Semerkhet gave a little smile, but it faded a moment later, and it never touched his eyes. He stood there as if he had something else to say.

"Is there something else?" the King asked, sipping the cool, red wine.

"Yes, Master," Semerkhet said, looking down and digging the toe of his sandal into the dirt. Tut perked up. What was making his valet so uncomfortable? "I… I heard something I wanted to bring to your attention. Presumptuous, I know, but it concerned me."

Tut nodded with a concerned frown. "Tell me, please."

Semerkhet swallowed and began, his voice distinctly uncomfortable. "Well, I was walking past Vizier Ay's chambers, and I heard him talking to someone. I think it might have been the General and the Treasurer. The Vizier sounded pretty upset. I didn't hear the whole conversation, but it was something about you being, well, sickly, and that... someday... when he was the Pharaoh, there wouldn't be any money left for his lifestyle or his tomb. I distinctly heard the words, 'We have to get rid of him before he and his naïve generosity bankrupt the entire country.' He... he sounded angry enough to kill, Your Majesty." Semerkhet swallowed again, bobbing his head in a nervous bow. "I just thought I should tell you," he finished, the phrase running together into one anxious word.

The Pharaoh took a shuddering breath, then reached out and patted Semerkhet's arm with an encouraging smile, gratified that his friend was making eye contact with him. Semerkhet nearly flinched, then blushed at actually being patted by his master.

"Thank you, Semerkhet," Tut said in what he hoped was a confident, reassuring tone. "I will deal with it."

Suddenly the squawking of the birds sounded like fear and anxiety. And a few of them had begun to fight.

The sun grew low, and Tut made his way back to the Temple of Amun-Ra. It was time for the Sunset Ceremony. Tutankhamun and the priests stood outside the temple, but this time they did not enter it. Instead they stood watching the sun set, and as it set, Tut bowed his head and began the evening prayer.

Hail to thee, who settest in the region of life, Atum, father of the gods.
The double doors are opened for thee in thy horizon at thy setting towards the earth to illuminate the west.
Thou causest the gods to set in the earth,
thy followers, they, who are in thy retinue,
o soul holy of utterance,
begetter of the gods,
who endued himself with his unknown form,
thou first-born,
great is he in his mysteries.

They paused for a moment of reflection, of private prayer. *Make me the strong Pharaoh I am supposed to be*, Tutankhamun silently asked, just like he did every morning, every evening. *And tell us… when the time is right to try again.* The sun continued to set, shadows growing longer. The High Priest bowed to the Pharaoh as he walked away, walking home in the growing dark. But even as they had acknowledged the beauty and majesty of nature through prayer, there was still… emptiness.

"Does he even hear me?" Tut asked as he and the Queen sat on the balcony in the cool evening breeze, listening to the whirring of the locusts roosting in the garden below, watching the pink sunset reflecting in the lotus-pools. The cool of night was a relief after the blazing hot day, even if it was the time when the mosquitoes came out to bite. On a table set between them lay the remains of the very last watermelon of the season, green rind picked completely clean of the sweet, pink fruit. Beside it sat two empty cups, which had been full to the brim with cool, refreshing licorice *mai-sus*.

"Who, love?" Ankh asked, leaning forward with a little frown.

"Amun," he said, glancing at the fading light. He sighed. "I prayed at the Sunset Ceremony tonight just like always... but I just don't... feel like he hears me. How many times..." He swallowed. "How many times have I prayed to be a strong Pharaoh? And nothing has changed. And how many times..." He took her hand. "Have I prayed for an heir?"

Ankh squeezed his hand, looking down.

"Sometimes I wonder..." Tut mused. "About Father. What he believed. I just feel... like we're missing something. Like we're reaching out to Whoever's out there, Creator, but we haven't quite found Them. But maybe... Father was onto something. Because whenever I come out of the Temple of Amun-Ra, back into the Sun, I feel better. The moment the Sun touches me. It's like I can feel this... *love*... reaching down and touching me. But I don't feel that inside the temple."

Ankh sighed, shaking her head. "I wonder the same thing. About Tawaret." She swallowed. "I've prayed so many times. But she's never responded." Then she almost chuckled, morbid as it was. "And the bull sacrifice, every single day at lunch... What does that accomplish? Do we know that the gods really require it of us? And what purpose does it serve? Does it—" She swallowed, a sudden thought touching her heart like the warm rays of the Sun. "Does it stand between us and our sins like the lamb's blood Father said the Hebrews put on their lintels the night Uncle Thutmose died? Does it have any meaning at all... or is it just wasted death?"

"So how do we find out the truth?" Tut asked.

His sister sighed, giving him a little smile and shaking her head so the silver beads of her braids gave a little jingle. "We keep looking."

They looked out at the horizon, the fading light of the sunset. And the warmth touched the King's heart again.

"Semerkhet brought something interesting to my attention," Tut said.

"What was it?" his wife asked, brushing a mosquito away.

Tut sighed, then swallowed. There was no way to tell her other than simply to tell her. He lowered his voice. "He overheard something the Vizier was saying... and now he's convinced Ay wants to kill me."

Ankh gasped, eyes going wide, and grabbed his hand, her henna-dyed nails digging into his skin. Her beaded braids rang out a cry of alarm as they swung wildly. "Kill you?"

He shook his head and she listened in growing horror, squeezing his hand tighter and tighter. "Something about 'getting rid of him before he and his naïve generosity bankrupt the entire country.' I've always trusted Ay... and I don't know what to think. Don't know what I *want* to think." He sighed, looking down. "I don't even want to imagine Ay wanting to hurt me, but how can Sem be wrong? You don't mishear something like that. But I don't know who I can ask, who I can trust, even what questions to ask. If... if something really is going on, first of all they'll only lie about it, and secondly, I don't want to put myself in even more danger by flushing it out too quickly." He looked at her. "What can I do?"

Ankh sighed, looking down at their entwined hands. "Ay... he has a lot to gain from stopping you from re-imagining the budget. And he's been in charge a long time, ever since you were crowned.

238

Now that you're of age and starting to make changes of your own…" She sighed again. "I feel the same way. I want to trust him, but I'm not sure if we can. Something like this… is serious. Too serious to explain away… too serious to ignore."

"But what can we do? How can I find out what's really going on?"

She looked up at him with the face of a confident, experienced young politician. He knew that whatever she was about to say was right, and that he could trust her wisdom. "Actually, I think flushing it out quickly might be the best plan. Go at it all out, really innocent. Totally direct. Like you just want to know. Be the sweet little boy he's kept you all these years. You'll catch him by surprise, and he won't be able to tell for sure if you know something and you're being sneaky or if you honestly just want him to tell you."

Tut nodded. "Then I'll tell him my valet told me something interesting I want to clarify—"

Ankh put her hand on his arm, green beads chiming as her braids swayed. Even the *uraeus* on her diadem seemed to be telling him to wait. "No, no, don't tell him Semerkhet told you. Don't name any names."

He frowned. "Why not?"

"Because if you say Semerkhet told you, Sem will be dead by morning, whether he heard correctly or not."

Tut blinked. "You think so?"

She just nodded sadly.

"You've seen what the Vizier can do. Remember when he turned Semerkhet into a scribe?"

Tut frowned. "But I reversed it."

She shook her head, beads clinking. "Well, next time it won't be reversible. You keep opposing Ay, he will keep fighting back harder."

"So are you saying we should stop fighting?"

"No, I'm saying we need to be careful. And don't give him any openings. This is war, my love."

The King shuddered. "Well, I'm glad to have you with me. I wouldn't know what to do."

She gave a little smile. "You're learning. Just like with everything else. And I'll always be here."

Ankh took his hand, and they sat together in silence, trying to peer into the future. They couldn't.

She sighed. "This is how politics works, my love. It's a deadly game of thrones and relationships. No, just say there's a rumor going around and you're curious. Then watch his face, watch his body even more than you listen to his words. If he gives even the slightest sign of being upset… you'll know he's lying when he tells you he never said any such thing. Because the one thing he won't do is say the rumor is correct."

Tut gave a little smile. "How did you get so wise?"

"Watching Mother," she said. "She reigned as Pharaoh for three years after Father died. Moved us back to Thebes, helped us move on…" She closed her eyes and clenched her strong little hands. "Until the day her horse was spooked… and she fell, and it kicked her, right in the face… and she was gone." She looked up at him. "And then you were Pharaoh."

Tut looked down and swallowed. He had never wanted to be Pharaoh at the expense of his own mother.

Ankhesenamun blinked. "But I think that if you catch him by surprise, you can get him to tell you something useful."

Tut put his arm around his sister, kissing her on the cheek. It was almost dark now, and time to go in, the first stars appearing in the deep blue sky. "Thank you, my dear Queen. Truly you are the Lady of Wisdom."

The Queen closed her eyes with a shudder as the sound of her brother's tapping cane faded. He was going to bed, but she was going to stay up a little longer. She had things to think about.

The Vizier. In a moment, a sentence, everything had changed. And now his disdain of the Pharaoh did not seem so innocent.

There was no way in the Two Lands that Semerkhet had misheard him. When politicians were heard plotting, that was exactly what they were doing.

She put her arms around herself as the evening chill deepened. It felt like this game they were playing was turning into a war.

Things would go on, she knew. Ay would keep playing this game, this war, move by move. Until he either brought the Pharaoh under his control or eliminated him. Or until the King and Queen brought *him* under control… or eliminated him. Because the one thing the Vizier was not going to do was leave Tut to rule as he saw fit. Nothing had ever been as clear as that. But what would the Vizier's next move be? And what countermove could the Queen and her brother offer? How could they evade him before he trapped them? And what other pieces were in motion on this gameboard? What allies of his, of theirs, would add their infinite complexity to this game in which they were squaring off?

A mosquito flew by, landing on her neck. She brushed it away before it bit her, but it brought with it a glimmer of memory, of death. Of her own big sister's death from overnight ague in the very first year of their brother's reign. And as the insect had touched her neck, it had felt as though a noose was being placed. A noose was already in place about Tutankhamun's neck. And only by trading moves in a deadly game of strategy could they hope to win.

Suddenly, Ankhesenamun was afraid.

Tut and his Vizier sat playing *seega* in his study the next day, a reward after another dull history lesson. Tut loved history, but not the way Ay told it. Although the way things were going, he felt as though they might be making history right now. Vaguely he wondered who would be reading his story in the future. At least it was less hot in the study this time, although it was still warm. Today he had on a short-sleeved tunic instead of a kilt.

It was the years of the Hyksos now, the dark time after the Thirteenth Dynasty when a large region of Egypt had been ruled by immigrants from Canaan who had multiplied, risen up, and formed their own dynasty contemporaneous with a reduced kingdom under native Egyptian rule. Some said that they were the descendants of the Canaanite Vizier who had moved his whole family to Egypt, or at least their relatives. Some even whispered that it was their population growth and formation of their own dynasty that had inspired Pharaoh Ahmose the First to gain control of them by forcing them to build cities and work the fields, he or his successors finally crippling their increase with the cruel edict that every male child should be drowned in the Nile. Hyksos, Hebrew, what was in a name?

But those were stories Tut had heard from his father. They weren't in the histories Ay was reading from. The papyrus the Vizier was reading to Tut said simply that these Canaanite invaders had arrived during a famine, grown in strength, taken control of parts of Egypt, and eventually been defeated and "cast out" earlier in their very dynasty, the Eighteenth. And now the Hyksos were gone. Just like the Hebrews.

"I heard something interesting yesterday," the Pharaoh said into the stuffy silence.

Ay looked up from considering his next move. Through the window, the sun was making a rather interesting pattern of shadows out of his wrinkles. "Tell me."

"A rather odd rumor going around the palace staff. Apparently one of them was walking by your chambers and happened to overhear part of a conversation, and now they're all under the impression that you were telling the General and the Treasurer that you intend to… what was it they said, 'get rid of me before my naïve generosity and I bankrupt the country.' I just wanted to hear your perspective. Are the servants hearing things?"

Ay moved his game piece. A rather foolish move, Tut thought, one that would allow Tut to corner or capture all of his remaining pieces within two more moves. When they played, it was usually Ay who won. Strange.

"I am afraid that the slave misheard me, My Lord," Ay said eventually, running his gnarled finger over another of his game pieces without moving it. "I was telling my loyal fellow courtiers that I was afraid that you and your splendid generosity would damage our economy, yes, and I admit that my… concern… was starting to get the better of me, but I said, 'teach him wisdom,' not 'get rid of him.' The royal decisions do lie with you now, of course…" Tutankhamun's breath caught in his throat— was the Vizier handing him the reins of power? "…in ever-increasing measure," he continued, and the Pharaoh wilted. "But you have not yet attained your full measure of wisdom. I intend to be with you every step of the way, offering my own experience and… support."

The Pharaoh nodded as he made a bold move to hem in Ay's remaining pieces. "Thank you for clarifying, Vizier. I'll admit, they really had me worried for a moment there."

"Shall I have the Superintendent of the Works of the Palace have all the slaves beaten for their foolishness?" Ay asked, old eyes brightening. Almost absentmindedly, he made a final fruitless move, withdrawing his piece to the safety of the corner, where, although it could not be captured, it would no longer be able to move.

Tut shook his head. "No, thank you. When has slave-beating ever gotten us anything but trouble? A hundred years ago, the Prince saw an overseer beating a slave, and he came over all homicidal and ran away to the desert, and we know how that went. Someone made a mistake, that's all. But sometimes… the servants are the ones who figure things out." He moved his piece, completing the game by definitively cornering the four pieces the Vizier still had on the board.

"Indeed, O Mighty King," Ay said. He looked at the board. "Ah. I see you have won. Splendid game. I… I wish you a splendid day. All life, prosperity, and health."

And Ay excused himself.

Tut sat back and looked at the gameboard, Ay's badly-played pieces and his easy win still in place. They were playing a game, he could see. Where it would lead them remained to be seen.

The sun was warm, but the breeze was cool. So Ankhesenamun got a cup of *mai-sus* and sat in the pavilion, sipping it and thinking.

Thinking about the other conversation she had had with her brother.

She wondered too. About the gods and goddesses they prayed to, made offerings to, whose images the priests bathed, dressed, fed, and asked questions of. Just like… It was blasphemy, but no one would hear the thoughts that she kept inside her heart. Just like her and her sisters, dressing and feeding their dolls.

But their dolls had never spoken to them. And neither had the silent gods and goddesses of the temples.

Something was missing, she thought, shaking her head. A gust of wind made the beads of her wig jingle, and she felt a sudden warmth on her face as the Sun came out from behind a cloud.

She smiled as she felt it. Somehow it felt… like what was missing.

Tut sat down next to Ankh, who was relaxing in the pavilion, enjoying the Paophi sunshine and the sweet fragrances of the flowers over a cup of *mai-sus*. She sat up as soon as she saw him, bending toward him secretively.

"What did you find out?" she asked in an eager whisper.

"He said he was misheard."

She raised an eyebrow. "Really."

"And he lost the game."

She nodded. "Interesting. He's definitely lying."

"So what do we do now?"

"We watch. And we wait. We don't make any sudden moves. We just made our move, so his is next." She sighed, reaching out to take his hand. "But we have to be ready for whatever might come."

22   The King of Peace

"Your Majesty?" Tut looked up. Horemheb was standing in the doorway of his study, waiting for an invitation to enter.

"Come in," he said, beckoning. Horemheb stepped into the King's study, looking around appreciatively at the walls full of shelves, fully stocked with papyrus scrolls. As always, he was neatly dressed in his full military uniform. Likewise, the Pharaoh had prepared for the meeting by putting on his circlet, although he had not gone so formal as to wear the false beard or hold the crook and flail. His walking-stick was leaning on the edge of the desk, but he hoped he wouldn't have to use it for awhile. His foot was bothering him today. "Sit down, please."

"Thank you, Your Majesty." Horemheb sat down in a chair across from the desk where the King sat looking at tax and import data. The cat, who was curled in Tut's lap, lightly hopped to the floor, pausing to look questioningly up at the General and slink past him out the door.

"What did you need to speak to me about, General?" Tutankhamun asked after Horemheb had sat in stoic silence for nearly thirty seconds.

"The military budget, O Mighty King. As you review your economic plans for the entire nation, I wanted to make a recommendation regarding the military budget."

"What is your recommendation, General?" Tut asked.

Horemheb swallowed. "I believe it needs to be increased, Glorious Lord. As they stand, the military's current funds will not allow us to defend Egypt from her enemies over the next year."

246

"Is that so?" Tut asked, stacking a few of his documents together and setting them aside. A burst of pain jolted through his foot, and he pressed his lips together, forcing himself not to react. He was a strong Pharaoh.

"Yes, My Lord," Horemheb continued confidently. "I also recommend quickly taking action to regain control of the territory your father lost in Amurru to the Hittites, and to prevent them from claiming any more of our northern lands." He smiled at the thought. "Through such victories, you will become as great as your ancestor Thutmose the First!"

Tutankhamun gently shook his head.

"Thank you for your suggestions, General," he said softly. He saw Horemheb blink in displeasure at the word "suggestions." "You have a great deal of experience in the art of war, and I appreciate your input. However," he said, sitting up a little straighter, taking up a little more space in his chair, "we are going to take a different approach."

"And what approach is that, O Great Morning Star?" Horemheb asked, a hint of contempt creeping into his voice.

"That of peace," the Pharaoh said. "I have no reason to believe I will ever go into battle, so it is my intention to serve my country as a King of peace. I want to make friends with our enemies, even the Hittites. Just as my diplomatic grandfather did." He smiled. "And I will become as great as my ancestress Hatshepsut."

Horemheb swallowed, eyes flickering. "I would not wish to see the Pharaoh's goodwill lead Egypt into subjugation by the Hittites."

"Neither would I wish to plunge us into war while we are still recovering from the disaster with the Hebrews, as well as from my father's unique policies," the King countered. "If we can foster peace and friendship with the nations around us, we may be able to avoid entering into a war for many decades, allowing us to rebuild our economy and return to our full strength. Then, if one of our neighbors moves against us, we will be ready. We must seek peace for the present in order to obtain the time to rebuild."

He paused, steepling his fingers. "By how much are you requesting I increase the military budget, General?"

"By at least ten percent, Your Majesty," Horemheb said hopefully, scooting slightly forward in his chair.

Tutankhamun nodded. "I will give you five. But you are to take no military action to retake Amurru. Territorial expansion is not my priority, and therefore, as my loyal General... not yours." He paused, tapping his chin as he thought. "Actually, General, I believe I will send you to the Hittites."

Horemheb blinked, a hint of a frown creasing his forehead between his eyebrows. "Why, My Lord, if not to fight?"

"With gifts," the King said, spreading his hands. "Seeing the greatest General in Egypt peacefully bearing gifts will surely demonstrate to the Hittites how Egypt wishes to establish peace and friendship with them. I also wish you to go to the Mitanni, and to Nubia to check on our territories. Show them that we can move toward a peaceful future together."

Horemheb sat in silence, formulating a reply. "O Mighty King, a Pharaoh must show strength to his neighbors, not weakness."

Tutankhamun raised an eyebrow. "Was Pharaoh Hatshepsut weak when she focused her reign not on war, but on trading and building?"

"Pharaoh Hatshepsut was different, O King for Whom the Nile Floods," Horemheb said uncomfortably, not meeting Tut's eye.

248

"Then do you suggest I hand the throne to my Queen?"

"No, My Lord," Horemheb said even more uncomfortably. Now he appeared to be trying to read Tut's tax data upside-down.

The Pharaoh smiled. "Then see to it. We will approach our neighbors in peace, establishing friendships with gifts and greetings. I wish to be a King of peace, General. And I will need your help."

Horemheb got up from his chair and bowed. "As you wish, Your Majesty. All life, prosperity, and health."

Tut watched the General leave the room as the cat padded back in. He gave a satisfied sigh. This just might work.

Horemheb left three days later with a squad of men on horseback. They led camels laden with gifts for Egypt's neighbors; grain, wine, pottery, papyrus. Egypt was sending its best, even ox-hides, glass beads and vessels, and fine linen. And one small, confused giraffe. The King had decided to re-gift it to whichever nation Horemheb thought would react best to it. The King smiled as he watched the caravan begin its journey. These gifts would prove their goodwill to their neighbors.

"Why have you sent the General to the ends of the earth?" Ay asked over dinner. Menhet, the flute player, and a dancer were entertaining them, but they weren't paying attention.

Tut took a bite of beef, and chased it down with a sip of wine from his blue cup. His foot was feeling a little better, a great relief. "I was talking to the Queen," he said, "and she said that if I couldn't lead my country into war, I could be a King of peace. So I have sent the General on a mission of peace and diplomacy that I hope will keep war far from our gates for the rest of my reign."

Ay nodded, Adam's apple bobbing as he swallowed. "Indeed, My Lord. Have you thought about how we might need him at home?"

Tut shrugged. "Why? If this works, we may be able to decrease the size of our army, leaving more funds available for the support of the needy, the growth of the economy, and the promotion of education. I have a plan, Vizier."

Ay looked at him. Tut saw no confidence on the old man's lined face. The Vizier swallowed again. "Indeed, Son of Ra. And the needy... they are your first priority?"

The King nodded. "Yes. And they will be until no one in Egypt is needy any longer."

Ay nodded. "Indeed."

"More wine, Your Majesty?" a female servant asked. The King was pleased to see her meeting his eyes, truly looking at him, without a trace of fear.

"Thank you, Tentamun." He was pleased that he remembered her name.

Ay stood up, sudden rage on his face. "How dare you look at the Pharaoh with such disrespect? Get out of his exalted presence!" Hastily setting her serving vessel on the table, she fled the room in tears.

Tut looked at his Vizier. "Excuse me?" he said simply.

"What has gotten into that girl— what could possibly have possessed her to make her think herself worthy to actually look into your eyes— as if she were equal to you—"

"She looked at me because I extended royal permission to do so," the King said firmly. Slowly Ay sat back down. "I've issued a

250

royal proclamation that no one is forbidden to look at me any longer. When I look at them, they can look back at me. When I talk to them, they can reply. And when I smile at them… I hope some of them will smile back."

"I heard of no royal proclamation, My Lord," Ay objected with a questioning frown.

"I distributed it directly through the staff," Tut explained, taking a sip of wine. "I thought that would be more direct. And less subject to interruption."

"Is that so, Lord of Perfect Laws," Ay spat, slouching back in his chair with a bitter look almost as ugly as one of his son's sneers.

"It is," the King said. He cleared his throat. "Tentamun, please come back in," he called. Slowly she reappeared, shaking from head to foot and wiping away tears. "The Vizier has something he wants to say to you."

Ay glared at the Pharaoh as if to say, "I do?" then visibly swallowed back his anger. "I apologize for my unwarranted harshness," he said smoothly, barely managing to keep his nostrils from flaring in disgust. "I was not aware of the Pharaoh's decision." Tut nodded at him, raising his eyebrows. Ay glanced at him questioningly, then continued. "I… wish to thank you for serving us every day."

"It's my honor," she whispered, glancing briefly into both of their faces before her eyes returned to the safety of the floor. Then with wishes for life, health, and prosperity, she excused herself.

Tut continued with his dinner. So did Ay. The silence between them was uncomfortable, but for the Pharaoh, it represented one more small victory.

"I had a meeting with Horemheb," Tutankhamun said to his wife as they sat in the garden, watching the purple evening sky reflecting on one of the lotus-pools. Whirring locusts roosted in the sycamore and fig trees, the pink roses, fragrance wafting in the evening breeze, seemed almost purple in the deepening dusk. In the distance, they could hear the gentle lapping of the pools, the shifting of the loyal guard who stood watching over them. Sometimes, they only needed one. The evening was cool, cooler than those of the past week. It felt good.

"Hmm?" she asked.

"And I told him what you said about being a King of peace."

She grinned, looking almost embarrassed. "You did?"

He smiled at her, waving away a mosquito before it could land on her arm. "I did. And I told him that as part of being a King of peace, I wanted him to go to our neighbors with gifts. I'm sending him to the Hittites and the Mitanni, and to our territories in Nubia. If we can reestablish these friendships, we may never have another war with any of them again."

Ankh nodded, putting her arm around him so he could lean against her, his head on her shoulder. In the darkest part of the sky above them, the first stars began to twinkle. "Oh, I hope so."

They sat in silence for a few minutes, then she gave him a squeeze around the shoulders that made him chuckle.

"You excited about your birthday?" she asked. "It is next week, after all."

"About my birthday, yes, about the party…" He gave a playful shudder. "Hope it's not like last year. There were way too many people and they stayed for way too long."

His sister winked at him. "Well, it was your coming of age."

252

"How many people did you say there would be for this year?" he asked her.

"Just the dignitaries from around the country who want to congratulate you," she said. She shrugged. "Maybe… maybe a few dozen, but nothing compared to Tribute Day."

Tut nodded. That didn't sound too bad. "Well," he said, smiling as a sudden idea popped into his mind, "I want to have it in the afternoon. Serve lunch and dinner, and then…" He chuckled. "Thank everyone for joining us." He put on his distinguished politician voice. "I am the Pharaoh, and I don't want my party to last all night."

His sister chuckled, cuddling closer as the night grew cooler, a breath of relief that gave just a hint of the cold weather that was to come. "The Pharaoh gets what he wants," she agreed. "Especially on his birthday."

The future was on its way, Ankhesenamun thought as her brother gave her a kiss and headed inside to bed. The future they were building together. And it was beautiful.

Then she chuckled. *Well, look at that*, she thought proudly. *My ideas, being signed into law. What do you know.*

Tut dabbed his face with the linen towel as Semerkhet helped him dry off after his shower that evening, relishing the feeling of having all his makeup washed off. He hadn't been too tired to think, so all Semerkhet had to do was pour the water for him and scrub his back. Now that Kahotep was retired, Nuya was called upon on the nights when the King was too tired to do anything but sit there and be washed. Although he was thriving in the scribe department, he still made a very good valet, and he was honored to help when he was needed. Ptahmose was a good assistant to Semerkhet, but he didn't help with bathing.

"Beautiful day for a journey," Semerkhet said lightly, helping the Pharaoh hobble to the bed to put on his nightclothes.

Tut nodded, sitting down carefully and continuing to dry his face.

Semerkhet swallowed. "The staff," he said, "they're all curious as to where General Horemheb's caravan is going... especially with such an interesting assortment of cargo. Grain, wine, the little giraffe from Tribute Day... Half of them think we're going to war, and the other half think we're making some unheard-of new treaty with one neighbor or another." He swallowed again. "They're very curious. And a bit concerned. They keep asking me what's going on, but I don't have anything I can tell them." He glanced at the Pharaoh, making eye contact for a fleeting moment.

Tut smiled. "Well, we're not at war," he said, and Semerkhet's shoulders dropped in relief. "On the contrary. I've sent Horemheb on a mission of peace to the Hittites, the Mitanni, and our territories in Nubia, bringing gifts and working to establish friendship with our neighbors. If we can gain them as allies, we may be safe from war for the next hundred years."

Semerkhet began to help Tut put on his sleeping-tunic. He gave the King a smile. "Oh, I hope so."

23 Power

Then came the Pharaoh's birthday, toward the beginning of the hot month of Paophi, the last truly hot month. It was a splendid affair, a grand royal feast with food and drink from distant lands, musicians, dancers, acrobats. Dignitaries from all over Egypt, members of the government who did not work in Thebes or Memphis, had traveled to the palace for the celebration, and sat eating and chatting at the splendid tables in the royal feasting hall, being served by staff members who seemed just a bit more cheerful, just a little less shy, less fearfully reserved, than they had a week ago. Jewelry clinked and bright colors shone in the torchlight as the upper crust of Egypt celebrated. At least the staff would get to share in some of the bounty at tomorrow's lunch.

Ay stood up just as one song was ending.

"We want to thank you all for coming such a long way to celebrate the Pharaoh's nineteenth birthday with us, and for bringing such fabulous gifts," he said, sweeping his arm toward the stacks of furniture, jewelry, and folded clothing. It had been just like Tribute Day all over again. Except indoors, which had been an enormous relief. There were a lot of guests, but many of them were contentedly chatting among themselves, so the Pharaoh only had to talk to one or two people at a time.

The Vizier smiled. "And I also want to take this opportunity to make an announcement. One year has passed since the Pharaoh came of age, and today, I am officially stepping back from any and all regent duties. I will remain as Grand Vizier and as the Pharaoh's advisor, but the Pharaoh now stands alone, in full power, the leadership of Egypt falling solely to him. All hail

255

Pharaoh Tutankhamun, Lord of the Two Lands, Ruler of Truth, the Strong Bull, the Living Image of Amun! All life, prosperity, and health!"

The guests cheered wildly, echoing the Vizier's wishes for life, prosperity, and health, and Tut felt his head spin. Ay was no longer regent in any capacity? He was truly ruling alone now?

Ay was giving up power by doing this for him. Maybe... maybe he could be trusted after all.

The Queen blinked as the guests cheered. A sense of shock was still echoing through her. The Vizier had just declared himself no longer regent.

She clenched her hands, nails biting into her palms. She had been right. The moment had come. Ay was making his move. Reeling her baby brother in by making him trust him. And something else was coming, she could feel it in her bones. Something else the Vizier had planned.

This was the first step. The Vizier had placed the noose; when would he jerk it tight? And could Ankh free her brother from it before it choked him? Only history would tell how all this would go.

Ankhesenamun milled around the party after Ay's announcement, greeting guests, thanking them for joining them for the celebration. Fine ladies and gentlemen sat on benches around the grand hall, sipping wine and *mai-sus* and snacking on grapes, nuts, and honey-cakes. The culinary department had outdone themselves; there were even sweet, sticky date loaves molded like lucky crocodiles, and bite-sized confections made from tiger nuts, honey,

256

dates, and spices. As the guests ate and chatted, Menhet played her flute and dancers swayed and twirled.

As the Queen approached, Mutnedjmet and Amenia, wives of Horemheb, and Meryt, the wife of Maya, stood and inclined their heads respectfully. They looked like pretty little dolls, dressed in graceful gowns of white linen, cones of scented wax perched on their heads and slowly dripping down their faces as clouds of expensive perfume wafted around them. Amenia and Mutnedjmet looked almost alike, tall, willowy, and statuesque, images of Isis herself gliding gracefully about the feasting hall, diaphanous white robes shimmering around their slender bodies. Meryt was beautiful too, a little older, a little more serious, a little more… bitter.

Fine jewelry hung heavily on their necks and arms, intricately beaded collar-necklaces, rings and bracelets of solid gold. Their wigs were even longer and more elaborate than the Queen's, their nails were dyed red with henna, and their makeup was superb. Each had brought along her own handmaiden, bustling around her mistress, adjusting her wig, handing her her bronze mirror for a quick touch-up. And under her arm, each carried a small, yippy dog, scrawny little things with light brown fur, large, pointed ears, tiny, pointed noses, jeweled collars, and henna-dyed nails just like their mistresses'.

The ladies had rich husbands.

The Queen smiled at them. "Wonderful to see you ladies." She bit her lip, holding back her pain, then smiled at Meryt's round belly. She had known that they were expecting, but she had not seen the Treasurer's wife since getting the news. "Congratulations," she whispered through dry lips.

"Thank you," Meryt simpered, a dimple showing in her round cheek. She put her arms around her belly, hugging it, and the Queen had to interest herself in a loose thread on her sleeve. "Oh, I do hope it's a boy," Meryt sighed. "Carry on his father's name, grow up to be a big, strong man just like him."

The Queen raised an eyebrow. "You did name your daughter Mayamenti," she pointed out.

Meryt sighed again, looking wistful, almost disappointed. "But it's just not the *same*... I love her so much, but a son like his daddy... That's what every wife wants to give her husband."

Ankhesenamun nodded. Why she was subjecting herself to this, with the tears just under the surface, she wasn't sure. She was the Queen, she could thank them again and excuse herself the moment she chose. But there was something else tugging at her heart. Something else she had to say.

"My mother was Pharaoh after my father died," she said. All three of the ladies swallowed, glancing away at the reference to the Heretic no one was allowed to talk about, nervously playing with their jewelry. "And my oldest sister was Queen alongside her." She gave a little smile. "The politics of gender was not quite as important to my parents."

Amenia looked at her with a hint of discomfort, fiddling with her green-beaded braids. Even their jingling sounded tinny, uneasy. "That was a... unique situation."

The Queen nodded. "It was indeed. And a unique family to handle it." She sighed. "But my point is, being a wife is about more than having sons... about more than giving birth to your husband's children." She smiled at Meryt. "So don't discount your daughter," she said. "She's here, and she's healthy. And she could grow up to be Treasurer... Vizier... Queen... Pharaoh. My mother did."

They looked away, all three of them. And Ankh could sense that this was getting a bit intense. It was... it was getting intense for her, as well. This was a conversation they needed to have, but here, at her brother's birthday party, among a large assortment of guests, was not the time to have it. Another time, another place, would be best. A private party, just for the four of them. That's what she would tell them. That they could continue this conversation over tea sometime, if they wanted to.

But then, Amenia smiled. And so did Mutnedjmet.

"I would like to hear more sometime," she said softly.

"So would I," Mutnedjmet said.

The Queen smiled at them, excitement touching her heart. "Maybe we could have tea sometime."

And they nodded.

Then the topic returned to men. "My husband is the handsomest," Meryt said proudly a minute later, batting her eyelashes at Maya, who was attempting to discuss something important with Vizier Pentu while his frivolous wife distracted him. "Just look at his long nose, his strong chin... We're going to have the handsomest little boy that ever was."

"Yes, if you think a camel is handsome," Mutnedjmet tittered. "*Our* husband is the handsomest," she insisted. "Big, strong soldier, fighting off the barbarians with his great big arms and his strong chest..." She and Amenia sighed adoringly as if they were about to melt onto the floor like the scented wax cones on their heads. "Oh, what do you think he would accomplish if *he* was Pharaoh..."

The Queen blinked. And shook her head. Horemheb *was* technically Tut's Crown Prince, until the day Ankh's brother had a son of his own. But Mutnedjmet was just being silly. Too silly for Ankh to allow herself to be offended.

"Well, maybe you find a bull-neck attractive," Meryt replied, looking down her nose.

"I always thought the Pharaoh reminded me of a cat," Ankh said thoughtfully. "Not in his face, but in his personality. He's not the friendliest person, but if he likes you, he'll go right to you." She smiled. "And I suppose his big, beautiful eyes and his sweet little nose make up for his... teeth." She glanced over at him, where he sat at a table, alone in the crowd, resting his foot and taking a break from conversation.

The ladies just looked at her. No one ever mentioned the Pharaoh's teeth.

"Well," Meryt said after an uncomfortable silence, "when my son is born, he'll be just as handsome as his daddy." And she stroked her round belly. It hit the Queen again, harder this time.

Ankhesenamun sensed that she had done enough consciousness-raising for one day and got up.

"Thank you again for being here," she said sweetly, through the growing lump in her throat. "I'd better check on my husband." Biting back the pain, she walked away from the ladies, looking around at all the other guests, taking in the sights and smells. She had a job to do. And she had a role to play. This was her responsibility as Queen.

But that didn't mean the King didn't see it in her face. He looked up with a smile as she approached, then paused, his own face changing as he saw Meryt. Together they sighed. And he squeezed her hand.

260

Pentu and Usermontu joined the Pharaoh as he sat sipping his favorite white wine from Tribute Day.

"Hiring has begun for the construction of the new schools," Usermontu reported, numerous chins wobbling as he smiled.

Tut returned the smile, carefully avoiding showing his teeth. "Oh, that is good to hear. When do you think the schools will be able to open?"

"Well, we've been doing some calculations," Pentu replied, "and if everything goes as planned, at least two should be able to start classes by next year. As we discussed during the conference, all of them should be open five years from now."

"And they're all to welcome both male and female students," the Pharaoh reiterated.

"Of course, Glorious Lord," Pentu said, inclining his head. "We wouldn't have it any other way. And neither would my sister." He smiled.

Tut smiled back. "Neither would mine." He nodded at both his courtiers. "Thank you, gentlemen. I'm glad to hear that progress is being made."

"You have a great legacy ahead of you, Great Morning Star," Pentu said. "Because age… is no indicator of wisdom, courage, or success." He smiled. "I can't wait to see you get more done in ten years than Pepi the Second did in ninety-four!"

The Pharaoh just chuckled.

"My Lady?" Ankh looked up. Treasurer Maya was raising a hand slightly, trying to get her attention. Putting on a smile, she crossed the room to join him.

"Hello, Treasurer," she said as he bowed… not very deeply. "Thank you for joining us in celebrating the Pharaoh's birthday."

"Wouldn't miss it, My Lady, wouldn't miss it. My Lady…" he said a moment later, "did the Pharaoh happen to tell you about the new directives he passed recently?"

Ankh took a sip of her wine and tried not to roll her eyes. How had Maya managed to forget that Tut had plainly explained that most of the ideas he was presenting were his sister's?

"Yes, he did," she said politely. "I was very proud of him."

Maya sipped his own drink. "Yes, he's lowering taxes, introducing a minimum wage, increasing palace staff, opening new schools… He's even opening a school for ladies. I wonder what they'll teach there…" He tapped his chin. "Well, what do women do all day… sewing? Cooking? Laundry? Taking care of… you know, taking care of babies?"

The Queen bit her tongue to keep from either guffawing out of pure horror or throwing her drink in the Treasurer's face. Or telling him to go jump in the Nile.

"I imagine they'll teach a lot of things, Treasurer," she said calmly. "And I'm sure these schools will make a great difference in the lives of many people. Good day." And she excused herself to go have a good laugh before she threw up.

After the party, Tut and Ankh, tired but glowing, headed outside into the early evening. The royal artist stood there with a large piece of papyrus stretched over a frame, as well as a variety of pens and a supply of ink. Tut had put on his blue crown, as well as a light tunic over his kilt, and had brought out his crook and flail. Time for a picture to commemorate this special birthday.

262

Ankh put on her own crown, then took her place beside him. And Tut planted his feet, trying not to grimace as he placed his weight on the left one. Slowly, he let go of his walking-stick, letting Semerkhet set it aside, handing him his ceremonial crook instead. He didn't mind that in most of his royal portraiture, he was shown with his cane. It was the truth, plain and simple. But it was his birthday. And as Pharaoh, he had the right to be portrayed as he chose. So for just a few pictures, he wanted to be shown standing on his own two feet, no walking-stick in sight.

From where she stood facing him, Ankh reached out and took his left arm in her hands, one hand gently grasping his forearm, and the other nearly under his arm, supporting some of his weight. And she smiled up at him.

Tutankhamun looked down at his sister, her smile, her stance, the way she was physically holding him up. Helping him keep his balance, offering support, helping him to get the portrait that he wanted. In the stories of the gods and goddesses, in the portraits of couples throughout history, the message was the same. Wives supported and protected their husbands. And here was his wife, smiling up at him encouragingly as she planted her own feet, bearing up under the weight he was sharing.

There was nothing to do but smile back in gratitude.

The artist was happy with his sketch, so Tut sat down for a moment, handing his crook and crown to Semerkhet, who replaced the crown with the Pharaoh's favorite wig and a delicate circlet with a tiny golden *uraeus*. As he slipped out of the tunic, choosing to appear bare-chested for the second portrait, Ankh took her jewelry off, also opting for a bit of variety. After handing her his own bracelets to be set aside, Tutankhamun slowly stood up again with the Queen's help.

The artist was quick, but as he stood there, Tut's left foot burned, and it became ever more difficult to keep his balance. But Ankh was there, cradling his left hand in hers, her right arm supporting him.

"You're doing fine," she whispered as sweat began to bead on his forehead, gathering along the edges of the heavy wig. "He's almost got it. This is going to look so good…"

He just gritted his teeth and tried to smile.

"And… we're finished, Your Majesties," the artist said just as Tut's legs were starting to shake properly. Nodding emphatically at Semerkhet, Ankh got both hands under Tut's arms, and very, very lightly, he rested his hands on her shoulders. Not to make her bear any more of his weight; just to keep his balance.

Semerkhet flew over to the fig tree where the Pharaoh's walking-stick was leaning. A moment later, Tut had it firmly in his hand, and was bent over it like an old man, left foot sighing in relief as he was finally able to take the weight off of it.

"Fank you," he whispered, catching his breath and standing straight again. He was still the Pharaoh, after all. Even after such a long day. And he still had to look as regal as he could.

The artist just bowed, and with a wish for life, prosperity, and health, he was gone, off to take his sketches and turn them into a painting, a carving, or a pair of statues. Vaguely, Tut wondered what medium would be used.

Then a pair of warm arms were around his waist, and Ankh's wig was tickling his chin. "Good job," she whispered.

"You did all the hard work," he whispered back gratefully.

She just popped up onto her tiptoes and kissed him.

264

Tut leaned his head on Ankh's shoulder as they sat together on the bed that evening, sorting through a few of the presents he had received today. Among them was a lovely matching ring and necklace, but the best gift was possibly the fact that no one had given him a cane. Or a giraffe, like he had sent off to a new home among the Mitanni or the Hittites. Another precious gift, of course, was the enormous bouquet of flowers that his sister had prepared for him, its sweet fragrance and bright colors sure to cheer up even the most stressful week ahead. Still another gift, apparently from the gods, had been that his foot had hardly hurt at all today, except for those few minutes he'd spent standing without his cane, and that the day had not been unreasonably hot. He was still exhausted, though, from all the people, all the noise, and he was rather glad that the party was over.

"I think we can trust him," he said, remembering the Vizier's stunning proclamation. "I really think we can. Did you hear what he said? I'm standing alone now. He's not going to be interfering anymore, telling me what to do, getting in my way. It's going to be all me... all us."

Ankh sighed, gently stroking his wig. Sometimes she was his wife, and sometimes she was his big sister. "I just... just don't know, love. Even this... It could still be a ruse. Trying to get you to trust him. I've seen it before in Mother and Father's court... That's politics. Next he'll try to get you to do something risky, see if he can still control you. Might even emphasize how it's all your decision, now you're grown up, but he'll give you some sort of suggestion." She paused, still stroking his head. "And you're going to have to decide what to do."

265

He nestled into her side, enjoying the feel of her warm fingers running through his wig, over his forehead. It was still too warm to really snuggle, but that felt nice. "I'll be careful. And whatever he says, I won't be rash. I'll take the time to think about it, and we can discuss it together before I decide anything." He smiled and closed his eyes, feeling like Bastet being petted. "We'll be fine."

Something good had come out of the party, Ankh thought, trying to set aside what the Vizier had said. There was nothing to do about it until the next day. But Amenia and Mutnedjmet had told her that they wanted to hear more about her perspective on womanhood. She would have them over for tea very soon.

Meryt hadn't seemed as enthusiastic. But the Queen would invite her too. And she would hope that she could make a difference in all three of their lives.

The Queen was proud of them, Amenia, Mutnedjmet. And she was excited to share with them what she herself had learned. And in her mind, she began to prepare what she wanted to share with them.

While she chuckled to herself. Because she remembered what the Treasurer had said, explaining her own policies to her, quite poorly.

What would Mother say?

She'd tell her daughter to pay him no mind. That his opinion was not worth her spending any time or emotion on.

Ankh smiled. And she let it go.

His wife was wise, the Pharaoh reflected. No matter what happened, she seemed to know what to do, drawing on her greater experience, greater wisdom, and the knowledge passed down to her by her mother and grandmother. As Akhenaten had focused on his faith with Nefertiti as his co-regent, his mother, Queen Tiye, had focused on politics, the dowager Queen making at least some effort to keep up friendly relations with their neighbors. Alongside her husband, Tut's grandfather Amenhotep the Third, Queen Tiye had been very much like Ankhesenamun, wise advisor and confidant to her Pharaoh husband, an active politician in her own right, the power beside the throne.

He smiled as he thought about the great change that the day had brought. Ay was no longer regent. The world was ahead of him.

The noose was definitely in place, Ankhesenamun thought as she got ready for bed after the party. Ay had made the move she had expected, tempting Tut into trusting him by offering what looked like the gift of sole power.

But was the gift poisoned?

She shook her head. Time was moving forward, each decision they or the Vizier made altering the course of the future. There was no telling what would happen. But she promised herself that she would carry all her political skill with her, wherever this strange future might lead them.

24   Taking Responsibility

The next morning, things were different. Ay was no longer regent, so that meant that Tut had to do everything himself. That meant conducting the morning meetings, welcoming local leaders, members of his government, and envoys from neighboring nations to see what the Pharaoh could do for them.

That also meant wearing all his finery. He sat in the throne room, crook and flail held crossed over his chest, false beard of magnificence attached to his chin, his whole body weighed down by his double crown and jewelry. He had to look royal, after all.

"O Mighty Pharaoh," a Mitanni nobleman begged from where he lay prostrated on the floor before the god-king, "please send Egyptian troops to Kadesh and protect us from the Hittites. As he pushes his borders south, King Suppiluliuma threatens to take us over completely. In the days of your father we asked Egypt for help, and received none— now our plight is worse than ever; we have lost a great deal of land and fear for our future. We lay no claim to Kadesh, but if the Hittites retain control of it, we fear they will destroy us. You approached us in friendship… Now we ask for your protection."

The envoy swallowed. Then he continued. "The people of Amurru need you, too. Their land lies between the kingdoms of Mitanni, Egypt, and Hattusa. They keep to themselves and pay tribute to those in power even as borders change— they were loyal to your father before the Hittites took their lands from Egypt— but the longer this conflict lasts, the harder it will be on them. Their home has become a battleground. So it for their sake also, Mighty Pharaoh, that I beg the help of Egypt. All that they want is the opportunity to pay taxes to a strong Pharaoh who will protect them from the fury of the Hittites."

He could help, Tut thought. With their superior armed forces, Egypt could save the Mitanni and the people of Amurru from the Hittites. And with so many innocent lives at stake, how could he justify doing anything else? As Pharaoh, the opportunity was suddenly in his hands to save them all.

He smiled. Would that be his legacy, using the strength of Egypt to save her neighbors from their common enemy, preventing that same enemy from threatening Egypt herself, and who knew what other parts of the world?

He thought of the people of his own country, his own capital city, of the poverty and ignorance all around him, which he had promised himself he would fight til his dying breath. The Mitanni and the citizens of Amurru were people too. And if he could relieve some of their suffering, like he was relieving that of his own people, wasn't that the right thing to do?

He couldn't do nothing.

For a future of peace... he was going to have to condone a war. But after the war, that peace would be established. And everyone could live safe and free, able to pursue the lives they wanted to live in prosperity and security. He couldn't justify not getting involved, not helping. The future of the world might depend on it.

Tutankhamun nodded very slightly, careful to keep his double crown from falling off his head. It was the right thing to do. It had to be.

"General Horemheb will support your army with his," the Pharaoh promised. "He visited your lands quite recently, did he not?"

"We were honored to receive him in peace," the envoy responded. "But now… now we ask for his help in battle."

The Pharaoh nodded. "We will take Kadesh back." He paused. "I am not my father. Whatever he did, or did not do… as I now stand as Pharaoh, I will use the might of Egypt to protect your people and free your lands, and the land of Amurru, from our common enemy."

The ambassador slowly rose, keeping his eyes carefully averted. Now that he was upright, Tut could get a better look at his dark beard, his olive skin, his pointed cap, his long white robe with its red accents. He was a human being. And so was the Pharaoh.

As the envoy left, offering a "hail to thee, Lord of the Two Lands" and the traditional wishes for life, prosperity, and health, Tut felt a twinge of uncertainty in the pit of his stomach. Should he really be sending Egyptian troops to Kadesh? Was that really the decision of the King of peace?

But such an act would protect the Mitanni and the people of Amurru, he told himself. They needed Egypt's help. And as Pharaoh, he could offer it.

Then the foreman of one of the school-building projects arrived for the approval of the shipment of the necessary limestone from the quarry at Kurna, and a royal architect with questions about the expansion of the staff quarters to account for the influx of new gardeners and cooks. Tut signed documents and offered counsel, acting like a Pharaoh for the first time in his life.

It was a little hard to hear some of the requests, however, since most of the visitors spent so much of their meeting time on their faces before him. And, of course, every time one of the petitioners left, he heard the words, "Hail to thee, Lord of the Two Lands; all life, prosperity, and health!"

By the time the morning ended, he was exhausted. But satisfied. Because he was doing it. Being Pharaoh. And so far, halfway into the first day, it was going all right.

Tut sat at lunch, enjoying his meal of roast goose, fresh cheese, a cup of *mai-sus*, and two kinds of figs. He could truly enjoy it because he knew it was safe, Semerkhet had confirmed that no one had slipped poison into it. And he could enjoy it because, now that the morning's meetings were over, he had been allowed to take off his heavy jewelry and his double crown, exchanging them for his favorite pendant necklace and a simple circlet.

On the other side of the royal feasting hall, Ay and Nakhtmin were eating together. Kilt season was over, and Tut was quite pleased to be wearing a long-sleeved linen tunic. Not quite cool enough for an outer robe yet, but the hottest part of the year was behind them. As delicious as the *mai-sus* was, he knew that its season was almost over; it was a cold drink for hot days. Soon it would be time for cups of chamomile and peppermint tea, warm drinks for cold days.

A young female servant was silently pouring a drink for Nakhtmin, refilling his cup with red wine. He looked up from drawling a story to his father and a disgusted grimace came over his face.

"What's the matter with you? I wanted white wine! Didn't you see I had white wine? Are you blind, or just stupid?"

Recoiling, she jogged the serving vessel, splashing red wine over her dress— and Nakhtmin's fine white tunic.

"You clumsy little camel!" he roared, grabbing her arm. His angry face had gone as red as the wine. She squealed, struggling to cover her head as he raised his other hand to strike her. He dropped the cup and she dropped the serving vessel. Wine went everywhere.

The other servants stopped what they were doing, but no one spoke. No one moved.

The Pharaoh stood up, a hand on the table. "What is going on here?" he asked in his loud, impressive proclamation voice. Pain shot through his foot as he suddenly put too much weight on it, but he ignored it.

Nakhtmin dropped the servant's arm. Sobbing, she took shelter in a corner of the feasting hall, where an older kitchen maid comforted her.

"That little fool started by pouring me the wrong wine, and then she dumped it all over my new tunic!" Nakhtmin spat viciously. "I'll have her beaten."

"No." Tutankhamun raised a hand, dark eyes flashing dangerously, eyebrows lowering like stormclouds.

"No?" Nakhtmin asked incredulously, lip curling.

"No," Tut repeated calmly. He paused. "Did she pour you the wrong wine out of spite?"

"Out of stupidity is more like," Nakhtmin replied.

"And did she splash wine on your tunic intentionally? Or maliciously?"

"No…" Nakhtmin said slowly.

Tut shook his head. "I saw her make an honest mistake and then respond in fear to your raised voice. I did not see her do anything deserving of punishment." Tut paused. "And she is my servant, under my authority, and therefore my protection. I, and I alone, will decide how, and when, she is to be disciplined."

Nakhtmin looked bitterly at the King. Tutankhamun regarded him calmly, refusing to drop his gaze first. Calmly, but with eyes

272

of lightning and eyebrows of thunder. The Vizier had risen to his feet, but stood saying nothing, face unreadable. Finally Nakhtmin looked away, face twisting in an ugly sneer.

"Excuse me," he said, and strode out of the hall, wine-stained tunic billowing behind him. Ay followed him. Meanwhile, three other servants had silently appeared, beginning to clean up the mess as those who had paused in horrified silence returned to their work.

Tut sank back down, wincing. Jumping to his feet like that was painful, and wobbly. After giving himself a moment, he grabbed his cane, got to his feet again, a bit more carefully this time, and walked over to where the young woman was still crying, cowering in the refuge of the corner. Semerkhet followed him.

"What's your name?" he asked softly. His eyes, his face, were gentle now, the storm passing as the sun began to shine through the clouds. Softly, he smiled.

"Sh-Shepset, Master," she stammered, wiping away her tears and straightening her lopsided wig. Tut could see that she was just a little older than the Queen. She kept her distance, chin tucked so she wouldn't make eye contact with the Morning and the Evening Star. But at least she hadn't thrown herself facedown on the floor before him.

The older maid backed away, giving the Pharaoh a semi-private audience with the young woman. The three servants who had come to clean up the spilled wine had silently disappeared with their handfuls of wine-soaked rags.

"Shepset," he said gently, "please look at me. It's all right."

The woman gulped, then slowly turned her tear-streaked face to him, cautiously meeting his eye. Dislodged by her tears, her eyeliner was running all over her face.

The Pharaoh gave her the same encouraging smile she had missed a moment ago. Still overcome by shock, Shepset continued staring back at him. "I'm sorry he shouted at you. I saw what happened, and it wasn't your fault. Is your arm all right?"

Shepset glanced at her arm. Tut nodded at Semerkhet.

"May I?" Semerkhet asked her. She nodded. Very gently Semerkhet touched her arm, inspecting the damage. Tut peered over his shoulder. There was no scratch, only the possibility of slight bruising. Her dress was ruined; the wine had turned almost half of it a dull pink. Such a stain might be even beyond Khenut's skill to clean.

"Doesn't look too bad," the King said, giving her a reassuring smile, which was returned with a very watery one as she wiped her eyes. "Just maybe a little bruise." Tut swallowed with a solemn sigh. "You're my servant, not his," he said, "and that means you're my responsibility. So I get to take care of you. Keep you safe. And it's my honor. But I'm not doing a very good job, and I'm sorry. I'll do better, I promise."

She stared at him with tear-filled eyes, not knowing what to say. Finally she stammered, "It's all right, M-my Lord. Th-thank you."

"You're welcome," he said with a smile. He did not hide his teeth from her. "And I want to thank you all…" He looked from Shepset's face to that of the older kitchen maid, who stood silently listening, "for everything you do. We couldn't run the palace without you."

274

"It's m-my honor, Your M-majesty," she stuttered. And after dropping to her knees to clasp her hands and bow her forehead to the floor, she got up and staggered away.

Tut watched her go. Today he had made something right.

Ankhesenamun sat before her mirror, letting Meresankh touch up her makeup and restyle her wig before the afternoon began. As she worked, accepting first the makeup palette and then the wig comb from her assistant Tia, the handmaiden regaled her Mistress with stories of life among the palace staff.

"So Ramose told Menhet that Neferkare was flirting with Hemetre; that's the nanny of Lady Meryt's daughter, of course, and Menhet said that first of all, that was none of his business, but that secondly, she knew for a fact that Hemetre would rather be bitten by a cobra than let Neferkare get within arms' length of her, which is unfair, really, because everyone says it's General Nakhtmin, Neferkare's Master, of course, who's an unpleasant little—"

The Queen cleared her throat. "Meresankh?"

And her handmaiden paused, biting her tongue. "I'm sorry to gossip, My Lady," she mumbled, then turned as if to get something.

Gently, Ankh caught her hand. "It's all right," she said with a smile. "I love your stories. But all good stories…" She chuckled, and finally Meresankh returned the smile. "…have a beginning, a middle, and an ending."

Meresankh laughed. "Yes, My Lady." And with a curtsy, she went to put away the Queen's makeup.

Tutankhamun chuckled to himself as he sat reading in his room, taking a bit of a break after lunch. He had done it. Because as he compared how he had handled Nakhtmin's behavior today as compared with the big mess that had erupted in his defense of Semerkhet earlier in the season, he could see how far he had come. And he was proud of himself. Horemheb had been right. He could use his righteous anger to create positive change, rather than letting it explode into something everyone would regret. And practice made perfect.

He chuckled again. Looking at it another way... that truly had been good practice— for making decisions for the sake of his country. Tut smiled. He had handled that episode like a Pharaoh.

25   Education

Ankhesenamun looked up from the poem she'd just finished reading out loud. They had come to visit her,
Mutnedjmet and Amenia and Meryt, and they were
lounging comfortably in her private sitting room,
snacking on dates, figs, tiger-nut sweets, and almonds while the
silent handmaidens they had brought along with them kept the
warm, still air moving with fluffy ostrich-feather fans. It had been
a tiny bit awkward, as always, for them to walk through her royal
bedroom to get to the sitting room, but that was the way the suite
was arranged. And Ankh didn't mind letting her guests see her
room.

The Queen enjoyed a quiet afternoon alone with her brother, her
handmaiden. But she also enjoyed some more company now and
then. And when she felt like seeing different faces, she would
invite certain acquaintances over for tea.

But this wasn't just any tea party. This was the continuation of
the visit that had begun at the Pharaoh's birthday party. And Ankh
wondered if they would return to the subject they had been
discussing… and what she could teach them today.

As usual, all three of them were wearing a little too much
makeup and perfume, their fine linen dresses just a little too tight, a
little too revealing. In the corner, Ashait, the blind harpist, was
serenading them, nimble fingers finding each note with ease, even
though she would never see the strings she was playing. Three tiny
little dogs were sniffing around the sitting room, occasionally
tussling with one another or trying to get into something they

shouldn't. Their red nails clicked on the floor as they roamed restlessly, their jeweled collars glittering in the torchlight.

Meryt sighed and shifted in her chair; she was bigger than ever.

"He's moving," she said, smiling proudly. Ankh gritted her teeth.

"He?" she asked. "Can you tell?"

"Of course he'll be a boy," Meryt said, cradling her curve protectively. "His daddy needs an heir."

"He already has a namesake," Ankh pointed out. "Mayamenti. 'Her father endures'."

Meryt just sighed.

From a neighboring room of the palace came a sudden loud, hollow thump. A servant somewhere had dropped something. All three dogs went mad, galloping over to the door with a scrabble of manicured claws on the polished floor and jumping up, tiny little paws to the door, barking at the top of their tiny, high-pitched voices.

"Blossom! Stop it!" Mutnedjmet squealed, her sharp voice drowning out the yips and yaps of the tiny dogs.

"Bitsy! That's enough!"

"Poppy! Shut up!"

Finally they gave it up, giving angry little snorts before returning to stand under the table and wait. The startled Ashait, who had paused in her playing when the dogs lost it, resumed her song. And the surprised handmaidens carried on gently moving the air with their feathery fans.

Those dogs were exactly like their mistresses, the Queen thought. Or was it the other way around?

"Did we want to continue our conversation from the Pharaoh's birthday?" Amenia asked softly after silence had settled again.

278

"Yes," Mutnedjmet said, sitting up straighter. "We want to hear more."

The Queen smiled. They had been the ones to bring it up. They really cared. Then she swallowed. It was a heavy subject, after all. But here, in the privacy of her sitting room, they could speak freely, and could be as vulnerable as they chose to be.

Might as well slip right in, she thought. "Well, as I was saying, I believe that being a wife is about more than giving your husband an heir." She glanced down at her own flat stomach, then looked up at them again. "And being a woman is about more than being a wife."

Mutnedjmet gave a sad little smile. She, too, had lost two children at birth.

"But being the mother of the firstborn son is an honor like no other," Meryt said, stroking her stomach smugly.

Ankhesenamun shook her head with a little smile. Here, in the privacy of her own sitting room, she had also given herself permission to speak freely. If it got deep, and they needed them, she had plenty of handkerchiefs. She swallowed, considering how direct to be. Then she decided.

"You make it sound like you're afraid your husband won't love you anymore if you don't have a boy."

The three just stared at her.

"We have suffered great loss," she said softly, "but that doesn't mean we aren't still standing together, side by side. We're partners for life, through all the joys and sorrows, helping one another in every way we can, no matter what happens. We're a team."

Then Amenia sighed. "It's all I ever wanted… to bear my husband a son."

"And I hope you will, one day," Ankhesenamun said with a gentle smile. "But I hope even more that you can see who you are outside of being a mother, outside of being a wife."

Meryt popped a grape into her mouth. "You make it sound like you don't like being married."

Ankh shook her head. "I'm very glad to be married. I'm very glad to be standing beside my husband, helping him as much as I can with what I know, what I remember from our parents' time on the throne."

Amenia stared. "You tell him what to do?"

Ankhesenamun chuckled. "I am his big sister, after all. And he appreciates it. He knows I know more about politics than he does, and he wants my guidance. So I'm very glad to be married, but it doesn't define every element of who I am. I have my own interests, my own concerns, my own ideas. And so does he. Being his wife is not the sum total of who I am. And being my husband is not the sum total of who he is."

Mutnedjmet and Amenia looked at her in silence. And then they smiled.

But there was more to ask. More to talk about. And boldly, Ankh moved on to the next subtopic she had planned.

"So what do your husbands do all day?" she asked.

Three birdlike little voices chorused in a single word. "Work."

The Queen raised an eyebrow. "Work. That's it? You mean they don't talk about it, don't share what they do, don't ask your advice?"

Amenia shrugged. "Why would they? All a man wants after a long day is to be looked after." She smiled, leaning forward slightly, lowering her blue-painted eyelids alluringly. Ankh tried not to blush at how much cleavage she was showing. "If you know what I mean."

Ankh shook her head with a little chuckle. "Well, that's all well and good, but there's so much more to marriage when you work together."

"But what could there even be that we could work on together?" Mutnedjmet asked, looking up with a careless shrug. "We don't talk about work because I couldn't understand… I'm a woman, and he's a big, smart man."

Ankhesenamun looked at her in no small amount of horror. "Excuse me?" This was unacceptable. *I wish my mother was here,* the Queen thought. *She could slap some sense into you. Well, I'll do it.*

She fixed Mutnedjmet and the others with a firm gaze. "Listen here, sister. If I'm smart enough to come up with brand new laws, and I am, because I have, you're smart enough to understand how the government functions. Sit down and I will explain the government to you." She cleared her throat. "It's like the ripples created by a flower falling into one of the pools outside…"

And just as she had described it to her brother, the Queen explained to the ladies how the bureaucracy in Thebes and Memphis kept the rest of Egypt wealthy and strong, and how Egypt herself had her place among all the nations of the world. They stared.

"…so that's what your husbands do all day," she finished. "They have their own part to play in the ripples that extend from the palace out to the edges of the world."

Amenia sighed, picking up her tiny dog and petting it. "You seem to know more about what our husbands do than we do. And

I'm still not sure how we can find anything to talk about. Their work and what we do at home are so different."

Ankhesenamun shrugged. "There are lots of things. Ask him about his day, ask if there are any issues he's still working on, and if you have any ideas, tell him."

"Men don't want ideas," Meryt said, stroking her stomach. "Men want love. They're tired when they come home, and they just want to relax... they don't want to debate politics."

Ankh shook her head, blue beads jingling under her gleaming diadem. "Maybe it's because we're also siblings, but the Pharaoh and I have always shared ideas. And we're both richer for it."

"I don't know why you bother," Mutnedjmet said with a careless sigh. "You've got it all, you don't need anything else. What higher status could there possibly be than Great Royal Wife?" She smiled smugly, running her fingers through the braids of her heavy wig, golden beads tinkling luxuriously. "I'm the wife of the General, and that makes me very happy."

Ankh looked at her. "But do you see him every day?"

Mutnedjmet looked down with a little sigh. "No... He's... busy. Very, very busy."

The Queen raised an eyebrow. "Must be, if he never comes home. Maybe a little *too* busy."

"He usually sleeps in the barracks," Amenia explained. "But when he comes home, we make him *very* happy." Her posture changed, and the tightness of her dress became even more unbearable.

"I'm sure you do," Ankh said, keeping her eyes on Amenia's face.

Then Mutnedjmet sighed again. "At least you see your husband every day."

282

Ankh swallowed. She knew that Amenia and Mutnedjmet were little more than pretty trophies claimed by the General.

"But when my son is born," Meryt said with a wistful sigh, "Maya won't be so busy. He'll come home and watch his little boy grow up. Our son will be the greatest athlete of his generation… He'll race horses, play hockey, lift weights, throw the javelin… And his Daddy will come to all his competitions. And he'll be so proud."

"But Meryt," Ankh said softly, "what if it's a girl?"

The wife of the Treasurer crossed her arms over her stomach, protecting the child inside from even hearing that it might not be a boy. She shook her head. "He's a boy. You'll see."

"But what if?" Ankh asked.

Meryt shook her head again. "He won't be."

Ankhesenamun got up and popped an almond into her mouth. Under the small, glass-inlaid table where the snacks were arranged in delicate little terracotta bowls, Meryt and Mutnedjmet's dogs were sitting silently at attention, ears up, just waiting for a crumb to fall.

The Queen sighed. Meryt had a few months yet for her mind to be opened to the possibility of delivering another daughter.

"It's a woman's job, Your Majesty," Meryt said, as if it was obvious. "To give her husband sons."

Ankh shook her head, fighting back a sudden flare of anger. Was Meryt seriously suggesting that in not yet having given birth to a healthy heir, she had not yet done her job? She released a deep breath. The Treasurer's wife didn't know any better yet, but today, she would learn. Ankh would teach her.

The Queen gave a little smile as she continued. "Maybe… but there's so much more to it. More to marriage… and more to life. Having children is an important part of life… but it's not all you can do."

"Makes me feel like a failure," Mutnedjmet said softly. Ankh turned to her, resisting the urge to throw her arms around her. She shook her head, beaded braids tinkling as they swayed. "Like I'm a disappointment to him."

"No, no," Ankh whispered. "Don't ever say that. You're not a failure… and neither am I."

Both looked down at Ankhesenamun's flat stomach. "Yes, Your Majesty."

"If there's one thing I've learned," the Queen said, "it's that there's more to being a woman, more to being a wife, than giving your husband sons."

She and Mutnedjmet shared a sad smile.

"You're his partner in life," the Queen said. "The good, the bad, going through it all side by side. And that's true whether you have ten children or none… in this world."

Horemheb's wife nodded. And she gave a tiny smile.

The Queen looked at the wife of the Treasurer. "I just want to say…" she said to Meryt, "that boy or girl, your child could grow up to be anything. And your daughter could grow up to be anything. Every child is born with unlimited potential, and every child should have the opportunity to grow up to be anything they choose. Your daughter is blessed not to have any financial limitations… She could receive any education you choose to give her, follow in her father's footsteps to be Treasurer herself." Ankh swallowed. "Mayamenti has so many opportunities that the children who live on the streets of Thebes and Memphis could only dream of. So don't limit her. I hope she'll go to one of the new schools when they open."

The wife of the Treasurer just closed her eyes with a sigh.

Mutnedjmet gave a deep sigh of her own.

"I don't..." she said slowly, "don't think I'm as happy as I thought I was."

Amenia fiddled with her ornate necklace, nodding at her husband's other wife. "I don't think so either," she agreed. "Because now... I see what's missing. Being friends with Horemheb."

Mutnedjmet looked down, and Amenia squeezed her hand. "And seeing..." Her voice broke. "Seeing myself as more. Everything I could be."

"Everything you will be," Ankhesenamun said warmly, smiling at her friend. "Everything you already are."

And Mutnedjmet smiled back.

Before long they were ready to go, getting up and gathering their things, tiny little dogs held carefully under their arms. Their servants took their fans, ready to follow their mistresses. "It was lovely to see you all," Ankh said, standing up as well.

All three bowed deeply to the Queen. So did their servants.

"Always an honor to be invited," Mutnedjmet said, eyes flickering to Ankhesenamun's face as she gave her a little smile.

"C... could we come back sometime?" Amenia asked. "There's so much we want to ask you."

Warmth rose in the Queen's heart as she smiled at them. "Of course. I would be delighted."

Meryt didn't say anything. Just offered a nod.

And all three of the ladies were gone. Ankh smiled as she watched them go, followed by their bustling servants, fans in hand. Amenia and Mutnedjmet were going to come back, she thought with a smile. She was excited about what she would be able to teach them.

But she wondered about Meryt.

"Day one done," Ankh heard. Her guests had gone, and she was sitting alone in her sitting room, sipping a cup of chamomile tea. And now the soft tapping of a familiar walking-stick was sounding in the doorway.

She looked up as her brother came into the room, bent wearily over his cane but glowing. The Queen got up, setting her teacup aside, and walked into his arms, gently putting her arms around him. He put his free arm around her, holding her to his heart.

"How'd it go?" she asked into his shoulder.

She felt him shrug. "Satisfactory," he said finally. Gently he pulled away, and she looked up into his face, which was tired but proud. "I think we can do this, Ankh."

The Queen squeezed his hand. "*You* can do this." And popping up onto her tiptoes, she pecked him on the cheek. "My dear Pharaoh."

He just smiled. And she smiled. Slowly but surely, his confidence in himself was growing, just as surely as his wisdom.

"Got you something," she said with a smile.

He looked at her. "Hmm?"

Crossing to her dressing-table, Ankh picked up a bouquet of lotus flowers and presented them with a flourish. "My Pharaoh," she said with a smile.

With his free hand, Tut accepted the flowers with a smile of his own. "Thank you, love," he said, bending his head to inhale the sweet fragrance. "Almost as pretty as you." And she stepped closer, into his arms. The sweetness of the flowers was almost as sweet as their love for one another.

What a big day it had been. Tut slipped into bed after his shower, Bastet curled up warmly under one of his arms. And he was proud of himself. His first day standing alone as Pharaoh. And he had done well for himself.

He smiled. Another day lay ahead of him. And he wondered what it would bring.

His sister was right. He could do it.

Tut ran his meetings every morning; met with dignitaries, businessmen and women, architects, and merchants who brought ideas, problems, and questions.

But with his newfound responsibility and authority came a new reliance by the staff. And they began asking him the questions they might once have asked the Vizier.

"My Lord, what side dishes do you want with tonight's roast gazelle?"

"Son of Ra, are you satisfied with the condition of the royal chariots?"

"Great Morning Star, did you by any chance want to commission any new jewelry?"

"Glorious Lord, what do you think of the garden this season?"

There were so many questions, in fact, that Semerkhet began fielding them for him without being asked. He would walk with the

Pharaoh to and from meals, scaring off staff members with innocent questions and sending them scurrying away. "The Pharaoh is busy," he would say rather coldly, stepping slightly between Tut and the hopeful enquirer. "If you have a formal question, you can bring it to tomorrow morning's audience."

So much that Tut had to turn to him and say,

"Sem, it's all right. It's my job to answer their questions. I appreciate the fact that you don't want me to get sidetracked, but it's all right. I don't mind."

And unwillingly, the valet stepped back and let the questions rage.

26 History

"Tell me a story, Ankh," Tut said one cool afternoon. He had another headache, and he was not up for a third game of *seega*.

"All right." She stroked his head, and he moved a bit on the couch so his hands wouldn't fall asleep as he lay there with his head in her lap. "Let's see…" She smiled. "What about the Mystery of the Hebrews?"

Tut smiled too. That was one of his favorites. And it was a mystery that had never been solved. He closed his eyes and got comfortable.

Ankh cleared her throat and began the familiar story. "The Hebrews… They destroyed our grandfather's Egypt from the inside out. Their God, I-AM, sent ten plagues, so it was said, and killed Uncle Thutmose, who was the Crown Prince. Father was called Prince Amenhotep then, of course. But what happened with the Hebrews… was only whispered," Ankh said, "and was never preserved in any of the official records. The story goes that the adopted son of Hatshepsut had murdered someone. Then he had run away and gone missing. He was gone forty years; everyone thought he was dead. But he'd gone to Midian and turned into a shepherd. Apparently the Prince got converted to some crazy desert nomad religion and got convinced that the God of the crazy desert nomads wanted the slaves freed. And with what happened next…" Ankhesenamun shuddered. "All of Egypt wondered if he had truly found something out there.

"Father saw it all," Ankh said. "Saw the Prince come back and turn his walking-stick into a snake. Saw the Nile turn to blood, saw the fiery hail, the days of darkness like being blind, the hordes of insects, saw his big brother die on the night that every firstborn son died. And when he grew up and became Pharaoh, he changed his name to Akhenaten to honor this strange desert God Who had been powerful enough to tank the economy of the greatest nation on earth. Father said He was the Lord of Light, and he called Him the Aten. And Egypt called our father a heretic."

Tut remembered his father telling him and Ankh and Meritaten those stories in a whisper, looking up so the priests wouldn't hear him telling it to his children. Though this Lord had killed his brother, Akhenaten felt that He had made him Pharaoh for a reason, and he had to honor the Aten above all other gods, finally forbidding the worship of any god other than the Lord of Light.

"He felt like we did," Ankh continued, giving a little shiver despite the warmth of the day. Her beads jingled. "Like we felt... the night the sickness came. He felt like that... on the night that he said that the Angel of Death came."

Tut shuddered. He remembered. And he thought of his father as a little boy, losing his big brother on that terrible night just like he had lost his big sisters. And he wondered... what was true.

"And we remember Grandmother's stories, too," Tut said.

His sister smiled. "Mm-hmm. She was Father's mother, of course, and she remembered even more than he did. She couldn't explain what had happened, but she remembered. She always told us that she didn't... didn't know why Uncle Thutmose had died, but she knew that something, Someone, powerful was at work."

Ankh sighed, looking far away, back into the stories her father and grandmother had told her. Slowly, steadily, her tiny, warm hand continued to stroke her brother's aching head. "In any case, Egypt never saw the Hebrews again. Or the army that Grandfather sent after them. Not a single soldier came home. And all the rescue party that followed their trail a week later found was broken bits of chariots washed up on the shore of the sea on the eastern border. No one could ever swim that sea. But the search party found no sign of the Hebrews. Nothing. And they didn't find any soldiers who could tell them what had happened." Ankh shook her head. "Six hundred chariots," she said, snapping her fingers. "Gone like that."

"They hated him for what happened, didn't they?" Tut asked. "Hated our father for what happened."

She nodded with a sad sigh. "Yes. A generation after all those strange things happened, when he started changing things… all of Egypt came to hate him. And they called him a heretic for saying that Egypt had been wrong about everything, that the God of this wayward Prince was not only the greatest, but the only One."

"What do you remember?" Tutankhamun asked his sister.

"I don't…" she said slowly, "really remember much of it myself, but Mother and Meritaten told me what it was like. And I can hardly imagine. The priests didn't get to take care of the statues in the temples anymore, to keep the actual gods and goddesses happy. Father took the statues away, and the ones he didn't take, the priests hid. He said that all the images and statues were idols. And he had the statues destroyed, and the names of the gods hacked out of inscriptions, even if the men he sent had to climb all the way to the top of an obelisk to erase a name. He didn't even want to see the word 'gods,' because there was only one God."

"What about the birthdays of the gods, if he didn't believe in them?" Tutankhamun asked.

Ankh shook her head. "All the festivals were canceled. That was the way we had kept track of the year for centuries. And he took it away. The Opening of the Year, the birthdays of the gods, the Hathor Festival, the Opet Festival. No more celebrations, no more ceremonies that let us all know that we were forgiven of our sins. Father said that the Aten would offer forgiveness now. And he changed his name to Akhenaten, 'Effective for Aten,' because even referring to Amun in his name was idol-worship."

"So what about the old temples, the traditional ones?" Tut asked. "And the priests?"

"He fired the priests," Ankh said, shaking her head with a confused little rattle of beads. "All of them. Even when the priesthood had been in the family for generations. Everything that made life make sense was disappearing before our eyes. All for the Aten. To keep Him from sending ten more plagues to punish Egypt again for not turning to Him. Father was going to turn all of Egypt to the worship of the Aten to keep them safe from His wrath... whether the people liked it or not.

"He built a new city," Ankh said. "Akhetaten. And he filled it with temples to the Aten. And we all lived there. And Tasherit and Rure and Setepenre and you were born there."

"Did anyone go with them?" Tutankhamun asked his sister. "To the new city?"

"A lot of people did, actually," she said. "There were a lot of courtiers and servants who believed he was right. But for most of Egypt... it was... it was a religious civil war, and the people were caught in the middle. And they didn't know what to do. Father had told them that everything they had believed was wrong, but he

292

hadn't replaced the old forms of worship with something new, something they could participate in. He didn't start a community priesthood to the Aten, or tell the people what sacrifices to make and how. Just promised them that he and Mother were praying for them, and that everything would be all right. To trust... and be grateful. And nothing else."

"How did the people feel about that?" the Pharaoh asked his sister.

The Queen sighed. "For so long, the people had worked for the gods, had fed them, bathed them, played music to them, and that was their way of being sure of a good future. If they gave the gods what they demanded, the gods would answer their prayers. And now here was a God Who demanded nothing. And there was nothing they could do to please Him, and to make sure that He gave them what they asked for.

"It was all so strange," she said with a shudder. "Nothing made sense anymore. It was as if... either he was crazy... or he was right."

"What do you think?" Tut whispered.

Ankhesenamun shook her head, beads jingling. "Meritaten believed. So did Tasherit and Meketaten. Rure and Setepenre were too little to understand. But I..." She swallowed. "I was never sure."

"And neither am I," Tut said earnestly. He and his sister shared a look. A look that wondered who was right. And what was true. But there was no answer.

"I do wonder, though, what it all meant," Ankh said softly. "I remember the day that the Sun disappeared. You remember that, don't you?"

Tut nodded. "Mm-hmm." He shuddered at the memory. "Strangest thing I ever saw. Like something... like something was covering the Sun. And I never..." Tut swallowed. "Never heard Father sound like that."

Ankh sighed. "Father thought that the Aten was hiding Himself from him, even though he'd tried so hard to honor Him, because He was angry that some people in Egypt were still worshiping idols."

Tut shook his head with a sigh. He still did not understand the event that had followed their sisters' deaths. No one really understood it.

"The Sun just disappeared," his sister repeated simply. "Right in the middle of the day. The way... the way that Father believed the Aten revealed Himself, gone. Just gone. Without warning. And no one knew if or when it would come back."

Tutankhamun shook his head. "I remember you kneeling down to hold me and keep me inside... and Father ran by, and I could just see him, kneeling there in the courtyard and crying. I hadn't heard him cry since the sickness came."

Ankh remembered her father screaming at the sky. "And he said, 'Why do You hide Your face from me? Why do You turn away? Do not abandon us!'"

"But it came back," Tut continued. "And he stopped crying to watch it come out again."

Everyone else had wept in relief when they saw the light begin to grow, felt the warmth touch their faces once more, as the darkness had passed, slowly revealing the Solar Disc once more. They had all shielded their faces at its glorious return, but the Pharaoh had not, gazing directly into the bright, loving beams of their returning God. He never took his eyes off the reemerging orb.

"His eyesight was never the same, either, was it?" Tut asked. "Didn't staring at the Sun burn his eyes, and they never got completely better?"

Ankh nodded. "Mm-hmm. And three other members of the court were stricken completely blind. And Father thought that even as He came back, the Aten had still punished them for failing to honor Him completely."

"Was Father right?" Tut asked softly. "What did Mother think? What did she say?"

"She believed in the Aten too," Ankh said with a sigh. "Father was the priest, and she was the politician. But they both believed."

Tut grabbed his walking-stick and got up, stretching one arm, then the other. He had been sitting for long enough, and his headache was quite a bit better.

"Don't stop there," he invited his sister, beckoning with his free hand. "But let's go down to the kitchen. All this remembering is making me hungry!"

Ankh chuckled, following him. and they made their way down the long hallway that led to the royal kitchens.

The Queen gave a sad little smile as they walked. "You remember our sisters?" she asked.

He chuckled. "Mm-hmm. All those smiles, those sweet little voices, all that running. They were always chasing one another, around the palace, around the grounds. But even when it got noisy, it was always happy noise."

Ankh nodded. "It was. Do you remember their names?"

"I don't remember what they mean," Tut admitted.

"Neferneferuaten Tasherit was named after Mother, the name she took when Father became *Akhenaten, Neferneferuaten-Nefertiti*. Although we just called her *Tasherit*. And then when Father made Mother his co-regent, she became *Ankhkheperure Neferneferuaten*. And then as Pharaoh, she took the throne name *Ankhkheperure Smenkhkare*."

They entered the royal feasting hall, finding their way across it to the small, inconspicuous door that led to the kitchen. "And Meritaten was called *Mayati*, and Neferneferure was *Rure*. And you were *Tut* and I was *Ankh*. I guess we thought Meketaten and Setepenre's names were short enough not to need nicknames."

"So many good memories," Tut said with a chuckle. "I was the only boy… and I remember the day I learned that boys and girls were different from one another. I was two, and we were at a party. And I met the Viceroy of Kush, and I introduced myself as the youngest sister."

Ankh laughed too. "Surrounded by girls. Stands to reason you'd think you were one!"

They had reached the kitchen, but stopped at the door. Tutankhamun swallowed, face falling. The next part of the story was not so happy. And Ankh shared his sigh as they remembered together.

"And then everyone got sick," he said heavily. "And we had to hide. And wait."

Ankh nodded. And they remembered.

They didn't go into the kitchen. Instead, they sat down at the high table, alone in the empty, silent feasting hall, as empty and silent as their lives had become after the epidemic.

"What do you remember about that?" she asked softly.

"Some," he said. "But not a lot. Tell me."

296

"They all started coughing," Ankh said. "And running fevers. Grandmother, then Tasherit. And Mother and Father... they didn't tell us that there was danger. But they didn't say there wasn't. And we weren't allowed to leave the palace."

"And then everyone else was coughing," Tut said. "Rure, Setepenre, Meketaten. And then... and then that night came..."

"They put us in your bedroom," Ankhesenamun said. "And they told us to stay out of the way, stay quiet, stay safe. They lit one lamp for us, and I told you stories about the pictures on the walls, about the gods and kings all the way back to the pyramids. And I sang to you, every song I knew, and told you riddles and played guessing-games with you, everything I could do to keep you distracted. Keep you from crying."

"I didn't know what was going on," Tutankhamun admitted. "It was late— I just wanted to go to bed. And I wanted Mother and Hetty, and I didn't understand why they couldn't come in. And I was hungry."

Ankhesenamun chuckled. "We snuck down to the kitchen to get someone to give you some dates. You always did have a sweet tooth."

"Speaking of dates..." Tut said, standing up and nodding at the kitchen door. Ankh smiled, following him inside.

They procured a large plate of fruit and nuts, and Ankh carefully carried it out to the pavilion so they could eat their snack in the sunshine.

Tut sat down, eating a handful of almonds. And he continued to remember, as well as he could, the night that their sisters and grandmother had died.

297

"Even Meritaten was busy," he said. "I could hear voices; her voice, the doctor's voice, Mother and Father, even Hetty, but they were too busy to stop and tell us what was going on. There wasn't anyone who could sit with us."

"So we sat with one another," Ankh said, reaching out to squeeze his hand. "I remember they kept asking Hetty to heat more water, make more mustard plasters. But nothing they could do... nothing they could do was enough."

"And Father was crying," Tut said. "I saw him in the hallway. He looked so sad."

"The doctors came to Father," Ankh said. "And they told him that this sickness was the gods' anger at his turning away from them. 'If His Majesty would only turn back,' the doctors said, 'his family might live.' But Father just looked at them. And he said, 'No, I trust in the Aten. He is able. And whatever may happen, we trust in Him.' And he did. Even with everything that happened."

"And then..." Tut bit his lip. "I heard Mother crying. Hard. And I knew something was wrong. Really wrong."

Ankhesenamun just squeezed his hand, the same strong, brave big sister who had rocked him in her lap on that dark night thirteen years ago. And she nodded.

"Then I only had two sisters," Tut said, fighting back tears as he remembered. "And Father said that they had joined the Aten."

Ankh nodded. "Four funerals," she said. "The laughter was gone. Six years old, seven years, eight, eleven... They were gone too soon."

She could still picture that night. Father had prayed so hard, prostrated on the hard, tiled floor of the hallway outside the bedrooms where Setepenre, Tasherit, Rure, Meketaten, and Grandmother lay coughing and burning up. He was haggard from

298

lack of sleep, the lines on his face deepened by the fast he had begun the day after the epidemic had struck. And in a voice Ankhesenpaaten had never heard before, he had begged the Aten to heal his family. But in the darkness of the night, it was as if their father's God had turned away. And the sound of their mother's grief was all he needed to know that the Lord of Light had not said yes.

"Grandmother was gone," Tut whispered.

Ankh nodded. She missed her knowledge, her stories, her age-old wisdom. Now Ankh's link to all the women of their illustrious past was severed, and she would never hear another wise word from Queen Mother Tiye. Would never again hear her say to sit up straight, to hold her head like a Queen, to speak with conviction, to mold the way people behaved toward her by the way she responded to their good or bad etiquette. The Matriarch of all Egypt, the mother of Pharaoh Akhenaten, was gone.

Tut shook his head. "And our sisters… were gone."

"Do you remember them?" Ankh asked softly.

"A little bit," he said, shrugging.

Ankhesenamun smiled. "Tasherit… She was the prankster. She used to steal honey-cakes from the kitchen, and one time she even released all our cats into one of Father's meetings!"

Tutankhamun laughed, vague images of an older sister who now lived on only as a story warming his heart. "I couldn't imagine letting cats out in the Vizier's office today!"

Ankh continued with a wistful smile. "And she used to climb up onto this one statue so she could whisk Kahotep's wig off his head when he walked by with a basket of laundry… and she always wanted to travel."

"Didn't one of them play music?" Tut asked.

The Queen blinked back tears as she nodded. "Meketaten. How could I ever have been so annoyed at that flute? I'd... I'd give anything to hear it again."

"One of them was just learning to read and write," Tut said.

"Setepenre," Ankh reminded him. She chuckled, shaking her head gently as she remembered. "Running around singing with that little bull's voice of hers, tripping up the servants, scaring the cats, playing chase..."

Tut just smiled.

"And Rure," Ankhesenamun said finally. "The quiet one. The wise one. Mother and Father's courtiers always said she should have been born a boy, because of what a good leader she would be... and they said... they said, 'why shouldn't she be?'"

"I remember her," Tutankhamun said. "She looked a lot like you."

"Actually, she looked a lot like you," his sister said. "Same sweet little nose... same wise heart." Ankh sighed. "Studying history, spending all day reading... she didn't like the parties like Tasherit and Setepenre did, but she had her own cats, Bastet's aunties, and she loved history. And she was learning..." She swallowed. "Learning about the past so that she could mold the future."

"What kind of Pharaoh would she have been?" Tut asked wistfully. His sister had no answer.

The Queen sighed. "Father believed the epidemic was a punishment for the idols people still had. And he worked even harder to clean Egypt from top to bottom."

"Five funerals," Tut said. "Grandmother. I remember..." he said softly, "I remember seeing her. She still looked so... wise. And her hair was all braided… They let me cut a braid of her hair, and I still have it… in a little b-box…"

He wiped away the tear that had escaped as Ankh squeezed his hand. "Then it was just the five of us," she said softly.

Tut shook his head. "No more laughter. No more joy. That was the beginning of the end at Akhetaten, wasn't it?"

His sister nodded. "And then one day Father died," she said solemnly, looking down at her hand, holding his as he listened to her story. "The Vizier… the Vizier had been so concerned, and he made sure Father took the nettle medicine the doctor had made, but his heart got worse and worse, until…" Ankh swallowed, then went on. "And the people… I think they were relieved, although of course they never would have said such a thing. His tired old heart… just couldn't go on."

Tut swallowed back his own tears as wavery memories of his father, all of which were from his sixth year or earlier, rose in his heart. "And Mother became the next Pharaoh. I think I remember her coronation."

Ankh gave a sad, proud little smile as she nodded. "Pharaoh Smenkhkare. She started to steer the nation back toward orthodoxy, back to what the people knew. And she said that although she believed Father had been right, there wasn't a lot of love in a state-imposed religion. People had to be free to choose to worship the Aten, or not. So she reopened the Temples of Amun-Ra, Horus, and all the others, and moved us back to Thebes. And she started up all the festivals again, and allowed the people to worship Aten, Amun, or no one." Ankh bit her lip. "Mother's reign began when you were six… and then when you were nine… we had that parade."

Tut reached over and squeezed his sister's hand as she looked down, more tears leaking from her closed eyes. "And the horse," she said in a choked voice, "and the blood. And she wasn't moving. And Ay said... Ay said, 'The Pharaoh is dead; long live the Pharaoh.' And it was you from that day forward."

"And then I was Pharaoh," Tut echoed. He could take up the story now. "And my throne name was *Nebkheperure*, but no one ever uses it unless they're having to be stupidly formal." He swallowed. "And we got married as soon as I was crowned. And the priests of all the old gods said that we should restore the old temples that Father had closed, and we had it done. The priests told us that Father had been wrong, and that we were going back to the truth... They said it was truth as old as the pyramids. That was when we changed our names. And we started leading the country ourselves... or at least, we started representing Egypt to the world."

"And then Meritaten..." Ankh said, "that same year, just when it started to get cold... Ay told us the ague had taken her almost overnight." She sighed, giving half a sad smile. "And it's been you and me ever since."

"And you've been here for me every step of the way," Tutankhamun said with a smile. "Standing beside me. Telling me what to do."

"Guiding you," she said with a wink.

He smiled again, giving her a little nod. "Guiding me. With your wisdom. Your experience."

His sister smiled back at him. "I've always been there," she said, "and I always will be. No matter what." And she leaned forward to kiss him on the forehead, her braids tickling his face.

302

They sat for a moment in reflective silence. They had been through so much. And who knew what the future held.

"I'm glad you remember so much," Ankh said, taking his hand. He nodded.

"So am I."

And together, they wondered what the future held. And they wondered what was true.

27   Growth

The month of Paophi wore on, the days slowly growing cooler. And Tut got his lesson on Tetisheri, Ahhotep the First, and Ahmose-Nefertari. But it was cursory, the Vizier still focusing on the military accomplishments of their husbands while those dear wives had stayed home and minded the house, even if the house was Egypt itself. Tut listened, and when the lesson was over, he found his sister in the study they shared.

"Tell me what really happened," he said immediately.

She looked up from petting the cat and trying to keep an apple out of her curious reach.

"About what?" she asked, giving him a little frown.

"About the Queens of the Seventeenth Dynasty," he said, sitting down in the chair across from hers. "Ay did his lesson on them, but it was all about holding down the fort while their husbands did the real work." He took an apple of his own from the fruit bowl on the table, crunching into it. "So tell me… How did they keep Egypt from falling to pieces while their husbands were at war?"

Ankhesenamun smiled, even as her heart frowned at the same time. That Vizier, de-emphasizing the accomplishments of her ancestresses, saying that they had only done as much, or as little, as any wife, nothing more than facilitating the great work of their husbands.

But then her heart smiled. Because her brother wanted to know the truth. He wanted to learn more, about what their grandmothers and great-grandmothers had done in centuries past. And she could tell him.

"Well, it all started with Tetisheri," she began, and he leaned forward in his chair, ready to hang on to every word. "Who saw the transition between the Seventeenth Dynasty and the Eighteenth…"

She went back after describing the accomplishments of the Dynasty Seventeen Queens, to make sure that he hadn't missed any important details of the reigns of the other female Pharaohs and powerful Queens of the past, Pharaohs and Queens who had brought them to where they were today.

And not just the women who had reigned as or in the stead of Pharaohs— women who had held other vital governmental positions, like Nebet, the only female Vizier in all of Egyptian history, who had served during the Sixth Dynasty, whose daughter had become Queen and served as regent between the reigns of her husband and son. And Ankhesenamun smiled at how fascinated Tut appeared to be. What a good brother he was. And what a good Pharaoh he was growing up to be.

The Queen's blood came every month, healthy, normal, but telling her that this month, there was no royal baby. And yet… now when she felt the cramps, tended to her body's needs as her monthly purification took place, she didn't cry angry tears before the image of Tawaret, demanding to know the reason her prayers had not been answered.

Now that they had decided to wait, Ankh had peace. They had set their hopes and dreams aside for the future. The monthly arrival of her bleeding reminded her that she still had the potential to have more children when the time was right. Someday, their hearts would call on them to try again. There was time.

Tut kept learning. Kept studying, kept researching. Diving into the papyri in the royal library, he researched the legal system; the mechanics of law, order, human rights, criminal and civil cases, and the different punishments that were typically applied to different crimes. And he learned that there were always options from which a judge could select the most appropriate consequence. And that as the highest judge in the land, Pharaoh could punish the accused exactly as he or she saw fit. Pharaoh could have someone executed for sneezing during a meeting, or could pardon a murderer with a snap of their fingers. He or she had complete jurisdiction over everyone and everything in Egypt.

As Pharaoh, he would not be limited, obligated by the legal system to respond to a particular problem in a particular way. He would be able to follow his heart, and his own best judgment.

Still the staff had questions for the Pharaoh. Like whether he was satisfied with the way his birthday feast had turned out, how his favorite shoes were holding up, whether he wanted any new rosebushes planted. And gritting his teeth, Semerkhet stood back and let the Pharaoh answer his own questions.

Just not the pettiest ones.

But there was always time. Time to decompress with his friend, for Tut to sit at his dressing-table while Semerkhet put away his jewelry and ask him how the latest horse race had gone, whether the defense of the hockey team from Tjenu was better than the offense of the team from Behdet. And he didn't just ask so he could let the gentle tide of words wash over him as he settled into the drowsiness of evening, he really wanted to know.

Because the things that mattered to his friend mattered to him.

"So now I'm the 'pretty little Queen'," Ankh said to Meresankh one night after dinner.

"Says who?" her handmaiden asked as she put away a series of freshly-cleaned wigs.

"Says Treasurer Maya," the Queen said angrily, resting her indignantly folded arms on the dressing-table at which she sat. "Ran into him at dinner. And he wanted to know what I wanted in getting my hands dirty in politics, and if it really made me happy. Said I should just enjoy the palace and appreciate the things I have."

"What did you tell him?" Meresankh asked.

"Told him I appreciated everyone who'd gotten us here. Kings and Queens. And reminded him that my Mother was both. And I told him that I wanted the people of Egypt to have enough money to be able to enjoy pretty things of their own."

Meresankh smiled. "And what did he say to that?" she asked sweetly.

"Nothing, because I left!" Ankh said triumphantly. And together, she and Meresankh laughed out loud.

As their laughter faded into delighted chuckles, the Queen found herself putting out her hand. And Meresankh's smile disappeared. But tentatively, she extended her own, and they joined hands in a clasp.

Then Meresankh's smile came back. And so did Ankh's.

But although the Queen had no doubt that her brother could do it, he was still young. So young. And she found herself swallowing back genuine misgivings as he told her about the planned campaign to Amurru, intended to protect the Mitanni and their neighbors from the Hittites.

"Should we really be fighting their war for them?" she asked gently.

Her little brother just gave her a hopeful smile, full of goodwill toward the world. "Aren't all the countries of the world like one giant community?" he asked. "And just imagine the ripples it will create. All the people whose lives will be better once the Hittites are pushed back."

For once, Ankhesenamun had no comeback.

Tut smiled again. "Besides, it's Horemheb leading the campaign, not me. The King of peace isn't going anywhere."

"Oh, you're going places," his sister said with a smile, giving him a peck on the cheek. "You'll go far."

"Ready, My Lady?" Meresankh asked.

Ankhesenamun adjusted the linen kerchief wrapped around her bald head and nodded. It was the end of a long day, and, retiring to the Queen's chambers a bit on the early side, they were ready for some sticky fun.

Meresankh turned to the dressing-table Ankh sat at and picked up the little bowl of frankincense, honey, and ground grain. And together they laughed as Meresankh applied it first to the Queen's face, then her own. They looked rather grotesque at the moment. But the masks would leave their skin glowing.

Then, even as she laughed with her friend, for that was the only word to describe Meresankh, Ankh's heart began to ache. And she remembered doing facials with Mother, Meritaten, Meketaten. The fun. The connection. The togetherness.

308

Then she looked at Meresankh, smiling merrily at her with the sticky paste of honey and frankincense on her face. And she smiled. Because this felt the same as those times she was remembering.

Like being with a sister.

Later that week, the General came home. The King and Queen went out to see the small parade that heralded his return, cheering Thebans lined up along the main road to greet him and his men as they rode home in their fine chariots. They had returned with a variety of gifts, Tut noted with satisfaction; gold, animal skins, ostrich feathers, woolen textiles, glass of a different style than was produced here in Egypt. At least some of the interactions had been successful.

Tutankhamun gave Horemheb a few hours to rest and freshen up, then summoned him to his study. The General strode in, still carrying his helmet under his arm.

"How was the mission, General?" the Pharaoh asked, setting aside the documents he was looking over.

The General gave a deep bow. "The Nubians and the Mitanni accepted our gifts with joy, Glorious Lord, and offered gifts of their own. A young Mitanni Princess was delighted by the giraffe. The Mitanni remember your grandfather and look forward to moving into the future as allies, and the Nubian governors of our lands in Kush report that things are going well."

"That is good to hear," Tut said, nodding his head. He chuckled as he imagined a small Princess leading the giraffe around with a bridle. "And the Hittites?"

Horemheb looked down, his air of proud satisfaction fading. "My Lord, the Hittites actually refused to speak with any of us. I fear... I fear that we may have offended them by even attempting to contact them. I applaud your intent, but I wonder if there will be consequences."

Tutankhamun inclined his head. "Thank you for going, General, and thank you for your report. I hope that your mission will strengthen our presence in Nubia and our alliance with the Mitanni... and it has clearly shown us the way the Hittites feel toward us."

"I would like to commend the son of Commander Seti," Horemheb said proudly. "A young man named Paramessu, just a little older than Your Majesty. I see a lot of potential in him." He tapped his chin. "I believe he is related by marriage to the Viceroy of Kush."

The King inclined his head. "He sounds as though he has a bright future ahead of him."

Tutankhamun sighed, looking out the window. Then he smiled at Horemheb. "It's good to see you again, General."

Horemheb inclined his head. "And you as well, Your Majesty."

"I remember..." Tut chuckled. "I remember, when I was a little boy, just after my coronation, you were always the one who could calm me down when I was being... unreasonable."

The General also allowed himself a small chuckle. "It was my honor, Great Morning Star." Then he gave a sad, wistful sigh. "My wives and I may not have children... in this world... but you brought out something of the father in me. With the greatest respect, may I say that that statue of Thoth was particularly well-aimed. As was the walking-stick against Kahotep's knee. We both still bear the scars."

310

"They wouldn't let me play outside," the King explained, re-membering one of the roughest afternoons of his entire career as a ten-year-old. Heartbroken by his parents' death, confused by the recent move to Thebes, and utterly overwhelmed at suddenly finding himself Pharaoh, he had found being told he couldn't go out and play simply too much to deal with. The day had begun with the palace staff learning to fear the wrath of a screaming ten-year-old armed with a walking-stick. It had finally ended with Ankh, the only person in the universe who was allowed to tell him to stop doing anything, sitting him down and telling him that throwing a royal fit when he had big feelings was undignified and beneath his station. After that day, he had never thrown another tantrum. Except that one time, when Nakhtmin had shouted at Semerkhet. Tut sighed. "They still won't."

"Well... as you say, Your Majesty," Horemheb said after a moment, "you can be a King of peace, if that is what you choose. And we have made excellent progress today."

Tutankhamun smiled at the General, a happy smile from a Pharaoh to his loyal servant... a sad smile between two fathers who could hold their children only in their dreams. "Thank you."

The King smiled as the General left with the usual wishes for life, prosperity, and health, making sure to close the door behind him. That was one of the longest, and the friendliest, conversations he could remember ever having had with Horemheb.

That night there was a small feast in celebration of the great General's successful mission of peace to the Mitanni and the Nubians. High-ranking officials and their wives sat in the sumptuous royal feasting hall in the warm light of the torches on the walls, clinking glasses, feasting on roast beef and ostrich, spiced mutton, and elaborate cakes as musicians and dancers entertained them and perfume filled the air. And admiring the gifts offered by the Nubians and the Mitanni, which lay in glorious stacks toward one end of the room.

After a bit of entertainment, General Horemheb cleared his throat and stood up from where he had been semi-reclining at the table, one arm around each of his pretty little wives. The musicians, who were preparing for their next song, paused, waiting, as did the dancers. Tut looked over. Was he going to make a speech?

"Tonight we celebrate Egypt's successful overtures of peace towards our neighbors, the Mitanni and the Nubians. You can see the glorious fruits of our mission," Horemheb said, sweeping his arm toward the piles and piles of luxurious gifts. "And it is all thanks to the wisdom of our glorious Pharaoh Tutankhamun, the Lord of the Two Lands. It was his plan to reach out to our neighbors, and I am honored to report the success of his ideas."

Tut squeezed Ankhesenamun's hand and they smiled at one another. They knew whose the idea had been.

"...our Pharaoh may be young," Horemheb was continuing, "but he shows wisdom beyond his years. I am honored to declare my loyalty anew, and to serve as his General. All hail Pharaoh Tutankhamun, the Strong Bull, Ruler of Truth, Lord of the Two Lands! All life, prosperity, and health!"

The guests applauded, echoing his good wishes for the Pharaoh, and Horemheb sat down. Time for another song. The King smiled. Horemheb was his to command.

"So, what are your thoughts on the tax cuts?" Amenia asked the Queen as they stood sipping wine and listening to the music.

312

Ankh nearly spit out her wine. Was it working?

"Ah…" Caught by surprise, she could barely formulate an answer.

"Mutnedjmet and I have to admit that we don't have a full grasp of the way taxation even works," Amenia continued. "Are farmers taxed on what they harvested that year, or some sort of established standard?"

The Queen blinked, trying to get the words out smoothly as she struggled to phrase the explanation clearly. "It… each year during Inundation, the government measures how high the Nile has risen that year, and they use that figure to calculate how much grain can be grown per field. And the farmers are taxed a particular fraction of the predicted harvest. If the harvest falls short, they still have to pay, but if they gather more than they expected, it all belongs to them; they just have to pay the standard portion."

Mutnedjmet, who was standing at Amenia's elbow, took a sip of her own wine. "Mm-hmm. That is interesting. So what happens if—"

Suddenly, from across the room, Horemheb looked over, waving at his pretty little wives. The ladies squealed and giggled, fawning and blushing as they squeaked, "There he goes!" Ankh shook her head. Were they really crushing over their own husbands?

Then it came to her, a phrase to describe how they were behaving, and she chuckled. "Big, strong man syndrome." That was what they had. As far as they had come, initiating conversations about how taxation worked, they still had a long way to go.

The next day, the Pharaoh had another history lesson. And it seemed that Ay had reconsidered the way in which he had glossed over the reigns of the female Pharaohs and Queen Regents he had spoken of so superficially just two days previously.

"If the Lord of the Two Lands wishes to learn about the women who have led Egypt under... unusual circumstances, that is what he will learn about," the Vizier said smoothly. "Let us begin with Hatshepsut."

Tut sat up straight, mind and heart ready to receive the useful information and heartening inspiration he was sure was coming. "When Pharaoh Thutmose the Second died after a relatively short reign, his son Thutmose the Third was too young to rule. The boy's stepmother, his father's wife Hatshepsut, took power as regent, over time elevating herself to Pharaoh with the future Thutmose the Third as her co-regent. She did not hand the reins of power to her stepson when he came of age, instead retaining the throne until her death. Upon his succession to the throne, Thutmose the Third erased her name from historical records, chiseled away her reliefs, and dismantled her monuments, taking his place as the next Pharaoh and restoring *ma'at*."

The Vizier swallowed delicately. "Thutmose the Third had been tied to his stepmother's apron strings too long. When he finally had the freedom to strike out as his own Pharaoh, his own man, he let the world know who wore the crown."

Tutankhamun squirmed. What was the Vizier trying to say?

Then the elder statesman came out and said it. "Hatshepsut, the wise, caring regent, took her stepson's throne. You and your sister may say you're partners, but will she do the same to you? Or is it time..." Ay smiled, an air of inspiration in his look. "Is it time for you to prove who wears the crown?"

314

The Pharaoh looked down. Now he was squirming with the way that the point the Vizier was making…

Was sort of a point.

Tut saw the General again later that day. And this time, he had an order to give.

"General?"

Horemheb looked up from checking that his dagger was sufficiently polished. The torches set in the walls of the hallway in which they stood gleamed on the metal of the armor he wore even indoors.

"Yes, O Great Morning Star?"

"I've made a decision… although I hope you will not think that my determination to be a King of peace has changed."

"What decision, My Lord?"

"I want you to plan a campaign to Kadesh, to free it from the Hittites and prevent them from destroying the Mitanni and their neighbors in Amurru," he said. Horemheb gave an audible gasp, standing up straighter as his eyes widened. "This does not change the fact that territorial expansion is not my ultimate goal," the Pharaoh said firmly before the General got too excited. "Protecting our weaker neighbors from destruction by a common enemy is. Are we strong enough?" he asked the General.

Horemheb nodded. "The military has been rebuilt since the day your grandfather's army went missing on the mission to bring back the Hebrews. It has been a process… but yes, My Lord. We are strong enough."

Tut smiled. "Good. I want you to prepare an army of sufficient size to assist the Mitanni in pushing back the Hittites so that they, we, and the rest of the world will not be overrun before the end of the year. I will tell you when to launch it. And when you have done that…" the Pharaoh said, letting just a hint of the thunder creep into his stern expression, his dark eyebrows, "I want you to come home, General. As a King of peace, I want to use Egypt's strength of arms to protect our neighbors and our borders, not to take over the known world. Is that perfectly clear?"

"It will be my delight and honor to clear the Hittite scum from Amurru," Horemheb said with a bit of a feral growl, gripping the handle of his dagger more tightly, knuckles showing white. "Now that our army is rebuilt, we will use its strength to remove them from the region."

"Only from the regions that we and the Mitanni lost," Tutankhamun said firmly. "I don't want you taking over Babylonia while you're gone. And I don't want you to leave until I say so."

"Understood, O King for Whom the Sun Shines," Horemheb said. He looked down, then back up at the Pharaoh. "Wh… when does Your Majesty plan to send me?"

Tut smiled at the General. "Soon," he said. "Soon."

Horemheb gave a little smile of his own, offering a deep bow and a wish for life, prosperity, and health. And he walked away, glowing with excitement.

Tut, however, still felt a twist of uncertainty as he watched him go. Somehow, he felt that this would not be over quickly.

28   The Ruler of Truth

The Pharaoh and the Vizier played *seega* in the garden that evening, listening to the birds twittering in the trees as the flowers fluttered in the cool breeze. There were still a few mosquitoes, but ague season was practically over for the year, so they weren't worried. In the valley below the town of Thebes got on with its evening bustle, a low chatter of sound reaching the palace when the wind was just so. Even at this distance, soft orange torchlight was visible from some of the larger buildings.

Closer to hand, Treasurer Maya's wife was scolding her little girl for playing in the dirt. Well, he supposed that since the little girl's dress was just as ornate and elaborately pleated as her mother's, it would be a shame to get it dirty. And the child had so much jewelry on that Tut was surprised she could play in the dirt at all. Then he sighed. People who were blessed with children should let them play in the dirt. It looked like Mistress Treasurer had another little one on the way. He hoped she would let her youngest pick flowers and gather pebbles.

"You might want to teach your son better manners, Vizier," Tut said into the silence.

"Is that so?" Ay asked, moving his game piece. Internally Tut smiled. He was closing in on one of Ay's pieces, moving to trap it so any move it made would be doomed. "What has he done wrong?"

"Abused a servant in front of me," Tut said as he made his move. "And in front of you."

"The girl with the wine?" Ay asked in a careless tone, considering his next move... in terms of the game as well as in terms of the conversation. He looked up at the Pharaoh. "It *was* a new tunic."

"Hardly justification for screaming at her, bruising her arm, and threatening to hit her," Tutankhamun said. "Besides which, if he hadn't shouted at her, she wouldn't have spilled the wine on him."

"Shepset is a clumsy girl, My Lord," Ay said. His gnarled old hand hovered over the gameboard as he considered one move, then another. "Rather like the handmaiden my dear wife used to have." Tut bowed his head respectfully. Lady Tey, the wife of the Grand Vizier, had died two years previously. "It's not my fault you have incompetent servants."

Tut looked at the Vizier. "Can you think of another example of Shepset being clumsy?"

The conviction in Ay's voice was not convincing. "She's just... just generally clumsy."

Tut raised an eyebrow. "Really." He sighed. "Well, I want you to tell him I won't stand for any more threats and violence. As I told your son, as my servants, they are under my authority, and it's my job to discipline them as I see fit. It's my responsibility to protect them from anyone who might mistreat them." He paused, looking firmly at the Vizier. "*Anyone.* I also don't appreciate *your* overzealous defense of the front hall of the palace from mud while it's still raining. I saw you order a beating for that young man a few weeks ago."

The noblewoman had taken her little girl back inside, pulling her by the hand and squawking at her in a voice that made the King think of the birds he had received on Tribute Day. "Mayamenti, just look at your dress! That cost your wonderful daddy two weeks' wages, and you've got it all dirty! Get inside!" The child struggled to keep up, tripping on the hem of her long dress as her mother yanked her along and fretted at her. Poor little girl. And poor baby that was yet to come. Hannu, the guard who stood protecting the Pharaoh and the Vizier, coughed uncomfortably as he watched them go.

"The state of the palace must reflect the proper prestige and majesty, Son of Ra," Ay replied, still pondering the game. "No matter the weather."

"But the staff are only human," said Tut. "There is only so much they can do, and they cannot be held responsible for the weather or its impact on their work. And as those who provide for them by giving them the opportunity to work, we must forgive them for being only human." He paused, eyebrows darkening. "That's an order."

Ay glanced up at him, then looked back at the board. "Yes, O Great Morning Star." And he moved his piece, evading the trap Tut had been setting up.

Tut watched him make his move, clearly slithering out of any further conversation. He sighed. All this responsibility was giving him a headache.

But more responsibility was soon to come with the next day, when one of the head scribes came to the Pharaoh's study with a report. Tut had already fielded an application for the use of the space necessary to house the builders who were going to construct the new schools and a dispute as to what section of the staff quarters was going to be expanded for the use of the new cooks and gardeners, and he was tired.

"We regret to inform you that the tombs of three officials buried just outside Thebes have been found robbed," the scribe announced, standing stiffly at attention with his eyes carefully averted. The King noticed how perfect his wig was— had he taken a moment to restyle it before entering the presence of the Pharaoh? "And we regret to inform you that Sennedjem was found to be the ringleader."

Tutankhamun blinked, setting aside Horemheb's written report on the mission to Nubia and the Mitanni. Sennedjem? His tutor from childhood? A tomb robber?

He had no choice but to deal with this as Pharaoh. Now, it was his responsibility, rather than the Vizier's.

"Have him brought in," he ordered. "We will handle this."

Quickly, the Pharaoh reviewed the lessons he had learned. And he held them firmly in his mind. He knew what to do. And now it was time to apply what he had learned.

An hour later, Tutankhamun sat in his throne room with his crook and flail back in his hands, his *nemes* on his head, and his false beard of magnificence on his chin again, staring down his former tutor, who stood before him in chains, flanked by two uniformed guards bearing spears. At the two sides of the King sat his courtiers, Viziers Ay, Pentu, and Usermontu, Generals Horemheb and Nakhtmin. The gods and kings in the paintings on the walls around them seemed to frown down at the prisoner. The Pharaoh could feel the presence of the people around him, but he was focused. He had work to do.

"You stand accused of robbing the tombs of three officials," Tut said simply. "What is your response?"

320

Sennedjem did not meet his eye. The skinny old man was shaking, knobbly knees knocking with fear, wig lopsided on his bald head, makeup smudged. "G-g-glorious Lord," he stammered, "I th-thought we needed the g-g-gold. The ec-conomy's still a m-m-mess, and I th-thought that if we p-p-put some of the t-treasure back into the b-budget..."

"Yes, the economy is a mess, and we do need gold," Tutankhamun said, "but not like this. You should be pleased to hear that all the funeral goods you stole have been returned to their proper place."

Tut sighed as he looked down at the thief, ready to pass judgment.

"Sennedjem, I'm ashamed of you. You're fired. No longer part of the royal court. You are no longer Fan-bearer on the Right Side of the King. The Pharaoh has spoken."

Sennedjem stood shaking, his face pale. He twisted his hands together as he considered his sentence. "F-fired, O M-m-mighty K-King?"

"Yes, Sennedjem, fired," Tut said firmly, eyes flashing. "For stealing from our ancestors and desecrating their final resting places. Be grateful it's not worse."

"So what does—" Sennedjem asked rather pathetically.

"It means you no longer live at the palace," the Pharaoh said. "It means go to your chambers, get your things together, and start seeking accommodations elsewhere. Now go." Tut raised his dark, stormy eyebrows at the guards, who took Sennedjem's arms and began to lead him from the throne room, still blinking in a state of shock.

Tutankhamun looked at his remaining royal court, who were also blinking in a state of shock. No one spoke. Only stared.

Finally they rose from their seats and bowed, barely more than whispering, "Hail to thee, Ruler of Truth; all life, prosperity, and health!"

"That will be all," Tut said, getting up, carefully descending from the dais with his walking-stick, and walking slowly but majestically toward the door, leaving them to their stunned silence. Stunned that he had taken such decisive action… yet intrigued by the fact that he had been so lenient. Tomb robbers were usually executed.

Nakhtmin was the one who could be trusted to say what everyone was thinking.

"I hope you know that tomb-robbers are usually hanged," he drawled, looking scathingly at the Pharaoh. "Rather obvious, really. But I suppose…" He looked down his nose at the Pharaoh, eyes narrowing scornfully. "You have time to learn."

Tutankhamun swallowed. What a sweet person.

But he had a response. And, of course, whether or not his response held up to Nakhtmin's scrutiny, the decision was his. He was the Pharaoh. And Nakhtmin was not.

"Actually, General," he said pleasantly, "I've done my research and decided that this is appropriate. I don't need to kill him. Sennedjem has lost his honor, his reputation, his home at the palace, and any hope of ever being employed again. He's completely and utterly disgraced. And when he dies, he will not be able to promise Ma'at that he never committed theft… He may even forfeit the right to be buried in his own tomb. And that's punishment enough. As Pharaoh," Tutankhamun said, giving the son of the Grand Vizier just a hint of the eyes of thunder and lightning, "it's my responsibility to determine the most appropriate response to every issue that is brought before me. And I believe I have done so." He smiled. "Thank you."

Nakhtmin just walked away, followed by the other courtiers. After all, the Pharaoh had already dismissed them.

Tut watched them go. He had used his authority as Pharaoh. And it had felt good. And he had followed his own best judgment, choosing not to execute someone who would learn a much stronger lesson through having to navigate life with no home, no career, and no reputation. He knew he had done the right thing.

But that wasn't the issue, he thought as his court left the room. The issue was getting them to see his authority.

Tutankhamun moved his game piece. He and Ankhesenamun sat in her private sitting room a few hours after Sennedjem's trial, surrounded by comfortable pillows and graceful paintings. Just like his, her private sitting room was a nice little space a bit different from the bedroom but not as formal as the study. It was a good place to play *seega*. The days were growing cooler, the Pharaoh observed with satisfaction. The month of Paophi was drawing to a close. And he was delighted to wear a long-sleeved tunic and a cozy blue robe. And to need a blanket at night. It wasn't quite cool enough yet for the second blanket, and some days were still too warm for an outer robe. But the season was changing.

"Good move, Your Majesty," Ankh said, studying the board. Her hand hovered over her one remaining piece, long sleeve of her dress fluttering as she pondered how to escape him. Finally she moved… then bit her lip. "I think you beat me," she said with a smile.

He made his final move, capturing her final piece. "I think so too." Tut grinned at her, showing his big teeth.

She put her hand over his with a proud smile. "Good game."

"I learned from the best," he said.

Ankh squeezed his hand. "I heard what happened with Sennedjem. And I'm sorry he did something like that, but I'm so proud of you." She smiled down at the gameboard. "It's like I was saying about the game; you're taking action, taking charge. Not letting them decide what happens anymore. With Sennedjem, and with all the decisions— about the schools, about the staffing." She sighed. "So you're not just a better game-player... you're a better Pharaoh."

He just smiled. One day, he would be a truly great Pharaoh.

But the day wasn't over yet. As afternoon drew toward evening, Tut went to his chambers to let Semerkhet and Ptahmose help him change back into his finery, a long-sleeved tunic and a dark blue robe, large, heavy, beaded earrings, and a heavy collar-necklace with matching bracelets. He also wore a circlet, and his false beard of magnificence, in addition to a more formal pair of shoes and a walking-stick that brought the whole look together. Tonight he had a dinner to attend, discussing the future of the schools that were being built with the architects who had designed them and some of the instructors who would run them.

Ten people sat there at the high table when he entered the royal feasting hall, ten wise, mature adults, ready to work with him to lead Egypt toward the greatest possible future. He was one of them now. The Pharaoh took a deep breath, tightening his grip on his walking-stick. He had gotten through Tribute Day. And he had gotten through meetings before. He would be fine.

"Greetings," he said, giving a professional nod. They all rose, offering deep bows and "hail to thee's" in return, jewelry glittering in the lamplight, beaded wigs clinking and delicate linen fluttering as they moved. Then they sat down again, Tut struggling to get comfortable as his foot throbbed. Why did it always insist on being the most painful when he had work to focus on?

"Thank you for joining me tonight," he said, taking a sip of white wine from Tribute Day.

"It's our honor, Glorious Lord," said a tall, stately older woman whose outfit was simple and professional but whose eye makeup rivaled the Queen's. One of the instructors lined up for one of the new schools in Memphis, she would be offering training in midwifery and herbal medicine.

"We wanted to show you our proposed schedule for the lessons that will be offered at the school that will open next year," a younger man said. He was one of the architects, but he was also going to be teaching architecture. His broad, muscular shoulders, powerful arms that boasted a number of scars, and large, wide hands with their chipped fingernails gave Tut the sense that he would teach many of his lessons out on the field, giving his students hands-on experience.

The Pharaoh accepted the papyrus he offered. And he smiled. The schools were more than an idea. They were on their way toward welcoming students. And they were going to change the world.

On their way to lunch one day, Tut and Semerkhet paused at the sound of angry voices just down the hall.

"Who died and made you Pharaoh?" a whiny voice was pouting.

"What I am *saying*, you little snake, is that you can't talk like that to the servants in front of me!" a deeper, older voice replied.

"Excuse me," Tut said into the middle of the argument that was taking place in the hallway. Between Nakhtmin and Horemheb, apparently. The older General was backing the younger one against the wall, his dagger gleaming where it hung from his belt, ready to be unsheathed in a heartbeat. A few feet away stood Raherka, staring silently at his feet as the two noblemen argued.

Horemheb and Nakhtmin looked up, Horemheb's mouth closing on the angry words he was about to continue pouring out and Nakhtmin elbowing him out of the way with a scornful scoff.

Blinking, Horemheb remembered himself and bowed to the Pharaoh. A moment later, Nakhtmin went to the trouble of bobbing his head.

"Your Majesty," Horemheb said shortly, "I was merely correcting the son of the Vizier, who seems to have forgotten your new policy of treating the staff as *human*."

Nakhtmin scoffed again. "This old windbag had the gall to call me out for correcting a slave for bringing me the wrong—"

"The human beings who work at the palace are not *slaves*, Nakhtmin!" Horemheb shouted, temper flaring again.

"But would any *human* be *stupid* enough to—"

That was when Horemheb reached for his knife.

At a nod from the Pharaoh, Semerkhet took Raherka by the arm and walked him away to a safe distance.

"It seems as though we have a problem," Tutankhamun said in his clear, ringing proclamation voice. Swallowing back their rage, both men looked up at him in silence, bitterly avoiding one an-

326

other's eye. Horemheb flared his nostrils as he blew out an angry breath, and Nakhtmin pursed his lips as though he'd eaten an unripe jujube. "General Nakhtmin, General Horemheb is correct. My new policies forbid the abuse of staff members. And I am afraid that threatening them is an infraction. Horemheb," he continued before the older General could look too pleased with himself, "this new policy also applies to other members of the royal court. So I'm afraid that we can't have you threatening one another in public. If you feel the need to fight, do it on your own time. Now please," he said gently, "be on your way."

The two glowered at one another, then Nakhtmin put his nose in the air, turned on his heel, and walked away. Looking exhausted, Horemheb sank down on the nearest bench.

And he put his head in his hands. Concerned, Tut hurried over to stand beside him.

"What's wrong, General?" he asked.

Horemheb rubbed his face, then looked up with a heavy sigh. "I'm ashamed of myself. I've done exactly what I counseled you not to. I'm a terrible example."

Tut sat down beside him, shaking his head. "We all have people who drive us to the edge." He chuckled. "Remember that other time?"

Horemheb returned the chuckle, a small smile lighting his face as he nodded. "I do."

"That was Nakhtmin, too," Tut said with a sarcastic sigh. "Sounds like he didn't learn his lesson." He paused, then smiled again. "But I did."

Horemheb gave another sigh. "You did. And you helped me not kill Nakhtmin today just like I helped you not kill him."

The Pharaoh chuckled. "Exactly. Where would he be if you hadn't taught me those skills?"

The General looked down at the dagger at his hip. "Dead," he whispered.

Tut wasn't sure how to go on from that. "Well," he said a moment later, "you did teach me. And then I was able to turn it around when you needed it. So thank you."

Horemheb shook his head at the Pharaoh's circuitous logic, then stood up with another little smile. "No, thank *you*, Your Majesty. All life, prosperity, and health." And with a little bow, he was gone.

Tut watched him go. The man had taught him so much... and yet he himself still struggled. And although it had ended well today... somehow Tut doubted that the saga of Nakhtmin versus Horemheb was over.

Later that day, Tut's sister said she had something to tell him. And he listened in rising vexation as she described her interactions with the Vizier and the Treasurer over the past week.

"I could punish both of them," the Pharaoh said, gripping the handle of his walking-stick as he rose from the chair in his sitting room with an indignant frown. "Trying to tell you what you can and can't do... Who do they think they are?"

Ankh rose from her own chair, giving him a little smile as she shook her head, beads jingling. Gently, she reached out to take his free hand in both of hers.

"I'm all right," she said softly, rising onto her tiptoes to peck him on the cheek. In spite of himself, he smiled at her. "Just because they're wrong about everything doesn't mean I have to take it personally."

Now Tut really did laugh. "Well, I'm glad you see it that way," he said, pressing a kiss to her forehead. She stepped closer to him, and he put his free arm around her, holding her close.

"We're changing the future, you and I," Ankh said. "They just need to catch up."

At dinner, the Queen's brother was laughing. Semerkhet served him his roast beef and stewed onions, taking a quick bite as well as a sip of wine from Tut's blue lotus cup. And as he ate, they chatted about last night's hockey game.

"So the forward from Gebtu took a swing, and Raherka dived... Ptahmose intercepted the ball and shot it toward the Gebtu goal and Hepu blocked the goalie so he couldn't stop it..."

Ankhesenamun shook her head with her own chuckle, beaded braids jingling. And she smiled at Meresankh.

"Those boys and their sports," she said.

As the days went by, Tut got into the new routine of daily meetings and decisions, sitting there on his throne in his crown, crook and flail crossed over his chest, as the people of Egypt brought him their problems, questions, and proposals. At the end of each day, he told his sister about who he'd met with, what they'd spoken of, and asked for her counsel. And together, they would prepare a plan or a response for him to deliver, her wisdom and experience joined to his authority. They were one Pharaoh, really, leading and guiding their country together— he would lead, and she would guide... through guiding him.

And every day got a little easier. Although he had to get up a little earlier in the mornings, because not only was he now responsible for officiating the Sunset Ceremony every night, he had to run the Sunrise Ceremony as well. Somehow, with all the honor and power that came with his new responsibilities, the carefree laziness of childhood was being taken away. But even as he made judgments that would improve the lot of all the citizens of Egypt, he still wondered… what his legacy would be. And he still felt… like something was missing.

Ankh was proud of her brother. As the days went by, she watched him get into the swing of conducting meetings, making decisions. He asked for her guidance, and she offered it gladly, but he was the one ultimately making the decisions. And he looked and sounded like a Pharaoh.

But along with the majesty, there was something. A dissatisfaction in his voice, his manner. A discomfort. And she wished that he could see that he had already become the King of peace he aspired to be.

29   Rebirth

ut even as politics grew ever more stressful, there were events that took their minds off of the strange new things that were beginning to become normal. It was time to set aside politics for the moment and turn their thoughts to things above. It was time to observe the Opet Festival.

Semerkhet did not speak as he helped the Pharaoh dress, holding the ceremonial *was*-scepter in his hand. It wasn't that sort of day. This was the Day of Rebirth, but for rebirth to occur, it must be preceded by death. This was a day to think.

Tut passed Ankhesenamun, standing in the hall in a long, white dress with wide, starched sleeves. He smiled and touched her hand, but neither spoke. Not even a good-morning. It wasn't that sort of day. She was going too, but only as a spectator, celebrating the joyous element of the festival like all the citizens. The real work of the day belonged to the Pharaoh.

After a quiet breakfast, the King and Queen silently walked through the gardens, to the giant pleasure-lake that was sparkling in the morning sun. Climbing into the waiting barge, they took the short journey across the massive pond, entering a canal that carried them past the royal harbor and onto the waters of the Nile.

They sailed to the Temple of Amun-Ra, listening to the happy hubbub of the crowd on the nearby shore, the music, the laughter that had already been going on for over a week and would continue after today. But they were quiet. After today, they would join the celebration. With them were the images of the god Amun-Ra, which the citizens had been thronging to see since the festival had begun, and those of Mut and Khonsu, Amun's wife and son. Today the Pharaoh was going to seek Amun's blessing on the new year.

The people stood waiting in a thronging crowd, every person in Thebes anxious for the ceremony that would secure blessing and prosperity on the next year.

This temple that they were going to visit today had special significance to the King. He had ordered the building of several sections early in his reign. But even that was not something to think of just now. It wasn't that sort of day.

They disembarked and walked slowly toward the temple, along the stately avenue of sphinxes of sand-colored stone which guarded it. Tut's *was*-scepter tapped on the lane of packed earth as he walked, doing double-duty as a walking-stick. Priests in kilts of fine white linen, heads and bodies shaved completely hairless as a sign of purity, were carrying the statue of Amun-Ra on a small palanquin draped in gauzy linen curtains, preparing to put him back into his sacred inner sanctum within the temple. Outside, the King and Queen paused. Amun would let the Pharaoh know when it was time to approach.

Ankhesenamun looked up at Tut and squeezed his hand. He squeezed it back with the shadow of a smile, and she stepped back, giving him space. This was his work to do.

"The great god Amun-Ra delights in the presence of Pharaoh Tutankhamun," High Priest Parannefer said, opening his arms in welcome, the leopard-skin he wore draped over his shoulder swinging as he moved. The Pharaoh swallowed and entered the temple.

It was dim, and the smoke and fragrance of incense filled the air. Somehow he felt himself shivering as he left the warmth and light of the Sun behind, entering into the cool darkness of his

332

people's best effort to connect with the Divine. Oil lamps sat in dim recesses, casting flickering shadows on the painted walls, pictures of gods and goddesses, some with human faces, others with the heads of animals. Above them, the grand image of Amun-Ra stood silent and imposing, his stern face appearing and disappearing in the shifting light. There was no warmth in the cold light of those flickering flames.

The Day of Rebirth also applied to the Pharaoh's divinely-appointed rule. And Tutankhamun stood still as the priest poured water over his head, ceremonially cleansing him for his audience with the god.

Tut wore no crown, only a simple wig. But as he stood before the image of Amun-Ra, the priest brought out the red and white crowns of Upper and Lower Egypt and placed them upon the Pharaoh's head one by one, intoning the words of the coronation ritual Tut remembered from ten years previously.

This was Tutankhamun's first Opet Festival, the first year that the responsibility of interceding for his nation, the gravity of the renewal of his reign, applied to him. Every other year since his coronation, Ay had done it for him. But now he was an adult. And the responsibility was now his.

With one last prayer by the priest, one last promise from Tut to lead his people in truth and justice, the re-coronation was complete. He was ready to be Pharaoh for another year.

Now it was time to represent his people to the gods, to intercede for his people as their king. Slowly the Pharaoh set aside his cane, resting his hip against a nearby table for support instead. Hands raised in worship, the Pharaoh prayed. Prayed for his people, prayed for his wife, prayed for himself. Prayed for all of Egypt to be strong and healthy in the coming year. Prayed for strength for himself, renewal, further healing as he continued to recuperate from the ague. Prayed to become the strong Pharaoh he was supposed to be. Prayed for the dry, harvested lands to be restored as the yearly floods came and rejuvenated the earth. Prayed that the new schools would open ahead of schedule; for the well-being of every single one of the human beings who lived in the country he was now leading. Prayed for the Mitanni and the people of Amurru to be safe, that the Hittites would change their ways. Prayed for the forgiveness of his sins, the forgiveness of all Egypt. Prayed... prayed for fertility. Maybe one day, he and Ankh would try again. How could a god answer a prayer that had never been prayed?

His prayers complete, Tutankhamun took his cane and made his way toward the offerings that had been prepared by the priests. Head bowed in reverence, he offered the table that had been arranged, laden with food, drink, and fragrant incense.

"May the gods hear your prayers, O Mighty King, and pour out their blessings upon all Egypt," the High Priest said. Tutankhamun straightened up. His intercession for his nation was complete. He gripped his walking-stick and slowly, respectfully, walked from the temple, back into the bright warmth of the Sun, the Sun that stopped his shivering and filled him with something he knew was right, was real, was true. He felt more connected to the divine right now, simply walking in the Sun, than he had in the grand temple.

But despite the time he had spent in prayer, he felt... empty. Amun was so silent. He had heard no divine words, felt no answering warmth in his heart. Just like the silence every day during the lunchtime prayers and sacrifice, silence broken by the words of the priests, not the god himself. There had been nothing. Only his own words, his own hopes, echoing into silence. As he slowly

334

limped away, weak foot aching as his *was*-scepter tapped on the ground, he hoped it would be enough.

Ankhesenamun also prayed, while her husband was in the temple. Standing in the bright sunlight, she asked Tawaret for what she always did… a beautiful little boy to rule Egypt after Tutankhamun. Or a beautiful little girl to rule Egypt after her father. Either one. As long as… as long as it was blessed with health.

Why can't I do what I'm supposed to do, she asked. *Why can't I be what I'm supposed to be? I'm the Queen of Egypt, Great Royal Wife of the Pharaoh. It's my job to give birth to his heir. Why can't I?*

Head bowed, she asked the goddess of fertility for the blessing she longed for the most. But she felt no response, heard no divine words. There was nothing there but her own hopes. And her empty womb. And the silence.

Someday. Not yet. One day they would try again. Yet for now… there was silence.

And yet, in the warm rays of the Sun, there was a whisper. A whisper of hope. A whisper that told her not to give up. Someone could hear her prayers. Whether or not it was Tawaret. And Someone loved her. Somehow she could feel that love in the warm touch of the Sun… a Love she remembered from somewhere in her childhood.

And that love told her that someday, the time would be right.

Ankhesenamun closed her eyes. She had more questions than she had answers.

The people cheered as they saw the Pharaoh emerge from the dark temple. His royal intercessions were complete, and they would be blessed. Because the gods of his grandfather were listening. Raising one hand majestically, he tried to smile at the people—without showing his teeth. And he hoped they were right.

Tut was quiet when he came out of the temple, his prayers complete. Ankh took his free hand, and they made their way back to the barge, ready to take the journey back to the palace. Maybe she would join the festival later, for a little while. Because she could tell he didn't feel like it.

His limp was more pronounced; he leaned more heavily on his walking-stick than he had this morning on the way to the temple. It had taken a lot out of him.

Ankhesenamun sighed as they got into the barge, ready to go home. He didn't want to mingle with the crowds, loud, hot, and rowdy. And now she thought of it… she didn't either. They had too much to think about. Maybe tomorrow… and just for an hour or so. If they felt like it, once they had both rested.

There was purpose in all of this, she knew. All the pain. All the suffering. All the struggle. And one day they would find it. They just had to keep looking.

That week, the King and Queen remembered Senebhenas as her second birthday arrived, the date they had selected, about a month after she had come so early into the world, to call hers. Two long years since they had seen her, held her in their arms, whispered to her how much they loved her. Although… they still whispered to her when memories of the precious moments they had spent together ached in their hearts, the days that had seemed to go on

336

forever while passing as quickly as a breath. Together they got down the basket of baby things they had gathered for her; the swaddling, the tiny doll, the ribbons that would have gone on her first tunic. With sad smiles, they commemorated their precious daughter, finding peace alongside the pain as they remembered that they would not be separated forever.

30   Legacy

Slowly Tutankhamun made his way past the grand portrait of Grandfather Thutmose, who sneered down at him with the usual disappointment. He swallowed, choking up on his walking-stick, trying to ignore the ache in his foot.

What kind of Pharaoh was he, he wondered bitterly. Tapping around with his cane, as far from the battlefield as the Queen, as the Treasurer's little girl. He was pathetic. Even with everything he and the Queen were accomplishing... of which he really was quite proud... he was still not what a Pharaoh was supposed to be. He was not yet the strong Pharaoh he prayed to become every single day at the temple. He was still waiting for that prayer to be answered.

At this morning's meeting, from which he had just come, he had authorized a trade agreement with Punt, exchanging fine linen for ebony and ivory, and approved a shipment of building stone for the housing that was being built for the laborers who would build the new schools, as well as the clearing of the land immediately adjacent to the current staff quarters, which were being expanded to accommodate the new gardeners and cooks. He had also dispatched messengers throughout the entire nation, from Tamiat to Napata, spreading the word that soon, five new schools would be opening, two trade schools in Thebes and two in Memphis, along with a medical school in Thebes. It had been a busy, productive day so far, but he was still feeling... less than.

So he had gone back to his room to have Semerkhet and Ptahmose help him change out of his heavy crown and put away his false beard, and was going to try to get on with his day. However he was feeling about things at the moment. Then it had been time for prayers at the temple, accompanied by the usual bull sacrifice. The silence of the god and the suffering of the bull hadn't done anything to improve his mood.

He sat down to have lunch; roasted duck, flatbread spread with fresh cheese, and sweet, hot dumplings, fried balls of dough drizzled with honey. Ankh had already eaten, and was out in the garden, watching the birds. It was much easier for her to maneuver her way outside than it was for him. Semerkhet made sure that the Pharaoh's meal wasn't poisoned, and Tutankhamun began to eat.

That was when he noticed his dining companion.

"Hello there, Your Majesty," General Nakhtmin drawled, hoisting his glass of Tut's favorite white wine in a not-entirely-sincere salute. "How are you today? How is your, uh, foot?" He glanced down, as if he wanted to examine the Pharaoh's odd foot.

Tut pulled his feet closer to himself, away from Nakhtmin's eyes. No one was allowed to discuss his feet, or even acknowledge that they didn't match. Apparently no one had told Nakhtmin.

"Shame about you not wanting to take over the rest of Nubia," Nakhtmin said, taking an ostentatious sip of wine, heavy bracelet glittering on his wrist. "Although…" Again his hooded eyes seemed to glance toward Tut's feet. "I'm not sure whether you'd be leading us on campaign."

Tutankhamun gritted his teeth, squeezing the stem of his blue lotus cup until his knuckles went white.

"Maybe not," he said stiffly. "That prayer has not yet been answered."

Nakhtmin shook his head. "I suppose not." He gave a scornful little chuckle. "Wonder what your legacy will be," he mused thoughtfully. "Boy-King, I suppose. Not an empire-builder. Lowered taxes and established a minimum wage, for good or for ill… and decided that Egypt doesn't need slaves to build our great monuments… and you have quite an impressive collection of shoes… and, uh, walking-sticks. How many do you have now? I know you got a few at Tribute Day. What does that bring it to, two hundred?"

"A hundred and thirty-nine," Tut said through clenched teeth.

"Hmm… thought it was more," Nakhtmin murmured, taking a bite of duck. "Well, anyway… You might be remembered for your… fashion sense… but when it comes to our borders… I don't know; I wonder if you'll lose even more land than your father did."

Tut forced himself to take a bite of flatbread, following it with a sip of wine. Hard as it was, he had to be the mature one. Although, when it came to Nakhtmin, being more mature was not difficult.

"Well, I am only nineteen," he said stiffly. "I suppose I have some time to make a legacy for myself." He swallowed. "And maybe… eliminating poverty and promoting education will be more important than expanding our borders."

"Maybe you'd be too tall to be a soldier anyway," Nakhtmin said thoughtfully. "I mean, it is a bit… unnatural how tall you are." He chuckled, pointing a be-ringed finger. "That's what you remind me of… an ibis. With those long, skinny legs and knobbly knees." He gave a disdainful little snort. "If I was that tall, I'd have the legs to get me around."

"What makes you think any of this is my choice?" Tut muttered under his breath, clenching the stem of his glass.

And finishing his meal, the Pharaoh excused himself, the clouds of cloying perfume that surrounded the little General sticking to his own clothing.

340

Too late, he realized he hadn't finished his dumplings. He shook his head. In his annoyance at Nakhtmin, he had let them get cold anyway.

"Careful, Your Majesty. Watch your step!" Horemheb danced out of the way as Tut almost plowed into him, lost in frustrated thoughts.

"Excuse me," he said, continuing on his way.

"The maids just cleaned the floors that way— don't slip!" Horemheb said cheerfully, if a little patronizingly. "Don't want you to get hurt." Then he chuckled... in a way the Pharaoh didn't like. "This isn't the battlefield, after all. And you're not exactly Thutmose the First. It is too bad, though," he continued, shaking his head in what might have been mocking sadness, "that the gods saw fit to..." He paused, glancing down at Tut's feet, the walking-stick clutched in his hand. "Well... maybe you'll be a... different... kind of Pharaoh. A... special one." He gave the Pharaoh the smile one would give a very young child.

Tut just gripped his walking-stick and kept going.

Straight past Maya. Who was not looking where he was going. Again Tutankhamun had to change course to avoid a collision, and Maya blinked as he saw who he had almost run into.

"Careful, Glorious Lord," he said. "Can't have you falling to your death without an heir." He swallowed. "What a legacy that would be."

Clenching his teeth, the Pharaoh kept walking, even though each step hurt as much as his growing frustration. Nakhtmin, Horemheb, and Maya's insincere wishes for life, health, and prosperity clanged like broken bells, meaningless noise. As meaning-less as his own efforts to get them to respect him.

"What's wrong, Glorious Lord?"

Tut bit back a rough "Excuse me" as he recognized User-montu's creaky voice. He stopped, turning to face the Vizier. The old man stood across the hall, multiple chins quivering as he stopped walking.

The Pharaoh sighed and arranged his features into a polite smile, leaning more heavily on his walking-stick as they stood facing one another in the hallway.

"It's just Horemheb and Maya and Nakhtmin, they don't like me, they don't respect me, they don't think I'll amount to anything and they seem to be enjoying making me feel worse about every-thing," he said in a frustrated groan.

Usermontu shook his head. To Tut's satisfaction, the old man was looking right at him, straight into his eyes. "For shame. What did they say?"

Tutankhamun gave a bitter little chuckle. "Well, Nakhtmin compared me unfavorably to an ibis, Horemheb said I'd never be a soldier and called me 'special,' and Maya commented…" He grit-ted his teeth— "about me not having an heir."

Usermontu shook his head with a disgusted frown. "Shame on them. But well done. Nineteen, and you're more mature than any of them. That maturity will go far."

Tut tried to smile. "How do I prove myself?" he asked, yearning aching in his voice. "How do I show them I can be the Pharaoh they think I never will be? That my legacy…" He chuckled as Nakhtmin's comment replayed in his mind— "that my legacy will be more than my collection of walking-sticks and shoes."

"You've already begun," Usermontu said with a little smile. Tut smiled back as the old Vizier looked right at him, looking into his eyes as though they were both human. "Ordering taxes to be lowered, slavery to be limited, schools to be built. You have a great legacy ahead of you, Great Morning Star." He swallowed. "On or off the battlefield."

Tutankhamun nodded. Usermontu was right. And there was no scorn in his voice, his words. He was merely stating what he saw.

Then the elderly Vizier chuckled. "I have something for you, actually, if you'd like it," he said. He reached into a bag he was carrying and pulled out something wrapped in linen. As he revealed his gift, the Pharaoh smiled. His favorite honey-cakes.

"Honey-cakes make everything better," Usermontu whispered, handing the King the linen-wrapped package.

Tut took it in his free hand with a smile. "Thank you. They do."

The Pharaoh paused. Usermontu was a very old man; he would have been practically an adult during Akhenaten's childhood. Was he someone Tut could ask about the Hebrews?

"Usermontu..." he said slowly, "changing the subject... Can you tell me anything about a long time ago, when my father was a little boy, and the Hebrews and the army all disappeared? It's not in the history Ay's been reading to me, and he doesn't want to talk about it."

Tut saw Usermontu take a deep breath, stand a little more stiffly. The old Vizier swallowed carefully.

"Your Majesty..." he said slowly, not meeting the Pharaoh's eye, "those things happened... a long time ago. I will say that no one... quite... understands what happened, and there are different… opinions. Those events certainly… influenced… your father, but what god willed them, and why, I'm not sure."

He released a long, shuddering breath. "The important thing now is to move forward with what we have. And you're doing that, promoting education, fighting poverty, seeking peace and friendship with our neighbors. Whatever happened in the past, and why, I can see you guiding us into a glorious future."

And with a bow and a wish for all life, prosperity, and health, he let the Pharaoh continue on his way.

Something had happened, Tutankhamun thought. Whatever the details, whatever the cause, something had happened. His father's stories were based, in some way, on the truth. But what did that mean?

But the day wasn't over yet. Early that afternoon, the Pharaoh had another history lesson with Ay. The study was cooler today than it had been lately, and even if that was the only good thing that happened today, Tut was grateful not to be sitting there actively sweating as he tried to focus on the endless stream of useful information that was issuing from Ay's mouth.

"…and Thutmose the First took over Nubia and campaigned in Syria, expanding Egypt's borders to their greatest extent," he read in his dry old voice.

Tut swallowed. Again, the great warrior grandfather was coming back to haunt him, taunt him, with his accomplishments, accomplishments Tutankhamun would never match.

"How will they remember me?" he asked sadly, leaning his head on his hand. He hardly knew why he asked; maybe he just wanted to get it over with.

344

Ay set aside the papyrus and smiled warmly at the Pharaoh, the boy he had practically raised.

"Your reign, my dear boy," he said gently, "may well be remembered as one of the most peacefully uneventful periods in all of Egypt's history. Sometimes…" He looked off into the middle distance, not a good sign. "Sometimes, not changing the status quo… is wise. You will be protected, dear boy, by your loyal courtiers, who will always be there to guide you." Ay swallowed. "You need the help of others, dear Pharaoh. And you will always have it."

Tut looked down at his knees with a sigh, shielding his feelings from the Vizier. Just as he had expected. Yet another "loyal courtier" telling him they didn't think he'd be able to accomplish anything, amount to anything. Telling him that he might as well remain a child, because then he would be safe, safe from the things he wouldn't be able to handle.

Ay was never going to let go of him.

31   Respect

Tutankhamun shared the honey-cakes with Ankhesenamun as they sat together on the balcony that afternoon, listening to the birds singing in the garden below. A gentle breeze wafted the fragrances of the flowers toward them, making the golden beads in Ankh's wig jingle. Tut smiled as he wrapped his green outer robe closer around himself. It was getting cooler. Here was a little gift from above, toward the end of a long, frustrating day. Another gift was that there were no longer nearly as many mosquitoes.

"These are good," she said, wiping her mouth as she finished one. "What's the occasion?"

"Usermontu gave them to me," Tut said. "I had a bit of a… rough afternoon."

Ankh's eyebrows contracted in a little frown. "What happened?"

He sighed, the frustration and embarrassment coming back as he recounted the conversations he and his courtiers had had.

"They just make me feel…" Tut sighed, leaning back in his chair as the cool afternoon breeze ruffled the fine black braids of his wig. "Make me feel like I'll never amount to anything. Feel… weak. Like a pathetic little kid, a helpless little cripple. Like I'll never be the strong Pharaoh I'll have to be to get them to believe in me. Take me seriously. Respect me enough not to insult me to my face." He swallowed. "I don't know how to be strong."

His sister leaned forward and took his hand. "You *are* strong," she whispered. "And you always have been. And…" She swallowed, feeling a lump in her throat. "There's a purpose. To all of it. I know there is. We might not know it yet… but we have to keep

346

searching til we find it. And we will." She sighed, squeezing his hand. "But don't ever let anyone tell you you're not strong. If they think that, they don't know you very well. Because you are the strongest person I know."

Giving his sister half a smile, Tut lifted her hand and kissed it. "And you're the strongest person *I* know."

Then Ankh chuckled. "I got something for you, actually," she said, getting up. And Tut grinned as his sister presented him with a beautiful bouquet. "Thought it might cheer you up."

Already Tut was breathing in the sweetness of the blossoms, admiring their bright colors. "You went around to the far side of the gardens," he observed, running his fingertips over the velvety petals of the lotuses she had gathered. "That's the only pool with purple lotuses. And who helped you reach the red roses? I imagine it wasn't Meresankh."

"Hannu," Ankh laughed, rolling her eyes playfully. "The bodyguard. He said he knew you'd like them."

"I love them," Tut said, taking another deep breath of their fragrances. He could feel his stress melting away as he drank in their beauty with all his senses. "I thought the blue lotuses were gone."

"I found a couple more," Ankh said, her dimple deepening with satisfaction.

"And these are the first chrysanthemums I've seen," he said, marveling over their bright red and yellow.

"They were hiding under the fig tree, the tall one, next to the rose bush," the Queen said. Tut nodded, picturing the exact spot.

"Look at this color," he whispered, losing himself in the swirling depths of the red roses. "And the smell... And this jasmine… it's almost pink. I don't think I've ever seen pink jasmine."

"It's doing that this year," Ankh said with a little shrug. "And the blue lotuses lasted and lasted, and the poppies were really big… Every year's different, isn't it?"

Tut gathered the flowers into one hand and opened his other arm to his sister.

"This is *our* year," he whispered, gently holding her close as she stood beside his chair, her little arms around his neck. "The year we make a difference."

He had confided in his sister. And now he wanted to confide in his valet. But where was he? Tut tapped around the palace with his walking-stick, looking for Semerkhet.

Just as he was beginning to feel worried, a familiar laugh sounded behind him. Relieved, Tut spun round and limped toward him. Semerkhet stood there in his blue hockey uniform, sweat and elation all over his face. His nine teammates were crowded around him, laughing and playfully shoving one another as they recounted the details of whatever they'd just been doing.

"Did you see that save?" Amenmose was saying, throwing an arm around Semerkhet's shoulder and almost knocking him over. Sem grinned, playfully pushing him away. "All hail the greatest goalie in Upper Egypt!"

"Well, how about you?" Semerkhet said with a chuckle. "The way you knocked the ball out of the air before it landed but still managed not to brain Sennefer—"

Another teammate cut in, gesturing animatedly. "And that dive that Kamose did, straight between Neferkare's knees—"

Now a third interrupted, gesticulating even more wildly. "And how Raherka scooped it off the ground before Sennefer could get it and still managed not to get run over by Amenmose—"

Tut shook his head with a smile. How he had he forgotten? Semerkhet had had hockey practice.

He didn't say anything. Just stepped back and let them go by.

Tut walked down the hall, Bastet padding along beside him. He'd spent a little while reading in his private sitting room, and he needed to get up and stretch before heading down to dinner.

"Your Majesty?"

Tut paused as he heard the younger Vizier greet him, then saw him approach from across the hall. Pentu smiled up at him, a sweet, gentle little smile that almost reminded him of Ankh. The other politician could tell something was wrong. Even after the Pharaoh's rest, his heart was still hurting.

The King smiled politely, shifting his weight so his painful foot could rest during their conversation. "Yes, Pentu?"

"Your Majesty," Pentu said with a warm smile, "Vizier User-montu told me how… immature the others were being. And I also want to commend you for how you've handled it." He sighed. "They just… don't understand that… there are many different types of strength, all equal in value. They haven't looked back to see how strong you have been your entire life, and how strong your heart and mind are. It takes a special Pharaoh to lower taxes and open new schools, all while deferring the purchase of any additional slaves for an entire year and limiting the expansion of the military budget."

He winked, and Tut knew that in his use of the word "special," there was nothing but respect. "You've shown them what your priorities are, what kind of Pharaoh you intend to be. So don't let them get you down. When your ideas lift us out of this economic depression and lift the less fortunate out of poverty, they'll see that you were right."

Tutankhamun smiled. "Thank you, Pentu. That's just what I needed to hear." Then he chuckled. "But you know that all the ideas belong to the Queen," he whispered.

Pentu chuckled too. "I know, Great Morning Star. Egypt has been blessed with a wise Pharaoh and a wise Queen. It takes wisdom to listen to wisdom." The young Vizier looked like he wanted to reach out and give the King an encouraging pat on the shoulder, but restrained himself. "Your time will come, Glorious Lord." And Tut gave him a grateful smile.

Then Pentu swallowed. "I can't say it's the same… but as the youngest of the Viziers, sometimes I've felt like my ideas receive less weight. It's good… it's good to be among other young politicians. Because like I said… age doesn't always equal wisdom." He winked again.

And together, they chuckled.

Tut sighed and shook his head as Semerkhet touched up his makeup before dinner. Hockey practice had been a great success, and the Pharaoh had enjoyed hearing about it, but now it was his turn to tell his story of how his day had gone.

"I thought I was getting through to Horemheb," he said in frustration.

"What's wrong?" Semerkhet asked, outlining the Pharaoh's left eye with kohl.

350

Tut fought the impulse to shake his head while his friend was doing his eyeliner.

Bitterly, Tut described the General's disheartening comments. Frowning in concern, Semerkhet turned away for Tut's eyeshadow, and the Pharaoh shook his head, braids swinging.

"I just thought… He was coming to me for relationship advice, and he was the one who helped me that time I got so angry, and then I helped *him* when *he* got angry. And whenever we talked, I felt like it meant something. Like we were going to be able to exchange ideas. Like maybe we could trust one another. And now I don't know. He just…" Tut bit his lip. "Really dithappointed me." He sighed. "And I don't know… don't know if I can get him on my side. I feel like… if he had to pick between listening to me and listening to the Vizier, I don't know who he'd pick. I don't know if *he* knows who he'd pick."

"He'll see," Semerkhet said, brushing the braids of Tut's wig out of his eyes. "He'll get his priorities figured out. But just remember… When someone else is wrong, you don't have to take it personally."

And Tut laughed.

Before long it was time for the Sunset Ceremony. Tutankhamun stood before the temple, watching the sun set. *Make me a strong Pharaoh*, he prayed, just like he did every morning, every evening. *The Pharaoh I am supposed to be.*

The evening sun shone down on him, warming his face, his heart, with its gentle rays. It was saying something to him, telling him something. But he wasn't sure what.

Semerkhet got him ready for bed, and he fell asleep, Bastet curled up warmly against his side, the extra blanket he'd been waiting for all year tucked warmly around him.

Then he was walking down the hall to lunch, past the grand portrait of Grandfather Thutmose.

"What a disappointment you are," a deep voice boomed. Tut stopped, looking up at the painting to see that it was… moving. Grandfather Thutmose himself was actually looking down at Tut, a scornful sneer on his carved and painted face. "Hobbling around the palace with your walking-stick. I'll bet you can't even lift a sword. Feeble little cripple. You're an embarrassment, the pathetic little Boy-King. And that's all you'll ever be. One day they'll find your tomb, and that's what they'll call you. The Boy-King."

He shook his head. "What a grandson. I'm ashamed of you. You'll probably bring my dynasty to an end, too. You're a failure, a failure of a warrior, a failure of a father. A strong Pharaoh has strong sons and expands Egypt's borders. And you've done neither. You're a disgrace. Unworthy to be Pharaoh. Useless, weak. How do you expect me to be proud of you? You'll never amount to anything."

Tut tried to formulate a response, but before he could come up with anything, the portrait had gone perfectly still, his grandfather back in his static pose of preparing to smite an enemy. The strange conversation was over.

But it still hurt. Stung and angry, Tut gripped his walking-stick and kept walking, foot hurting with every step.

Bastet's purring suddenly made him look for her. And he was waking up, the cat in his arms. He was safe in bed, away from any talking portraits. It had all been a dream.

He rolled over, holding Bastet to his heart. It had only been a dream... but it still hurt.

"I've got to do something," he murmured to the cat. "*Something... Ugh...*"

But he still didn't know what.

"Tell Bastet the goddess to send me something," he asked her. "Anything. Anything tho I can prove that I'm a strong Pharaoh."

She just looked at him. Then she laid her head down and closed her eyes. She was going back to sleep.

Tut sighed and closed his eyes again. Maybe she was right. There wasn't much he could do about it in the middle of the night. He could think, and plan, in the morning.

What could he do, he groaned to himself all through the next day. He had to do something, had to prove himself to be the strong Pharaoh he was supposed to be. Had to show his people how strong he was. Restlessly he tapped around the palace, searching for whatever it was he was meant to be doing. Like he had just before he and Semerkhet had gone on that hunting trip a few months back, he felt like if he didn't find the legacy he was supposed to pursue, he was about to go crazy. This desperate, bored frustration was getting stronger every day.

What would he be remembered for? And how could he get it started?

32   The Politician

The Pharaoh called another meeting. Ay, Maya, Horemheb, Nakhtmin, Pentu, and Usermontu joined him in the throne room, preparing themselves for the Pharaoh's next royal recommendation.

Except that now, they weren't just recommendations. Now in his full power, the Pharaoh would be very hard to veto.

This time it was easier to go in, he found. Easier to look at those six faces before him, waiting to hear what he would say. This time, he was somewhat looking forward to it. This time, he felt... he felt a little like a Pharaoh. Felt a bit of that confidence, that power, that he had felt coursing through his veins when he had fired Sennedjem, reprimanded Nakhtmin. He could do it. He knew he could. Because he had done it in the past.

Sitting in his own chair across the room, Nuya the scribe was preparing a pen, getting ready to take the minutes of the meeting.

"I see we haven't yet lowered taxes," Tut announced from his throne, showing off a piece of papyrus containing the most recent tax data. The *nemes* on his head, the crook and flail in his left hand, and the false beard on his chin showed he meant business. "I thought we discussed this."

"We did discuss it, Glorious Lord," Ay said from where he sat in his chair, one of the semicircle of courtiers who sat facing the royal throne. "But your benevolent proposal has not yet been approved."

"Proposal?" Tutankhamun asked, kohl-lined eyes flashing under dangerous dark eyebrows. "I am the Morning and the Evening Star, standing alone in full power. It will be as I say. And I say that we are lowering taxes, effective immediately."

"Must it be immediate?" Maya asked, leaning slightly toward the King as he tried to pull him back from a change like this. "The schools you're building are very expensive, Ruler of Truth. Keeping taxes as they are would help us to pay the builders, as you have insisted, especially considering your... generous... new minimum wage."

Tut shook his head. "No. Dock the pay of the bureaucracy if you have to, but how will the people ever be able to afford school if taxes remain so high?"

"The Pharaoh is right," Pentu said before anyone else could register their shock. His bright, clear eyes shone with the same dreams as the King and Queen were seeking to implement. "What is the point of building new schools if people won't be able to go?"

Nakhtmin gave a tiny grunt, frowning at Usermontu, who sat beside him. But he said nothing. Had he been about to ask if there was any point in building the schools at all, but been silenced by a kick to the ankle?

"By how much does the Pharaoh recommend we lower the tax?" Usermontu finally asked, hope for a compromise clear in his grandfatherly voice.

"By at least ten percent," Tut said immediately.

Maya looked at the papyrus of tax data, doing calculations in his mind. "We can manage five, Glorious Lord," he said finally. "Perhaps we can increase the cut to ten next year."

"Decreasing the tax by even five percent will put a noticeable strain on the... bureaucracy whose pay you are suggesting we dock," Ay said smoothly. "I advise caution, My Lord."

"Why can't we cut it by ten immediately?" Pentu asked in his high tenor before the Pharaoh could accept the compromise. His sleeves fell back, revealing his pointed elbows, as he gestured. The ugly looks the others gave the young Vizier as he spoke almost frightened the Pharaoh; as much as Tut was pleased that someone agreed with him, Maya almost looked like he wanted to hurt Pentu, and all Ay would do was stare as Nakhtmin shook his head with a disgusted sneer. "I am sure we could cut spending in other areas to make room for the tax cut. We could decrease military spending, for one thing. And I'll accept the largest pay cut myself."

"If we decrease military spending, how can we defend Egypt from her enemies?" Horemheb asked immediately. The King had to remark at how smart his uniform looked today. "My Lord, it's my opinion that the military budget must stay exactly where it is. Although your mission of peace toward the Mitanni and the Nubians was very effective, the Hittites are encroaching on our territories in the northeast, and we'll need all the funding we can get to continue holding them back, O King for Whom the Nile Floods. The five percent increase you graciously granted may be the only thing standing between us and takeover."

"And I think the military budget should be expanded," Nakhtmin said. As usual, he was leaning back in his chair, one foot resting on the opposite knee. The gold rings he was wearing glinted in the light of the torches that lined the walls, and the usual clouds of perfume permeated the air around him. "When you sent Horemheb on your mission of peace, you forgot to underline the importance of expanding our southern borders."

"Thank you, Nakhtmin. I already discussed an expansion of the military budget with Horemheb; if you care to refer to this report—" Tut held up a piece of papyrus— "I think you'll see that I agreed to raise it by five percent, and to send troops to Kadesh later this year to protect the Mitanni and their neighbors in Amurru from the

356

Hittites. Moving on, I'll accept a five percent tax cut for now," Tutankhamun declared, subtly gesturing at Pentu to drop it while glaring at the son of the Grand Vizier. "And ten next year. The military budget will remain as it is for the moment, and the minimum wage will be officially established at its agreed-upon rate. Thank you, gentlemen." Nuya's pen scratched as he finished taking down the Pharaoh's proclamations, recording for posterity the decisions that had been passed today.

As one the others rose and bowed, voices chanting, "Hail to thee, Ruler of Truth; all life, prosperity, and health!"

Then they filed out, and Tut shook his head at the goodhearted smile on Pentu's face. That was the last time he ever saw it.

It was more technical than he had thought, the Pharaoh realized. He could propose an adjustment to a budget category, order the building of a school, demand the cessation of the slave trade with Nubia, or direct the lowering of taxes, but if his decrees comprised nothing more than verbal suggestions to his royal court, they would remain exactly that. Anything he genuinely wanted to make happen, he had to put into writing and stamp with his signet-ring.

Ankhesenamun and Tut sat on the balcony after evening prayers, watching the sun set and listening to the locusts whirring in the garden. The colors of the trees and flowers were fading as the light dimmed, reds and pinks sliding into soft browns, greens darkening into blue and then a deep gray. The water sparkled in the dying light, lotus-pools reflecting what sunlight was left. The nights of the end of Paophi were beautiful.

Finally it was time for long sleeves, sometimes even cool enough for outer robes. Finally, the mosquitoes were gone. And they would stay away for a good while, usually until the Season of the Harvest.

"What changes have you made so far?" Ankhesenamun asked into the stillness.

He adjusted his arm around her delicate little shoulder, holding her closer and resting his cheek on her head.

"Well, we decreased taxes by five percent," he said. "I wanted ten, but they said we might be able to go to ten next year. It's not quite what I hoped, but I'm still pretty satisfied. And we're moving forward with the minimum wage, and with ending the slave trade."

"Five percent," Ankh said appreciatively. Her head moved against the side of his face as she nodded. "That'll be meaningful. Keep a lot of bread on the table."

Tut nodded. "I hope so."

Ankh could see him growing with each day that passed. And she was proud of him. But she was always there for him. And when there was something he didn't know, he came to her. And she told him.

The other thing he could always count on was the flowers. Somehow she always knew when he had a big meeting. And when he tottered into her room or to join her on the balcony, she had a bouquet for him; daisies, poppies, anemones, lotus blossoms. They always made him smile, always helped restore him with their beauty after the long, overwhelming day he had had. And they always reminded him of how much his big sister loved him.

Occasionally, though… his big sister could be just the tiniest bit annoying. She would fuss over his formal outfits, making sure he looked perfect for his meetings when Semerkhet had already gotten him all arranged. Was his crown straight; was he really wearing that belt with those shoes? And she would remind him of things they'd discussed four or five times already, making sure he was prepared for his meetings, knew what he was going to say, knew, even, who he was meeting with. And he gritted his teeth and let her.

But at the end of a long day, he could let it out, set free the big day and how hard the Queen was working to help him. Even if she was working a little too hard, and her help was turning into henpecking.

"Oh, girls," he groaned, sitting down in front of his mirror one night to let Semerkhet remove his heavy wig, set aside his gleaming jewelry for the next day. Silently, Ptahmose took each piece, quietly putting them away. "I love her so much, but sometimes I wish she'd just stop trying to arrange me to death. And I wish she knew she doesn't have to remind me ten times what not to say to the Mycenaeans!"

His valet shook his head. "That's big sisters for you," he said with a sigh that told the Pharaoh he understood only too well. "They love us so much, don't they?"

Tut chuckled and shook his head. "They sure do."

And he smiled. Sem got it. Just like a brother.

Semerkhet, too, struggled, though. Struggled to stand back, to stop protecting his lord, master, and friend from all the questions and comments that came his way from every direction. And

359

sometimes he would still dismiss a hopeful chef or gardener with a look. Sometimes, the Pharaoh did not even notice.

Semerkhet was that good.

But even though the burden of responsibility sometimes weighed heavily on his shoulders, Tut found the time to relax and do the things he loved. He went to every horse race and hockey game that he could, cheering his friend on to victory, encouraging him in defeat. And between the games and races, he and Sem would go hunting in their chariot, or just out for a joyride, Stormy and Flash thundering ahead of them as they tore around the empty racetrack or loped through the grasslands, spooking ducks at every turn. He was the Pharaoh, after all, standing alone in full power.

He could do anything he wanted.

33   Pentu

Every week or so, Amenia and Mutnedjmet would come and have tea with the Queen. And they would talk— about life as women, about their men, about life. She shared the Queens List with them, taught them about the same powerful women she had taught her brother about, about the mighty legacy that stretched back before the building of the pyramids. Shared with them what her mother and grandmother had taught her, how to use feminine strengths in a world led by men.

And what she had learned in her own life, becoming stronger with every loss she suffered, becoming a mother to Egypt itself. Working alongside her brother, marrying her greater political experience and wisdom to his authority as Pharaoh, guiding him as he led their nation. Finding joy as the power beside the throne… and being civil and sneaky, sweet and deadly, when she had to. Approaching each day with both courage and cunning.

A Queen did not have to become Pharaoh for her decisions to echo through history. And Amenia and Mutnedjmet could become the power beside the throne in their relationship with Horemheb. And… they could learn to define themselves not in terms of being his wives, but in terms of being their own beautiful, unique, individual selves. And they… could learn to define themselves not in terms of whether they had had the opportunity to raise children. They could allow themselves to heal, to feel, to mourn, and they could find peace. Find joy again, when the time was right. And find themselves stronger than before.

Ankhesenamun and Mutnedjmet had carried children. Children they had been forced to say goodbye to almost before saying hello. Amenia had never had a child.

But none of them had failed. Ankh made sure they understood that.

Every time they met, Ankh taught her friends something new, something they could apply to their own lives. And when the ladies left, they were smiling. Even if tears had been shed. And Ankh was always proud when she watched them go. Because they were growing so much.

They were growing as people, no doubt about it. But they were also growing as friends to the Queen. And she knew she could trust them. And that one day, if she needed help, she would be able to turn to them.

She was a mentor, Ankhesenamun thought to herself. And that was something to be proud of.

Whenever his daily responsibilities were complete, Tut always found the time to take a turn around the garden, no matter how tired he was. Because it was so lovely out; the cool breeze, the gentle sunshine, so bright and loving, the joy of not having to swat mosquitoes away every two minutes. And he and his sister played *seega* in the garden or on the balcony as often as they could. The Pharaoh was proud to see his strategy improving; he considered every move before making it, placing his pieces carefully and thoughtfully as each game began, then taking the time to envision the outcomes of each potential move before choosing it. Sometimes, he won. Between games, he would listen to her accounts of the great Queens of the past, join her on long strolls through the gardens, anything they could think of that would get them outdoors for just a little longer.

This was a glorious time of year. The beauty of his favorite time of year helped him set aside the stress, the weariness, that he was quickly realizing was part of the job of Pharaoh. At the end of each day, no matter what, he found the time to get outside.

The day after their approval, the Pharaoh again gathered his inner circle for the signing of the tax cut and the official establishment of the minimum wage, the cancellation of the purchase of any additional slaves for the year, and increase to the military budget. This was the third meeting they had had, and this time, he didn't even feel a twinge of anxiety. He looked around the throne room, counting faces. Ay, Maya, Nakhtmin, Horemheb, Usermontu…

"Is Pentu running late?" he asked.

"Vizier Pentu will not be joining us today, I am afraid," Ay said carefully. "He has been taken ill with ague."

Tut nodded, shielding his thoughts. Ague. How strange. This was not mosquito season. He turned to Nuya, who was taking the minutes.

"Nuya," he said, "please take this down to Pentu after the meeting so that he can sign it."

As he spoke, there was a sudden rustle of fabric. The Pharaoh glanced around to see Treasurer Maya suddenly sit up straight just as the Grand Vizier's gnarled old hand tightened on the handle of his walking-stick, his Adam's apple jumping as he gave a convulsive swallow. For a moment there was silence, Vizier and Treasurer looking at their respective sandals.

"I will take it to him," Maya said finally, his voice loud in the hush that had descended. He smiled rather stiffly, shifting uncomfortably in his chair. "I will deliver it," he said again, "with your best wishes for a speedy recovery." The Treasurer smoothed his robes, still not looking at the Vizier, whose neutral expression appeared very intentional. He was still looking at his sandals.

The Pharaoh nodded, smiling pleasantly. "Very well. Thank you, Treasurer." And he put on his signet-ring.

They signed it without Pentu, and it was official. Tutankhamun's loyal subjects would pay five percent less in annual taxes. But there was an odd taste in Tut's mouth as he signed this agreement into law with his signet-ring. Because he felt that he was getting in very deep.

It was time to return to Memphis. The staff packed everything into boxes, Semerkhet and Meresankh feverishly overseeing the work of the other servants, ticking items off their lists to ensure that nothing was lost or stolen. Tut tried to keep out of the way of Semerkhet and those the valet was directing, but he couldn't seem to find anyone to talk to; Horemheb and Maya had their own packing to oversee, and Usermontu was going to pack the contents of his office himself. Pentu, also, was not in evidence; the Pharaoh assumed that he, too, was overseeing his packing. Assuming he was feeling better, that was. Tut gave a sigh as he thought of the cheerful young Vizier, then pushed the other politicians to the back of his mind. Ptahmose had just dropped an armful of walking-sticks, and Semerkhet was struggling to squash a stack of linen robes into a chest. He might as well at least offer to help.

Once the caravan of baggage trains was loaded, they all packed themselves into carts and wagons for the long journey north. Tut always missed the lake in Thebes when he was in Memphis, but Memphis had the best hunting. All in all, it was a wonderful luxury to have the opportunity to spend half the year in one capital and half in the other.

The season was changing. The wind was cool, and it was time to exchange short sleeves for cozy robes. The Queen sighed as she oversaw the rearrangement of her wardrobe. And she remembered two years ago, wrapping her warm robes around her curved belly, feeling Senebhenas kicking. Those were the days… when everything had been all right.

"Have any of your maidservants had the ague lately?" Tut asked his sister as they sat together in his Memphis bedroom. He shifted his weight in the chair; this was one of the days when he couldn't get comfortable. His foot hurt too much. So much that he had hardly left his room all day. It was lovely, though, that the day was relatively cool. His tunic, and Ankh's dress, both had long sleeves. Warmer clothes for a cooler day. Every year, the seasons made their rounds. And every year, in the months of Athyr or Sholiak, the heat finally faded.

Ankh looked up from playing with the cat on the floor and shook her head, the red beads on her wig tinkling. "No. It's too cold for the mosquitoes. They all run away and hide when the weather finally turns." She sighed, giving a little smile. "So that's why the servants have been eating outside. Because it's so nice out."

"That's what I was thinking," Tut said thoughtfully. "But Pentu wasn't at the signing of the first set of changes we're making, and they said he was out with ague. Strange."

Ankh sighed, giving a little frown. "Yes. Strange."

"My Lady?" Meresankh was standing across from Ankh's bed, one of the Queen's bracelets in her hand. She fiddled with it as she spoke, eyes lowered. Her hands were trembling.

"Hmm?"

"My Lady… I've been thinking… about the Pharaoh's new tax cuts. And I don't know… if they're wise. Could you counsel him to reverse them?"

Ankh blinked. What was going on? Her handmaiden, interested in economics, telling her what to tell Tut?

Meresankh looked at the Queen, and there were tears in her eyes. And Ankhesenamun understood.

"Who was it?" she said softly. "Who talked to you?"

"Treasurer Maya," Meresankh said, her voice a scared whisper. "I'm sorry… I'm scared, My Lady. Something's going on. Something's wrong."

"I know." Ankh stepped forward and wrapped her handmaiden in a gentle hug. She was warm and soft. The servant shuddered, then relaxed into the Queen's embrace. Ankh had never hugged Meresankh before… like a dear friend, the friend she had become to the Queen. "But it's not your fault. Don't pay any mind to anything the Treasurer tells you to do. But if you do hear anything else, come and tell me right away, all right?"

Meresankh looked up and nodded, her makeup running down her face. And alongside the anxious fear, the Queen caught another glimpse of the Light shining in her eyes. "I will."

366

Ankhesenamun paged through the Queens List she kept so carefully put away, being that it was the only copy in the world. Right now she needed wisdom for herself. Because something was wrong. Politics was brewing. And she wondered what her brother's royal court would do next. And how many of them would live to see next year.

Queen Ahhotep had seen her country through a war, guided it confidently as they had waited to see if her husband would come home from that war. He had not, but his widow had stood in the gap, serving as regent until the heir to the throne was old enough to rule. And her grateful son, Pharaoh Ahmose the First, had recorded her deeds, telling future generations that his mother had taken care of Egypt… *She has looked after her Egypt's soldiers, she has guarded Egypt, she has brought back her fugitives and gathered together her deserters, and she has pacified Upper Egypt and expelled her rebels.*

A war was coming, Ankh thought as she put away the documents, carefully stacked among other histories. But with the knowledge and wisdom that had been passed down to her from the generations upon generations of women who had gone before, she would know what to do.

"Sem," Tut said one evening as his valet helped him get ready for bed, "I was thinking… today… it's been a year, hasn't it? A year since you first came to the palace, helping Hetepheres?"

Semerkhet smiled as he turned down the covers of the Pharaoh's bed, taking his walking-stick as the King slowly sat down.

"That's right," he said. "That is today." He sighed. "A whole year."

Tut lay down, then reached out to squeeze his friend's hand. "A good year." He chuckled, thinking back over that year, all they had learned over the past twelve months. All they had learned about one another. "Hard to remember now... When you first started, we weren't even friends."

Semerkhet shook his head with his own chuckle, bending to tuck the Pharaoh in. "I never would have imagined calling the Morning and the Evening Star my friend." His voice dropped to a whisper as he smiled. "But I'm so glad that I can."

The month of Athyr went on. Again day and night were balanced, and another festival was due. And even with all of the politics they were fighting their way through, Ankh and Tut went out into Memphis. They needed a breather.

The people of Egypt gathered to celebrate the changing of the seasons— and the Hathor Festival, which, for most participants, involved large amounts of alcohol. The Pharaoh and the Queen celebrated just long enough to get pleasantly tired, which wasn't very long, what with the heaving crowds, blaring music, and high levels of general rowdiness, and then made their way back to the palace, which was nearly empty. All the staff were out getting merrily drunk.

The Pharaoh didn't drink much. The wine was good, but one glass was enough. One time when he was fourteen, he had gotten himself thoroughly drunk, and woken up the next morning so hungover that he'd sworn to himself not to repeat his mistake. And he never had. Ankh, too, drank carefully, enjoying the rich flavor of the imported wine while being cautious not to cross the line between feeling pleasantly mellow and being unable to walk home.

They chatted to one another as they came back into the quiet palace, not expecting to see anyone. Then the Queen paused mid-sentence.

"Oh, hello, Meresankh." Her handmaiden was standing there in the front hall with a tiny old lady— the Granny she had told the Queen about.

"Your Majesties." Meresankh gave a graceful bow, as did the midwife. Then, quietly, they walked away, toward the staff quarters.

Ankhesenamun shrugged as her handmaiden walked away. That was the third religious festival Meresankh had missed.

The King thought about his cheerful Vizier every day. Life went on; no one mentioned him. Finally, after he and the Queen came back from the Hathor Festival, the King decided to bring it up himself.

"Ay," he said, coming across him in the hallway under the grand painting of Grandfather Thutmose, nearly identical to the one at the palace in Thebes, "how is Pentu? Last week you let me know he was sick, but I haven't heard anything since. Do you have any news?"

Ay's lined face became very solemn. Tut's stomach twisted. "My Lord... I was just coming to tell you... Vizier Pentu died this morning. The ague took him much more quickly than anyone could have imagined."

Tut's head spun, and he clutched his cane. Dead? Smiling, happy Pentu, who always had a kind word and a small gift for everyone he saw? Dead?

"Do you need to sit down, Great Morning Star? I understand this must come as quite a shock… My heart bled when I got the news. Gave me a bitter taste of how I might feel if my own son Nakhtmin died."

Ay's lips were moving; sound was coming out. The words moved slowly through the air, coming distorted to Tut's ears, as if through water. *Quite a shock… heart bled… own son…* He tottered over to a bench and sat down, holding his head. So healthy. So young.

So implausible.

Because healthy people rarely just up and died from the ague. They suffered in bed for a week or two, and then got through it. It didn't make sense. Pentu could not have died from the ague.

"I can't believe he's gone," Tutankhamun whispered for Ay's benefit. That at least was true. Then he looked up. "Can I see him?"

Ay grimaced. "The King for Whom the Sun Rises would not wish to see his mortal remains. He's scarcely recognizable."

Tut gave himself a tiny nod. Ague did not disfigure those it took away. "How sad," he said simply, shaking his head mournfully. "I should have liked to have said goodbye."

"The embalmers have taken him, and we shall all say goodbye at his funeral in seventy days," Ay said. He put a consoling hand on the King's shoulder. "Excuse me, My Lord. I'll leave you in peace. All life, prosperity, and health!" And the Vizier walked away.

Tut sat staring into nothing. Dead. How, he wondered. Poison? Drowning? Suffocation by pillow? Staged accident? Or a simple knife to the throat? It had to be something external; otherwise why would Ay have claimed the illness had made him unrecognizable? Whatever the truth was, Ay knew it.

Because Tut knew Pentu had been murdered.

34 Meritaten

Tut hobbled out to the garden, where Ankhesenamun was sitting in the pavilion, enjoying the sunshine and the cool afternoon breeze, listening to the birds chirping and admiring the bright daisies and sweet-scented roses. The hot half of the year had ended, the Season of Inundation passing into its second half with the month of Athyr. The month when the mosquitoes finally subsided. The Treasurer's little girl Mayamenti had sneaked out and sat playing in the dirt in nothing but her under-tunic, her elaborate dress carefully set aside. Woe betide her when her mother caught her. Hannu, the usual guard, stood stiffly, his eyes flickering over to her when he could no longer restrain himself. He, too, knew what trouble she would be in.

"Can we talk?" Tut asked breathlessly. He looked around, hoping no one was listening. "Inside?"

"What's wrong?" Ankh said immediately, hopping to her feet with a worried frown and hurrying solemnly behind him as he hobbled inside as quickly as possible, cane swinging through the air with his rapid strides, foot protesting with every step. But he ignored it and went even faster. This was more important.

They hurried to his bedroom without speaking, looked both ways, and locked the door behind them. Tut collapsed on the bed, panting, and Ankh sat beside him. Bastet hopped up on the bed with them. Whatever was going on, she wanted in on it too.

"What's wrong?" Ankh said again, taking his hand and searching his face. "Tell me."

"Pentu's dead," he told her.

Ankh went pale. "What? How?"

372

"I don't know," he said, shaking his head. "Ay said last week that he had the ague; that's why I asked you if any of your maid-servants had had it."

"I remember," she said, nodding. Her eyes bored into his under anxious eyebrows. "Well?"

"Well," he continued, "Just now, I met Ay in the hallway, and I asked him how Pentu was. And he told me he'd died of the ague this morning... but that I couldn't see him, because he was disfig-ured."

"But the ague doesn't disfigure people," Ankh said with a sus-picious frown. The silver beads on her braids echoed her questions as she shook her head. *Just as she had feared. His courtiers were killing one another. The dam of polite tolerance was breaking. When all the anger, all the mistrust, all the selfishness, came pouring through, where would that flood carry them?*

"I know. So that's why I think they slit his throat or suffocated him or ran a horse over him, something visible. It's just all wrong... It's the wrong season for ague, ague doesn't usually kill healthy people in a week, and ague doesn't disfigure you. Pentu was the only person who wanted all my proposals to go through without any changes; the tax cuts, the minimum wage, the schools, the hiring, the immigration. And he agreed with me that we could do it all without slaves. Ay didn't like that he agreed with me, and neither did Maya. I think... I think they did it." He swallowed, giving a shudder. "I wonder if that's what would have happened to Semerkhet if I had mentioned him to Ay by name."

The Queen gasped, face blanching as she suddenly swayed where she sat. Tut put a steadying arm around her shoulders—what was wrong; was she going to faint?

"What? Are you all right?"

She shuddered, regaining her balance. And looked at him with horrified eyes. "Meritaten," she whispered hoarsely.

Now the King was the one feeling lightheaded. He swallowed, eyes closed against the terrible truth. The day, all those years ago, in the first year of their reign as the little Pharaoh and Great Royal Wife, when Ay had come with the bad news that their big sister Meritaten had died almost overnight of the ague, at the age of seventeen. They had not been allowed to see her mortal remains. They had not questioned that they were not allowed to. They had not thought to.

"Same time of year," Ankhesenamun whispered, eyes brimming with tears. "Not mosquito season."

Tutankhamun pulled her close. He was in too much shock to speak. A thousand thoughts ran through his mind, memories, plans for a violent revenge, the question of what to do next.

"He killed her," he whispered finally. "Ay killed our sister."

Ankhesenamun began to cry into her brother's shoulder. "Now you're not safe," she said through her sobs. "If they'd k-k-kill our sister to get her out of the way, if they'd d-d-do that to a Vizier just because he agreed with you, what will they do to *you*?"

Tut held her and thought. He had no answer to give her.

What would they do to him?

And what would they do to her?

Sitting beside them, the cat snorted, as if to tell them she had known all along that the Grand Vizier was a traitor.

"You look worried."

"Hmm?" Tutankhamun looked up from staring blindly at his own reflection in his bronze mirror as he sat at his dressing-table that evening. Semerkhet was standing over him, warm brown eyes full of concern. Outside the window, the locusts were buzzing in the trees as the deep blue of the twilight sky slowly faded into black and one by one, the stars twinkled into view. But the King had not watched tonight's brilliant sunset after leading evening prayers at the temple. And even if he had, it would not have made him feel any better.

Tut sighed and met his friend's eyes. Semerkhet looked back kindly, but most importantly, comfortably, as if he were no longer afraid of being incinerated by the Pharaoh's gaze. "Yes. I am worried. If you never have a week like I have just now, it'll be too soon."

Semerkhet's eyes flickered toward Tut's heavy collar-necklace. "May I?" he asked softly.

It was getting late, and Tut's shoulders were stiff and weary from the weight of the beaded collar as well as the weight of the world. His whole body was tense and exhausted, and he was fighting a headache. And his foot hurt more than usual.

"Thank you." Carefully, Semerkhet removed the King's necklace and put it away for him. He returned and stood behind him, their faces reflected side-by-side in the mirror. He brought his hands up, letting them hover over the King's tense shoulders. "May I?"

Tutankhamun gave his valet the ghost of a smile. "Thank you, Sem," he whispered. And folding his arms on the dressing-table, he rested his forehead on his hands.

He felt Semerkhet's hands gently touch his shoulders, slowly beginning to rub away the stress of the day. Tut sighed and closed his eyes. Sem always knew what to do to make him feel better.

"I heard about Vizier Pentu," Semerkhet said sympathetically as he slowly kneaded the King's shoulders. "I was so sorry."

"You know he didn't die of ague," Tut said.

The movement of the valet's hands stopped, and Sem dropped to one knee beside the Pharaoh. "What do you mean?" he asked in a horrified whisper.

Tut sat up again. Sadly, he shook his head, braids swinging. "I mean," he said softly, "that politics is turning deadly." He kept the second terrible discovery, the horrible truth that the Vizier had killed Meritaten as well, to himself. It would be too much to burden his friend with that too. That revelation could wait.

"I was right," Semerkhet gasped, voice breaking. "When I heard him say he wanted to get rid of you, I thought he sounded angry enough to kill— now he's killed Pentu, and he'll kill you, too!" Tut almost jumped as Semerkhet grabbed his hands, nails digging into Tut's skin. "Be careful, Morning Star. Other people can be replaced, but you... you can't."

Tutankhamun gave his faithful servant half a smile. "I'll be careful," he promised. Slowly Semerkhet let go of his hands, clearing his throat and looking down as if he were embarrassed. "I'll be safe."

With a heavy sigh, Semerkhet stood up again. Gently, he returned his hands to the Pharaoh's shoulders.

"Are you sure they did him in?" he whispered, gently beginning to squeeze the Pharaoh's shoulders again. But Tut could only nod sadly. He was sure.

In the mirror, Tut saw Semerkhet bite his lip. "Well... I suppose it couldn't have been the ague. Wrong season... and it doesn't just kill strong, healthy people like him in a week."

The Pharaoh folded his arms on the desk again, sighing as he laid his head down. Slowly Semerkhet's ministrations were starting to loosen up his stiff shoulders and neck, helping his tired body relax. Already his headache was beginning to fade.

Tut shook his head against his wrist. "No. It doesn't. But something did. And the next question is what Ay will do next. *Who* will be next. Will it be me; will it be the Queen? And what can I do to keep us safe, keep Egypt safe, short of executing him?" He sighed. "I never thought I'd say this, but it's... strangely tempting; to throw him in prison, at least. If it wouldn't cause a civil war."

The valet's shock seemed to be fading, but his determination to help wasn't. "You could play into his hands," Semerkhet said, pressing his thumb into a stubborn knot under the King's shoulderblade. Tut sighed as he felt it slowly melt away, sinking into the chair, into the table he was leaning on. Somehow Semerkhet's gentle hands were making even murder plots feel a little less immediate, a little less deadly. "It worked before, when you asked him about that, uh, rumor. Ask his advice on some major issue, like you trust him. Get back in one another's good graces, and then he'll stop seeing you as a threat. Don't give up on your plans, cancel any of the decisions you've made, but just... step back slightly. Throw him off the scent. And reconsider how you might step forward again."

Tut surprised himself with a little smile. A bit of wisdom and a ten-minute massage from his valet had been exactly what he needed to put him to rights.

"Thank you," he whispered again. "I'll do that."

Semerkhet gave a tiny chuckle, warm hands returning to the King's shoulders, slowly kneading them again. They felt much better; Semerkhet's gentle touch had relieved the stiffness of the long, stressful day. And now the soft movement of his friend's hands simply felt good. "Now rest. You don't have to be the King of the world for the next fifteen minutes."

Ay had killed their sister. Ankhesenamun closed her eyes, trying to sleep, trying to push away the images of her older sister's wise face that kept presenting themselves before her closed eyes, a sweet face she had not seen for so many years. And a sweet face she had not been allowed to see after Meritaten's sudden death. It seemed so obvious now; she had disappeared from their lives in utterly the wrong season for a death from ague, and there was no way that ague could have disfigured her face, or anyone else's face, unless Ay wished to argue that the sight of a red, swollen mosquito bite might disturb them. Poor little children. They had been so little. So innocent. So naïve. So trusting.

So much for trust, she thought, rolling over, curling into a little ball. And now she and her husband had to move forward, figuring out who to trust, how to move forward, how to get their nation under their control.

That was what made it even sadder, she thought. Right now Meritaten, the wise, experienced young politician, was the person they needed the most.

Ay had killed their sister. Tut lay in bed that night, Bastet in his arms, trying to sleep as thoughts rushed through his mind. All those years ago, when the tiny King and Queen had gotten the terrible news that Meritaten had died overnight of ague... they had been too little to question why they couldn't see her, too young to see the holes in the story. He couldn't trust Ay, because he had

378

killed the Princess, and for all Tut knew, he might have been responsible for Akhenaten's death, too. Goodness knew much of the government had hated the Pharaoh, especially in those dark later years. He couldn't trust the Vizier. But he had to make the Vizier trust him.

35   The Warrior King

"Ay, I need your wisdom," the King said, beckoning to his Vizier from where he sat on his royal throne, his formal staff in his hand. Today, with so many decisions to make, so much politics to play, felt like a good one for the throne room. "What is the best course of action as the Hittites threaten our borders and our neighbors?"

Ay looked pensive, pressing his fingertips together and examining them closely.

"The Pharaoh is of age now, and the decision lies with him. But my advice would be to fight. Reclaim Kadesh for Egypt. Your father allowed the Hittites to take a great deal of land from us, and it's time to take it back. Show the Hittites the might of Egypt, demonstrate what they will be up against if they dare to oppose us any longer. Launch the campaign you spoke of; fulfill your promise to protect the Mitanni and the people of Amurru from obliteration. And I do believe," he said carefully, as if he wasn't sure how his next words would be received, "I do believe that the message would be that much more powerful if the Pharaoh were to lead the armies of Egypt himself."

Tut blinked. All his careful planning of throwing the Vizier off the scent, all his intentions of carefully regaining his trust, playing the political game, were gone as quickly as if they had been swept down the Nile. His prayer was being answered. If he was being called to go off to battle, then he must be strong. That was what he could do, the solution to his desperate, bored frustration. And maybe... maybe this was his legacy being revealed, as well. Maybe he *would* be a great Pharaoh of conquest, take back all the

380

land his father had lost and more. Maybe he would make Grandfather Thutmose proud.

The Mitanni didn't really need Kadesh all that much, did they? They just needed the Hittites to be wiped off the map.

That was what they had said, after all. That they laid no claim to it. That they just needed Egypt's help in neutralizing the threat of the Hittites. The people of Amurru, too, just needed to be able to sleep soundly, knowing their homes and villages were safe from marauders from the north. And they honestly wanted to be Egyptian again.

"Do you really think I could?"

Ay gave a little smile, all the lines on his face rearranging themselves as his old lips curved. "The Pharaoh is strong. And you would be perfectly safe. You can trust your men to protect you even as you show the world the warrior King. Such a fearsome hunter should have nothing to fear as an archer fighting from a chariot." He paused again. "Your heart is full of love and concern for the less fortunate, but I fear that if you focus every one of your decisions on them, you will be perceived as weak. Let the Queen cry for the poor, Glorious Lord. Your people need their warrior King."

The Vizier sighed. And he continued. "Think of the Mitanni, Great Morning Star. They need you. Every day that you delay their plight grows worse; more of their towns fall to the Hittites and more brave lives are wasted. Keep your promise to them. And…" Ay gave the tiniest chuckle, as though he was trying not to sound rude. "Now is the time, My Lord. The time for you to change your image from that of a courageous but reclusive Boy-King… to demonstrate your strength to the world." The Vizier paused again.

"To disentangle yourself from the Queen's loving guidance, to begin doing more than simply enacting her... philanthropic... plans... To prove who wears the crown."

Again, the discomfort squirmed in Tut's stomach. But he squashed it down and smiled as it was drowned out by the glorious words, *now is the time.* "You are wise, Ay. I will proceed as you advise."

As quickly as he could, Tut hobbled into the study to find Ankh, barely hearing Ay's wish for "all life, prosperity, and health." Sometimes it was her study, too, when she felt like reading or writing somewhere other than her bedroom or her private sitting room.

"We're going to Amurru!" he announced.

She got up, leaving the letter she had been writing. What was he saying? It didn't make sense. "What?"

"I asked Ay what he thought the best course of action would be against the Hittites, and he said we should attack. And..." He paused, glowing with pride. "He said I should lead the army myself."

Ankh felt herself go pale as her heart began to race, an instant of lightheadedness making her feel as though she'd missed a step going downstairs. "He wants you to fight? Darling, are you quite sure he isn't trying to kill you?"

The King laughed. "Ay, kill me? The man raised me. And he's as old as the pyramids. I trust him. I mean, I've had to do away with some of his policies, but as a person, as a guardian, I trust him. And I want you to trust me."

"What were we saying about not letting Ay make the decisions for you any longer?" she asked in a rather horrified whisper. "And about how he would try to get you to trust him and do something risky? And…" She swallowed. "How you said that you would be careful, wouldn't be rash, that you'd think about it, and… and talk to me about it before you made your decision." She wiped away a tear, feeling angry at her baby brother. "You promised." Ankh grabbed his arm, not gently. And he frowned. "I'm your big sister, Tutankhaten. And I'm telling you… this isn't safe. Why don't you trust me anymore?" She looked up at him with the question on her face, eyes full of angry tears. "I thought I was your advisor."

He'd blinked at his old name, but now he gave her a soft smile. Tut put his free hand over hers, and she let go, taking his hand instead. "I do trust you," he said softly. "And you are. You're my Vizier, not him. But I'm… I'm growing up, Ankh. And you… you won't be able to protect me forever. As much as I would love you to. We're both adults now. I'll always be your baby brother, and you'll always be my big sister, but… I can't hide behind you anymore. I have to do this. And I…" Now tears were swimming in his eyes too. "I need you to let me."

She stepped into his arms and hugged him, and he hugged her back. As big as she was, she couldn't protect him from everything. And she couldn't hold him back from what he believed he needed to do. Or even if she could… it would be wrong.

She couldn't even get her arms around him, she realized. He'd been her baby brother his entire life, but as if for the first time, she realized just how big he was. And she felt small.

"I know," she whispered. Slowly she let him go. From her arms, and from her control. From… her protection.

He was an adult now. Facing the cold world outside the loving embrace of her arms, the shadow of her wings. And her arms felt empty without him.

"Kadesh is so... so far away," Ankh said, frowning at him earnestly. "It'll take you almost two weeks to get there. Are you sure you want to go so far away?"

He sighed, looking pensive again. "I know," he said. "It is a ways, isn't it?"

She bit her lip, trying to think what she could possibly say. "I'm proud of you," she whispered through the tears that filled her eyes. "I'm so proud of how you are growing and making more of your own decisions, but this is the one thing I wish you would have asked me about first! I know I said I was looking forward to the day you would no longer have to ask me what to do, even the day we'd disagree and the decision would be yours to make, but I didn't mean like this! I thought when we finally disagreed on something it would be which side of the river a new school should go on or whether to lower taxes by five percent or seven percent. I never thought... never thought it would be this. Never thought I'd see you marching off to war."

Her baby brother blinked back tears. "I know," he whispered. "I never did either. St... strange, isn't it?"

But even as Tut wiped away his tears, the excitement returned, the thrill of what was about to happen. And he grinned.

"The Vizier said it was my decision, and I'm deciding to go with what he suggests." He put his free arm around her again and kissed her forehead as she vaguely patted his shoulders. "And it *is* a long way, but it's my opportunity to go on my very first trip on this scale and see how I do! My prayers have been answered. I finally know what I'm supposed to be doing. If I'm getting the opportunity to go off to battle, I must be stronger than I thought."

"But you've always been strong," Ankh whispered. She reached out and touched his chest, his heart. "In here."

"This is it!" he said, smile shining like the sun. "Finally!"

Ankhesenamun swallowed. "If the gods want you to go… then have they changed your feet?"

Tutankhamun looked down. In his excitement, he had forgotten the pain, almost forgotten the chore of using his cane.

His feet looked the same as they always had.

"Has anyone ever been healed like that?" she whispered.

"Well…" he said, "I'll probably be fighting from my chariot, so it's not like I'm going to have to run anywhere." He kissed her again, still dizzy with excitement. "Come on! Let's go pack."

The Queen stood there as he merrily danced out of the room, lightheaded with shock. Right now she could not even process what was happening.

"General?"

Horemheb looked up as the Pharaoh came striding down the hallway. Quite quickly, in fact. As quickly as he could go.

The General bowed. "Yes, O Great Morning Star?"

"Pack your bags," Tut said with a smile. "It's time for our campaign. We leave at dawn."

"Yes, Glorious Lord," Horemheb said with another bow. And he set off, Tut was sure, to literally go pack his bags.

"This is part of your plan for throwing the Vizier off the scent, right, Master?" Semerkhet asked as he walked around the Pharaoh's bedroom with a list and a pen, ticking off the things the other servants had packed for the trip. "Going to Amurru? You don't actually mean to fight, do you?"

"What do you mean?" Tut asked with a little laugh, bending over the open chest where his leather-and-scale armor lay carefully arranged. "Of course I'm going to fight! This is what I've been dreaming of my entire life! And now it's finally coming true... We're going to get out there in our chariot and show the Hittites who's in charge!"

Semerkhet swallowed. "As the Pharaoh wishes." Half a moment later, Tut barely noticed him whisper under his breath, "We?"

"He's going to war," Ankhesenamun whispered blankly as she sat at her dressing-table that night, Meresankh picking out a sleeping-tunic for her. Outside the locusts were whirring an endless "Why... why... why..." into the deepening night.

Her handmaiden almost dropped the linen tunic. "When?" she whispered back.

"Tomorrow morning."

Meresankh closed her eyes, knuckles whitening as she gripped the fabric. "We will pray, My Lady. We will all pray."

Ankhesenamun closed her eyes as well, clenching her own fists as she struggled to hang onto what was left of her brother's childhood as it was cruelly yanked from her grasp. "I hope that will be enough."

Meresankh gave a little sigh. "It will be." As she opened her eyes, the Queen saw peace and assurance in her handmaiden's eyes as well as concern. Where was that peace coming from?

386

Then Ankh felt the tears begin to fall. "I just know there's something going on," she sobbed. "I've seen it before, when an advisor wants to get rid of a Pharaoh… they manipulate them, gain their trust and then strike… And they don't like him, none of them do; they hate his policies. *Our* policies. And if he's in danger, am I? These ideas are mine, and he's told them. Will they get rid of him to stop these new policies being enacted, or get rid of me to stop the ideas? And why won't he let me help him?" She hugged herself, remembering how empty her arms had felt when she had released him from her protective embrace. And they would feel empty until he came home.

The Queen felt a soft, gentle hand come to rest lightly on her shaking shoulder. Meresankh had never touched her like that before, a caring gesture from a friend to a friend.

"He wants to keep you safe." Meresankh sighed. "When he gets back, you can decide together what to do next."

The Queen swallowed back her tears. "If he gets back." She sighed. "But I'm supposed to keep *him* safe. I'm his big sister. He's my baby brother, the only sibling I have left. I should be protecting *him*."

There was a pause. Then slowly, Meresankh whispered, "Is Semerkhet going too?"

The Queen nodded. "I think so."

Now Meresankh was the one who was crying.

Ankhesenamun sat alone in the garden, no game-board on the table beside her. Her brother was indoors. But even if they had been sitting together, neither of them felt like playing a game.

Servants stood in little knots around the enormous garden, extending their break-times as long as they could to enjoy the glorious, cool weather. And she was glad that they were enjoying it. She was, too. Or she would have been, if not for the thousand things that were happening, the thousand worries chasing one another around her heart.

A breeze ruffled the leaves of the trees, the petals of the flowers in the garden, the surface of the lotus-pools. And she shivered, pulling her long-sleeved gown closer. For once it was not refreshing to shiver in the chilly breeze of Athyr. Because the shudder that ran down her spine felt like fear.

Something was coming. And she was going to need all her wisdom to navigate it, and all her strength to bear it.

"Just tell me why," came a voice over his shoulder.

Tutankhamun looked up from where he'd been resting on the couch in his private sitting-room, perusing a papyrus on military strategy. Had to read up, after all.

His sister stood above him, face solemn, eyes red, a handkerchief crumpled in her hand. Slowly, he sat up with a sigh.

"I know I can't stop you," she said, "but at least tell me why."

Tut swallowed. "I have to show them I'm strong," he said simply.

"But why won't you listen to all the reasons it's a bad idea?" Ankh asked, frustration in her voice. "I thought I was your advisor!"

Tut looked up at her. And slowly, he stood up. And looked down at her.

"Yes," he said, his voice sounding harsh in his own ears. "And that's the problem. The Vizier says everyone thinks I'm tied to your apron strings. I need to change my image. Show them who wears the crown."

He looked down at his sister. She was standing as still as a statue, eyes closed, jaw tight, hands clenched. She said nothing.

And then she did. "All I want is to keep you safe."

Nineteen years of loving protection taking on the quality of overbearing henpecking, he went on, heart beginning to race as a pounding began inside his head, the same pounding as when he had gotten into that fight with Nakhtmin. "I don't want to *be* safe. I want to *be* King and *look* like I'm King. I don't— I don't need you."

His sister looked up at him, eyes slowly filling with tears. Then she turned and left the room.

Tut fumed for the rest of the day. She was wrong; he knew she was wrong. Well, she was right about a lot of things, but about this, she was wrong. He could do it. He would be fine. It was the right thing to do. Why couldn't she see that? Why did she want to prevent him from saving hundreds of Mitanni from the wrath of the Hittites, keep him from proving himself as Pharaoh? What was wrong with her? Why didn't she understand? Wasn't she the one who was always telling him that he could do anything he set his mind to? Why couldn't she see that this was the opportunity he'd been waiting for all his life?

Ankh put away her third handkerchief and took a sip of the tea Meresankh had brought her. Her baby brother. Her precious baby brother, telling her he didn't need her any more. Telling her he didn't value her input, didn't want her anymore as his advisor.

Telling her that her desire to keep him safe didn't matter to him. Nineteen years of loving wisdom shattered, lying broken on the floor as though he had knocked over a precious statue... knocked it over on purpose. And pain filled her heart as she remembered every bitter word he had said.

Did he... did he love her anymore?

Thoughts of what the morning would bring filled the Queen's heart to overflowing. And she reached for her fourth handkerchief.

The King did not sleep well that night. The night was chilly... but not in the cozy way that the first cool nights of the year usually made him smile. This was a coldness that was getting into his bones, making him shiver... with fear.

To go... to stay... If he stayed, backing out on his offer to fight for his country, he would be branded a coward. The child he looked like, the child everyone thought he was. He would remain the Boy-King, the pathetic little princeling who was Pharaoh only in name, and only because he was an orphan, his powerful Pharaoh parents dying before him. Demonstrating weakness would only invite Egypt's enemies to prey on her, knowing that the Pharaoh was a helpless child, unable to stop them. If he was an adult, standing firmly on his own two feet (so to speak), he had to show everyone that he was brave and courageous, the Strong Bull, the roaring lion that would devour Egypt's enemies for her.

He looked at Bastet, lying beside him. "What should I do?" he whispered. She just looked at him with her large, thoughtful eyes, giving a long, slow blink. She was saying something, he knew. He couldn't help but think she was telling him to stay.

390

Tut rolled over in bed with a sigh, putting his arms around the cat and holding her to his heart, feeling her warmth, her reassuring presence. There was no longer any question. He had to go.

But if he went, he would be giving up the one thing guaranteed to him by staying.

Safety.

The Queen stared at the ceiling, the moonlight streaming through the window slowly moving, counting the hours that she had lain awake. Tomorrow morning. He was leaving tomorrow morning. To go to Kadesh. To war.

It had happened. The Vizier had pulled the noose tight, the trap he had set when he had ceremoniously given up his power as regent. And Ankh was no longer sure she could extricate her baby brother from this tangle before it was too late. Already she could hear him choking.

She thought of the excitement she'd seen on his face. She was proud of his passion for helping their neighbors, but the way that he had thrown all caution to the wind the instant this "opportunity" had been presented… just went to show that even if they were of age, nineteen-year-olds didn't always make the wisest leaders.

She shivered and pulled her blanket closer. It was early for it to be this cold, and it felt like a sign. But not a good one.

He had to do this, she knew. To take care of his country, to win the respect of the politicians. And he had to do it for himself. All in all, it had to happen. He had to go. But going wasn't the issue.

What if he didn't come back?

Ankhesenamun reached up and put her arms around her brother's neck as he stood awkwardly in his chariot, a crowd of a thousand Egyptian citizens cheering the warrior King as he rode off into battle. It was the seventh day of the month of Athyr, and the early morning was chilly, a damp mist hanging in the air. But that hadn't kept anyone home. Word had spread that a war was on, and most of the palace staff along with what felt like half of Memphis had come to see the King off.

But not just to see him off. The curious crowds had gathered simply to see the Pharaoh, to catch more than a glimpse of the mysterious young King who spent most of his time either within the walls that surrounded the palace grounds or shrouded by the curtains of a palanquin. And so the people stood on tiptoe, squinting as they tried to get a good look at the Boy-King, see how tall he was, how strong, how muscular, see if they could get a glimpse of his foot. They had seen him serve Egypt from childhood as a beloved figurehead, seen him take power at his last birthday, but they had never seen him ride off to war. The merry hubbub felt like a cross between Tribute Day and the crowded marketplace of downtown Memphis. There was a feeling of celebration in the air.

But not for Tutankhamun. Now that this was real, the elated bubble he'd felt swelling in his heart when Ay had suggested he lead his nation to war was slowly beginning to deflate. A nagging worry he could not define, some word, some phrase, some clue, had chased him through his dreams last night, leaving him poorly rested. All this joyous screaming was just giving him a headache. And he kept finding himself shivering.

"Come home safe," the Queen whispered. There was love in her voice, even as he heard a stiffness, a sense that he was not quite

392

forgiven for yesterday. In fairness, he wasn't quite sure if he had forgiven her. But he hugged his sister back. Because he loved her.

"I will," he said, leaning his right hip against the side of the chariot to take some of the weight off of his left foot. "Be safe while I'm gone," he whispered even more softly.

He could hear her frowning against his shoulder, feel her stiffen in his arms. "Why? What's wrong?" So something was going on. Just like she had feared.

He shook his head. "It's just... politics. I... I'd feel better about going if you didn't move forward with anything while I'm gone. Just... maybe don't even talk to Maya. Or even Ay. Just lie low for a little while. I... I don't know. I just don't know." He sighed. "But I'll be back soon. And then we can decide what to do next."

She nodded, giving him a smile. "As soon as you get back."

Ankh gave him a squeeze, then turned her face up for a kiss. Then she was gone, melting into the crowd. Tut felt his stomach twist as she disappeared.

Semerkhet was going too, as the Pharaoh's charioteer. He stood beside the King, the reins in his hands, ready to go. Suddenly a young woman darted up through the crowd, reaching out and taking his hands. Tut chuckled as he recognized Meresankh. He looked away, trying to give them privacy as they exchanged their goodbyes, but could not help but notice Semerkhet's head dipping down as he bent to kiss her on the cheek. An instant later she was gone, swallowed by the throng just like the Queen. Tut smiled at Semerkhet, who looked slightly embarrassed. Both were leaving their lady-loves behind.

Now Ay was stepping forward, preparing to send the Pharaoh off with a short speech.

"Pharaoh Tutankhamun, Egypt watches with pride as you prepare to defend her and our neighbors against our common enemies in Amurru. You have led us with your heart at home, but now you prepare to lead us abroad with your sword. Go forth and lead us to glorious victory! All life, prosperity, and health!" As one the crowd echoed his words, a thousand voices wishing the best for the King.

The crowd roared, screaming and jumping itself silly as its Pharaoh rode by in his chariot. It was time to go to war.

Ankhesenamun clenched her hands as she watched him drive away in his chariot, working very hard to remain upright, harder than any of the members of the joyously hysterical crowd could tell. He was going to war. Not something she had ever imagined.

The Queen put her arms around herself as a shiver shuddered through her. It was cool this morning. But that wasn't the only reason she was shivering.

She thought back a minute or two, to the feeling of her brother's arms around her, the goodbye kiss he had given her. And the words he had spoken after rousing her worries with the phrase, "be safe—" "it's just politics." She shook her head. "Just politics?" What kind of a thing was that for him to say to her, the established young politician who had taught him almost everything he knew?

When they were younger, twelve and seventeen, thirteen and eighteen, she had comforted him with the same phrase, and he had smiled, knowing that his sister was keeping him safe from the machinations he didn't fully understand yet. Still didn't understand, not like she did. And had somehow gotten himself into this tangle, this demonstration of bravery that might endanger his very life. He was learning, learning quickly, and she was very proud of him, but he was still young... so very young.

She was the politician, not him. If he tried to do this all by himself, not letting her help him, he was going to end up in a situation from which she could not save him.

Had he already?

She had let him go without fully making up. Was it just possible... that that was a regret she would carry with her for the rest of her life?

Her baby brother was out of sight, a cloud of sandy dust in the distance and a low, distant rumble of chariot-wheels the only signs of his departure. Ankh turned and began to follow the crowd of servants and courtiers back into the palace. It made no sense for him to smile at her and say, "It's just politics." As if he was the politician and she was not.

Something was very wrong.

Author's Note

L et's start with a basic question that must be asked of every work of historical fiction— how accurate is my story? Why do I have King Tut seeking to solve the mystery of the Exodus of Egypt's Hebrew slaves? When reading about Pharaoh Akhenaten, Tutankhamun's father, it struck me how his religious reforms, beginning with honoring the Aten, a sun god, above all other deities and ending with the worship of any other gods being outlawed, evoked the Exodus of the Hebrews from Egypt. Not many people may associate King Tut with Moses, but the evidence I found was too strong to ignore, and added a beautiful and unexpected deepening to the entire story.

The Date of the Exodus

Biblical archaeologists have dated the Exodus to the 18th Dynasty of Egypt. This is possible through going back 480 years from the 4th year of Solomon's reign (1 Kings 6:1), which provides a date within the decade of the 1440s BC (although some estimates, such as the one discussed in *Tutankhamun: The Exodus Conspiracy: The Truth Behind Archaeology's Greatest Mystery*, place the Exodus as late as 1413 BC, during the reign of Amenhotep the Second).

Another clue is metal-containing coral formations found at the bottom of the Red Sea, believed by adventurer Ron Wyatt to be Egyptian chariot wheels from the Eighteenth Dynasty. Akhenaten, who lived during this dynasty, is also known to have had an older brother who died during their father's reign; he was not born the heir to his father's throne. I found the death of the royal family's firstborn son to be very significant. Furthermore, Akhenaten's father, Amenhotep the Third, ordered the manufacture of hundreds of statues of the goddess Sekhmet, who was associated with plague. Could this have been in response to the ten terrible plagues they were witnessing?

The Exodus is often dated by Biblical archaeologists to a little over a hundred years prior to Tutankhamun's birth, with the future Pharaoh Hatshepsut being identified as Moses' adoptive mother and Thutmose the Third, Akhenaten's great-great grandfather, being the Pharaoh who would not let God's people go. Amenhotep the Second, the next Pharaoh, is also a candidate, as both Thutmose the Third and Amenhotep the Second can be dated to having reigned in the 1440s BC, and both were predeceased by their eldest sons. The younger son of Amenhotep the Second, who ascended the throne after the death of his older brother, actually left us a piece of writing stating that he had become Pharaoh through divine intervention.

If his great-grandfather Amenhotep the Second was the Pharaoh of the Exodus, Akhenaten, therefore, may have been responding in amazement to the military exploits of the nation of former slaves who, under the leadership of Joshua, conquered every piece of land they walked on. It would have been very clear that their God was with them.

However, I feel strongly that Akhenaten's religious reforms must have been inspired by very recent events, in an attempt to honor the mysterious God Who had tanked Egypt's economy, destroyed its army, and freed its slaves. So for the sake of drama, I have telescoped events in an intentionally vague fashion, making Akhenaten's older brother, Crown Prince Thutmose, the firstborn son who died during the tenth plague, and his revolution based on what he had seen during his own childhood.

According to my chronology, the elderly midwife Merneith would have been around twenty when the plagues came, and the Hebrew Prince's (Moses') birth and adoption by Hatshepsut would have taken place about a hundred and thirty years before this story is set, rather than the approximately 200 years that are usually considered to separate Hatshepsut and Tutankhamun.

The reigns of the Pharaohs are literally "set in stone," but the lengths and even the order of their reigns are always subject to re-consideration. Although we usually date the Exodus to the 1440s BC, we don't know for sure which Pharaoh was reigning at that time! We don't even know Akhenaten's birth year, although I have gone with the hypothesis that he died at the age of fifty when Tut was six years old. If Akhenaten and Tut lived sixty-five or seventy years before they are typically dated, Akhenaten's childhood could easily line up with the Exodus as dated to the 1440s BC.

The dating of Ancient Egyptian events is viewed differently by different scholars and is always subject to adjustment. In the grand scheme of so many centuries of history and so much ongoing uncertainty, an adjustment of seventy years (from Tut reigning 1332-1323 BC to reigning 1402-1393 BC) is not as extreme as it might sound. If, on the other hand, the Exodus took place as late as 1413 BC, as suggested in *The Exodus Conspiracy*, and Tut reigned as early as the 1350s, moving Tut's reign back by thirty years and the Exodus forward by thirty years in relation to their typical dating, then Akhenaten's reign would have taken place between 1380-1363, leaving plenty of room for Akhenaten to have been a child in the year 1413 BC. The dating of Hatshepsut's life by different historians varies to such a degree that Moses' birth being set during the 1490s BC, rather than the more typical 1520s, could still line up with her childhood. In short, whether the Exodus took place during his childhood or in the years of his great-great grandfather, we can clearly connect Akhenaten's religious revolution to this shocking series of historical events.

The Pharaoh who Searched for the Light

Akhenaten's harsh shutdowns of temples and removal of images of traditional gods evokes the uncompromising action taken by Old Testament King Josiah to eliminate idolatry after the rediscovery of the Torah scrolls. Severe though both may seem, both leaders were facing religious emergencies, and Akhenaten may have feared that the longer Egypt continued worshiping false gods, the angrier the Aten might become, and the greater the risk became of Egypt facing further punishment— did they want to invite ten more plagues?

Viewing Akhenaten as a sincere seeker of the God of the Bible, I have chosen to capitalize the pronouns of the Aten, in Whom I see Akhenaten's attempt to define the God Who had performed so many signs and wonders in Egypt. As I agree with Akhenaten that the traditional deities such as Ra and Horus were idols, I have chosen not to capitalize their pronouns.

It is true that Akhenaten had the names of the gods, and even the pluralized form of the word "gods" hacked from statues. There were never any idols of the Aten, only images of the royal family at worship. In references to the Aten mercifully reaching down to humanity, extending His love like friendly hands or the rays of the sun, I am alluding to Akhenaten's depiction of the Aten in the form of sunrays terminating in outstretched hands.

We don't know what killed Akhenaten, but I portray his death as heart failure after so many years straining to honor the God he both loved and feared while dragging an unwilling nation along with him, a nation that would not "see the light." I mention his "tired old heart" and also describe symptoms of early heart failure.

I also partially follow the reasoning of Kara Cooney, who suggests in her book *When Women Ruled the World* that Akhenaten may have died after being horrified to see his beloved Sun disappear in a solar eclipse, and that he may have interpreted the earlier epidemic that took at least two of his daughters as a plague sent in punishment for further idolatry. This sign from Heaven may have been the point at which Akhenaten redoubled his efforts to wipe out polytheism.

There is no real evidence that Akhenaten's eyesight was damaged by staring at the eclipse, but I feel that under the circumstances, this makes sense. I also theorize that a number of unnamed courtiers were stricken completely blind, and that the Pharaoh would have seen this mysterious affliction as divine punishment.

It also interests me how although practically everyone agrees that the Ancient Egyptian deities were legendary, that is, not literally real, few Egyptologists consider most Pharaohs to have been "bad" or "crazy" for having believed in them. Akhenaten, however, with his love for a single deity with haunting similarities to the God of the Bible, is considered by many to have been a "bad" King or to have been psychologically disturbed. The question is what this reveals about our own biases.

I also describe Akhenaten as wishing to serve his people as priest more than as Pharaoh, because what we know about Atenism suggests that the royal couple served as the sole mediators between the Aten and the people. I wonder if this is one reason that this new way of connecting with Creator never caught on; if the people had been provided with a way to worship, and perhaps been allowed to form a community priesthood to the Aten, they may have felt involved enough in the new faith, connected enough with the Divine, to become emotionally invested in it and take it to heart.

However, the Sun King may have had a dark side. Cemeteries that appear to belong to the workers who built the city of Akhetaten (known to archaeologists as *Amarna*, a name I will also use to refer to the royal family) reveal skeletons of children and youths, and suggest that they were both overworked and abused. Did Akhenaten himself resort to abusive child slavery to build his new holy city, or should these burials rather be connected to the reign of his father, Amenhotep the Third? If so, what city was Amenhotep forcing them to build, if not Akhetaten? Or did Amenhotep the Third begin the building of the new city, perhaps during the coregency he may have shared with his son?

The economic depression associated with Akhenaten's reign may also be evidence for his having ruled just after the Exodus. Perhaps he inherited a destroyed economy from his father, from whom the Hebrews escaped, and then further depleted their limited funds by making honoring the Aten the highest priority. Maybe Akhenaten was left to clean up his father's mess, rather than Nefertiti having to clean up his, as some Egyptologists say. Going back a generation, Amenhotep the Third, the father of Akhenaten, was actually the Pharaoh who began to raise the Aten to prominence. Was that because of what he, as the Pharaoh of the Exodus, had seen?

Will we ever know?

A Hidden Disgrace

It's no wonder that in Ancient Egyptian records we don't find obvious references to abuses of enslaved Hebrews, the ethnic-cleansing murder of Hebrew babies, the Ten Plagues that tanked Egypt's economy, the death of Pharaoh's firstborn son, and the sudden disappearance of all the slaves and the army Pharaoh had sent after them. The whole Hebrew affair was terrible PR from beginning to end, and the Ancient Egyptians were all about PR, glorifying their Pharaohs as deities and claiming military victories after a stalemate (Battle of Kadesh, fought by Rameses the Second against the Hittites). Those who lose wars, military or supernatural, seldom brag about it afterwards. If anything, the Egyptians would have hidden their interactions with the Hebrews as well as they could!

In my telling, I have Egyptians such as Ay accept that Egypt once kept Hebrew slaves, who all disappeared one day, but I portray most of them as unwilling to accept that a series of miracles, a foreign God essentially declaring war on Egypt, was what allowed the Hebrews to leave for freedom. I also describe Akhenaten himself as only telling his children their history in a whisper, cautious of what the priests and politicians might do if they heard him. Furthermore, the Egyptians living only one generation after the plagues have chosen not to preserve these events in their historical records, instead hiding them from the world and from their own descendants as well as they can by claiming that the reign of Amenhotep the Third (who I have chosen to identify as the Pharaoh of the Exodus) was remarkably peaceful.

An argument brought by various scholars against the historicity of the Exodus is based upon the lack of clear evidence from an

Egyptian perspective that they kept Hebrew slaves. However, this may be yet another example of PR; conscripted laborers or indentured serfs may not have been identified by the Ancient Egyptians as "slaves," but to describe such hard labor being performed by people who had no option to leave and were beaten if they didn't work fast enough as "slavery" is in every way appropriate, even if they were earning the minimum wage. Should we really expect them to have bragged about such things?

The Mystery of the Hyksos

I also draw a connection between the Hebrews in Egypt and the Canaanite community referred to as the *Hyksos*. Parallels include the fact that both arrived in Egypt in enormous numbers from Canaan beginning around 400 years before the Exodus and settled in the eastern Nile Delta. Both grew in strength and numbers, and became a threat to Egypt's status quo. And both left Egypt very suddenly, pursued by the Egyptian army through the Sinai Peninsula.

The Hyksos are also believed to have been a multi-ethnic group, and we learn in Exodus 12:38 that those who left Egypt in the Exodus constituted a "mixed multitude," which, as emphasized in some translations, included many who were not Israelites. It may be, too, that the term "Hyksos," which simply means "rulers of foreign lands," was applied by the Egyptians to all the different people groups who came to Egypt in Joseph's day to buy grain.

The Egyptians considered the Hyksos to be foreign "invaders," and after forcing them out of Egypt, erased the evidence that they had gone so far as to set up a rival kingdom with its own capital. In the same way, the Egyptians concealed the enslavement of the

403

equally Canaanite Hebrews, as well as the entire saga of the Ten Plagues and the Exodus. In fairness, if most archaeologists accept the theory that the Egyptians concealed the Hyksos occupation, why should we not accept it as credible that they did the same in regards to the abusive slavery and murder of the Hebrews, the plagues, and the Exodus?

If we take the statement, "The Hebrews have grown numerous; if war breaks out, they could join with our enemies and destroy us," as a response to the rival dynasty of the "Hyksos," and the action the Pharaoh takes being their military defeat and enslavement, eventually culminating in the murder of great numbers of small children and the sudden total disappearance of these outsiders, the Hyksos and Hebrews appear to be much more alike than different.

Three verses, Exodus 6:1 (Then the LORD said to Moses, "Now you will see what I will do to Pharaoh: Because of my mighty hand he will let them go; because of my mighty hand he will **drive them out** of his country.") Exodus 11:1 (Now the LORD had said to Moses, "I will bring one more plague on Pharaoh and on Egypt. After that, he will let you go from here, and when he does, he will **drive you out** completely."), and Exodus 12:39, ("With the dough the Israelites had brought from Egypt, they baked loaves of unleavened bread. The dough was without yeast because they had been **driven out of Egypt** and did not have time to prepare food for themselves."), line up in a clear manner with the hypothesis that the Hebrews can be identified with the Hyksos that the Egyptians claim to have "driven out."

Such was the focus on PR of the Ancient Egyptians that I can easily imagine the sudden disappearance of all the slaves after a series of ten deadly miracles being recorded for posterity as the

Egyptians themselves heroically "casting out" those horrible invaders. The description by the Egyptians of the Hyksos as a "plague" is an invention of my own, but I wonder if the embarrassment and confusion after these remarkable events may have been so great that even the Pharaoh who chased the Hebrews into Sinai might not have been identified. (My theory treats Ahmose the First's defeat and subjugation of the Hyksos (casting them out, not of Egypt, but out of their strongholds and out of power) and their expulsion into Sinai (*Pharaoh will drive you out*, Exodus 11:1) as separate events).

I don't believe that evidence that the Hyksos were polytheistic rules them out as the Hebrews. After centuries living in Egypt, many of them may have forgotten the God of Joseph and become completely integrated into both Egyptian culture and religion. Moses' arrival may have meant the Hebrews' return to the worship of the God of Abraham, Isaac, and Jacob.

Furthermore, in a later clash with the Hyksos at the beginning of the Twentieth Dynasty, the Egyptians describe expelling this new wave of invaders and taking a great deal of silver and gold from them. Could this be the silver and gold jewelry that the Hebrews had taken from Egypt in the Exodus?

Joseph, the Canaanite Vizier

Pharaoh Senusret the Third of the mid-1800s BC is considered by many Biblical scholars to be the Pharaoh who appointed Joseph as his second-in-command in preparation for and during the seven-year famine. Another candidate is his father, Senusret the Second. Amenamhat the Third, the son of Senusret the Third, is also associated with a great canal still known as Bahr Yussef.

Thousands of years later, this period in Ancient Egyptian history and the Pharaohs who led it are connected with the Biblical and Quranic figure of Joseph, or Yussuf. The building of Joseph's canal during the mid-1800s BC strengthens the dating of the Exodus to the 1400s BC.

The book *Tutankhamun: The Exodus Conspiracy: The Truth Behind Archaeology's Greatest Mystery* refers to the candidacy of Senusret the Third as the Pharaoh who welcomed the Hebrews, as well as the identification of the Hebrews and the Hyksos as the same people. I have even found a reference to the immigrants that Senusret welcomed having been engaged in building Egyptian monuments, and to the idea that the peaceful immigrants eventually "[came] to power as the Hyksos." Large numbers of Canaanites are also known to have visited Egypt during the reign of Senusret the Second, and the earliest known usage of the term *Hyksos* dates to the reigns of Amenamhat the Second or Senusret the Second. This general period in Ancient Egyptian history was also associated with famine, and possibly even plague.

As he was taken to Egypt at the age of 17, and lived to be 110, Joseph lived under the reign of, and perhaps served as vizier under, multiple Pharaohs. The entry of the Hebrew people into Egypt during a period of famine being placed within the Twelfth Dynasty lines up nicely with the Exodus taking place in the Eighteenth Dynasty, after 430 years in Egypt, and the fact that Egypt's capital was in the Fayum (Eastern Nile Delta) during the Twelfth Dynasty also strengthens the other elements of this line of reasoning. It is also easy to envision Moses traveling back and forth between the Hebrew community in Goshen and the Egyptian palace in Memphis.

The translation of "Zaphenath Paaneah," which is an English transliteration of *"Tsophnath Pa`neach,"* a Hebrew transliteration of the name given to Joseph by the Egyptians, comes from Creation.com. Patrick Clarke's reconstruction of Joseph's name in its Egyptian form is *"Df3n'ty P3nn'i3h,"* and it has been translated as "Overseer/Minister of the Storehouse of Abundance; He of the Excellent/Gracious Spirit." The use of the number "3" in English transliterations of Ancient Egyptian words to communicate a certain use of the sound "a" has been adjusted to a simple "a."

Sobekneferu, one of the female Pharaohs discussed by Ankh and Tut, was the granddaughter of Senusret the Third, and her reign was also affected by low Nile inundations that caused famine in Egypt. Kara Cooney's book also refers to Egypt being sustained during this lean period by grain stores "amassed from the years of plenty." Had Sobekneferu followed the example of her grandfather or great-grandfather and his wise Canaanite vizier, who had had enough grain stored to feed the known world during the famine of their time?

To sum up, clues as to what elements of Ancient Egyptian history line up with what points in Biblical history are there if you squint. However hard they may have tried, the Egyptians could not completely obscure the work of I-AM in their country.

Disabilities in Ancient Egypt

The quotation from the *Instruction of Amenemope* comes from a real wisdom text composed at some point during the New Kingdom. The concepts found within it were an important part of Ancient Egyptian culture from as far back as the First Dynasty. If, however, the *Instruction of Amenemope* was written after Tut, it could actually have been written in response to his reign. The existence of such a high-profile person with a disability could very well have improved the lot of special-needs Egyptians of all social classes.

People with dwarfism were treated with great respect and had the opportunity to become high-ranking officials. Blind people often became musicians or poets, and deaf people were provided with a full education using sign language and the written word. Dwarfism and deafness, in fact, seem to have been considered to be unusual gifts. From the *Instruction of Amenemope*, we also see that etiquette forbade impeding a person with mobility challenges, and that readers were expected to offer understanding and compassion to those with learning disabilities or psychiatric differences. Tut was not rejected at birth or held back from the throne because of his clubfoot, and when he became Pharaoh, he was treated as such.

The Pharaoh's ownership of 139 walking-sticks and over eighty pairs of shoes is historically accurate. I enjoyed researching his footwear, and discovered that he owned several of the earliest known pairs of orthopedic shoes; they were clearly specifically designed to stay on his special feet. As a person with spina bifida and a wearer of leg braces, I nodded appreciatively when I saw pictures of Tut's orthopedic shoes with their special straps, thinking to myself, "Yes, those would stay on." Based on personal experience, I can attest to how difficult backless sandals are to wear, and how vital good shoe design is. The eighty pairs of shoes belonging to Tut, however, cover a range of sizes from child through adult, so he would not have had eighty pairs of shoes in his closet at any one time.

Tut's ownership of over a hundred canes and several pairs of orthotic shoes backs up the interpretation that he had significant special needs from birth. Staffs would have made beautiful and practical gifts for the rulers of neighboring countries, who must have known he had a walking challenge, to offer him. Although I have not followed these lines of reasoning, it has been suggested that linen straps found attached to several of Tut's chairs and thrones were designed to help him sit upright. His 145 pairs of underwear also lead us to wonder if he had bladder or bowel challenges.

The specifics of Tutankhamun's special needs have been debated over the years. A scan in the mid-2000s, whose conclusions were strengthened by an additional examination in 2014, revealed a clubfoot on his left side. His right foot was pathologically flat and was missing a few bones, and he had a painful bone disease in his left foot. This is not something he would have been born with; this is a disease that would have developed, although the challenging ways that his two feet were shaped would have affected him from birth.

As visualized by a mannequin that serves as a reconstruction of the Pharaoh's entire body from head to toe, his clubfoot caused his ankle to bend inward dramatically; as a result, he would have walked with most of his weight being borne by the lateral edge of the sole of his left foot. His left foot was also angled slightly inward. Radiological images of this foot also seem to indicate that his "footprint" would only have included the front part of his foot; his heel may not have touched the ground.

In a tomb known as KV21, the mummies of two royal women of the 18th Dynasty have been found, one of whom may represent

Ankhesenamun. An examination of her mummy indicates that like her brother and husband, she had clubfoot, but both of her feet were affected. To simplify the story, I have described another of Tut and Ankh's sisters as having two feet similar to Tut's left one.

As I have portrayed, Tut did have large front teeth and a partially cleft palate, although how it affected him is not known (I gave him an intermittent lisp and mentioned that as a baby, he had been difficult to feed). He also had a significant overbite, which is why I mention that Semerkhet has more chin. It is also debatable whether he had scoliosis or whether the curve in his spine was the result of the mummification process.

It is surprisingly unclear how tall the Pharaoh was. Estimates have ranged from 5'5" to 5'8" to possibly even the rather towering 5'11", in an era when most adults were under 5'6". I have chosen to describe him as being at the taller end of this range, as it serves my story well; as the heir to the throne and a fragile child, he would have been lavished with good nutrition, which would have enabled him to grow to his maximum potential height based on genetics. Babies were traditionally nursed until they were three years old; therefore, Tut being nursed until he was five is unusual, and only takes place because he is a frail child.

In contemporary artwork, Tutankhamun is often shown either holding a cane, usually in his right hand, which is consistent with having a clubfoot on the left side, or seated, even when doing activities one would generally do standing. There are even pictures showing the King and Queen together in which Tut is not using his walking-stick, but Ankh appears to have a very firm grip on his left arm, possibly helping him stay upright while a royal artist sketched them. In more than one case, also, when depicted with a cane, the Pharaoh is shown visibly taking the weight off of his left foot.

410

In fact, this is why I believe one particular image often described as depicting a male Smenkhkare and Meritaten, his Queen, is actually a picture of Tut and Ankh— the male figure is shown leaning on a walking-stick, quite obviously taking the weight off of his left foot. What other young man in the Amarna period used a cane and had a challenge specific to his left foot? And loved flowers, because the Pharaoh in this scene is receiving a bouquet from a Queen, as Tut is often depicted receiving flowers from Ankh. Even as they honored the Pharaoh as a god, the royal artists were acknowledging his special needs; why on earth would a Pharaoh be shown with a cane, an indication of physical weakness, if they didn't genuinely need one in real life?

Furthermore, based on my own conjecture, I have described Tut as beginning to use a cane at around the age of twelve. This is the point in childhood when the proportion between a kid's strength and his or her weight changes and the monkey bars are no longer so easy. For Tut, this could very well have been the point at which his unstable left foot was no longer able to reliably carry him without the support of a walking-stick, especially since many boys experience a growth spurt at this age. Since I portray him as growing up to be very tall, his feet would have had to work harder to get him around than if he was shorter and smaller, and a cane would have been even more of a necessity as he became a teenager.

As a toddler, although he may have gotten around more slowly and fallen more often than other small children, his desire to follow his loved ones around the palace and get into things would have been much stronger than the challenge that walking presented. Since clubfoot is not in and of itself a painful condition (his painful bone disease arose later in his childhood or youth), a two-year-old Tut would not have had the disincentive of pain to slow him down. He would have gotten around just as quickly as he could.

As we can see, Tutankhamun's special needs can be clearly identified, through examinations of his mummy and considerations of the portraits and personal belongings he left behind. Let this remind us that the manner in which a person gets around has no bearing on their abilities as a leader. To sum up, the fact that he became Pharaoh at all, that the royal shoemakers invented orthopedic shoes for his benefit, that he had as many walking-sticks as he needed, that he had all the support he needed to remain neat and tidy and sit up straight, and that when he died, he was buried in a solid gold coffin show us just how much Tutankhamun's people respected those with special needs in general, and how much they loved him in particular.

Family is Forever

Tutankhamun and Ankhesenamun's loss of two infant daughters is tragically historical. The mummies of two baby girls, one of whom had been born at around twenty-four weeks of pregnancy, and the other, who may have had spina bifida, having been born at around thirty-six weeks, were found in the Pharaoh's tomb. Examinations have suggested that the younger daughter was still-born, while the older one got to look into her parents' eyes. No record has been found of how old Tut and Ankh were when their daughters were born.

I think the older daughter must have had spina bifida. One or both of her parents had a clubfoot (see *Disabilities in Ancient Egypt*, above), which can be related to neural tube conditions like spina bifida, and her father had cleft palate, also a neural tube

412

condition. There must have been a health condition that caused her to pass away as a newborn despite surviving to nearly full-term. It is possible, according to examinations of her remains, that she may have been as young as 31 weeks, but the theories of her having had spina bifida and being born at basically full-term reinforce one another.

Spina bifida would not have been treatable in Ancient Egypt, and although doctors may have attempted trepanning, strategic placement of holes in the skull, in order to relieve the pressure created by hydrocephalus, she is not likely to have survived long enough for the operation to be undertaken. Even if the doctors were able to see that the child's life could theoretically be saved if her back was closed up, they did not have the technology required for such an operation. Ultimately, before germ theory and modern surgery, no amount of herbal medicine could have protected a child with spina bifida from a fatal infection.

It bothers me when Tutankhamun and Ankhesenamun's daughters are referred to as "fetuses," or, as they are sometimes, completely ignored. Even worse, some books and documentaries even suggest that in their losses, Tut and Ankh "tried" to have children and were "not successful." I am also honored to be able to refer to these precious children as princesses— because they were.

Because the names of these two princesses have not been provided for us, I had the honor of selecting names with meanings I found fitting, one of which, *Senebhenas* (Health is With Her) I found through research, and the other of which, *Mereneferet*, (Love and Beauty) I constructed based upon my desired meaning. Children born with medical concerns were often given names related to good health, to bless them with that same good health.

When they were first discovered by Howard Carter, the two infant princesses were the youngest mummies ever found. Since their discovery, the mummies of even younger babies have been discovered. Let this remind us of the incredible love parents have had for their children in every era of history.

Glimpses of Real Life

Honey-cakes and molokhiya soup were real foods enjoyed in Ancient Egypt. The soup is made of minced molokhiya leaves, garlic, and broth, and is still eaten today. Tiger nuts, from which sweets were made, are actually a tuber, but have a flavor similar to that of nuts and are employed in similar ways. Mai-sus, as I describe, is a cool drink made from licorice.

Winter in Egypt is colder than many Americans may imagine, receiving more rain than other parts of the year, and even getting down into the forties at night in Luxor, the modern city found on the site of ancient Thebes. These facts inspired me to describe very hot, mostly dry summers and winters with cool days, cold nights, and more rainfall. And, of course, what these characters consider to be "cold winter nights" is based on a "normal summer day" being over a hundred degrees. It is also true that the central and eastern regions of Turkey, within whose modern borders the Kingdom of Hattusa once existed, have snowy winters.

The board game of *seega* is real, although precisely how ancient it is is not known. The rules I describe are based on a reconstruction explained online. As my mother and I have discovered, it is as fun and challenging today as it is for my Pharaoh and his Queen.

Although white linen robes were the foundation of Ancient Egyptian clothing, dyes of many colors did exist. It was more common for white clothing to be adorned with colored embroidery or delicate stripes of color than for garments to exhibit a solid color. On the other hand, Tut himself is known to have owned a rather fantastic dark blue tunic decorated with a pattern of red flowers, so we can see that bright-colored clothing was available to royalty.

Malkata Palace, as it is known to archaeologists, was truly massive, and yes, it did have its own lake and attached servant quarters. It is also true that after the reign of Amenhotep the Third, the harem quarters of Malkata were used for storage.

My reference to Tut wanting his new policies to be applied "from Tamiat to Napata" is meant to give the same sense that "from New York to LA" would give in reference to America. Tamiat, practically on the coast of the Mediterranean Sea, is one of Egypt's northernmost cities, and Napata is very close to the southern border of Egypt established by Thutmose the Third.

Semerkhet's description of the palace staff being happy to "do their part" and knowing that everything they did could have a far-reaching impact was based on the structure of Ancient Egyptian society. Everyone had their place, and many believed that staying in one's own social class would help to sustain *ma'at*, or balance and order. By extension, though, a small positive act could ripple widely and make a surprisingly large impact.

Many other details are based in truth, such as Tutankhamun's ostrich-feather fan (an inscription on its long handle tells us that he hunted the bird himself), and the daily prayer-time and bull sacrifice. The Pharaoh also took part in a ceremony at sunset (the details of which I have invented, quoting excerpts from a prayer that refers to the sunset), and at sunrise. All the beauty products I mention have historical basis.

Cats were indeed loved and honored by the Ancient Egyptians. According to Herodotus, families whose pet cat had died would shave their eyebrows as a sign of grief, and deceased cats were mummified. By the year 450 BC, the punishment for killing a cat was death. Therefore, Tut's discovery of the stray cat is a horrible shock to him, arguably almost as disturbing as meeting the orphaned child.

Tribute Day, with all of its sights, sounds, and smells, was influenced by paintings found in the tomb of Amenhotep-called-Huy, the Viceroy of Kush during Tut's reign. These paintings show the Pharaoh receiving gifts from delegations from Nubia and from Western Asia, gifts I have specifically mentioned during the Tribute Day sequence (although the events in the paintings appear to be in response to Tutankhamun's successful rekindling of diplomatic relations between Egypt and her neighbors, rather than being a depiction of a yearly tribute festival).

I also portray other contemporaneous nations as bringing gifts that reflect their various resources. (Yes, the King does appear to have received a giraffe from Nubia, although what he did with it is not clear). My description of Egypt's peace overtures toward the Hittites backfiring is fictional, but I used it as foreshadowing, establishing Egypt and the Hittites as enemies.

Different scholars have aligned the months of the Ancient Egyptian civil calendar with the months of the Gregorian calendar in very different ways, but I have chosen to abide by the alignment provided in the *Encyclopedia of Ancient Egypt*.

Although I do not know precisely how many days the Opet Festival would have spanned during Tut's reign, it varied in length

416

over the centuries, growing from around ten days to nearly four weeks. The specific date of the Pharaoh's special intercessions on behalf of Egypt is also conjectural. All the other festivals I mention were real Ancient Egyptian celebrations.

The Sed Festival was a real jubilee usually celebrated when a Pharaoh had reigned for thirty years, and then every few years thereafter. It symbolized the Pharaoh's enduring strength and involved a ceremonial footrace intended to demonstrate that they were still worthy of ruling. The specifics of the celebration varied widely from Pharaoh to Pharaoh, so it is not out of the realm of possibility to imagine a Pharaoh who physically could not run demonstrating his or her enduring power in a chariot race.

Historical Fiction

Some details I did change, however; for example, I have, for plot purposes, divided the year into "mosquito season" and "not mosquito season," with mosquitoes disappearing during the coldest parts of the year, but resurfacing during warm spells. I have also divided time into familiar seven-day weeks rather than the ten-day "decans" or "decades" used in the period. Days are also divided into familiar hours, minutes, and seconds (although the hours vary in length throughout the year). My placement of Tutankhamun's birthday at the end of August is fictional.

Although I describe Khenut as being the leader of the palace washerwomen, in Ancient Egypt, laundry was done solely by men, as it was very heavy work performed on the Nile, and laundry workers were intrinsically at risk of being attacked by crocodiles or hippopotamuses. Khenut and her team, therefore, may be envisioned as being responsible for folding clean laundry and returning it to the royal quarters.

In Ancient Egypt, doorways within homes were generally covered with woven mats of reeds, which served to offer privacy, protection from the heat, and reduction of insect invasion. However, lockable doors existed in Ancient Egypt, and extrapolating the existence of lockable bedroom doors, in the palace, at least, allows the Pharaoh and Queen to discuss political developments in privacy. I also didn't mention the wooden headrests most Ancient Egyptians slept on, instead providing the Pharaoh with a more familiar type of pillow.

I also do not touch on the fact that Tutankhamun's coronation took place at Akhetaten; historically, the surviving members of the royal family may not have moved back to Thebes until Tut was twelve, and he was crowned at around nine. I portray Nefertiti, as Pharaoh Smenkhkare, moving with Meritaten, Ankh, and Tutankhamun back to Thebes almost immediately after Akhenaten's death when Tut is six. I also adjust the timing of the decision to reopen the traditional temples and move away from the Aten. Historically, Tutankhamun reopened the temples around the time that the capital was moved back to Thebes, but I have Smenkhkare Nefertiti reopen them during her three-year reign.

King Tut and Moses?

When I began my adventure in Ancient Egypt, I had no idea that the Exodus of the Hebrews was such an important part of King Tutankhamun's backstory, no idea that Moses and King Tut had anything to do with one another. I have repeatedly shaken my head in amazement at the clues I have found within Egyptian history, clues that remind us of the truth of the Bible and show us that the

418

work of God cannot be concealed by human beings. I will always be grateful for this amazing adventure and everything it has taught me. The truth of God's Word is demonstrated in every chapter of the Eighteenth Dynasty, if only we know where to look.

Glossary

Ague: malaria, a potentially deadly, mosquito-borne illness that causes weakness, fever, and chills

Bastet: ancient Egyptian goddess with a role related to various aspects of health, depicted as a lioness or cat

Crook and Flail: props the Pharaoh might hold, which symbolized his or her being a loving shepherd but also meting out discipline

Cuirass: tunic worn by Ancient Egyptian soldiers, constructed of various combinations of leather and metal. These became more common in the decades after Tutankhamun's reign.

Diadem: a term for a type of crown with a lower profile than the white crown of Upper Egypt, the red crown of Lower Egypt, or the double-crown. A diadem would fit closely against one's wig, with the only protrusion being the *uraeus* in the front. Also referred to as a circlet.

Henna: red dye used in various cultures to decorate the skin with beautiful designs, and used by Ancient Egyptians to color nails and dye hair. Soldiers colored their nails red before going into battle.

Hieratic script: a form of writing; a "cursive" form of hiero-glyphic script that could be written with pen and ink

Khonsu: Ancient Egyptian moon deity

Kohl: the eyeliner used by Ancient Egyptians to create the well-known cat-eye and to darken their eyebrows. Combined with blue-green "eye-shadow," it helped to protect the eyes from infection and from the bright sun. Both kohl and the "eye-shadow" were made from minerals.

Ma'at: both the name of an Ancient Egyptian goddess of truth, harmony, and justice and a term for these and related concepts. Upon death, Ancient Egyptians anticipated that their hearts would be weighed against the feather Ma'at wore in her hair; if their heart was too heavy, it indicated that they were unrighteous, and their heart was eaten by the crocodile-lion-hippopotamus beast, Ammut. They would not have the opportunity to advance to a happy afterlife in the Field of Reeds.

Natron: a naturally-occurring blend of multiple sodium compounds, which was used by the Ancient Egyptians to mummify the dead and as an ingredient in soap, as well as for various other purposes from insect control to leather-making, meat preservation, teeth cleaning, and laundry

Nemes: the head-cloth worn by Pharaohs in Ancient Egypt. The most famous example is worn by the Great Sphinx of Giza.

Palanquin: another word for a litter in which a member of the royal family might be carried, borne by servants

Pectoral: refers to a very large necklace that covers a portion of the chest

Sed Festival: jubilee traditionally celebrated when a Pharaoh reached his or her thirtieth year in power, and then every three or four years thereafter. Ceremonies included a ritual run that demonstrated the Pharaoh's enduring strength.

Seega: a board game played historically in Egypt

Sobek: an Ancient Egyptian god of fertility, depicted as a crocodile or with the head of a crocodile

Spikenard: an essential oil obtained from a plant of the valerian family, long used in perfumery

Tawaret: an Ancient Egyptian goddess of fertility, depicted as a grandly pregnant hippopotamus

Uraeus: the cobra-headed decoration seen on the front of many Ancient Egyptian crowns

Vizier: a sort of "prime minister;" a high official responsible for supervising much of the running of the government

Wadjet eye: also called the Eye of Horus; the famous eye-shaped symbol used in Ancient Egypt, representing protection, health, and royal power

Locations

Akhetaten (Amarna): Pharaoh Akhenaten's capital city, which he had built to honor the Aten and to enable a "fresh start."

Alashiya: Eastern Mediterranean neighbor of New Kingdom Egypt

Amurru: Region in modern Syria and Lebanon historically subjected to both Egyptian and Hittite control

Behdet (Edfu): Town near Thebes

Djerty (El-Tod): Town near Thebes

Gebtu (Koptos): Town near Thebes

Goshen: Region in the eastern Nile Delta settled by the Hebrews

Hattusa: Kingdom of the Hittites, located in modern Turkey

Kadesh: Town in the region of Amurru, which switched hands several times between Egypt and Hattusa

Kush: Region of Nubia under Egyptian control from 16th-11th centuries BC

Malkata Palace: modern name of the glorious palace built by Amenhotep the Third

Memphis (Cairo): Northern capital of Egypt, in the southern Nile Delta

Mitanni: Neighbor of New Kingdom Egypt located in modern Turkey and Syria

Napata: Town in the extreme south of Egypt, on the Eighteenth-Dynasty border with Nubia

Nubia: Southern neighbor of Egypt, comprising parts of modern Egypt and modern Sudan

Nekhen (Hierakonopolis): Town near Thebes

On (Heliopolis): Town in the southern Nile Delta, just north of Memphis

Retjenu: Neighbor of Egypt in the region of Canaan/Syria

Tamiat (Damietta): Town in the extreme north of Egypt, on the Mediterranean coast

Thebes (Luxor): Southern capital of Egypt, on the banks of the Nile in the center of the country

Tjenu (Thinis): Town near Thebes

Ankhesenamun's Queens List

Neith-Hotep: possible regent, possible Pharaoh (early first dynasty).

Merneith: regent for her son Den, possible Pharaoh (first dynasty).

Nimaathap: possible regent for her son Djoser (transition between second and third dynasties).

Khentkaus the First: possible Pharaoh or regent for her son. A title that can be translated either as "Mother of Two Kings of Upper and Lower Egypt" or "Mother of the King of Upper and Lower Egypt, *and King of Upper and Lower Egypt*" suggests that she may have become Pharaoh (transition between fourth and fifth dynasties).

Khentkaus the Second: bore the same titles as her predecessor, and may also have reigned either as regent or as Pharaoh in her own right (fifth dynasty).

Setibhor: wife of Pharaoh Djedkare. Her pyramid complex is larger, more elaborate, and "kinglier" than any other belonging to a Queen, and certain symbols and insignias were added to reliefs portraying her, which suggests that she may have succeeded her husband as Pharaoh or as regent for the next male Pharaoh (late fifth dynasty).

Iput: mother and possible regent for Pepi the First (beginning of sixth dynasty).

Ankhesenpepi the Second: sister of Ankhesenpepi the First, daughter of female Vizier Nebet, wife of Pepi the First, bore one of his successors (Pepi the Second), likely served as regent (sixth dynasty).

Nebet: vizier (sixth dynasty).

Nitocris: legendary female Pharaoh, considered to be final Pharaoh of sixth dynasty.

Sobekneferu: Pharaoh (very end of twelfth dynasty).

Tetisheri: mother of Ahhotep the First, powerful Queen and matriarch of royal family (transition between seventeenth and eighteenth dynasties).

Ahhotep the First: regent for her son Ahmose the First. Praised by her son for keeping Egypt in one piece, expelling rebels, bringing home deserters, guarding the country, and pacifying Upper Egypt (transition between seventeenth and eighteenth dynasties).

Ahmose-Nefertari: daughter of Ahhotep the First, mother of Amenhotep the First, may have served as regent for him. She may have founded the Valley of the Kings (early eighteenth dynasty).

Hatshepsut: Queen, then regent, then Pharaoh (eighteenth dynasty).

Tiye: wife of Amenhotep the Third, mother of Akhenaten. Worked as a politician to retain good relations with neighboring countries during her son's reign (eighteenth dynasty).

Nefertiti Smenkhkare: Queen, then co-regent, then possible Pharaoh (eighteenth dynasty).

Meritaten: Queen of Pharaoh Smenkhkare, who is speculated to have been her own mother Nefertiti (eighteenth dynasty).

Calendar

Season of Inundation (Akhet)
Thoth: 19 July-17 August
Paophi: 18 August-16 September
Athyr: 17 September-16 October
Sholiak: 17 October-15 November
Season of Emergence (Peret)
Tybi: 16 November-15 December
Meshir: 16 December-14 January
Phamenoth: 15 January-13 February
Pharmouthi: 14 February-15 March
Season of the Harvest (Shemu)
Pashons: 16 March-14 April
Payni: 15 April-14 May
Epiphi: 15 May-13 June
Mesori: 14 June-13 July
Holy birthdays
14th of July: Osiris
15th: Horus
16th: Seth
17th: Isis
18th: Nepthys

Selected Resources

The Holy Bible

Daily Life of the Ancient Egyptians by Bob Brier, A. Hoyt Hobbs

The Murder of Tutankhamun: A True Story by Bob Brier

Empire of Ancient Egypt by Wendy Christensen

Tutankhamun: The Exodus Conspiracy: The Truth Behind Archaeology's Greatest Mystery by Andrew Collins and Chris Ogilvie-Herald

When Women Ruled the World by Kara Cooney

Tutankhamun's Armies: Battle and Conquest During Ancient Egypt's Late Eighteenth Dynasty by John Coleman Darnell, Colleen Manassa

The Tomb of Iouiya and Touiyou: The Finding of the Tomb by Theodore M. Davis, Gaston Maspero, Percy Edward Newberry

Amarna Sunset: Nefertiti, Tutankhamun, Ay, Horemheb, and the Egyptian Counter-Reformation by Aidan Dodson

Monarchs of the Nile by Aidan Dodson

The Mysterious Death of Tutankhamun: Re-Opening the Case of Egypt's Boy-King by Paul Doherty

Egyptian Non-royal Epithets in the Middle Kingdom: A Social and Historical Analysis by Denise M. Doxey

Life in Ancient Egypt by Adolf Erman

The Medical Skills of Ancient Egypt: revised edition by J. Worth Estes

Oils and Perfumes of Ancient Egypt by Joann Fletcher

Growing Up in Ancient Israel: Children in Material Culture and Biblical Texts by Kristine Henriksen Garroway

"The Deeds of Suppiluliuma as told by his son, Mursilli II", *Journal of Cuneiform Studies, 10* (1956) by Güterbock, H.G.

The Golden King: The World of Tutankhamun by Zahi Hawass

Scanning the Pharaohs: CT Imaging of the New Kingdom Royal Mummies by Zahi A. Hawass, Sahar Saleem

Principles and Methods of Toxicology, Fifth Edition Edited by A. Wallace Hayes

The Pharaoh's Court by Kathryn Hinds

Conspiracies in the Egyptian Palace: Unis to Pepy I by Naguib Kanawati

Who Killed King Tut? by Michael R. King and Gregory M. Cooper

Powerful Female Pharaohs of Egypt by Jone Johnson Lewis (article published on ThoughtCo)

Sacred Luxuries: Fragrance, Aromatherapy, and Cosmetics in Ancient Egypt by Lise Manniche

Ghosts: A Haunted History by Lisa Morton

Ancient Egyptian Kingship by David Bourke O'Connor, David P. Silverman

The Hebrew Pharaohs of Egypt: the Secret Lineage of the Patriarch Joseph by Ahmed Osman

The Oxford History of Ancient Egypt by Ian Shaw

The Encyclopedia of Ancient Egypt General Editor Helen Strudwick

Chronicle of the queens of Egypt: from early dynastic times to the death of Cleopatra by Joyce Tyldesley

Tutankhamen: The Search for an Egyptian King by Joyce Tyldesley

Ancient Egypt: Its Culture and History by J. E. Manchip White

Acknowledgments

When I began working on this story in 2017, I had no idea that it would blossom into one of the most meaningful things I have ever created; the project I am the most proud of. Little did I know that I had begun the long pregnancy and labor that would bring my firstborn child of a story into the world.

Let me thank the many people who held my hands, encouraged me, and coached me during this amazing process. To my mother, Anne, this story would not be what it is today if you had not let me read it to you out loud three times in a row. You have cured my dependence on paragraph-length sentences, you have helped me mature in my application of balance and pacing, and you have answered questions I could not answer myself. I will be forever grateful for your support, your willingness to serve as my sounding board, and your second set of eyes and ears. Thank you for being to me everything Ankh is for Tut. And thank you for playing *seega!*

To my brave friends, thank you for reading this saga before the rest of the world. Thank you for your questions and your comments; all your wonderful observations that helped me understand what was coming across well and what needed further clarification. Thank you for helping me make this story everything it has become.

And to the Pharaoh and his family… thank you for inspiring me.